EDEN'S TRIAL

An Eden Paradox Novel

Barry Kirwan

THE EDEN PARADOX SERIES

The Eden Paradox
Eden's Trial
Eden's Revenge
Eden's Endgame

Praise for the book and the series:

"A science fiction thriller with terrific images and revelations." SF author Gary Gibson

"It's hard to put down this book, but at the same time you don't want to race ahead but instead savour the complexities of personalities and the well-crafted story line. There are new worlds and new enemies entwined with the main characters nearly as closely as their lovers. I can't wait for the next journey alongside the Eden pathway!" Lydia Manx, Piker Press.

Top Amazon and Goodreads reviews:

"Riveting plot, compelling characters - delivered everything I hoped it would."
"Brilliant, imaginative, original."
"Book two continues the success of its predecessor."
"Fascinating, fantastical science fiction. Deeper than anything I've ever read in this genre."
"Incredible alien races and intense pacing. Buckle up for the ride of your life!"

for Sheila

Contents

PART ONE – ATTACK ON OURSHIWANN

PROLOGUE

General William Kilaney awoke, disappointed to find he was still alive. He tried to raise his head, but a metal rod pressed the back of his skull, forcing his gaze to the floor. He knew this interrogator's trick – bend the body as a prelude to breaking the spirit. He willed his arms and legs to tug against the restraints, but whatever had stunned him on the space station had his limbs locked down cold. He'd seen his crew killed, and he had no false hopes about his own fate. He listened to his captor's footsteps. He had a hunch who it was.

"Why am I here, Sister Esma? That is you, isn't it?" The Alician High Priestess herself. He prayed the four transports off Earth had escaped. He'd told Micah to leave, just before they'd lost communications. If the ships hadn't left in time, it had all been for nothing.

"If you're after their flight plan, I never saw it. Torture me if you like, but it won't get you anywhere." It should be over quicker if he pushed her, if she lived up to the reputation she'd gained during the four-day assault on Earth.

He heard a faucet, the rinsing of hands: blood, he imagined, probably his own. Steel boots clacked across the metal floor towards him. He glimpsed them underneath drug-heavy eyelids: blue flow-metal with steel stilettos. So, not above vanity. Life held so few surprises.

Icy water drenched his head and neck. He gasped, shaking off as much as he could, squeezing it out of his eyes.

"Your battle tactics were quite unorthodox, General."

Her voice carried all the arrogance he'd imagined from the leader of the terrorist sect who'd plagued Earth for the last decade. But he allowed himself a smile.

"Gave your Q'Roth locust friends a run for their money, did we?" While the rest of the world had been frozen by fear and panic, his forces had accounted for a quarter of a million Q'Roth dead in five separate hits. It paled in comparison to humanity being all but wiped out, but it was something. He'd put up a fight and – he hoped – four ships had escaped with their precious human cargo.

"What do you want, Esma?"

Her cool fingertips anchored themselves on the back of his neck. Pain punched through his head as something was wrenched from the base of his skull. He blinked hard. A wave of nausea gripped him, then flattened out, dissipating. The skin on his hands and feet prickled as his muscle control returned. He flexed stiff fingers. Curiosity got the better of him. "What was that?"

"A device to download your recent memories, in case you were lying about their flight plan."

They made it. He hadn't admitted how much he'd needed to hear this sliver of good news, and let out a long breath. He hadn't been lying about not knowing their destination. When Micah had almost told him, he'd cut him off immediately. Twelve thousand had escaped. He drew comfort from that. But he'd been in pain from cancer for years. Truth was, he couldn't face any more.

"You have what you want. Let's get it over with, shall we?" He waited. She reminded him of a cat playing with a mouse.

"The Q'Roth Supreme Commander wants you."

Kilaney wished he'd gone down with his men; he'd damned well tried to. "For torture or a light snack?"

She snorted. "You should have worked it out by now, General. They do not eat human flesh – they feed on bio-psychic energy. It is a critical part of their maturation process. But to answer your question, neither. She wishes to recruit you." Esma sounded bemused.

He laughed; life held a few surprises after all. "Let me get this straight: I just nuked five of her ships and she wants to offer me a job?"

"She said you showed potential. The Q'Roth are consummate soldiers, like you, General. They respect your tactical ability."

The disdain in her voice didn't go amiss. He knew now, between the Q'Roth aliens and the genetically-altered Alicians, who his worst enemy was.

"Well, Esma, I'm Stage Four. The cancer's all that's holding this sad bag of bones together. Can't blow my nose without a transfusion. I have a couple of weeks, max. Anyhow, not sure it would look good on my resume." He wanted this over. He'd done his part.

"They can cure your cancer, extend your lifetime by decades."

She said it matter-of-fact, and he realised she wasn't lying. They could cure cancer. He felt as if she'd kicked him in the stomach. The disease had eaten away at him for four years, robbing him of everything he once was. Being offered a cure now was the worst torture he could imagine. He clamped his lips.

Her voice became earnest. "You have seen the Q'Roth in action, but that is nothing compared to what they can do. All you have witnessed are freshly hatched warriors – newborns, primal rage instilled into their genes. But now they have fed, they will mature into the most potent armed force you could envisage. They are the foot-soldiers of the galaxy, General, respected by hundreds of races."

And feared by most of them, he supposed. But despite himself he had been impressed. He'd seen them tear down a whole planet in a matter of days: shock troops, destroying infrastructure in the first wave, dismantling communications, reacting so damned fast to every counter-measure; all of this immediately after being hatched. He jammed his lips tighter and thought of his wife, taken by cancer four years earlier, of the thousands of soldiers who'd served under him over the years, all killed in the last days' carnage. All except Blake.

"General," she continued, pacing in front of him, "A war is coming. Not like the one you have just fought and lost, barely a campaign in Q'Roth terms. The Commander assures me it poses a threat to hundreds of races, maybe even the galaxy itself. She is interested in the creative tactics you demonstrated. She feels they could be developed. You are a soldier, General, and –"

He had to stop this. "The answer's 'no', Esma. That's final. Now, I've shown you respect, you show me some."

The boots disappeared from view. Involuntarily, he tensed. A section of the metal floor beneath him receded to reveal a window. The sight unpeeling before him snatched his breath away. Earth hung below, a dull orange ball speckled with boiling clouds and glowing embers where the nukes had gouged his planet's flesh. Even the oceans had taken on a sickened pallor.

His muscles fought against the restraints. He was furious to have even listened to her poison. *Eden*, he reminded himself. This had all been about Eden, and where there's the promise of paradise, there's always a snake.

"One day they'll find you, Esma; Blake, Micah and the others. And when they do, they'll kill you like a rabid dog."

She walked in front of him, so that her boots appeared to be standing on top of Earth. Her tone sharpened. "A task force is already hunting them down and will destroy them. But even if they do escape, General, humanity will perish." She bent forward, her cheek level with his. "Do you know why?"

He preferred it this way, niceties and bullshit expended.

She whispered. "If humanity escapes – a very small if – they will undo themselves." She stood up, grinding her heel against the glass, as if she was stubbing out his native North America. "It is only a matter of time before your valiant refugees do something wrong, and are cut down like the weeds they are. Galactic Society values intelligence above all else, General. I do not mean the odd genius here and there, but coherent intelligence at the species level. Now, does that description fit humanity's resumé?"

He bristled. "If we'd known there was sentient life out there – especially a society – it could have changed everything."

4

She tapped her toes on the glass. "I told them you would say 'no'."

He was about to respond when he noticed something. It was as if the world was changing colour, morphing into grey sepia. "What's happening, Esma?"

"The Q'Roth have finished. They do not believe in leaving loose ends. It is one of the galactic rules. After an incursion, the planet's atmosphere is removed. It is for the best, especially following nuclear detonations on this scale."

His eyes widened as whirlpools of smoke, like massive hurricanes, mushroomed around the globe. Glittering nuclear sparks snuffed out one by one, deprived of oxygen. The last whorls of atmosphere lost cohesion and flashed into space in a series of bursts that pricked his retinas. When the blotches in his vision faded, he saw Earth as no one ever had, as no one ever should. The oceans had boiled off into space, leaving smooth basins bordered by stark continental ridges. The planet was barren, dark, moon-like. Earth was... he didn't even want to think the word.

"Earth must lay fallow for ten thousand years. No race will be allowed into this system during that period. Which is why humanity never encountered anyone from Grid Society – Mars was also culled, not that long ago by Galactic standards. The ban on entering the sector was lifted only a thousand years ago, and the Q'Roth were first to stake a claim on Earth."

He heard a click, and the metal rod behind his head eased back. He raised his chin despite the stiffness in his neck, and stared at his captor. She was tall and long-necked, wearing a simple grey robe with the hood down. Her skin was pale, framed by jet black hair pulled back into a tightly braided ponytail. Broad, menacing eyes stabbed down at him over a hooked nose.

She spoke slowly. "You should thank me, General. You should actually thank all Alicians."

The conviction in her voice almost made him retch. He tried to gather enough saliva for the only fitting response he could think of, but his mouth was dry. He watched her strut in front of him. What he wouldn't give right now for a grenade.

"The Q'Roth first visited Earth a millennium ago on a scouting mission. Their intent was to return and harvest all of humanity, after their long hibernation period. But they needed an ally to fine-tune the attack nearer their waking period. They found my ancestor, Alessia, and the Alician order was born. The Q'Roth re-engineered a few of us, and then left. We have patiently awaited their return, and now we will have a new home, taking our place amongst Grid Society. We are humanity's evolution, General."

He took one last look at Earth, then faced her, speaking on behalf of his dead world. "You're an abomination, Esma, and Alicians are humanity's bastards. What's to stop the Q'Roth feeding on you and your sect, now you've helped them?"

She looked away. "We have an agreement, a contract, you might say."

He scrutinised her – there was something she didn't want to admit, a secret too important to confess even to a dying man. He shrugged. "Watch out for the small print, Esma. In my experience, deals with the devil go south sooner rather than later."

A bell chimed somewhere deep in the ship, and she glanced at her wristcom.

"Your time is up, General. As you do not wish to come with us, I am going to send you home." She touched a panel and a glistening shroud ballooned around him. The glass beneath his feet slid away. His feet didn't fall, supported by some kind of force-field. But a savage, biting cold gripped his soles, coiling around his ankles, drilling into his bones. He cried out with pain.

"It will actually feel warmer outside, believe it or not. Right now the field in contact with your feet is conducting your body heat to the outer hull, which is in darkness, fractionally above absolute zero."

A steady hiss forewarned him of the dizziness he began to feel. His thighs and arms struggled against the restraints, trying to lift his feet. Her voice sounded fuzzy.

"You see, General, even if humanity escapes, the only way they can hope to survive is to evolve beyond what they are. And the sad truth is that humanity would choose to die as they are, rather than evolve."

His eyes fogged as their water vapour evaporated. He closed his mouth. She touched another panel and his leg and arm straps released. He fell forward, the skin of his palms and outstretched fingers welding to the freezing layer separating him from hard vacuum.

His body wracked with shivering, knocking his teeth together. When he spoke, it sounded like he was underwater. He shouted to compensate. "They'll... survive." His arms were numb. Through slitted eyes he watched his hands turn a sickly wax colour. His breath ran out, his throat asteroid-dry. He hunted the last oxygen molecules inside his shroud. Her voice was distant, fading.

"I can see why the Commander was interested in you. Goodbye, General. Oh, and a word of advice: do not hold your breath."

Out of the corner of a frosting eye, he saw her hand, as if in slow motion, move to activate another control. He had no doubt what it would do. The force-field cracked apart beneath him like an eggshell.

As he tumbled into space, he knew he had only a few remaining seconds of consciousness. As the residual air in his lungs expanded to bursting, he let out a space-silent yell of rage. He squeezed his eyes shut to protect them as long as he could, suppressing needle-like jabs as nitrogen flashed out of his bloodstream into his joints, competing with the grinding ache from his bloating limbs. The naked glare of the sun slammed into him, searing his face like a whip with each turn of his somersault. None of it mattered anymore. His body convulsed, venting blood at every orifice. He choked off the idea that she might be right about humanity. Instead, he willed his last thought out into the void: *Prove her wrong, Blake. You and Micah can do this. Wherever you are, for God's sake, prove –*

CHAPTER 1 – UMBILICAL

Luke touched the sonic syringe to his neck. He hesitated, knowing there would be no turning back – one way or the other he'd be dead in twelve hours. He took a breath and drove his thumb down, feeling the click followed by a small hiss as the neurotransmitters surged into his carotid. A flush crawled across his face, followed by tingling, then scalding. He doubled over. Within seconds his respiration and heart rate slowed. His senses sharpened. He could easily read the writing on his desk on the other side of the room. Muted conversations in adjacent quarters amplified, allowing him to hear their dreary banter. For the first time, Luke detected the deep, leopard-like purr of the engines in the bowels of the gargantuan Q'Roth vessel, as its human hijackers mustered power for the final transit through deep space to their new home. He knew his role well enough, and accepted it: to see that humanity never made it to their precious new world.

He marvelled at the Q'Roth technology, then grimaced at the thought of the three thousand undeserving passengers who had stolen aboard this ship instead of accepting their fate back on obliterated Earth. Most humans talked of the Q'Roth *invasion* – but to him and other Alicians it had meant liberation, after centuries of living in the shadows, hiding genetic advances from their inferior human cousins. Mankind had squandered its chances. Time for an upgrade.

He zeroed in on a man walking beyond the curtained doorway. Luke inhaled the pungent odour of this passer-by who hadn't showered. He cracked his knuckles. Two weeks pretending to be one of *them*, letting them think they'd escaped.

He picked up the blue stiletto, a Q'Roth ceremonial dagger, a gift from Sister Esma herself. Surprisingly light. Yet nothing on Earth had been able to bend, break or melt Q'Roth metal, except a nuke. A thousand years old, and still micron-sharp. He cocked an ear at a measured gait nearing his doorway. As it slowed, his fingers coiled around the hilt. The curtain rustled open and he launched the blade. A hand, moving so fast that only Luke in his newfound heightened state could have seen it, caught the knife in mid-air.

"I see you've taken your accelerator dose, too," Luke said, grinning.

Saul raked the curtain closed and tossed the stiletto back to him, glaring at the thin red line drawn across his palm. Blood threatened, then retreated, leaving no trace. "And if I hadn't?"

Luke's smile faded. "I got carried away. It won't happen again."

"Don't ever stoop to their level."

Luke bowed his head. He needed to redeem himself with Saul, one of the Inner Circle. Despite looking just a few years older, Saul had survived the Purge, between the fifteenth and seventeenth centuries, when the Alician Order had been hunted down, tortured and executed under the pretence of the great witch hunt – in the silent Alician war against the now-defunct Sentinels. Just thinking about it made Luke want to tear the head off the first human he encountered. But such emotional recklessness was unbecoming. Strategy and patience, he reminded himself, citing two of the most vaunted Alician maxims. He swallowed his anger, alchemising it into cold-blooded purpose: why kill a few when we can kill them all?

Luke cleared his throat. "What about the other three ships?"

Saul drew his pulse pistol, checking the charge. "Decapitation strategy – we take out Blake, their leader, and all those aboard this ship. Louise will take care of the others."

Luke nodded. "Good enough for me." He'd only met Louise once, and had decided there and then that it was true what they said – the female of the species was deadliest, especially after her recent Q'Roth DNA transfusion, which had apparently honed her aggressive instincts.

He shifted on his feet. "I want to be the one to kill Micah." He sheathed the stiletto. His eyes blazed. "Of all the parasites on this ship, his death deserves personal attention. If it weren't for him, none would have escaped."

Saul holstered his pistol. "The kill is yours. I've seen the roster. He should be outside with us later today. Just don't underestimate him. Remember, Louise herself failed last time. Let's go, it's time to keep up our side of the bargain."

Luke felt powerful, like a jaguar on the hunt, every muscle, every cell's DNA united in single purpose. They slipped out of the room, disappearing into the hordes of human prey infesting the corridors.

* * *

Micah scanned the pasty, sun-starved faces around him while he sat in one of the ship's dozen grimy canteens. Yellow light seeped out of the walls and ceilings, highlighting every crease of worry. Nothing could hide the stooped postures of a people whose backs had been broken by unimaginable loss – the near extinction of the entire human race.

He stared into his daily bowl of brown, nucleic phyto-soup – Sandy called it *gloop* – and stirred it absent-mindedly. Four sticky nondescript globs in his slurry-like food made him think of their four stolen Q'Roth transports, holding the last remnants of humanity within their hulking interiors. The four captains, Blake, Vince, Rashid and Jennifer, each took a disguised route – in case the Q'Roth tried to finish the job of genocide – to a new planet everyone hoped they could call home. But he couldn't eat, despite the rumblings in his stomach. He felt like he was at a perpetual funeral, though it was two weeks since they'd escaped. Each time he tried to eat he imagined all the dead back on Earth who couldn't. *Survivor's guilt*, he knew, though having a name for it didn't help. His stomach seemed to understand, like a family friend at a funeral patting him on the shoulder, unable to offer any words that could make a difference. He laid the spoon down and tuned in to a conversation at a nearby table, two men with their backs to him muttering their grievances.

"So, anyway, this planet, whose whereabouts they won't even tell us, what the hell do they actually know about it? I mean, all they know is it's out there somewhere, right? Don't know shit about it otherwise, how could they?" The man poked the air with a knot of stale bread. "Like, is it *really* empty? Who's to say the Q'Roth ain't waiting for us right there, eh? I bet they don't even know if it has water, food, or breathable air for God's sake. And, it could be really hot or cold. I'm telling you, nobody knows shit about this planet."

Micah shut his voice out, letting the sound of cheap cutlery on plastic tables drown it, along with the other muted, Spartan conversations that hung listlessly in the stuffy, catacomb-like ship, their temporary sanctuary. Still, the thought that they were drifting in uncharted space, with smouldering Earth far behind them, did nothing to whet his appetite.

He'd noticed how people clung to their meagre possessions, no matter how basic or common-place, and if they met someone who was miraculously from the same town, they became instant life-long friends. In the 'evenings', people gathered around anyone who had music or a vid-player; the lack of sound on the ship reinforced how much everyone had lost, how many human voices had been silenced. For Micah, who like most had escaped with his skin and little else, the sheer rootlessness of it all created its own chasm of nausea inside his guts. He interlaced his fingers and rested his brow against them.

Many complained of space sickness, though the doctors argued there was no reason for it – no vibration, no sudden movements, and certainly no pitching and yawing. He suspected nevertheless that the term was apt – people were literally sick of space, there was no ground, no earth beneath them, just a heartless vacuum.

He searched for something positive. Looking around him, at least people's clothes weren't ragged – it had only been a couple of weeks – but he noticed how most were starting to wear any old thing, as if nothing mattered. Black was the favoured colour, only adding to the morgue-like atmosphere in this behemoth of a ship, with its bottle-green walls that felt like dead skin to the touch. The ship, after all, belonged to their enemy.

"Not hungry?" Sandy dropped down into the seat opposite him, having already started her bowl.

He shook his head.

She soaked up her own steaming mush with a chunk of black, vat-produced, rye bread, eating with gusto. He watched, fascinated. He slumped back in one of the ubiquitous white gel-form chairs. *Thank God you're here, Sandy.*

"It'll probably end up on the cockpit shield like last time," he said. "Want it?" He nudged the dish across the metal table. "Eating for two, after all."

She launched a glare from beneath her pine-coloured fringe, conjuring in his mind a wild cat staring through jungle bushes – not a predator as such, but lethal when cornered. He decided not to say any more on the subject. Anyway, he guessed no one would suspect yet – she still looked as fit as a Tycho marathon-runner.

"Hope he appreciates this, one day," she said frowning, pulling the dish towards her, lobbing rye meteorites into the primal, hyper-nutritional sludge.

"He?" Micah raised his eyebrows, but she ignored him. Watching carefully, he noticed she had to make an effort to swallow; and then he knew she hated it as much as he did. She was simply determined to put on a good show. It was due to her proper upbringing, he knew she would say, and she would be right – if only everyone onboard could make such an effort.

A gruff voice intruded. "Hey, ain't you the sonofabitch who got us into this mess?"

Micah twisted around to see two men, the closest with a face as scarred as a strip-mined asteroid. The second was bear-like, stubby features shrouded in muddy brown hair and a straggling beard. They looked like cloudpunks – which meant trouble, since they could no longer get their drugs or kicks playing dodgem on high-alt jet-bikes. Shoulders hunched like jackals, the type who would only attack weaker prey. It was obvious who they were addressing.

Micah turned back to Sandy. Her right hand had dipped beneath the table. She had a wry smile on her face, he assumed because she was aiming a pulse pistol at the nearest man's groin. Micah had the stun-pen in his pocket, but decided to leave it there – for now. He scraped his chair back, and rose to face the two ration-hollowed men towering over him. The smell of the nearest one's breath almost made him sit back down.

"I'm Micah Sanderson, and, well, technically I got you out of a mess." He tried to control his breathing, to appear calm, congenial even. His pulse pistol was in a locker four levels down, and these men were bone-breakers. He wasn't sure the stun-pen would take them both out.

"Shouldn't you be a little taller, less scrawny?" The closest one jabbed a finger into Micah's sternum.

"With a decent haircut!" spat the second, smirking.

Micah kept his arms loose by his sides. He noticed several other people rise from their seats. *This could get ugly.* Ignoring the second man, he stared the first straight in the eye. "What do you want?"

"What do I want?" A leer scrawled across his bony face. "What do *I* want? From our resident hero?" He turned momentarily to his comrade.

Micah saw the opportunity to strike – Zack had been giving him combat training – but let it pass. He'd always seen violence as the very last resort, usually so late it just underlined failure.

The man's unshaven face loomed close. He whispered loud enough so everyone could hear. "I want to knock a piece off the prick who made us all run away when we should've stayed and fought those mother-fucking locusts." Spittle decorated his lower lip. "You know, the asshole who has us cooped up in this garbage can flying to some Godforsaken planet where we'll starve to death or tear each other to pieces."

Micah stood his ground, guessing he was likely to be hit pretty soon. He continued to stare into the man's hungry eyes, the bloodlust welling up inside them. Micah didn't blink. Neither did the man.

"Try to leave his brain intact," Sandy said, still sitting.

"H-hey, Lady," the second man stuttered, clearly less accustomed to public speaking than his colleague. "S-stay out of it."

"No, seriously, his brain is what saved us. Might come in useful. The rest, well... He's pretty skinny, won't be much of a fight."

Micah struggled not to blink. He wanted to offer this man some mouthwash. Out of the corner of his eye he noticed an old woman walk up to the pair of them. *Now what?*

"Excuse me," she said, in an old lady's voice that could only belong to an ex-teacher. She tugged the man's arm. His brow creased. Micah suppressed an urge to smile.

"I said, excuse me!"

The man pursed his lips. "*What?* Go away, old woman!"

"I'm not *that* old! Look at me, young man!"

The man growled and whirled to face the diminutive octogenarian whose head barely reached his chest. "What the hell do you want, lady?"

Micah blinked several times in relief.

The old woman beckoned the man closer with a bony finger. He sighed and bent forward. She slapped his face with surprising speed and force. He stumbled backwards a step, more shocked by the act than from any real pain. He looked around him, then advanced on her, fist raised. "Why you old –"

A cracking noise announced an upturned table as Sandy sprung to the man's side, pulse pistol nuzzling his neck. Only the man's eyes moved, swivelling between the pistol's barrel and Sandy. His buddy made to move towards his friend, but two other men barred his way. Several others circled around him. Micah noticed three had picked up knives from the tables.

Sandy primed the pulse-laser weapon, causing it to emit its unmistakable hum. "This respectable lady is trying to teach you a lesson, one you can learn from. I, on the other hand, specialise in lessons you personally won't learn anything from, though others might."

He drew away from her gun. "Aw, C'mon, I wasn't actually going to –"

"I don't doubt it, not enough balls, but you're going to apologise anyway." She advanced, pressing the nozzle deeper into his neck.

"Sorry," he said, to the elderly woman. The pistol edged forward a few millimetres. "Ma'am," he finished.

The old lady nodded, chin up, somehow appearing taller than the man dwarfing her.

"Apology accepted, I'm sure. Now, you should go back to your room, young man. A cold shower and a shave will remind you not to bite the hand that feeds you, or in this case, protects you."

Sandy retracted the gun. The man stepped away, ready to leave, then paused, turning back to Micah, the fire extinguished in his eyes.

"One thing, *Mister* Sanderson. Next time we face the Q'Roth or some other enemy, do we stand? Or do we run, and keep on running?"

All eyes fell on Micah. He wanted to swallow but thought better of it. It was a good question, and ultimately it would be up to Blake and the others, not just him. But he had to answer, right now. He knew the correct answer, the logical one to ensure humanity's survival. But he'd learned the hard way that it's not always wise to be logical in public. Reluctantly, he imagined how his dead father would have replied. He cleared his throat, stood tall, made his chest proud, and addressed everyone present. "We stand, and we fight," he said. "But next time we make sure it's on even terms."

The man nodded. "Then I'll be there fighting alongside you." He and his friend left. A few of the people who'd rallied round Micah briefly met his eyes, then either sat back down or went about their business. The old lady patted Sandy on the arm. "Nice pistol, I don't suppose I can have one?" She cackled her way out of the canteen without waiting for an answer.

Micah restored the table, sighing at the puddle of gloop on the floor, but a couple shooed him away as he went to clear it up. He slumped back into his chair, facing Sandy, who had regained her seat, acting as if nothing had happened. He leaned forward, whispering. "Can we eat somewhere else tomorrow?"

Her eyes, the colour of hazelnut but sharp like a hawk's, offered him no quarter.

"No, Micah. From now on we eat here *every* day."

Two new steaming bowls appeared before them.

"So, *Mister* Sanderson," she launched, after thanking the young man who had set down the bowls before them, "is humanity still worth saving?"

He scooped up a large dollop of synthetic algae. His eyes swept around the room, and he saw the people there differently: subdued, yes, but strong and ready to fight, whether despite, or because of, their grief. He blew across the top of the spoon, to dispel the odour as much as to cool the soup. A smile spread across his lips. "Sure." He took a breath and opened his mouth. His wristcom buzzed twice. He didn't need to read the message. The fracas had almost made him forget what he had to do today. He lowered the spoon back into the bowl, and stood up. "Saved by the bell – it's time."

She gripped his sleeve as he passed her, stopping him momentarily. "Good luck, Micah."

It always unnerved him whenever Sandy was sincere. He preferred her legendary sarcasm any day of the week, but especially today.

Micah threaded his way across the camp-site on the fourth level, as large as ten football fields. He skirted around each tent's territorial markers of straggled possessions and chem-dry laundry hanging on makeshift lines. He averted his eyes, not wanting to get stuck in conversation with anyone about the inevitable, heavy questions to which he had no answers, much less what these people needed more than anything: concrete hope.

He reached the central spiral ramp. A solitary soldier who looked too young to be in uniform saluted him, and Micah dipped his head in response. It was sad that soldiers had to be posted to control access, but at least they needed only one – humanity's remnants hadn't descended too far out of control yet.

He'd gotten used to military deference. He was only twenty-five and had no rank or military background. But he'd been granted military status by virtue of being the one who had discovered the human race's fate early, uncovering the Alician plot – their millennium-old collusion with the Q'Roth – so helping a sprinkling of humanity to escape the Q'Roth cull.

At first he'd been embarrassed whenever soldiers, some quite high-ranking as far as he could tell, saluted him. He'd even tried saluting back, until Zack had one day told him not to, saying his hand was clearly non-military issue. Besides, Zack had pointed out, just because the soldiers were offering him respect, they didn't necessarily need it back.

Micah had never understood the military.

He strode down the wide, coiling slope, towards base level, the artificial gravity pulling him softly forwards, making him feel lighter. He knew it wasn't real, but it lifted his mood anyway.

At the bottom of the ramp he met a group of heavily-armed soldiers, deep in discussion. The only words he caught were "more nukes" and "seen off the bastards". It was a familiar military refrain: *if only we'd had more weapons*. The armed forces, what was left of them, had a hard time accepting that they'd been defeated by strategy and intelligence, and not just by bigger weapons. Still, he envied their disciplined lives: it would keep them from going off the rails long before everyone else. But he also knew that if the new planet didn't work out, and they were all confined to this ship for months or longer, then these stalwart soldiers could end up shooting people to maintain 'civil order'.

They turned to salute him. One, a major from the look of it, addressed him. "Good evening, Sir."

Micah knew he had to respond in some way. "Good evening, Major, evening men," he ventured, drawing inspiration from war vids he'd watched as a kid, before he'd learned to really hate war for what it was, having been taken prisoner just before the end of WWIII. Was it only ten years ago? He remembered hearing the cries at night from the wounded, the screams of his buddies being tortured... He applied mental brakes, backed out of that particular cul-de-sac, and re-focused. The major clearly had something on his mind, so Micah waited.

"Sir," the major said, "I had the great honour of serving with your father, the Gray Colonel, during the War."

Micah's guts turned to lead. He'd forgotten how much he loathed that particular label. They'd even buried his father – the great war hero – in a grey coffin. He dredged up a smile from somewhere, praying it looked half-real.

The major beamed. "Well, Sir, I just wanted to say it's an honour to serve again with a Sanderson. You did us proud on Eden, Sir. And, if I might add, the Gray Colonel's jacket fits you well."

He had to get out of this fast. He stood to what he presumed was attention, and violated Zack's directive, giving the major the best salute he could offer. "Thank you, Major. But without the military," he added, making eye contact with each of the men, "none of us would have gotten out of there alive." He offered his hand to the Major, who shook it with a bone-cracking grip. Micah managed not to wince.

As soon as he'd rounded the corner, he leaned against the wall and hung his head. *I'm not up to this.* This damned jacket, he thought, glancing down at his father's grey Air Force tunic, which he'd donned en route from the canteen. He'd put it on for a special purpose. Oh well, he thought, let's get this done.

He pushed off from the wall and marched forward, fixing on the hangar in the distance, not stopping to speak with anyone. He zoomed in on Zack – easily distinguishable from a hundred meters away – his gleaming, black, bald pate and gorilla-like frame somehow moving with the quiet, uncompromising ease of a sumo wrestler. His head turned this way and that every now and again, his gaze hawk-like never missing a trick. Micah always relaxed around Zack, though no one under Zack's command ever did. He quickened his pace.

"Hey, buddy, how's it goin?" Zack's voice boomed across the hangar. A few soldiers – this was a strictly military zone – stopped to see who had arrived, and to whom their commander would be so cordial. He paused just short of Zack's reach. Zack's bushy eyebrows knitted together, and he folded his ebony forearms. "Need a stim?" Zack said quietly.

Micah shook his head.

"Well, okay then, there she is," Zack said, pointing to the sleek, blinding white, Moonwalker-class fighter, a mid-range, one man space-jet. Its delta wings ear-marked it as a hybrid, able to operate in atmosphere as well as in space. Micah's throat went dry, and his stomach shrivelled. As a kid he'd dreamt about being an astronaut, but he'd never imagined how disorienting it could be in a small spacecraft, let alone the space-sickness: in the past week he'd thrown up during every single training session. This was the first time he'd be going out on his own in a Moonwalker, having been in a two-man Skyhawk until now.

He braced himself. "Is she – it's always a she, right?"

Zack grinned. "Because you're inside her, Micah."

"Okay, okay. Is she, er ... loaded?"

Zack's grin stalled. He approached and planted a heavy hand on Micah's shoulder. "She's ready, kid. Now, go do what you have to do."

Micah swallowed. He turned towards the craft, then paused, but Zack answered before he could launch the question.

"Blake's already out there, putting your training buddies Luke and Saul through their paces. I'll be on open-link comms. There'll be a bunch watching remotely on level eight, but they won't have comms with you."

As Micah marched to the ladder, a private handed him his flight suit, and saluted him. He took off his father's jacket and passed it to him. The guy received it like it was precious, and almost bowed. Micah made sure he didn't react, and then stepped into the cobalt-coloured, one-piece space-suit, zipped it up and activated the auto-seals. It sucked closed around him, making him feel like a vacuum-packed slice of soy-beef. He bent over to pick up his helmet. It was then he realised there was no sound. Everyone had stopped working and was watching. He strode over to the black torpedo slung under the port wing and laid a gloved hand on it. "*Safe trip,*" he whispered. He donned his helmet, and clambered up the short steps into the cockpit. Once seated, the chair automatically hugged the contours of his body. The transparent forward shield slid into place, cocooning him in silence. The fluidic metal dashboard lit up, casting a sapphire glow around him. Now, for the first time since waking, he really thought about the package he would soon be firing deep into space.

"Ease off the aft port thrusters," Blake said.

Micah marvelled at how Blake never lost patience with him, only raising his voice if Micah was about to crash into the mother ship, or over-compensate with thrusters until his own craft entered a 'tumble', an uncontrolled spin ending with the pilot's intestines serving as interior decor. He couldn't see Blake's Moonwalker – he didn't blame him, best not to get too close. Micah wasn't adept at this, but Blake had insisted he train to be a Captain, to develop the physical skills to match his analytic ones: *the trappings of leadership are important.* At least, he thought, Luke and Saul are out of harm's way, on a recon mission.

He complied with Blake's monotone instructions, though it was all so damned counter-intuitive. None of his years of gaming and holo-sims when he'd been a kid had prepared him for the reality of flying in a straight line when there was simply no measurable gravity in any direction. Pick a star, he thought, *focus.* He selected one, and the oscillations gradually came under control. Micah was an Optron analyst, and Zack, the best pilot left alive, confided in him that this was his biggest problem – these craft had to be flown by feel. If you tried to think about it too much, he'd said, your brain was going to explode, sooner or later.

He relaxed a little, and maintained a straight line for twenty seconds without any appreciable yaw or wavering. For the first time, he saw Blake's craft pull up beside him, three wing-widths to starboard.

"Keep your eyes fixed on whatever star you're looking at, Micah."

He nodded inside his helmet and looked at the tiny speck of light in amongst the carpet of stars draped around them. He'd only realised after leaving Earth and Eden just how *dark* space was. But for the first time he felt in control of the ship. His shoulders dropped.

"You've got it," Blake reassured him.

Zack's voice cut in. "Hey, you've made me a rich man, Micah, you just wrecked the sweepstakes' prediction back here! They were sure you'd puke again!"

He smiled, but it didn't last. It was now or never; he couldn't do this unless he was in control of the craft. "Which way is Earth, Commander?"

"You're pointing in her direction, as far as we can tell after fifteen fractal transits."

Blake's gravel-like voice fit the occasion. Micah flicked up the lid covering the red push-button on the joystick. He paused.

"You have to say something first, Micah, some words," Sandy said.

He was taken aback, hearing Sandy. But then he remembered Zack had wanted to train her in battle comms, on account of the cutting edge in her voice.

"We've split the comms links," she said. "Blake is going to give a eulogy for everyone else, relayed to level eight. This line is just you and me. No one else can hear. No one alive, that is."

This time, her tone had none of its usual acid-coating. He wished she'd known his mother. There: he'd been avoiding that word all day. The image of his Mom rose up in his mind, triggering a cascade of scenes and emotions, from his early childhood, to three days ago, when she'd slipped away from him in the hospital wing on the fifth level, with an air of serenity, knowing she would at last join her long-dead husband.

Micah had managed to rescue her in the last days of the Q'Roth onslaught, but she'd been wounded, and she was just too old, the doctor had said. Micah had another opinion, however, as his Mom had always been so strong: she'd survived just long enough to see that her son was safe, and then, resources depleted, and too plain tired to countenance another adventure, she'd finally let go of life.

She'd had one last request: she didn't want to be buried on the new planet. She wanted to go home. He'd protested that it was impossible, but she'd gripped his wrist with withered yet firm fingers, and said "you'll find a way." It was the last coherent thing she'd uttered.

She hadn't been alone in this request. Many had been fatally wounded in the exodus, and seventy-four on Blake's ship had perished in the past two weeks since departing Eden. The Chief Medical Officer had been having a hard time determining what to do with the cadavers – all freezer storage was reserved for food and med-supplies, and the few relatives onboard had railed at the thought of their loved ones' bodies simply being dumped in space. So they'd cremated all the bodies, and placed the ashes in a torpedo casing, which he now aimed towards a dying planet God alone knew how many light years away. It would probably never get there, of course, instead winding up in some star's gravity well. But it was the best they could offer, a symbolic gesture.

Somewhere in the main ship behind them, a gathering of relations and friends was taking place, and various priests, rabbis and mullahs were casting prayers over these souls who had almost, but not quite, made it.

He realised he'd been silent for a while. He cleared his throat, his right hand locked around the joystick. "Sandy, I've never told anyone this before. When I was born, it was during one of the last outbreaks of the nannite plague. The hospital was infected and, well, my Mom was locked in with everyone else, under quarantine. In two days almost three hundred people died. When they pulled me out of her, they left the placenta attached, kept me incubated, as independent from the external environment as possible. Everything was contaminated, you see. So they cut the umbilical very late." He coughed. "My father used to joke that that was why I was such a mommy's boy, never able to break the ties with her. Truth is – "

"Incoming! Break off Micah, now!" Zack shouted.

He was trying to process what Zack could mean, but he'd been trained to react first and think about it afterwards when a CO yelled at him. He yanked the joystick hard to port as his right foot rammed the main thruster pedal. The move spun him around one-eighty degrees and displaced him fifty metres. He watched in disbelief as a white missile tore past him. Blake's craft lurched around and streaked behind him, in hot pursuit.

"Can he make it?" Micah asked, guessing the target was the mother ship.

"If anyone can, he'll do it," Zack said. "Micah, listen, I don't know who fired – Luke or Saul. Maybe they're both in on this. They're headed your way. No one comes past you. Arm both your... *damn!*"

"I know," Micah said. He had one live and one empty torpedo – well, not entirely empty. He knew better than to ask questions of Zack, as he'd be helping Blake take out the missile, relaying nav data and time to impact.

"Micah, listen, it's Sandy, all hell's breaking loose back here."

"Has Blake reached it yet?" He strained his eyesight looking for any telltale movement of Saul and Luke ahead of him. His radar showed no signals, so they must have switched off their transponders and employed stealth mode.

There was a pause. "No – it's going to be tight. He's already pushed eight G's just to track it. We've just found two dead soldiers in armaments, and two nukes missing."

Great, he thought, they have live missiles instead of dummies. "Shut the hangar doors, Sandy. Those Q'Roth ships are tough bastards. At least one survived a nuke attack, remember?"

"The doors are jammed open, and the two spare Moonwalkers have been disabled. They planned ahead."

"Move the ship, then!"

"You know we can't move between jumps, not for another four hours, not until the engines are recharged."

Micah knew that and more. He guessed what Sandy and everyone else would be thinking: *Alicians.* It meant they had at least one, probably two, and maybe more Alician spies aboard, with a simple objective. He flicked up the protective cover on the live torpedo, and nudged the joystick forward.

"Sandy, I'm going to need to concentrate for a while."

"Okay, Micah, good lu–"

"Micah. What are you planning exactly?"

"Hello, Saul." He'd hoped it would be Luke; Saul was the better pilot. He wondered why they hadn't fired the other nuke. How long had it been now? Thirty seconds? No detonation yet. Maybe Blake had made it, and wing-tipped it off course.

"Why, Saul?"

Luke answered, his voice higher-pitched than Saul's. "Loose ends, Micah, an intelligent race doesn't leave any. You're smart enough to do the math. *Intelligence.* That's what counts in the galaxy. Only the clever survive, and Alicians are more intelligent, so humanity loses. *Again.*"

The blood rose into Micah's head, but he knew he had to stay carb-steel cold. A message flashed up on his screen. *Missile diverted and destroyed.*

"Seems our flight instructor is as good as his reputation, eh Micah? But he can't stop a second one, he's too close to the ship now, and his fuel will be low after that little sprint."

"Micah, missile disabled," Zack cut in, "but Blake's now way over the other side of the ship. What's your situation?"

Micah was surprised – whatever he answered to Zack, Saul and Luke would hear. Zack must know that. He decided to play along. "On intercept. I can maybe take out one – but I don't know who has the nuke. Instructions?"

"Take out Saul."

Now he was perplexed. With their transponders de-activated, he wouldn't know which craft was Saul's unless he was close enough to see into the cockpit. What was Zack up to? But more importantly what would Saul and Luke do next? He had to outflank two Alicians – humans genetically altered with Q'Roth DNA. Ideally, they'd want to get closer, just to make sure with their last nuke. They could split in two directions, giving them a 50:50 chance – no, Alicians wouldn't trust to luck. So, they would take him out first, together. And both were better pilots than he was. How could he take down even one of them?

"Micah, Blake here, don't respond. I'm on a split channel, so Luke and Saul can't hear me. Set your starboard weapon to heat-seek, and disable its proximity protection. Then key in TX-24-03-64-2."

He tapped the code into the fluidic keyboard; it felt like pressing down on liquid mercury. Even as he wondered what the code was, Blake filled him in, audible through his helmet's left-ear speaker.

"It's Saul's training mission log from yesterday. Your missile targeting device has a fast-acting neural net. When you fire it will recognise Saul's piloting characteristics from his evasive manoeuvres and lock onto him. Okay, no more time, move to intercept. You'll only get one shot. Wind up your engine to max, but apply the forward thrusters in reverse. You'll black out when you release them and catapult forward, but it means their missiles won't be able to get a target lock. You can do this, Micah."

He swallowed. Blake had saved his life twice before, he reminded himself, so why not a third time? He tapped the required console symbols, then jammed his foot on the left pedal till it reached the floor. The Moonwalker stuttered and vibrated with a teeth-juddering intensity, then settled down and pitched forward, gathering speed despite the brakes being full-on.

"Micah, you're no match for either one of us, let alone two. This is suicide," Saul said.

"Bring it on, Micah, this is going to be like an old-fashioned turkey shoot," Luke added.

Good, while you keep talking, I know you're not firing. He understood what Zack was doing. By saying *take out Saul*, he was trying to throw them off-balance, to break their teamwork rhythm. He had to join Zack's game.

"Maybe so, Saul, but you're coming with me." There, that should do it. There was an odds-on chance Saul held the nuke, being the better pilot – unless they'd already thought of that.

Blake's voice cut in. "I said *full* throttle, Micah, hit the turbo."

He prodded the dashboard in front of him. A shrill whining noise made him check where the ejector release was, in case the ship tore itself apart. After three seconds of banshee vibrations, his ship accelerated, pressing him deeper into the warm embrace of his gel-seat. His eyes blurred with the accelerative pressure. He remembered his training, and tapped the right side of his joystick to switch to computer-audio, since he couldn't read any of the data.

"Four hundred, four-fifty, five-sixty..."

His eyes re-focused. '*... stabilising eight hundred kph.*'

He silenced voice-comp and punched up the radar onto the plazshield: two green blobs appeared a hundred and eighty klicks ahead of him, closing. They were moving at a slower speed. They could have accelerated too, but since the torpedoes couldn't lock on at closing speeds in excess of fifteen hundred klicks, it was clear they wanted to kill him first.

"Micah, get ready to release the live one. When I say 'now', fire it and then cut the brakes."

Fuck! If it doesn't lock onto one of them, it'll track me, and I'm dead: I can't outrun a torpedo.

"Micah," Zack said. "Soon as you've taken out Saul, pivot and pursue Luke. Blake's re-fuelled, he'll be there soon."

He watched the radar – they both accelerated towards him, but one edged forward – that must be Luke.

"Now!" Blake shouted.

Micah squeezed the missile release and then flicked the brakes off. He cried out as he was engulfed by the chair, his eyes rammed backwards into their sockets. His tongue retracted and his cheeks tried to shear away from his skull. His chest felt as if a space-craft had landed on it. He heard a shrieking alarm, recognising it as the warning for pushing G's way beyond pilot tolerance, half a second before his brain switched off.

"... up, Micah, WAKE UP!" Sandy screamed at him.

He opened his eyes, then shook his head. "I'm... I'm back online. What happened? How long –"

"Thirty seconds. One ship is down, you're chasing the other one."

His head was still reeling. "Which one?"

"Hey, Micah, just me and you, now, pal, see if you can catch me before I take out the trash."

Micah scrutinised the radar screen – Luke was ahead, but not by much. Why hadn't he fired yet? And where were Zack and Blake? He shoved hard on the joystick, exceeding recommended maximum tolerance.

His head raced. Saul was gone, but Saul would have had a missile lock alarm seconds before Micah's missile hit him, so if Saul had had the nuke aboard, he'd have launched it; so Luke must have it.

"Micah, this is Blake. I'm on intercept, but I need two minutes. Distract Luke if you can. He won't fire until he's in the red zone."

He figured it out. The first nuke they had launched long range, using the element of surprise, not counting on Blake's reactions and pilot skills. But by now Zack must have assembled targeting scanners and pulse lasers from the open Hangar. Once Luke launched the missile, it would fly a straight course, and maybe, just maybe, Zack could shoot it down. But if Luke got close enough, then it wouldn't matter, the blast would cripple or destroy the ship.

He was able to close the gap because Luke wasn't flying in a straight line, as otherwise Zack could target him. Micah tried to distract him.

"Hey, Luke. Why didn't you just detonate the nukes inside the ship?"

Luke snorted. "You missed a lecture, buddy. The nukes each have a lockout: they need command codes from Blake and Zack to activate them. Otherwise, they make a mess, but don't detonate."

Nearly in range. He capitalised on his own intrigue to try to stall Luke. "Then how –?"

"Out on recon we exceeded Zack's surveillance range. We uploaded an attack simulation, convinced the nuke's tactical computers that the hierarchy had been destroyed, and the mother ship re-taken by the enemy. The two ships had no option but to verify against each other, then they disabled the lockouts. Some of my handiwork, actually. Fear is always the key, Micah, even with computers. So, you want to see a nuclear blast at close range?"

Micah had already had a ring-side seat, twice. He picked out the blue-hot engine ahead of him jumping around like a frantic mosquito, and just as hard to swat. But the pattern wasn't random – it never was with people, genetically upgraded or not. He switched into Optron analyst mode and did the calcs. Luke's erratic pattern would defeat normal targeting scanners, and Blake was going to be thirty seconds too late. He made his decision. He tapped several rapid commands into the console and then let his mind follow the movements, tracing the zigs and zags in a mental 4-D grid. His breathing slowed as he tracked Luke, using the part of the mind known as the reptilian brain, homing on his prey the way a cheetah runs down a gazelle. All his fears, his inhibitions were suppressed, and now that he had a target, flying to hit it was much easier than navigating open space.

'Hey, Micah, you been practicing?' Luke said.

Micah didn't – couldn't – respond, his left brain was disabled, his right brain reflexes completely in charge. He was closing fast.

'Hey! Micah, I'm going to fire, man, if you get any closer!'

Micah deployed the fast landing grapple, a metre-long metallic hook designed to catch a braking line if hot-landing in the hangar. He inverted his Moonwalker and flicked his joystick down. There was a deafening grating noise, like trucks colliding, as his Moonwalker slammed into Luke's undercarriage, the grapple penetrating Luke's hull.

"What the fuck?" Luke shouted.

Micah had to do it now. He tapped a single command and his torpedo – with the ashes of his mother and seventy-three others aboard – fired, still locked down to the wing of his craft. He set the port thrusters on full so that the two bound craft careened to the right, slewing away from the ship at a right angle. "Goodbye, Luke."

Micah punched the eject button.

He catapulted away, spinning like a drunken gyroscope. He caught flashes of the pirouetting ensemble as Luke tried hopelessly to bring the two shackled ships under control. Micah counted down. Two. One. Goodbye Mom.

The darkness of space flashed brilliant white as the torpedo's ion engine cut in and instantly overloaded, igniting the entire fuel cell. The incandescence wasn't nuclear – if it had been, then he knew he wouldn't be scrunching his eyes closed with pain – he'd be vaporised. Luke hadn't reached the red zone, and he hadn't detonated. It was over.

Micah did a rough calculation of which way he'd been facing when he'd ejected. Figures, he thought, as he carried on spinning at speed, further away from the Mother-Ship.

CHAPTER 2 –
PREMONITION

The nausea had mostly passed. Micah knew he was flying at almost the same velocity with which the ejector seat had propelled him half an hour ago, but he had no real sense of motion, since relative to the stars he wasn't moving at all. At least he'd been able to apply his suit's micro-thrusters to stop the spinning and tumbling; dying alone in space would be bad enough, he didn't need to suffer it watching his last moments through a vomit-encrusted visor.

He recalled one of Zack's flying lessons, maybe a week ago...

"*Space has no compassion*," Zack said, lecturing him and the other trainees, leaning forward on sturdy black forearms, wiry eyebrows meshed together beneath a shiny bald pate. "It ain't like the sea – there you have a chance, you can trust in Lady Luck if all else fails. Ain't so with space – you always need a Plan A, definitely a Plan B, all the way up to Plan F. That's the one you apply when all hell breaks loose and you find yourself shouting... Well, I don't need to spell it out, do I? Oh, and I shouldn't have to say this either, but I will: never, *ever*, abandon your craft. Chances you'll be found are?"

"Zero," they replied, in chorus.

Never, ever leave your craft. A simple enough, intuitive rule. Try as he might, though, Micah couldn't figure out what better course of action he could have taken – he'd already be dead. They'd all be dead. He changed tack mentally, wondering if it would make any difference to his velocity or detectability if he adopted some position or other – foetal, maybe, or star-shaped. He considered his life so far: unhappy childhood, brooding adolescence, the usual teenage angst with girls which had endured longer than most. He'd spent his life wanting to be somewhere else –

away from his father, away from his job, not living with his Mom in their pokey flat. He'd always wanted to be an astronaut...

He raised his arm to view the data screen. Five minutes of air left. His long-range comms antennae had been ripped off his suit during ejection, so he couldn't even talk to anyone – Sandy, for example – in his last moments. Better for them, he supposed. He wondered what it would be like, asphyxiating – would he thrash around, try to take his helmet off? And then after dying, there was death itself. He'd always assumed it was like switching off a computer, an easy perspective to take when you're young and figure you've got another fifty years to come up with something better. He felt a shiver run down his spine as the full weight of death closed in on him. He imagined Death's bony fingers sinking into his flesh. He shuddered. "Well, Mum, looks like we're going to have a family reunion after all."

"Micah, you dumb sonofabitch, what did I tell you to never, *ever* do?"

Micah stared wildly in his field of vision, then powered his suit thrusters just enough to turn him around. Zack was floating towards him, tethered to his Skyhawk by a gossamer thread, carrying a white cylinder.

"Don't move, buddy." Zack's suit thrusters puffed wisps of evanescent air just in front of Micah. Zack flourished a hose and clamped it onto a valve on Micah's suit, and he immediately tasted fresh, cool air. He inhaled deeply.

"Zack, how'd you find me?"

Zack pressed auto-reel and they were gently tugged back toward the ship.

"What, you think I let rookies out here without emergency tracers in their suits?" He laughed so hard it steamed up his visor, misting his black features, but not his grinning white teeth.

"Christ, Zack! I thought..." He tried to punch Zack's arm, but in space, he realised, while there's no compassion, anger has no purchase either.

The massive black ship loomed before them as they approached at speed. Etched out in space, visible only because it obscured the stars behind, it created a towering, disc-like shadow as they approached side-on. The four-storey conning tower had the only windows on the entire vessel, glowing green oblong slits decorating its circumference. It protruded like a lighthouse, a head with menacing jade eyes craning upwards from the dish-like vessel. Zack accelerated and skated over the seamless, featureless hull that extended like a vast metal desert. Once they'd passed the tower, complete darkness flooded in, black as the tar-pits on Jupiter's Io. Micah could no longer see the vessel's surface beneath him, just the far edge where pin-prick stars re-asserted themselves.

Zack swooped over the rim and gravity-surfed down past the ship's seven floors and then dipped down to the underbelly, skimming back towards the ship's centre.

"Invert, see?" Zack said, not missing the chance to reinforce a valuable lesson in space-flight, namely to try to remember which way was up when you were coming back to the mother ship. He flicked the gyro-ball once with his left hand and rolled the Skyhawk. His right hand remained stable, cradling the joystick. Up ahead, a wash of yellow light spilled into space from the open hangar. Zack slowed down, and Micah could make out the other three Moonwalkers and soldiers milling about in the harsh lighting. He squinted, his vision night-adapted. He held his breath as the Skyhawk slinked through the shimmering force-field that nobody understood, which allowed them to go on recon missions without decompressing the entire ship and voiding everyone in the process. They slid smoothly to a halt, clamping into place with a welcome clunk. He breathed a sigh of relief as the plazshield above his head slid open again.

Blake was waiting for them as they disembarked. So were most of the soldiers and pilots.

"Not bad flying back there, Mr. Sanderson." Blake handed Micah a small pair of silver wings. "You earned them today, son." Zack started clapping, triggering a small round of applause and whistles.

Micah felt his cheeks redden, and nodded to his tall commander-in-chief, the man who led their small fleet of human refugees. Blake's ruddy hair framed a gaunt face, pock-marked from some battle or other during the third World War, which only served to emphasise his right to lead based on his extensive experience. "Thank you, Sir."

"Follow me." Blake turned and strode towards the briefing room. Micah got a congratulatory thwack on the shoulder from Zack, but otherwise he said nothing. As they headed away from the dissipating throng, he noticed an orderly cleaning up bloodstains on the hangar floor. So, he thought, they've been busy here too. He turned to Zack, who held up four fingers as they walked. Micah felt dazed. So, there had been six Alician spies onboard, and no one had guessed; two of them had been working right under Blake and Zack's noses.

The three of them sat down in the cramped, soundproof briefing room. Blake didn't waste any time getting to the point.

"Micah, in three hours we make the final transit to Ourshiwann. Vince and Jennifer's ships have both made contact in the last few hours via the Hohash – we're converging from our different routes, so the Hohash devices are in range again."

"And Rashid's ship?"

Blake pursed his lips. "We've heard nothing from the fourth ship. Nothing from Rashid, Pierre, or Kat. Since only you and Pierre could hold all the disguised flight plans in your heads, I need you to run through them."

Micah sat back – this was going to be tough, and he already felt wasted. "You mean right now?"

Zack answered. "Has to be, Micah, we gotta know if something's happened. If the Q'Roth tracked us somehow, or even our Alician pals... At the least, we can prep the Moonwalkers, go in guns blazing when we arrive."

Micah's shoulders ached. He got off the chair and pulled off his boots. He lowered himself into a half-lotus position, his sacrum wedged against the wall. The mental gymnastics he was about to undergo required physical props, in particular a straight and alert spine. Blake and Zack, out of politeness, squatted down next to him. He closed his eyes and began the breathing routine, imagining the void, just as he'd been taught back in Palo Alto by the Zen master who trained all Optron analysts. It wasn't so hard, given where he'd been just twenty minutes ago. It took five minutes before he could dredge up the package he'd stored in his mind two weeks earlier.

As a kid he'd always been good with numbers. But it was only when his teachers found he could visualise and multiply three-dimensional matrices that he was assigned more specialised schooling, first in mental imagery, then harmonic cipher-coding, and finally Optron reading. There had never been anything physical or medical done to alter his brain, excepting some specialised drugs, but it had altered the way he thought. Stuff often ran through his head of its own volition, processing, thinking sideways, looking for patterns and scavenging for resonances in events and data. Most of the time he could ignore it, pushing it backwards, downwards, like a radio you're not really listening to, playing somewhere in the house. But for now, he'd achieved complete inner silence.

He was ready. The rest of the world outside was blocked out, a vast emptiness. A red, cube-shaped package hovered in the middle of a starless night. Micah visualised the mnemonic ciphers and the package unfolded into the three-dimensional space in his mind. The fractal pattern he'd encoded took shape. It was a puzzle, four coloured snake-like tubes zig-zagging away from one blue-green ball in space and converging on another dusty brown one. He picked out the blue tube – their own ship – and counted the transits, the number of times the line changed tack. Then he counted the transits for the pink line, Rashid's ship. His head began to throb hard. A drip of sweat ran down his back. He didn't need to count again. Micah visualised the locking cipher and let the puzzle implode, after which it was swallowed up and bound once more inside the red cube. He observed his breathing for a few minutes, then creaked his eyes open. As he'd expected, everything around him, Blake and Zack included, was in sepia, but he knew it was a temporary side effect. It would pass quicker than the headache.

He heard his own voice as if from far away, his flat, analyst voice. "Same number of transits. Route longer. Some transits pushed engines. Longer recharge times. A day, maybe two, behind us."

Blake and Zack got up, helping Micah stand atop stiff legs. "Thank you, Micah."

"I'll prep a third of the squadron in any case," Zack said, "just to be sure, and have a couple of sling-jets on hot standby."

Micah didn't want to hear this. He wanted it to be over. At the same time he knew these two were right, which was why they were in charge. Blake spoke softly. "Micah, go get some rest."

He didn't need to be told twice.

When he reached his quarters after taking a needle-shower, he brushed aside the crinkled beige curtain not quite covering the oval doorway, and found Sandy cross-legged on the mat inside, a bottle of wine and two clean glasses next to her.

"Don't get your hopes up, Micah, or anything else." She raised an eyebrow. "You look like hell, you know that?"

He shrugged, too tired to think of a witty reply.

"It's the three week anniversary of this little fella" – she patted her belly – "being conceived, and his father being blown to smithereens by the Alicians."

He sat down next to her, did the honours, and poured the wine. He read the label. "Cabernet Sauvignon, 2032 – was that a good year?"

She clinked glasses. "Year I was born, which means it's a classic." Her face lit up with a broad, infectious smile.

He stared into the burgundy coloured liquid. His mind instantly did the math; Sandy was thirty-three.

She took a sip. "What's up? And don't say 'Oh, nothing really', Micah, I know you too well."

He took a long slug of wine, then another. It felt good, warming his throat. "Rashid's ship is late."

"That's reasonable isn't it? Didn't they take the longest route?"

He put down the glass. "Blake asked me to run the numbers again, and yes, it's reasonable, the numbers look... okay."

Sandy parked her own glass. "But numbers can lie, can't they?"

"Actually, no, they never lie, that's why I like them. It's just that, as an Optron reader, you deal with them so much that every now and again you get to glance behind them. You don't quite see what's there, you just know that, well, the numbers are hiding something."

Sandy topped up his glass. "So, what do you think, Q'Roth or Alicians?"

He picked up his glass, swirled the wine around, the way his father used to, he realised – and it no longer mattered. "The Q'Roth aren't like us. They've had their feed. I'm not sure they care what happens to us anymore. They're nomadic, they'll just move on."

"Alicians, then, our treacherous, genetically-enhanced, bastard cousins. Super."

They sat in silence, then Sandy raised her glass. "Well then, drink up, Micah. It may be a while before we can do this again." She tilted her head back and drained her glass.

Sandy was wearing her hair tied back today. He'd never seen her with her hair like that before, revealing how much her face was like a 'vee' from her temples to her chin. Her saucer-like eyes, which missed nothing, more than compensated. But in his mind, still in its post-analysis lucid state, a connection began to form. He took another sip, hoping it would go away. But as he savoured the wine, a different face he hadn't thought about for two weeks entered his mind: a striking, beautiful blonde with a ponytail. He gulped down more wine. He'd heard a disturbing report from Vince, just before they departed Eden, that Louise's corpse had gone missing, right before the end. She'd almost killed all of them, back on Earth. He really hoped she was dead. But the face stubbornly remained, no longer hiding behind the numbers. He felt a chill skitter down his spine. He held out his glass to Sandy.

"Say when," she said, pouring the wine.

Micah said nothing.

CHAPTER 3 – PIETRO

Rashid rammed the ankh key into the slot for the third time, but it was no use, the ship refused to move. He and two other crew members huddled in the mould-coloured control room whose curved walls made him feel like he was trapped inside the labyrinthine intestines of some giant monstrous being: dead, just not yet digested. They tried to make the Q'Roth vessel controls work, but everything was inert. Rashid bit hard on his lower lip. They'd already executed twelve perfect jumps, with the required twenty-four-hour intervals to recharge the engines. Something else was wrong, and meanwhile, they dangled in space like bait on a hook.

He'd planned to move closer to the storm-shrouded planet Pierre and Katrina were surveying in the Hohash scout vessel, when he discovered the mother ship had slipped into sleep mode. At least the two thousand human refugees aboard were unaware of their predicament – tensions since they'd fled a burning Earth two weeks ago had meant he might just as well have a manifest of gunpowder rather than people, a tinderbox ready to ignite at the mere hint of a spark. He glanced at Axel and Sofia, but their furrowed brows, reflected in the jungle green lighting from the consoles, told him they were just as confused and apprehensive. He hoped his own concern was better masked than theirs. On impulse, and because they'd exhausted all other options, he kicked the stand of the extruded grey console with his boot, which did nothing whatsoever for the controls. However, a voice lanced across the room from behind him.

"Engine trouble?"

He spun around to see the upper half of a woman, honey-blonde hair strained back in a ponytail, rending her eyes – which could otherwise have been considered beautiful – too elfin-like to trust. Her crystal-clear image, sliced off at the waist, stared back at him with an equivocal expression, hovering in the middle of the room.

A hologram, he assumed, though not like any he'd ever seen, and without any obvious source of projection.

"I wish to speak to Vince. Or Micah. Or even the legendary Blake Alexander."

Rashid jutted his chin at the seated woman. "All dead, killed on Eden," he lied. "And – you must excuse me – but we have not been introduced."

A smile flickered like a nascent flame and was gone. "Louise."

He narrowed his eyes. He'd heard enough about Louise – an Alician assassin – from Micah and Vince – to presume that he, his ship and its two thousand frightened souls were in grave trouble. Yet she was supposed to be dead. He decided not to question the obvious, but she must have read his expression.

"Vince gave me a headache, but I'm all better now," she said, mock sweetness.

He knew Vince had in fact put a hole clean through her skull. He brushed it aside: it didn't matter how she was here. He rebuffed the idea of asking the clichéd question of what she wanted. As he suspected, he didn't have to wait for her to get to the point.

"I've taken remote control of your ship. Perhaps that possibility didn't occur to you when you stole it?"

He grimaced. Of course it had, which is why each of the four ships fleeing Earth and Eden had taken separate, fractally-coded pathways to the Ourshiwann home world, transiting to distant jump points, only entering each destination just before the next jump. He glanced over to the empty wall-space where the Hohash mirror-device normally resided. Pierre and Katrina had taken it to the nearby planet, looking for water. It meant he had no way to communicate with the other ships to warn them. Still, at least Pierre and Katrina might survive.

He suppressed his mounting curiosity at how this holographic projection could transmit both ways, if indeed, he wondered, it was a hologram. She looked real enough to touch, except for the obvious fact that the lower half of her body was missing. *If she can interact with me – if she can hear my voice and see my actions, maybe this hologram can sense and transmit pain back to the real Louise...*

She stifled a yawn. "Give me the coordinates of your final destination and you may live. If not, I will jump your ship into this system's star."

Rashid heard Sofia gasp and Axel take a step backwards. Sofia, a dark-skinned woman in her thirties who he'd been getting to know in the two weeks since leaving Eden, touched his arm. "Rashid –"

He tensed his body, standing to attention, and faced Louise. "How do I know you'll keep your word?"

Louise didn't answer immediately. Instead, she interlocked her fingers and flexed them outwards. The bone-cracking noise whipped across the control room.

She smiled. "Rashid, is it?"

He nodded, not blinking. He remembered learning as a Rajasthani child how to catch a cobra, or at least to judge when one was going to spit venom. At age nine he'd lost his best friend in that deadly village game. He wondered if there was some way to grab this cobra's throat before she could strike.

"Well, I'm not after you, or your sorry baggage." She waved a hand dismissively. "I'm after Vince and Micah. They killed me, and I need –" she leaned forward, "really, I *need*, to repay the privilege." She reclined, folding her arms. "Give me your flight plan and I'll leave you with one jump possibility, following which your ship's navigation database will corrupt. There's a planet nearby with oxygen, though it's a tad heavy on sulphur. You might survive, after a fashion."

He heard Axel hovering near the doorway, and he understood. The young engineer had married only three weeks ago and knew where he wanted to be when... Rashid shut out everything except the cobra. "Give us some time to decide, I need to consult with other members of the crew and the council," he ventured, guessing it would make no difference.

Louise shook her head once. "No, Rashid. You're Captain, so it's not a democracy. You have one minute before you get to see the inside of a star."

Rashid knew it was probably futile, but he'd kick himself if he didn't at least try. He reached over his shoulder with his right hand, felt inside the back of his collar, and found what he was looking for. In one smooth flowing movement he hurled the stiletto straight at, and through, Louise's left eye. The knife lodged into the far wall with a thwack. At his side, Sofia gulped.

"Nice aim," said Louise. She hadn't even blinked. "Fifty-five seconds."

He pursed his lips, then moved to the back of the control room. "Move aside," he said, brushing Axel out of the way so he could access the navigation console. "You're dismissed ensign."

'But Sir, I –'

Rashid seized him by the shoulders, and spoke softly. "Go to her. Now." He pushed so that Axel half-stumbled backwards, then turned and darted out onto the central ramp. Rashid tapped in a flight plan. Sofia shadowed him, peering over his shoulder as he stooped over the displays and controls. He heard her soft intake of breath as she recognised the decoy flight plan Pierre had created just before he had left. She clutched his forearm as he typed. His fingers chopped at the keyboard as if he was entering their death sentence. She whispered into his ear, her voice unsteady. "You're doing the right thing."

He'd have preferred it if she'd started clawing at him, begging him not to lie to Louise. He punched in the transmit command and walked back towards the hologram, steady, setting his jaw. "It is done."

Louise studied something outside the hologram frame. "I'd warn you that if it's a trick, I'll be back." She cocked her head, elfin eyes gleaming. "But there's no point, is there, Rashid? Well, it's been a pleasure doing business with you. Say goodbye to your girlfriend." The hologram dissolved into granules of flickering violet, then vanished.

He knew it would be fast. He met Sofia's wide, frightened eyes. He reached out to her, stroked her cheek with the back of his fingers. Everything froze, and shifted into the familiar mercurial shades that meant that the ship, together with him, Sofia, his crew, and its precious goods – a quarter of surviving humanity – had just jumped.

Rashid had no illusions about the colour he would see next, but its brightness was beyond anything he could ever have imagined.

* * *

"Don't think I'll be sending any postcards," Kat said.

Pierre allowed himself an evanescent smile, not on account of Kat's sardonic wit, but because it meant she was relaxed with him. He valued the friendship that was coming like spring, after a bone-chilling winter, even if she'd never shown any warmth to him in the prior three months travelling from Earth to Eden. No matter that she loved Antonia, either. Sex was as over-rated as companionship was under-rated, in his opinion. He wondered what might grab her attention. Humour wasn't his strong suit.

"Not human-sustainable in the long term. At least there's some water, if we can filter out all the chemicals. Also, the day-night temperature cycle would severely challenge human endurance." He cut himself off. She looked bored. He tried another approach.

"We haven't named it." There, that was better. Yet again, he was painfully aware of how his father's genetic experimentation on him as a child had instilled scientific brilliance, at the cost of basic social aptitudes. It had made for a lonely life so far.

Kat swivelled her closely-cropped, raven-haired head from the displays, and cast a look at him as if she'd just noticed he was there. She was short and of slight build, with a constant edginess about her, as if she trusted no one. Her pale blue eyes were almost grey, and she had a habit of looking people in the eye for a split-second, drawing her assessment, and then looking away. But this time her eyes lingered. Pierre shifted in his seat as her stare penetrated through to the back of his skull; he'd never believed the expression 'see right through you' could be taken literally until he met Kat. He cleared his throat and gazed resolutely through the portal, out into the toxic vermillion funk masquerading as this planet's excuse for an atmosphere, hoping the stars would soon re-appear to distract them both.

"Pietro," she said, finally. "That's what we should call it: stone – rock – you."

He'd been called a cold fish enough times in his life, but her sarcastic tone and crooked smile anaesthetised the insult, the net effect being the verbal equivalent of a friendly punch on the arm, rather than a nasty jab. She was playing with him, he guessed, because he was no threat to her or Antonia.

They had left Rashid and the other two thousand refugees on the Q'Roth transport ship in order to inspect the planet, the only one they'd encountered since leaving Eden, just to check if it was habitable, a back up in case Ourshiwann wasn't viable. They'd taken with them the ship's Hohash, one of five surviving alien artefacts – and their only ally – found on Eden. The Hohash resembled an upright, art-deco mirror with an oval gold frame, like he'd seen once as a teenager in the holo-museum in Reims. The memory tripped him up as surely as an astro-blader hitting an updraft. Reims, Europe, Earth itself, was gone, scoured clean by the Q'Roth, sucking the bioelectricity out of all living mammals, leaving empty, flaccid husks behind.

He felt a connection with the Hohash, the last remnants of the spider world harvested by the Q'Roth a thousand years before they raked across Earth. The Hohash were unique, like him. As far as he knew he was the only non-Alician genetically altered human left, genned for intelligence. He usually hid how fast he thought, though it had come in handy back on Eden. He guessed the Hohash too, must feel lonely. Only Kat could communicate with them, after a fashion, courtesy of the play-node embedded in her cortex. The Hohash had sensors far beyond human technology, which was why he'd brought it along. Rashid had protested at first – as far as their overly-polite captain could complain about anything – but Pierre had persuaded him there was little danger, and they'd only be gone a few hours. Besides, they hadn't heard from any of the other three ships, each equipped with their own Hohash, for over a week. Evidently the Hohash had limited range.

He registered a mental shiver. It had only been twelve days since they'd left Earth and Eden. It was just possible that some humans were still fighting – or more likely hiding – from the Q'Roth. But the probability was vanishingly small. The purge had been so efficient, so relentless and swift. Earth was most likely desolate, destroyed, devoid of life.

Pierre bent his mind back to the task. The Hohash sensors had explored the planet far quicker than he'd imagined possible, relaying the information back to Kat. But it had not been good news. They wouldn't last a week on this planet – *Pietro*. It felt good to have a planet named after him, he decided, even a dud one.

The claret-coloured clouds faded as black night sluiced in around them, the stars glinting all around; they were back in space. He felt a thrill run through him: an astronaut, the best job conceivable for an astrophysicist. He let himself imagine he and Kat were explorers on a months-long mission, just them on this small ship. A rare warmth suffused his lean frame. Yet as he turned to face Kat, he watched a frown form on her face, then morph into a grimace of shock. He glanced down at his instruments but saw nothing to be alarmed about.

"Something's happened," she whispered. Her face blanched, eyes distant as if seeing outside the ship.

He looked over his shoulder to the Hohash, whose fluid mirror surface showed a zoomed-in picture of the neighbouring sun. A flare gushed upwards from the corona, like a wave slapping against rocks, then subsided again. He knew the Hohash was tied into the ship's external sensors, and that they were watching something in real-time, but he didn't know what. Kat shrieked with such ferocity that he leapt out of his chair and rushed toward her, just in time to catch her collapsing body. He lowered her twitching, unconscious frame to the floor. Worse than her tremors was the stillness which followed as she lay listless as a corpse. He checked her vitals, and the diagnosis emerged soon enough – coma. He leaned over her. "Stay with me, Kat." He glanced at the Hohash, but its mirror surface no longer rippled, instead registering only a dull, charcoal-coloured fog.

For the next hour he steered the craft back to the rendezvous coordinates, but he already had a bad feeling about what he would find. When he arrived, he decided it would have been preferable to find wreckage, rather than nothing at all. The absence of data left too many uncertainties. He wondered how much longer the air would last in their small craft.

After a day spent loitering in space waiting to see if the ship returned, with the air beginning to taste of stale mushrooms, Kat still in a coma, and the Hohash inert, he powered up the engines and directed the ship back to Pietro. *I hope I was wrong about surviving only a week.* He recalled what Zack had said about him once, not that long ago: "When it comes to facts and figures, Pierre's never wrong." He gunned the engines. *Every rule has an exception*, his father had told him, more than once. He prayed his father was right.

* * *

Ukrull, a reptilian Ranger under instructions from Grid Central, who had observed the Q'Roth culling of Earth as per galactic protocol, had tagged undetected behind the Q'Roth hunter-seeker warship, until the Alician female calling herself Louise located a ship containing a reasonable number of the species calling itself *human*. Cloaking his ship with a spatial harmonic offset, Ukrull tuned in to the communication exchange between the two ships. It was depressingly primitive, involving serial rather than parallel processing, brimming with redundancy, and inefficient far beyond the point of irritation. All of this meant that monitoring the exchange required almost none of his attention. Of more concern was the Bartran slave-mind humming quietly to his right. Ukrull had been mind-plexing through his former colleague Shatrall's database on this erratic race calling itself humanity, and the claustrophobic yet unusually diverse biospheric habitat they called Earth. He noted a passing similarity to the Bartran's exo-skeletal appearance with an Earth-based creature called an armadillo.

A thousand Grid-standard angts – or nine hundred Earth years – earlier, Shatrall had experienced a gravitational shear-front caused by an unscheduled neutron star burst during a long-distance spatial jump. It had caused him to crash-land on this remote planet in a region the inhabitants called Tibet. The indigenous people had saved Shatrall after the crash, pulling him from the burning wreckage. Luckily, further contact had been minimal, and a rescue transport arrived within a few days, though the encounter had sparked a small religious sect, as was frequently the case with unofficial intrusions into nascent civilizations. *Sentinels*, they had called themselves, according to Shatrall's somewhat patchy logs.

Ukrull nudged the Bartran, but it maintained its stiff, vibrating posture. Sliding his claw into the recess in the Bartran's armoured back, he found the centre of focus of the creature's mind, in the control room on the transport ship, focusing on a single male biped. Ukrull hissed at what he perceived: *A blood debt! Was it possible?* Yet the genetic marker was there, corroborated in a natshuul by the ship's archives. He growled.

He composed an urgent message requesting instructions from his station master, but no sooner had he transmitted, than an alarm signalled a jump initiation on the Q'Roth transport. Ukrull's octospheric brain unleashed a cyclone of commands through his neural interface: raising his ship's shields to maximum, interrogating the transport ship's coordinates; calculating an intercept point inside the local star, initiating the extraction protocol for the single entity with the genetic marker, and then firing the engines to maximum. As his ship catapulted towards the system's sun, at the same moment as the Q'Roth transport vanished towards its doom, Ukrull realised he would arrive one natshuul later than required. He hoped this human species was more resilient than it appeared.

CHAPTER 4 – EDEN COUNCIL

Micah ruffled the towel over his wiry black hair and then evaluated the effect in the aluminium mirror: as usual it was no different than before he'd entered the field-shower. One good thing about his run-of-the-mill features was that over the past few weeks, while everyone around him gradually became more unkempt, dishevelled, and rough around the edges, due to the absence of life's usual little luxuries and fancy toiletries, he stayed exactly the same. But there was a family resemblance he'd rather not see in his reflection.

He'd never liked his father, and could never even in his thoughts think of him as 'Dad'. As Vince had remarked back on Earth, every hero has a dark side. He stared deep into his seemingly bottomless brown eyes, the main family trait. "Well, father, now Mom's with you, you'd better behave at last."

An impatient knock on the frosted door reminded him of the queue waiting outside. He wrapped the towel around his waist and bustled through the disgruntled line, avoiding direct eye contact, as everyone else did, in the status-levelling conditions onboard the ship nobody cared to name. No problem, he thought – now we've landed, we'll leave these leviathan ships behind soon enough, and get out into the fresh air of Ourshiwann. He'd heard that atmospheric testing had shown it was safe to go outside; the military were probably already out there. He quickened his pace.

The kelp-green walls sucked in sound. Initially he'd found it peaceful after the inescapable noise of city life back on Earth. That was until, like many others, he'd had recurring nightmares about waking up to find himself alone, deserted in the warren-like ship. He'd be running, lost forever inside the belly of the Q'Roth transport, slipping and sliding in the sweat the ship's walls exuded every twelve hours. The scientists said it was harmless, and it got sucked back into the walls within an hour, but still... He reached his small quarters and pulled closed the curtain that didn't quite fit. The lack of privacy did nothing for his insomnia. Still, having landed, having escaped the Q'Roth and the Alicians, he couldn't help but feel upbeat, like those rare Sundays his parents had taken him to Venice beach before the War. He grinned.

He laid out his crumpled clothes on the cot and sprayed them with Bio-Revite. Thank goodness someone had had the presence of mind to stock it before they'd quit Earth. Washing clothes regularly was out of the question until they found a stable water supply. He glanced at the label – maximum seven days use before washing. He shook the can and sprayed his clothes a second time.

Micah arrived late at the meeting. He wanted to sit next to Sandy, but on the one side sat Vince, uncompromising and tightly-wrapped, his bald head inclined back as he surveyed the gathering like a hilltop lion checking out the other animals on the savannah below. On the other side Ramires perched on the edge of his seat, as if about to get up and leave. He was the last living Sentinel – slick with sinewy muscles like a free-climber, his whole life dedicated to fighting a secret war against the Alicians. The black-haired Mexican had permanent six o'clock shadow under a thin moustache, and hooded eyes: whenever he looked into them, Micah wondered how many had seen nothing else after that face.

He gazed around the ivy-green oblong room situated in the ship's conning tower. It was one of only three rooms that possessed windows – four oval portals, one on each side, letting violet light stream in above their heads. He wasn't sure where the polished oak board-room table and straight-backed chairs had come from, guessing they had travelled along with the former IVS Chief Exec Shakirvasta, together with, so he'd heard, a container-full of tobacco. This well-groomed, lank-haired and oil-skinned mogul, one of the most powerful people on former Earth, should have been on Rashid's missing ship, but he'd joined Blake's instead, no doubt to build alliances during the voyage here.

Here, he thought: *Ourshiwann*, another planet, and not empty like Eden. He corrected himself – Eden had never been empty, instead proving to be a terraformed trap, its subterranean caverns brimming with Q'Roth hatchlings.

But it had been a relief to arrive on Ourshiwann. He longed to set foot outside where there was no roof above his head, to tread on firm ground that didn't ooze green mucus, making his shoes slurp when he walked, even if every photo he'd seen so far suggested this planet was barren. The ground looked arid, scattered bushes so dry they made eucalyptus look lush. He was no farmer, but he questioned if any of the crops they had brought would grow here.

Then there was the sky. Completely cloudless, it changed air-brushed colours at least four times a day, lending a surreal touch to the place, as if they were trapped inside a featureless painting. But he knew they had to make it work here, with no idea of where other habitable worlds might lie. Besides, another few months and they'd run out of food completely. Then it would get really ugly.

He drew himself back to the present. Blake looked up, noticing him, and flicked his eyes to the empty seat to his left. Zack already occupied the seat on the right, propping himself up on his dark forearms. Micah couldn't help but turn around to see if Blake had been indicating the spare chair to someone behind him, but there was no one else standing. He skirted around the table, all eyes following him, and sat next to Blake. The only limelight he craved was the glow of a computer screen. He did his best to merge with the chair.

Blake rapped the table top three times with his bare knuckles. "Let's get started."

He noticed how Blake's gravel-like voice drew everyone's attention. He considered his own voice, how uncommanding it was, inviting interruption.

"I declare the first meeting of the Eden Council open."

There were murmurs of surprise. The immaculately manicured Senator Josefsson, in a dark suit and tie no less, cleared his throat. He brushed a strand of his wavy greying hair that hadn't been out of place back to where it had been all along. "Excuse me, Commander, did you say *Eden*? Was that a joke? If so it was in remarkably poor taste." His mature good looks, hollowed out by three weeks of emergency rations, made him look like a well-groomed predator.

Micah regarded the only other suit around the table, the mogul Shakirvasta. The Indistani didn't miss a beat. *He already knew – he and Blake must have planned this.*

"So we never forget," Blake replied. "Eden was our name, not the Q'Roth name for that planet. We considered 'War Council', but there are mostly civilians on this planet now."

Josefsson's nose twitched. "And who is '*we*' exactly?"

"Fair point," Blake replied. "From now on, 'we' are this council. All significant decisions will be made here."

A diminutive, mousy-haired girl with a ski-jump nose and bottle-green eyes joined in from the corner of the table. Micah hadn't actually met her yet, but he knew she must be Jennifer, with the burly, bearded Greek genius, Professor Dimitri Kostakis beside her. Funny, he thought, they didn't look like lovers.

"I'm not sure democracy is what we need right now," she said, her voice slightly too loud, not quite steady. *Brave, but inexperienced,* thought Micah.

She continued, manufacturing self-confidence along the way. "The Q'Roth may still be hunting us, or the Alicians. After all, we're still missing our fourth ship."

The room temperature plummeted. All eyes shifted to Blake – this is what everyone wanted to discuss, but no one wanted to raise. Micah peered past Blake and

Zack to Antonia, whose lover Katrina was on the missing ship. Looking at her porcelain, ballerina's face, strafed his heart again. She didn't meet his gaze. Just as well; his feelings for her were a one-way street, but he couldn't seem to dodge the oncoming traffic. He leaned back heavily against his chair-rest, finding Sandy's level gaze upon him. He almost missed what Blake was saying.

"– remain at war, for the foreseeable future. But we have other pressing matters to attend to. Mr. Carlson?"

A man Micah didn't know rose heavily, as if the weight of the world was on his shoulders. Carlson had greasy hair, a straggly beard and a paunch shrivelled by rations. He leaned on the table, using plump fists for support, his forearms like two masts supporting a burgeoning sail-like chest. "My name is Julian Carlson, I am – that is, I was – Eden Mission's chief psychologist."

Micah noticed Zack fold his bushy black arms, and detected an almost subliminal snort. Blake remained steadfast.

"At Commander Blake's request, I've been taking stock of what you might call the collective state of our people on this new world since we arrived." He looked at each face, one by one, all around the table. Micah somehow felt at ease with this man, though he hated shrinks.

"Ladies and gentlemen, three words sum up that state: shock, grief, and displacement. Most are still deep in denial. That's the easy one, relatively speaking. Now that we've arrived and, well, this planet is not quite what we had all hoped for, anger will follow shortly, then depression. We've already had fourteen suicides in the past two weeks, the most recent two since we arrived here two days ago. Some of you are military, trained to be resilient. Most people we saved are not. They are trying to come to terms with –"

"Please, spare us the lecture, Mr. Carlson," Shakirvasta said, leaning forward in his collarless, jet-black suit. "None of us here are blind or inept. Your point?"

Carlson glanced from the Indistani to Blake, then continued, his voice less blustery, the wind knocked out of his sails. "They need a home, security and stability, and most of all, leadership." He sank back down into his chair.

Vince's voice sliced across the room before anyone else could react. "The first three are luxuries they can't afford. We're sitting ducks here. The Q'Roth know the whereabouts of this planet, and we stole four of their transports, which undoubtedly have transponders hidden aboard. They might just decide to have an after-dinner snack, or clean their plates. The only reason we're not yet dead is that *they* don't know that *we* know of this place." His eyes burned like a gas flame.

In the past month, Micah had come to admire Vince's directness.

Blake nodded, holding up a hand before anyone else could chime in. "Which is why we're here. We have several priorities, and we need to assign teams to execute them."

"And who exactly put *you* in charge?" Josefsson jabbed a chiselled fore-finger in Blake's direction. "You got us here, and we're thankful, but we need a government here on this God-forsaken planet!" He spread his hands, his eyes hawking for support around the table. Vultures like company, Micah reflected.

He expected Zack to spring to Blake's defence. But it was Shakirvasta who attracted attention by tapping a platinum cigarette box on the table, extracting a smokeless filter-tip. He lit it with restrained grace. He inhaled, eyes closed, then exhaled a halo of heat haze into the air. Micah smiled at the theatrics.

"My dear Senator," Shakirvasta addressed Josefsson, "I ran the only Titan corporation that survived the Third World War, so permit me a small indulgence in thinking I know when to opt for military rather than democratic control of a situation. There will be a government – the roots of it are here today – but right now, we need fast and precise decision-making that won't be second-guessed. And I believe that when Mr Carlson spoke of leadership, he meant our good Commander here, not a hastily-concocted committee to lead our people into a race between famine and annihilation, with a dead heat as the most likely outcome."

Micah was impressed. This scenario had been well-prepared by Blake and Shakirvasta. Blake was known as a leader and a man of action, but Micah hadn't figured him for political acumen, particularly in this case – he had the feeling Blake disliked everything Shakirvasta stood for.

Josefsson masked his indignation with a cough, and appeared to have enough political savvy to realise he'd over-reached. He shot Shakirvasta a searing glare before continuing. "I see. Then I bow to your judgement, this time. So, Commander, what are your instructions to us humble citizens of this new planet, whose name I have difficulty pronouncing?"

Blake folded his hands into a steeple, surveying everyone over the summit. "Our – she – wan. Ourshiwann. Don't anyone forget, they lost more than we did. None of them survived their Q'Roth incursion."

Micah knew Blake had witnessed the invasion of Ourshiwann, via the Hohash who replayed the events when it first made contact with Kat on Eden. Apparently Blake had been moved close to tears at the razing of this pacifist spider-world. Micah privately wondered if they were really all dead. Spiders lay eggs...

Blake stood up. "Currently, we have four sling-jets scouting the entire region, looking for any signs of life, food and shelter. We have four teams on the ground in the nearby spider city, making sure it's secure. Half of our scientists are already exploring soil-crop compatibility here on Ourshiwann, the other half on better weapons delivery systems in case the Q'Roth or our Alician cousins come looking for us. An engineering team from Jennifer's ship is trying to determine if there is a transponder in the Q'Roth ships, though progress is slow, since we still can't cut through Q'Roth metal. The remaining military are helping keep order inside the ships, which isn't easy, and frankly not what they're trained for." He paused, and then perused every face around the table – Micah felt he was being enlisted.

"Out there is a lost civilisation, a depleted one, but possibly far in advance of our own. Our good fortune today is that the spiders didn't fight back, so there was little collateral damage to their infrastructure. We know that in a straight fight with the Q'Roth, and even the Alicians..." Blake paused, appearing to chew on the next part, and then spat it out. "We'll lose. That's an honest tactical assessment, and you all know it, though it doesn't go outside these walls. So, ladies and gentlemen, I'm allocating resources here, that is, you people, to seek advantages from the deceased spider race, to learn from what we don't know, to give us an edge, even if it's just an outside chance."

Micah hadn't realised how much he'd needed to hear this bleak evaluation, and some of the tension locked up in his chest eased off. Blake was a good leader, he thought, decisive and smart too, unafraid to face reality. During the past few weeks when nobody had dared state their situation so candidly, fear had lurked in the shadows, draining his own and everyone else's energy and morale. But now it was out in the open, they could work on it, fight it, and fight together.

Vince leaned forward on honed forearms. "With due respect, Commander, this is no time for pussy-talk. Most likely assessment is the Alicians or Q'Roth or both intercepted Rashid's ship and either destroyed it or culled its passengers and crew. Pisses me off as much as any of you, I had twenty of my best people on that ship, but we have to move on fast. They *will* find us. It's a question of *when*, and most likely when is soon, in the next few days. The only priority is security, because we are so very *not* secure right now. Three days, people, and all of us could be taken out like that." He snapped his forefinger and thumb together.

Blake waited, as if counting to ten. He continued. "Vince, Ramires – you'll work with Zack on new defences and weapons. Try communicating with the Hohash – we could do with finding another of their phase-shifting scout ships if there are any left intact. Micah, Sandy, Professor Kostakis, and Jennifer – I need you to organise teams to explore the Ourshiwann city to see what we can use from there – including the possibility of shelter and... somewhere to hide. I don't think anyone sleeps easy in these Q'Roth slime-buckets."

Whispers started in several quarters around the table. Blake slammed his fist down hard on the table, stunning everyone into silence. He glared at it a while. "I'll be damned if we perish here!" He uncurled his fist. "Now, food. It's still a priority. We have three months to find new food sources or reap a harvest. Otherwise the Alicians don't need to lift a finger, we'll starve to death. Senator Josefsson, Mr Shakirvasta, Antonia – I'd like you to work with Carlson on organising a social infrastructure that will keep all our people from going over the edge – dealing with lodging, food allocation, and tasks to keep people busy, as well as medical issues, and grievances, of which there'll be plenty. Questions?"

Micah raised an eyebrow. Blake didn't miss it. "Mr. Sanderson, you have something to add?"

He reddened. "Rashid's ship," he said. "I know maybe it's gone, but we don't know for sure. Are we going to look for it?"

Blake spoke in a quieter voice. "Needle in a haystack, son, and we have no way to look for them. The codes in your head only give vectors, not distances travelled – we'd never find them. There are three empty chairs waiting for Rashid, Pierre and Kat in this council as soon as they arrive."

Micah watched Antonia's face turn to desert rock, bereft of hope. It summed up everything – they'd all been through too much, and the three-week trip had only served to make tensions chronic. The psychologist hadn't just been talking about the other people in the ships – he'd been talking about *everyone*, including all the people here in this room, even the military. Micah knew all too well how easy it was to let despair subdue action. Reluctantly he recalled one of his father's famous aphorisms – *when you hit rock bottom, kick hard.* He shot to his feet. "Well, what are we waiting for?" He strode around the table and grabbed Sandy's hand, to the sound of scraping chairs.

Out in the corridor, as they waited for Jennifer and Kostakis, Sandy tugged his wrist. "Was that balls or bravado back there?"

"My Dad, I guess. Hated him all my life, even after he was killed in the War, but these days he seems to be the only role model that matches up to these shitty situations."

She cocked an eyebrow, a wan smile spreading across her lips. "Must be balls then. I'm told they're hereditary."

Micah was relieved to see Jennifer and Kostakis heading their way, which would save him from any further repartee with Sandy; it was a game he always lost. But as the scientist couple approached, his eye was caught by Antonia heading in the opposite direction. She didn't look his way. He felt a squeeze on his elbow from Sandy.

"That's the trouble with balls," she said. "No intelligence."

Micah glanced down at her belly, concealing the foetus growing inside her, the legacy of her fleeting encounter with the legendary Alician assassin Gabriel. He caught Sandy's eye and raised an eyebrow.

Her grin shrank to a pencil-thin line. "Don't even think about saying it."

He shrugged, and held out his hand as Professor Kostakis' beaming, curly-haired, goatee-bearded face loomed in front of him.

* * *

Blake asked Zack to stay behind for a few minutes. Once the room had emptied and the door sealed, cocooning them in the gloomy, dank silence that pervaded the Q'Roth ships, Zack finally spoke.

"Don't know if you feel out of your depth, Skip, but I sure as hell do. Meetings? Fucking meetings with civilians? Glad you took charge back there. Vince was –"

"Vince is right. Listen, Zack…" But the words wouldn't come.

"I'm listening, boss. You got a burr up your ass, you need to spit it out." He frowned. "Well, you know what I mean."

"Doesn't go any further."

Zack clasped his hands behind his bald pate, leaning back. "Never does. You got an attack of the *maybe's* again, huh? S'bin a long time. Hey, let's go, you know I love this game. Bring it on!"

Blake nodded, the corners of his mouth lifting. "Okay. Maybe we should have stayed and fought till the end."

"Yeah, dead is so cool." Zack rolled his eyes.

"Okay then. Maybe you're right, I shouldn't be leading this… whatever it is."

"So we'll throw an election once this is no longer a *military* situation. Come to think of it, we can also throw a *serious* party. Is this the best you got?"

Blake hung his head, and spoke to the floor. "Glenda's getting worse. Cancer's eating her insides. The trip was really bad for her. Don't know how long she can hold on. Maybe I –"

Zack unlocked his fingers and stood up, then leant forward, inches from Blake's face. "Maybe you should make her fucking proud and give her the chance to die in peace rather than having the top of her head lobbed off and her brain sucked dry by a three-metre-tall locust!"

"Christ, Zack!"

"We done here, boss? We good now? 'Cos I got stuff to do, you know."

Blake nodded, and Zack loped out the door. "Thanks, Zack," he said, as he levered himself up. He heard Zack shout from down the corridor. "Don't mention it!" Blake allowed a smile. "You know me too well, old friend. What in hell's name would I do without you?"

* * *

45

Rashid awoke in darkness, unable to move or feel his limbs. The last thing he could remember was glimpsing the inside of a star, so he knew he should be dead; only the physical discomfort convinced him otherwise.

"Hello? Is anybody there?" There was no echo, so he knew he was in a confined area. He tried to move his fingers, but all he could sense was a tingling that he guessed was his hands. It reminded him of when he'd crash-landed on Eden a year ago: *a stasis field*. But then, he thought, he should neither be conscious nor able to speak. He heard movement, and for the first time he smelt something odd, like the drying, rotting seaweed he'd kicked around barefoot as a kid on his holidays in Goa. A rhythmic, clomping, dragging noise approached. His heart accelerated. He tensed, his head at least, which seemed to be out of the stasis field. In the unremitting darkness, Rashid perceived someone or something very close – a foul breath of rancid algae washed into his nostrils.

"Sarowan," it grumbled, a voice like rocks grinding, making Rashid flinch. *Sarowan*. The word resonated inside Rashid's skull. Rashid was born of a secret and all-but defunct clan called Sarowan, a clan of the Sentinels...

"You, Sarowan," the voice repeated.

The voice hurt his ears. *Sarowan*... But how could anyone know that? Unless... He had always believed the legends a childish myth. He'd not had time to think about it since leaving Eden, but the stories of his ancestors in Tibet saving an alien creature, calling itself a Ranger...

He understood it was asking him a question, awaiting a response. No point in hiding it anymore. "Yes, I am Sarowan. My ancestors –"

"Saved Ranger. Saved Shatrall. Before. Now save you. Blood debt paid."

Rashid stopped breathing as the enormity hit him. This Ranger had pulled him out of the ship and the star – before everyone else was incinerated.

"The others?" He had to be sure.

"Gone."

His mind raced: Sofia dead, two thousand people – all dead, erased by Louise, and her ship was still hunting Blake and the others.

He tried to swallow. No saliva. "Where am I?"

"Others close. Find you soon."

He heard a dragging sound, like someone lugging a sack of potatoes across the floor, and the thuddish clomp of a foot, or claw. "Wait! You must help us. *Please*. Louise will find us sooner or later. You could stop her!" He tried in vain to make his limbs move.

The dragging paused. "Not help. Observe. Your species survive or die."

He remembered from his Sarowan upbringing that this was supposedly the Rangers' creed – a kind of Darwinian non-interference. He resigned himself. "Then at least let me see you. Turn on the lights so I can see the creature my ancestors saved nine hundred years ago."

The Ranger made a strange, descending hissing sound, which Rashid interpreted as a sigh. "Lights already on. Apologies. Was late."

CHAPTER 5 – FIRST CONTACT

The Hohash's golden, oval frame lay inert, propped against the wall, its flow-mirror surface dark and still. Pierre walked over to it. "Wake up, damn you!" He punched its rounded edge, sending a reverberating twang around the seven-metre wide wok-shaped Hohash craft. He'd already tried numerous times to rouse Kat, who lay curled up in the recovery position like a sleeping puppy. To his chagrin, the dormant Hohash rose from the floor and buzzed back into life. He stepped backwards, just as it swooped towards him, stopping centimetres from his face. He stood his ground. "Sorry," he said, unsure why he'd bothered, since by all accounts these alien artefacts didn't understand human speech.

Now that he'd gotten its attention, he wasn't sure what to do. He'd spent the last three hours attempting to land on Pietro, but a sulphur hurricane engulfed the planet's only continent, causing him to abort atmospheric entry, as well as to seriously downgrade his earlier assessment of its habitability. He'd dawdled long enough above the planet's toxic ocean to extract oxygen through the ship's filters before retreating back out into space.

"It shouldn't end like this," he said.

The Hohash's mirror surface flickered into a ruby background, purple splinters of broken glass spattered across it. Pierre almost laughed, since the display mimicked his own bleak feelings perfectly. Then his brow widened – he understood. He remembered the time Kat had been immersed in communication with the Hohash on Eden, how she'd explained later that she had seen colours reflecting her emotions.

It was worth a try. He forced a smile. The Hohash image barely changed, except the splash became luminous and seemed to lift away from the surface. At first Pierre thought his premise wasn't correct. Then he realised his smile was only skin deep.

He closed his eyes and thought back to his childhood, trawling for one of the rare memories of his father that he still treasured, before he'd become one of the latter's illegal genetic test subjects. His *papa*, in his Sunday best, pushed Pierre on the garden swing, while his *maman*, in a floral wrap, clapped in time with the upswings. The sun beat down on his boyish face, the hinges creaking and straining at each shove in the small of his back. He inhaled the smell of fresh-mown grass, and pumped his legs higher and higher, Earth's comforting gravity tugging him backwards.

He opened his eyes. The Hohash showed him lush greens, a gentle breeze brushing across a field of tall grass. He smiled, and this time an orange light bathed the synthetic scene.

"Nice to see you two getting along."

He turned to see Kat rubbing her eyes, propping herself up on her elbows. He rushed towards her. "Are you –"

"Okay, yes. Feel like my head has been used as a zero-G hockey puck, though. Our friend there was in communication with me after..." She stopped, and sat up, pulling her knees to her chest.

Pierre crouched next to her. He wanted to take her hand, tell her it was all okay and, he realized, a whole lot more. He glanced back at the Hohash; steel-grey rain beat down on the grass, dissolving it.

"Tell me what you remember, Kat."

She rested her brow on her knees, muffling her voice. "Dead. They're all dead, Pierre. They jumped into the star. I saw it happen."

Pierre felt dizzy, as if his legs might cave in. and sat down beside her. "All those people. Rashid. All... I don't suppose it was an accident. If whoever attacked somehow retrieved the flight plan, the destination..." He let his head tip back against the metal hull. "And us? Then we are, as they say, really screwed."

She lifted her head, placing her chin on her knees, and uttered a short dry laugh. "That's unlike you, Pierre, you're normally the logical optimist."

He shrugged. He pictured the faces of Rashid, of others on board he could recall. He'd been there with them just yesterday. His scientific mind intruded, demanding more data on how it had happened – whether it had been a mistake, an attack, or sabotage. But his emotional mind gained a rare upper hand; two thousand people had just been vaporised, and he and Kat were almost certainly without hope.

The Hohash glided towards them silently, its flow-surface dark as a lithium mine-shaft. Pierre felt crushed; they'd already been through so much the past few weeks. He thought of Blake and Zack. What would those two do right now? They wouldn't give up, of course, but what would they actually *do*?

Kat sat up, leaning her head against the bulkhead. "The planet?"

"It's uninhabitable right now. Sulphur storm."

She sniffed. "Figures. And our friend here can't contact his pals?"

"Apparently not. I guess their communication only works over a certain range, they must be too far away."

Kat ran her fingers through her short-cropped hair. "Right now, Blake would say, *Options, people?*"

He nodded. "Yes, he would, but I'm not sure he'd get too many answers. Let's see, we're in a short-range craft that can't make long-range jumps like the Q'Roth vessels. We've little in the way of food, water for a while, and oxygen for a few days." And no one will ever find us.

He studied her profile, her dark hair cresting a boyish face. Without thinking about it, his eyes traced the contours of her body.

"Uh-oh." Kat said.

"What?" He followed her gaze to the Hohash, which was still relaying his emotions. Pierre reddened when he saw the display's crimson and purple loops which somehow conveyed a mixture of tenderness and eroticism.

"Sorry," he mumbled.

"Don't be. The Hohash never lies, you know. Any last requests?" She gave him a crooked smile.

His flush got worse. He stumbled for words. "Antonia –"

"Would understand if you just wanted a kiss."

Pierre frowned, trying to balance the equation when Kat's face appeared between him and the Hohash. Warm, moist lips met his. At first he held back, trying to remember a blog he'd read years ago that had rules on how to be a good kisser. But she clearly knew, and so he let himself be sucked into the embrace, amidst flashes of yellow and scarlet emanating from the Hohash. Blood rushed into his head and groin, and his hands fumbled towards her; he wanted to touch her, but didn't know how. Finally he worked up the courage to trace a shaky hand over the contour of her breast. She gently pushed herself back from him. He let go, his breathing ragged.

She sat cross-legged in front of him, calming her breathing. "All those months on the Ulysses, travelling to Eden, you never said anything."

He stared at the floor.

"Must have been tough." She looked sideways, then got to her feet.

"Pierre, you're probably the cleverest human left alive. There must be an option. Think, it's what you do best."

His head was still swirling. He took a deep breath, closed his eyes, and imagined himself back in his father's musty, book-filled study. Every evening after dinner, a form of ritualistic torture used to take place where his father tested him mercilessly with logical and mathematical puzzles. In his mind he wrote down in white chalk the predicates of their predicament, and its assumptions. He wrote down *we are alone*, and then paused. He flicked his eyes open.

"Kat, do you know prime numbers?"

"Of course, but... Oh, I see. You think it's a way of signifying we're intelligent, a sort of universal distress code?"

He nodded quickly. "We need the Hohash to broadcast prime numbers and our relative position in this star system."

"To whom, exactly?"

"Anyone that's out there, Kat," Pierre said, energized by the idea.

"That's a pretty long shot. Still..." Kat knelt in front of the Hohash and pointed an index finger to her temple. Instantly she slipped into a trance-like state. Pierre got up and paced behind her, waiting for her to 'return'.

She opened her eyes. "It's transmitting, broad spectrum. Anyone within ten light years should pick it up. I also encoded the emotion *distress* into the signal."

"Are you sure that was wise, it might summon a predator of some kind."

Kat cast him a sceptical look.

"Okay, beggars can't be choosers."

She sat down cross-legged again. "I guess all we can do now is wait." She patted the empty floor-space next to her with a palm. Pierre felt nervous; the kiss had already thrown him off-balance. He sat, the left side of his body touching hers.

"Pierre, was there anyone back home for you? You know, someone special?"

He felt his throat choke up. He shook his head. *Please, don't.* He clenched a fist behind his back.

She smiled. "You know, once, somewhere, sometime?" She paused, her smile faltering. "I mean, once, you know... right?"

He tried to focus on his breathing; he felt he was made of glass. All the rationalisations he'd built up inside himself over the years came tumbling down, amounting to nothing. He didn't dare look at the Hohash. But she did.

"Oh my," she said.

He thought the compassion in her voice would shatter him for sure. But instead he felt her hand caress his cheek, with a tenderness he didn't know she was capable of. He'd never felt so vulnerable. She kissed his neck, then parted his lips with her tongue. He heard the unzipping of her overall, and his hands managed to help her peel the ensemble off her shoulders down to her waist. She jumped up, and for a hellish moment he thought she'd stopped again. But she winked at him and pulled the suit off completely, underwear too. She stood naked above him, and then knelt down in front of him. She took his hands and placed them on her breasts, while her lips locked onto his. She slid his suit zipper all the way down to his crotch, where she gripped him hard, making him cry out. With the other hand she pushed him back down against the floor. He gasped as she mounted him, her mouth still welded to his, and twenty-nine years of mental discipline and programming finally fused.

Pierre felt the air getting thicker with overuse, yet his mind was curiously calm. The Hohash displayed an emerald sea under an air-brushed magenta sky. Kat lay next to him, her head resting on his hairless chest. He could have reflected on a wasted life, on all the potential loves he could have had, now he knew what he'd been missing. Instead, he chose to dwell on the moment they'd just shared.

"Thank you," he said, with more gratitude than if he'd just received the Nobel Prize.

She tapped his chest with her fingers. "Just don't tell my girlfriend, okay? And I'm still pretty much a girl-girl. Don't go ego-hyping on me."

Always the inquisitive one, he decided for once not to ask *why* she'd made love with him, and just accepted it. He thought about his parents. His father had sacrificed him to research, and his mother had consented, though she'd been upset about it. For one thing, the genetic tampering had made him sterile, so his line would end with him. He wondered if his father, when he'd been bleeding to death on that conference podium, shot by an Alician assassin, had maybe, just for a moment, had an inkling of regret about what he had done to his own son. For the first time in his adult life, Pierre didn't completely reject the hypothesis.

The Hohash began pulsing increasingly frequent random shades of colour. They hastily dressed while shielding their eyes from the rainbow light's intensity.

"What now?" Kat said.

Pierre guessed what it was – a response. The flashing stopped, and the Hohash mirror surface turned to a swirling cloud of grey. An indistinct figure appeared in the middle, as if walking towards them. He watched in fascination as it clarified – it reminded him of ancient Egyptian hieroglyphs, a dog-like creature in a ceremonial head-dress of golds, blues and blacks. As the picture crystallised into vid-screen clarity, they gaped at the figure, who gave the definite impression of staring back at them.

"Hello?" he tried.

"No sound, remember?" Kat said.

He wondered what to do. The creature stared at them, waiting, and Pierre didn't know how long it would wait. He gestured to the creature, first with his hands, to come towards them, then, seeing no reaction, closed his hands around his throat, as if choking, trying to communicate they were running out of air. The figure disappeared, and the Hohash face re-adjusted to its habitual mirror surface.

"Well," Kat said, "not too bad given our extensive experience with first contact situations."

Pierre slumped. "*Merde!* This is hopeless. I've always wondered why in all the sci-fi vids the whole universe speaks English, or else there's a handy universal translator somewhere."

"Lazy scriptwriters. Anyway, maybe it understood. Hey, we just found another race. You're a scientist, you should be ecstatic."

He smiled warmly. "Give this scientist a break, he's just discovered the opposite sex!" But his grin ran out of fuel. "We could try the planet again, at least gather some more oxygen."

"Maybe we could use the bathroom there. I've heard sulphur exfoliates pretty well."

He took her hand. "Kat, I'm really glad –"

The ship jolted hard to one side, and they both sprawled to the far wall. Pierre had the wind knocked out of him, and struggled into a crouching position. Kat had already sprung to her feet when they both heard a loud *thunk* from above. He looked out though the normally black portal and glimpsed the silver underbelly of a vessel attached to them.

"Oh fuck!" Kat shouted.

At first he didn't realise why she'd said it, until he noticed his feet and ankles were wet. A warm, transparent liquid trickled, then gushed into their craft, jetting through the air vents. Scrambling to his feet, he sloshed his way over to the environmental controls. Kat beat him to it, and slammed her fist down on it, but the console was dead. He stared in disbelief towards the four upper vents, out of arms' reach, through which the pink water surged.

"It doesn't make sense!" he said. The noise of their own personal waterfall made it hard to concentrate.

"They're going to bloody drown us," Kat shouted, as she waded over to the inert Hohash.

"But why?" Pierre was trying to think, but the fluid was already knee-deep. "Suits! We need to put the suits on!" she yelled, already tugging the two EVA suits from their holding rack. Pierre grabbed one and tried to don it. With only one leg in, he lost his footing and fell over, so that the liquid poured into his suit, dragging him down. Kat's hand hauled him up by the collar, and he managed to regain his footing. She already had both legs in hers and zipped it up to her neck, then helped him into his. The fluid was now waist-level. His suit had half-filled with the stuff, which he knew would be a real hazard if he didn't remain upright.

They both snapped on their helmets moments before the fluid reached their necks. They stared at each other, wide-eyed, as the whole ship flooded to the ceiling, leaving no trace of air. The gushing noise shut off. He heard only his laboured breathing, and the occasional creak from the ship's hull. He switched on his intercom.

"You okay?"

Her breathing sounded scratchy, but he sensed she was more pissed off than scared. "Bastards! Just when you think it can't get any worse."

He nodded inside his helmet. Then he noticed the single red light flashing on the inside of his faceplate. He knew what it meant: his suit's air cylinder was almost empty. He remembered he hadn't had time to replenish his suit's systems since his last sortie on Pietro.

She caught sight of his warning light. "Is that what I think it is?"

He laid his hand on her shoulder. "How's yours?"

"About twenty minutes. Look, isn't there some way we can shunt air from my system to yours?"

He shook his head. He saw another red dot flash, meaning his air was almost gone. He had maybe twenty seconds.

"Listen, Kat –"

"Dammit, Pierre, I don't want to lose you, and I don't want to watch you asphyxiate in front of me, you got that?"

Pierre stared at her. He thought of the last hour. Any last requests, she'd said. He couldn't have wished for more. His eyes etched every contour of her face. He sucked in one last breath, feeling the canister's resistance telling him he was out of time. "You won't have to, Katrina. This'll be quicker."

Pierre raised his hands to his helmet, and flicked open the seals.

CHAPTER 6 – GHOST TOWN

Micah and his three companions stood atop the jagged, wind-carved ridge, scanning the pale ruins of the spider city in the basin below, cradled by beige bluffs and cliffs. What was left of the hexagon-shaped city had been bleached white. Blake had said that in the Hohash rendition of events, there had been vivid colours just before the Q'Roth invasion. The colour had faded because the spiders had been slaughtered. Nothing remained of them, except the few Hohash mirror-like artefacts which had once served the spiders, and now cohabited enigmatically with humanity's refugees – the rest of the Hohash had self-destructed when their masters died.

He could barely feel the tangerine sun even now where it hung at noon under a mauve sky. A silver moon, mountainous rather than cratered, and twice the size of Earth's, dawdled near the horizon.

Inwardly, he sagged – *could this really become our home?* His former excitement at being on another planet had quickly waned in the bleak landscape and coolness of the sun. Yet he knew it was the only option at the moment. *Try to make this work*, he told himself.

The city resembled a giant tray of upside-down crockery which someone had dropped, shattering pieces whilst retaining the original pattern. The area around the city, in contrast, was luminous: quartz in the sand and rock, Kostakis had suggested. All except three of the city's Moorish spires had broken, snapped in two like sticks of white candy. The resultant image was of a skeleton picked clean by vultures, its bones cracked open by hyenas to extract the marrow.

He tried not to think of Earth's demise. Lately he'd been dreaming of people he'd known, mainly from work or the few stores he used to visit. They never said anything, just watched him with a deadly earnestness, waiting to see whether humanity would survive or not. The way they looked at him made him feel responsible, yet he didn't know what he could do. He shivered. So many people had nightmares these days, that no one ever asked anyone else if they'd had a good night's sleep.

"Magnificent!" Kostakis bellowed, spreading his arms wide. "An archaeological treasure. A gold mine!"

Micah was searching for a different, more tragic word. It ailed him to be reminded how weak and defenceless humanity was – the spider race was obviously vastly superior, yet they'd been culled as easily as a harvester reaps wheat.

"So sad," Sandy said.

Thank God you're here, Sandy! Micah knew why he needed her around: she centred him. He'd had leadership thrust upon him, and without her grainy black and white vision, her seeing-it-for-what-it-was counsel, he'd be like a man cast adrift in an asteroid belt. He turned to face the others. His analyst-trained mind clicked in for a few moments as he considered the best way to lead this team. *Know your people*, he'd read recently in a flash-book lent him by Blake. Sandy wasn't a problem – they'd both worked together for Eden Mission back on Earth, albeit in different areas, and had been thrown together by events.

Kostakis, the hefty Greek professor whose dual reputations for being a genius and a philanderer had rivalled each other on the gossip nets back on Earth, seemed paradoxically selfless. Micah guessed the goatee-bearded scientist had been so long at the top of his scientific game in the field of Gaiatics – the study of Earth as an organism – that he didn't have to prove anything to anyone anymore. His approach to everything, in stark contrast to Sandy's, was optimistic to the point of being puppyish. Yet like almost everyone else here on Ourshiwann, he'd lost all his family members and friends. Micah presumed he was one of those rare people who found light even in the dark. Or maybe this was heaven for a scientist, every sunrise bringing a plethora of discoveries to ponder.

Jen – he'd heard Kostakis call her that – was a different story. Her physical shape – a slightly dumpy mousy blonde with a tendency to show her cleavage more than most women did, and bright green eyes that spent a lot of time looking sideways at people when they weren't looking back – belied the facts. She'd come through when Earth had most needed it – she'd commandeered a Q'Roth ship, and nuked a legion of Q'Roth warriors during the final retreat. There was also a nasty rumour that she'd killed a man named Hendriks with her nanosword – the like of which no one except Ramires had ever seen – in order to enforce a command decision on Eden. Given that she'd rescued a quarter of the population, Blake had understandably given her a command role. And if there was going to be a battle,

Micah knew which side he wanted Jen on. He had a hunch that someone like Jen could make a difference.

His eyes re-focused – the analysis had only taken a matter of seconds. He cleared his throat. "Our mission is recon. A platoon of Blake's men did a basic security sweep this morning – no life signs. Our job is to look for advantages – water, food, shelter, weapons." He felt more upbeat now he was taking command. "So, let's go down and explore an alien city! Jen, you're sure you can drive that thing?" He jabbed a thumb at the all-terrain eight-wheeler behind them.

"It's Jennifer to you. No problem, just make sure your head-strap is tight."

Frowning, he approached the muscle-bound hummer 'rhino'. He clambered up into the front passenger seat. Jennifer gave him a look but said nothing. Kostakis seemed happy enough to sit in the back next to Sandy.

Jennifer shoved her foot down and the vehicle raced toward the precipice. Micah fumbled to get the Velcro belt fastened across his forehead just as the ridge's edge in front of him disappeared, and all he saw was the city and the sky. The vertigo was heightened by the insane engine scream as the wheels spun in mid-air. A sickening feeling in his stomach barely had time to register before a bone-cracking jolt pounded his coccyx and spine as they hit the incline. A whirlwind of dust and rocks hurtled past at a sixty degree angle. His seat juddered too much to even think about shouting *Jesus Christ, slow the fuck down,* for fear of shattering his teeth. In a minute that felt like ten, they skidded onto level ground, tearing at a muscle in his neck as Jennifer swerved the vehicle to a screeching halt. Pebbles peppered the back of the hummer. The rhino purred.

He tried to calm his breathing, unclipped the headrest and turned around to Sandy. The last thing they needed was for her to have a miscarriage, not that anyone except him and Vince knew about her pregnancy.

"Are you okay?"

Jennifer cut in. "Of course she and Dimitri are *both* okay. Inertial dampers work in the back, in case of med-evac, but not up front. Wanna trade places with Dimitri?"

Sandy gave the barest of nods to indicate she was fine. Micah shook his head. He stared across the flat plain, the city glinting in the distance. "Let's go," he said, then added, remembering a line from an ancient Western vid his father used to watch, "we're burning daylight." Given the twenty hour day-night cycle here, it seemed appropriate.

They skirted the perimeter for an hour trying to find a way in that wasn't blocked by fallen spires and debris. They stopped at a juncture where, as usual, oak-tree sized chunks of snapped white columns barred their way. "This'll have to do."

"Finally," Jennifer muttered, cutting the engine.

Micah knew he was in charge, but Jennifer unnerved him. She'd been captain of one of the four ships; he hadn't. He recalled another tactic from Blake's manual: *pre-emptive strike coupled with evade.* "I suggest we split into pairs, and meet back here in two hours."

"Are we done?" Jennifer said.

He cleared his throat. "Sandy and I will take the left side, it's West I think, and you and the Professor –"

"– will see you in two hours," Jennifer said, disappearing out of her side door to the ground below. "Don't be late, and don't forget your VHF radio," she shouted, not turning back. Kostakis popped the side door and leapt out, loping after her.

Sandy grinned at Micah from the rear-view mirror. "That went pretty well, don't you think?"

He noticed Jennifer had taken the ignition keycard with her. *Yep, real smooth.*

* * *

Jen felt she'd been superimposed onto a cartoon alien world. So clean: no dust, no decay, and no bodies. It was so different to how Dublin had been, both times: the first, after it had been nuked in WWIII; and the second, after the Q'Roth had counter-attacked, just before she'd stocked her ship with its human cargo. Carnage, charred buildings and corpses whose smell she could never forget, and dust she didn't want to ingest because of what, or who, it might contain. The anger simmered inside her, stoked up recently after she'd found out that her brother Gabriel, whom she'd thought dead since the end of the War ten years earlier, had been alive all that time, only to be murdered by the Alicians days before the invasion.

Images from WWIII popped uninvited into her mind like holo-spam – her time in the gangs after the sacking of Dublin and most of the Eastern coastline, running guerrilla incursions against the enemy. She'd learned to trust her colleagues with her life, up until she discovered her team leader had been collaborating, leading them on doomed raids. That had been the first time she really felt she'd killed someone – because it had been personal – even if she'd rewired a drone to do it for her.

She gnawed on a knuckle, remembering why she was here. She wanted to crack an Alician neck, but that wasn't likely. The Alicians or Q'Roth could arrive in space and eliminate mankind from a safe distance, without warning. That was what rankled her most, their casual brutality. She needed to find a new weapon, one that would surprise the Alicians; something to even the odds. She kicked a piece of debris, sending it skittering into a plaza. Where would she find a weapon here, on a planet of pacifists who'd made no attempt to save themselves? She should be with Vince and Ramires, not out here looking for hidey-holes.

She observed the alien landscape with a cool disinterest as she and her lover stalked their way past bland buildings interspersed with coiling paths and plazas, some square, others round. They came across starfish-like mounds, wide as houses and raised at the middle, and every fifty metres or so stretched diamond-shaped structures pointing to the sky. None of these had any obvious access or purpose as far as she could fathom. The city had obviously been planned according to a complex mathematical topographical construct, but she'd need to survey it from above to work it out. There was little decoration except an off-white shuriken motif, three concentric circles with sharp barbs peeling off the central disk, tattooed on every structure. She noticed that they were all slightly different, in the number of barbs, or their length or angle. *Numbers or names.* Dimitri carried a small omni-recorder, so they'd be able to download the data later and review it.

"Nothing higher than two storeys," she said, to break the silence.

"Yes," Dimitri said, "but look closer: no brickwork, it's made of extruded material, the same density all the way through." He squatted down and hefted a piece of rubble as white on the inside as on the outside. "This piece has been lying here for a thousand years, yet there's no sign of decay. It's as if it was broken off yesterday!"

Some part of her scientific mind wanted to be as enthralled as Dimitri, caught up in discovery, but her guard was up. She had no explanation as to why there were no signs of spider carcasses, dust, or of broken Hohash mirrors. She found herself staring into the dark shadows, half-expecting to see a giant furry spider-leg protruding. Her mother's side of the family had always been a little 'touched', seeing ghosts, reading Tarot cards and the like. And here was a ghost town, a whole race slaughtered in a matter of hours. The fact it had been a thousand years ago didn't dampen her sixth sense's acuity. She walked on.

She had to admit the architecture was elegant: coiling ramps instead of steps, and low buildings so the sky loomed large. After ten minutes, she'd seen roads that were flat and open, and others that fed into smooth glossy tunnels passing between the ubiquitous buildings she assumed were dwelling places. She'd half-expected to see massive webs, but of course these creatures could simply have looked like spiders, rather than being similar to arachnids back on Earth. They stopped in a plaza with a set of poles around ten metres high, spaced evenly apart by about a metre. Jen glanced sideways at Dimitri, but he shrugged – a gesture she'd never seen Dimitri use before. He laughed in response to her surprise.

"Maybe they're for spider gymnastics," he said.

"Trust a Greek to suggest an Olympic function." Jen replied, trying to disguise her lack of enthusiasm.

"Do you realise," he said, casting his gaze panoramically around the square, "how fabulous it is to know that there is so much here I do *not* understand?"

She stared at him, remembering the first time she'd seen him lecture in a vast auditorium. His energy, his zeal for knowledge, had hooked her from the start. She pointed to an oval doorway into one of the buildings. Her foreboding had passed.

"Time to increase our ignorance," she said.

They stepped inside. Darkness enfolded her. She held her breath and slipped her right hand into a pocket, gripping the smooth nanosword hilt. As she passed through the squat, round portal, she had to duck her head. The short tube opened up into a kidney-shaped room, about five metres across, with four metal hoops suspended from the ceiling. It was light inside, though there were no windows – somehow the opaque walls transmitted light from outside.

She couldn't tell where the walls and ceiling and floor ended – the room had the appearance of having been blown like a glass bubble. She had a hunch, though she couldn't explain why, that it was a bedroom, or some form of restorative room. She turned around to see Dimitri enter and straighten up.

"Fantastic! I do believe all their buildings are extruded or grown from the same material. Very impressive, very practical! Imagine the durability, the low maintenance!"

She nodded, then turned and took the access tube to a larger room, twice the size of the first. Six squat, metre-wide circular tables formed a ring. Each table or stool, made of the same bland white, non-reflective material, contained a central funnel heading underground. She drifted a finger across the nearest table – it looked smooth but was sticky to the touch, like brushed steel. She knew it meant the material was molecularly complex. She'd read back on Earth about a new research project into organic polymers with DNA-like coding, the idea being you could grow objects based on an inherent memory structure. The theory was, she recalled, that if you could do this, then objects and even buildings would retain their shape longer, since they 'remembered' what they should look like. She reckoned the spiders had mastered it.

"Polyphasic mnemonic plastics," she offered.

"Exactly! That's why I love you my darling! So clever, so quick, and so concise!" He reached over and took her hand, gently spinning her into an embrace as if they were on a dance-floor. She'd always been surprised that someone so large could dance so well. He kissed her fully. She opened her mouth to his, in case his tongue wanted to enter – maybe sex would be a good idea, she thought, a tonic for her dark mood. But no. He was overwhelmed by his first love, scientific curiosity. She envied him.

He drew back, beaming, still holding her hand. "So, my love, what are you thinking? Social? Dining function? Both?"

She peered into one of the downward channels. "Let's not forget defecation; they must have been quite intimate." They laughed. It felt good. She thought she'd forgotten how.

In the rooms they decided were bedrooms, Jen and Dimitri saw an oval, Hohash-shaped recess in the wall, underscoring the symbiotic relationship between the spiders and their mirror-shaped vassals.

"Their lifestyle must have been simple yet graceful," Dimitri said. "No artefacts, none of the paraphernalia to be found in any normal human's home, and no decoration; almost Greek in a way." He nudged her. She laughed with him, recalling their hot nights in his Spartan but airy apartment in Santorini, high above the waves.

They drifted through numerous open spaces and found more of the stools or tables with funnels, forming concentric rings or intersecting hoops. The sun had dipped in the sky, and cast long shadows across the open plaza. She glanced at her wristcom; it had been an hour already. She knew she should really check in with Micah, but he hadn't called, and she didn't feel like making the first move.

This is all very fascinating, she thought, but not why we're here.

A soft breeze triggered goose bumps on her neck. Instinctively, her guard rose again, the way it used to whenever an enemy drone had tried to sneak up on her team. She knew her period of respite was over. Her muscles flexed.

She turned the corner and stopped dead. Her hand slid into her pocket to draw out the nanosword.

Dimitri, taking one last backward glance at a particularly beautiful plaza with spiral ramps coiling up to a raised dais, bumped into her. As soon as he saw it, he jumped in front of her. Gallant, she thought, but unnecessary, and in any case she was the one with tempered combat skills. The nanosword was drawn, its barely visible electric blue blade humming softly. Muscles prepped, she glared through half-closed eyelids at the perfectly still Q'Roth warrior a few metres away.

"A statue!" Kostakis said, strolling up towards it, as if it was a bust of some long-forgotten Greek athlete. "Remarkably detailed."

Her instincts went into overdrive as he placed a finger on the marble white warrior sculpture's hipbone, level with Dimitri's chest. She held herself back in a semi-crouch, ready to spring, in case – by whatever means – it came to life. She watched with that hyper-alert detached battle sense, born from witnessing too many friends and lovers slain at close hand, while Dimitri traced the statue's contours with a finger. He'd never seen them in action, up close, as she had. When humanity had made its final retreat from Earth to Eden, she'd learned how quick and deadly they were, impervious to anything except the weapon she held in her hand. Or nukes. She'd detonated one in the last throes of battle on Earth, taking out at least a legion of the motherfuckers as they'd homed in on the human bio-signs.

Seeing it in alien white marble, rather than its blue-black metallic skin, made it only slightly less scary. Its trapezoidal head reminded her of a hammerhead, six gill-like slits that were sensors of some kind, a gash she knew to be its mouth, and six legs with downward-curving serrated thorns running along their spines. Most people described them as similar to a praying mantis, but she knew a better comparison: the mantis shrimp, a tropical armoured shellfish that shredded its prey with talons not unlike those she was staring at right now.

She'd witnessed a swathe of Q'Roth who'd raked through the last vestiges of humanity fleeing for her ship just before she quit Earth. They'd hacked men, women and children down, reaping their crop, their slit-like mouths opening wide before clamping down on their prey's heads, extracting the bio-electricity they'd come to Earth to feed upon. Part of their maturation process. Remembering the gurgling sound as each human was drained made bile rise up in her throat.

Dimitri withdrew his hand suddenly with an intake of breath. "So sharp!" He sucked at the vermillion blood oozing from a fingertip that had grazed one of the hooked barbs on a middle leg.

Jen didn't get it. "Why would the spiders build a statue of a mortal enemy, by all accounts a galactic predator?" It didn't make sense. "Stand back, Dimitri."

He turned towards her, the finger still in his mouth, accentuating the question mark framed by his eyebrows.

"I don't think it's a statue." She ramped up the power on the hilt of the nanosword and approached the monstrous effigy. She raised the sword kendo style, and with a *kiai* shout not far from a scream – pure bloodlust rising from the pit of her stomach – she leapt into the air and used her falling weight to drive the blade diagonally from the warrior's right shoulder, carving through all the way to its left hip. Stinging sparks needle-showered her as the Q'Roth soldier split asunder. In the heat of her bloodlust she mistimed it, and the upper half toppled toward her, its petrified claws spearing towards her head. Dimitri's arm swung around her waist and yanked her aside. She had the presence of mind to retract the nano-blade into its hilt with a flick of her thumb as the warrior's torso and upper legs thudded into the dust.

She lay panting on the ground, cradled by Dimitri, a serrated claw centimetres from her face. "Thanks," she coughed. "It would have been stupid to have been killed by a dead one." She felt Gabriel's presence, which seemed reasonable, given how close to death she'd just come. *Sorry big brother, got carried away, won't happen again.*

She felt the storm of anger inside her ebb, though she knew it would reclaim her soon.

"Good God," Dimitri said, as they got to their feet and inspected the sliced mannequin. Jen saw what she had expected. Where she had cut, there was a neat cross-section of Q'Roth anatomy: solidified intestines, vessels, and assorted organs.

Dimitri knelt down to study the creature's ceramic insides.

Jen stayed back. She noticed three cubic devices embedded in the ground, spaced equidistant around the Q'Roth warrior. A smile edged across her face. *Finally ... a weapon.*

* * *

Micah had to sit down. The high levels of oxygen made him dizzy. Sandy's lips were cherry red, and he knew his must be too. The buildings, the broken spires – everything was brighter, sharper, due to the combination of a higher partial pressure of oxygen and a lower overall atmospheric pressure. He wondered how long it would take to adapt to the sickly sweet Ourshiwann cocktail of oxygen, nitrogen, argon, and a few other gaseous compounds they hadn't yet identified. The smell reminded him of cloves, but an environmental scientist back on his ship had said it was an effect of the adaptation process – there was no real smell in the arid air. At least the rad-levels were exceptionally low, suggesting the spider race had developed more subtle energy sources.

His heart sank again. After their near-complete demise at the hands of the Q'Roth, he'd had plenty of time to ponder mankind's fragile destiny during his journey to Ourshiwann. By all accounts, based on what Kat had learned from her sessions with the Hohash, humanity was hopelessly beneath the high standards of galactic civilisation and technology, and – the bit he hated and feared most – the *intelligence* of the rest of the galaxy. Humanity was Level Three, and the scale apparently went all the way up to nineteen. The upper echelons in the galaxy would no doubt consider humans the way Micah considered insects back on Earth. Mankind had only escaped attention so far because the galaxy was so vast, and Earth was in a backwater, off the beaten track.

Humanity had escaped, but it was, so to speak, out of the thermo-cook and into the fusion-stove. Being an analyst, he'd run a hundred mental simulations, using a technique called cascading event tree analysis. He started from their flight from Eden to Ourshiwann – and considered potential events which could yet happen, with probabilities based on a range of mathematical distributions. At each 'node' in the tree, when an event happened, the result could either be success or failure. The trouble was, even when he postulated unlikely successes – miracles almost, like finding a friendly race who could communicate with them – the failures soon followed in multitudes. All his scenarios ended up with humanity either being enslaved, or becoming some alien race's tasty meal. A third typical endgame involved everyone starving to death while killing each other in an anarchic civil war. They were like toddlers stumbling along the San Francisco jetway in the dark: no handy guide-palms, no star charts, no idea how to communicate – that was it, he thought, *no idea* – no idea what was out here: we're naked, defenceless, and dumb.

What made it worse was that few others seemed to dwell on it. *Cognitive dissonance.* They lived in the immediate present, thinking about water, washing, and food. They were uncomfortable, sure, but as Carlson had put it, in deep denial. He imagined humanity as a fly caught in a spider's web, preening itself and wondering where its next meal would come from, even as its devourer approached.

He shuddered. The air temperature was lower than on over-heated Earth. Though he knew he'd acclimatise, he adjusted the temperature control on the cuff of his all-terrain jumpsuit. Immediately the incipient chill was chased away, and with it some of his morose state.

"No skeletons, no cadavers, no remains whatsoever," Sandy said.

It had been bugging him too, since the Q'Roth only fed on bioelectric energy, not flesh. Either the spiders had decayed completely, or... He had no inkling what the 'or' could be. He recalled how elephants, before they'd been extinguished during the third world war, used to scatter and crush the bones of fallen comrades, so that for centuries there had been myths of secret elephant graveyards. But there was no life here except maybe some insects and a few tiny rodents; no one to remove the skeletons or carcasses of the fallen spiders. It would have been useful to know more about them, he was sure.

"Maybe there are siroccos here, and the ruins have been scoured clean," he ventured.

"Almost no dust, no sand even in the city. Doesn't that mean wind and storms are unlikely?"

He shrugged. "We need to get underground. Up here seems to be just dwellings. The food and waste systems, maybe their entire industry, might be down below."

"Why not somewhere else, in another city?"

"Doesn't fit. Everything here speaks of simplicity and efficiency. And there's no obvious transport infrastructure. No, the answers are beneath our feet."

"Silly me, I forgot my bucket and spade." Sandy plonked herself down, next to him, and lay her head on his shoulder. He managed a smile, but she was right, they were getting nowhere. "You okay?" he asked.

"Just light-headed. Wondering what this new air is doing for Junior."

"You should tell one of the doctors, you know."

"Already did."

"Oh." He stared towards the other side of the plaza. "You and Vince getting on okay?" Her head shifted on his shoulder, then re-settled.

"Blake's a good man, don't you think? I mean a real leader."

Micah glossed over the change of subject. "Yes. This council idea, though. Not sure about Shakirvasta and Josefsson. They're a bit too..." He couldn't find the right word.

"Raptors," she said. "I've worked for enough in my time. Josefsson's blunt, but resilient and persuasive; born into power, a Dynastic politician. However, our Indistani mogul is so sharp you could cut yourself on him."

"He supported Blake."

She snorted. "He's biding his time, playing the long game. Bastard will probably dance on our graves." She nudged his shoulder. "Don't get on his wrong side, Micah."

Graves. What *did* the spiders do with their dead? He stared into the distance, through one of the glossy cylindrical tunnels. "Hey, we've never been into one of those."

Sandy lifted her head. "They're empty, just conduits. We can see straight through them."

But Micah was on his feet, marching towards the nearest channel. He stood at the entrance. It was like looking down the polished barrel of a rifle. He stepped inside, crouching, and walked a few paces. "I guess you're right. It's just a –" He didn't finish his sentence. He fell straight through the floor.

"Micah? *Micah!* Are you alright?"

He groaned, flat on his back. Getting up seemed like an idea that needed maturing before enacting. "Yes. Hurt my foot, but otherwise..." He got into a seated position without too much pain and rubbed his right ankle. It wasn't a big drop, but it wouldn't be easy getting back up. He fished the radio out from his knapsack. No signal. "Sandy," he shouted, "I'm going to toss the VHF radio up to you. It doesn't work down here. Call one of the mil crew on channel sixteen, tell them to bring some rope. Don't come any closer, or we'll both be trapped and no one will find us." He hobbled on his good foot, then lobbed the radio in an arc towards the smooth ceiling two metres above him. He sighed with relief when it passed straight through what must have been a hologram, or maybe just a clever passive optical illusion.

"Okay, got it. It's still working. I'll get out of the tunnel and radio for help."

Micah scanned the area around him. He was in a wide chamber, three metres high, with evenly-spaced femur-shaped pillars rising up from a dirty brown screed floor to a ceiling that stretched away in all directions, gloomy sepia lighting yielding to obsidian darkness within ten metres in any direction. Clusters of vine-green pipes hung like hospital drips from the ceiling, funnelling into rust-coloured boxes the size of a hover-car. He limped over to the nearest. It had two portholes, so he peered through one. It contained a mustardy liquid. Shifting around to the other porthole he saw a darker, oily liquid. Micah did the math: food and waste, most likely recycling.

Ourshiwann plumbing and nourishment. The question would be whether the food component was edible and nutritional for humans.

He limped back to the place where he had fallen through. He wondered how the spiders got in and out. Then a thought struck him – they could have hidden down here, when they were attacked. He whirled around, spooked, imagining one of the spiders lurking in the shadows. His logical mind tried to dismiss this as irrational, but he felt sure he was being watched.

"Sandy!" he shouted. "Sandy?" No answer. He heard a shuffling to his left. He fumbled for his pulse pistol but couldn't find it – it must have fallen out of his holster when he fell. He couldn't see it anywhere. "Who's there?" he said, immediately feeling like a soon-to-be dead schmuck in a cheap retro-slasher vid. Anyway, he thought, the spider race wouldn't know English or possibly any spoken language, since from all accounts their communication was entirely visual.

But he did get an answer, a lilting human voice. "Micah, is that you?"

Micah stared, open-mouthed. Rashid walked hesitantly towards him into the light, and almost tripped over a pipe. Micah realised that he couldn't see. Then, as Rashid's face came into view under one of the light sources, Micah saw why.

"Micah," Sandy yelled from above, "are you okay? They're on their way. And Jennifer and Dimitri called, they've found something... Micah, are you okay? Is everything alright?"

No, he thought, staring into Rashid's haunted, scorched face. We're a long way from alright. "Call Blake," he shouted. "Tell him..." *Tell him what?* Here's Rashid, alone, blind, without his ship, without two thousand people including Pierre and Kat. Vince had been right all along.

"Tell him to send a sling-jet. I've found Rashid."

Sandy didn't answer. He wasn't surprised. Despite himself, the analyst part of his brain kicked in with this fresh piece of data, another possible event in his mental simulation confirmed. Micah didn't need to run the calcs to know their outlook had just gotten a whole lot worse.

CHAPTER 7 – SUBTERFUGE

L ouise paced like a caged lion at the Holoseum sensing an approaching kill. But a nagging doubt kept rearing its ugly head. Since being shot in the back of the head back on Earth by her former partner and lover Vince, she'd been consumed by thoughts of revenge. However, the Q'Roth re-generation procedure had changed her. She could feel it, like quicksilver running in her veins. She'd gained a reputation as a ruthless killer long ago, but there had always been some warmth buried deep inside, embers somewhere of the fresh young teacher she'd been before the War and its endless killing. Now it was as if those embers had been snuffed out, leaving only burnt charcoal.

Each day it bothered her a little less. She had a suspicion Sister Esma may have asked the Q'Roth psychosurgeons to do some special 'rework' on her, to keep her on track so she finished the job. Alternatively, they'd had to use too much Q'Roth DNA to replace parts of her cortex blown out by Vince's pulse bullet. Either way, she didn't like it. She'd always been her own boss, in charge of herself. Louise had no qualms about following dark pathways, as long as it was her choice.

She watched her two fellow Alicians, staring rapt at their consoles – possibly more in order that they didn't have to face her, rather than because they were busy. Fine, let them sweat. She stared first at the Norwegian male, Jarvik, the original blond Aryan poster-soldier, muscles semi-flexed, proud cheekbones and a wide brow – she would have him again tonight, with or without Hannah this time. Her eyes flicked in the willowy Brit's direction. Unlike Jarvik's glacier-cool stability, Hannah was jittery as a sparrow, her straggly ginger hair swishing from side to side as she worked at her console. Louise decided she'd have them both tonight: she'd begun to doubt Hannah's loyalty, and had learned long ago how to unmask deception and betrayal during sex.

"Update," she barked, knowing Hannah would react first.

"We've isolated two trails, but haven't been able to find the third, even though we're scanning vast sectors of space. They appear to be using random jumps. We don't even know if they mean to converge somewhere. Their pattern is erratic. Maybe they're desperate, running blind."

Nothing new, she thought, Hannah was the least incisive of the two. She waited.

Jarvik spoke. "As yet we discern no strategy. However, we may have underestimated them."

Louise joined him at his console, a dull grey and blue affair rising from the floor with an angled flat-top luminous touch-screen. What she saw at first made no sense, but then her genetic recoding shifted up a gear, and she realised what the swirling data clouds meant. She'd learned, as they all had, not to try to translate this understanding back into human terms – that only led to confusion and migraines. Instead, she yielded to her Q'Roth DNA re-wiring, intuiting the data. Jarvik was right. She perceived a fractal pattern, too random to be accidentally plotted by humans. So, they weren't running blind, nor were they executing a search pattern – they'd known where they were going all along. But how was that possible?

She tried to recall the last moments before Vince had shot her in the head – the bullet had passed through her right hippocampus, so no amount of Q'Roth regeneration miracles could replace the memories he'd scorched. She'd been interrogating Micah, that much she recalled. He'd been telling her something, something key. But as she pressed at the gap left by Vince's pulse bullet, there was just a hole.

"Theorise." She waited, although she suspected the answer herself.

Already standing a head above her, Jarvik raised himself a little taller. "We assumed they knew nothing of the location of habitable planets. This hypothesis seemed confirmed when we intercepted the first ship close to a highly unstable sulphur-based world. Yet their apparently random movements are in fact synchronised. They are disguising their way to a rendezvous planet."

Five metres away, Hannah's slender, pretty face, with sharp eyes topped by a furrowed brow, reflected the jungle green data from her console display. She needed to stand on a small platform to operate the Q'Roth work-station. Abruptly she threw her head back and then launched her riposte. "They're low-grade humans – they have no star charts, and the Q'Roth transport ship's navigational databases are encrypted in Q'Roth Largyl 6. How could they possibly know of the existence of a habitable planet?" She folded her arms, careful to glare only at Jarvik.

Louise held up her hand. "Enough. It doesn't matter how. The data are clear enough for anyone with Level Five intelligence to see. Hannah, correlate the information you have with the Q'Roth star-chart and Jarvik's analysis, and pinpoint their destination. I believe you'll find it's the most recent planet culled by the Q'Roth, a millennium ago. Somehow they've divulged it from one of the ship's Nav databases." *Micah.* "When it's confirmed, plot a course." Her eyes stayed fixed on Hannah, daring her to voice objections about uncertainties, probabilities, or unsolvable goal projections. To her satisfaction, Hannah merely nodded and returned to her screen.

Jarvik didn't gloat or show even a trace of smugness. How nice it is to work with an advanced race, she mused. "Follow me," she said, heading to the small spiral walkway which connected all five decks of the Q'Roth hunter-destroyer class warship, shaped like a squatting crab, its six extendable legs like claws. They walked in silence to the next high-ceilinged level. Jarvik hesitated momentarily as they passed her bedchamber. She continued down, leaving the living quarters and medical area, Jarvik tagging behind, to the engine compartment. Rather than being noisy, this part of the ship sucked in sound. Louise felt as if her head was underwater. She knew it was a side-effect of the pseudo-singularity system that created time-space pressure differentials, allowing them to 'jump' across light years of space. One of the enhanced techs had tried for a while to explain before they'd left Earth, but had ended up shrugging and walking off, pointing with his index finger towards his head.

This gesture was something all recently-genned Alicians had grudgingly taken to doing – the genetic enhancement didn't kick in overnight. The surgery and biochemical alterations would be followed over the next thirty to a hundred years by corresponding natural growth and changes in the brain, courtesy of a new gland inserted just in front of the pituitary, hooked across the corpus callosum, beginning the neural bridging of the normally separated left and right hemispheres of the human brain. The gland, and the hormone it secreted, followed a biorhythmic cycle, and would finish the work the surgery started, leading to a new, upgraded brain structure with vastly superior neuro-transmitters. So, whenever an Alician only half-understood something, or intuited it but could not yet verbalise it, they would point to their heads as if to say *not cooked yet.*

Louise led Jarvik towards an area reserved for martial training. His brow furrowed as he glanced toward the tough tatami covering the floor in the corner of the engine room. She knew why – he had never come close to winning a practice bout with her in hand-to-hand combat, and still carried recent bruises. Then he stared at her, his hard blue eyes unwavering. She pointed to a leg-width conduit which ran up one wall behind the training mat. He studied the unremarkable pipe-work.

"I don't –". He stopped. Something had happened. Jarvik stepped onto the mat within arm's reach of the alien pipe, staring at it.

He remained there nearly three minutes. His physique reminded her of Michelangelo's David. Then it happened again. For the first time since she'd met him, she saw on his sculpted face the brow-widening of uncertainty, a lack of complete conviction. His lower lip dropped a full centimetre.

Jarvik's gaze dipped to the floor, as he calculated the implications of the spasmodic dark flushes whose shadow he'd seen in the tube, like swirling iron filings. He faced Louise, composure restored, but darkened by his inference. "Nannites. We have been sabotaged. We do not have the tools onboard to extract them, though the humans might. We have maybe a week before the engines fail catastrophically and the hull is compromised."

She nodded. She hadn't thought it would be so soon, or so catastrophic, wondering if the nannites were meant to be there as some kind of engine upgrade. But Jarvik was never wrong about engines. It meant they had no chance to go back and retrace their steps and find the other Alicians – even if the route Sister Esma had given her was correct, which she now doubted.

"Our beloved leader, Sister Esma, has given us a one-way ticket." She raised her voice to prevent the ether from sucking the volume out of her words. "Now we too, as well as our inferior cousins, need to find that planet."

"Do we continue with our mission to eradicate humanity?"

"Do you follow me or Sister Esma?"

Jarvik answered without hesitation. "You are my leader. I serve you."

Good, she thought, as otherwise I'd have to kill you right now. She considered Hannah, and estimated that she too would prefer not to be on a one-way suicide mission, though more out of survival interest than allegiance to anyone.

"Go back to the bridge," she said. "I believe our mission parameters have just broadened. I will join you shortly."

Once Jarvik had left, Louise walked to a sealed room on the same level. She keyed in an access code and stepped inside the purple-lit compartment, locking the door behind her. Her fingers traced the edge of a vat, as she listened to the susurration of minute bubbles popping at the surface of the green liquid. Peering in, she could just make out the features. "Nearly done," she remarked.

She'd had to sleep with the genetic engineer to get him to install it before she quit Earth, and hoped she'd never need it. But Sister Esma had lied to her. For Louise it wasn't an issue of betrayal – such pointless and narcissistic emotions were beneath Alicians – she could see Sister Esma's logic. What mattered more in Alician mores was cunning, thinking ahead, and ultimately survival, and Louise had those in spades – Sister Esma had taught her well.

* * *

Blake stood outside his command tent listening to the flapping of the beige canvas in the afternoon breeze. The dry air tasted sweet. He'd awakened to find his skin cold, though not enough to make him shiver. The temperature ranged between twenty-three Celsius at noon and twelve at night. They'd been lucky to find the climate so hospitable, though of course there might be substantial seasonal variations.

The extra oxygen made everything appear sharper – one of the doctors had said they would adapt within a couple of weeks. The mountains some twenty kilometres away glared purple, though at dawn they glowed green. He knew they would ebb with an ocean blue tinge before nightfall. He longed for clouds – the shifting palette of sky colours was a constant reminder of how alien this place was.

He wondered why the water kept running from the mountains, with no obvious source like rain. The Professor had suggested that millennia ago the spider race must have attained weather control, though he had no idea how.

He watched the dust-trails from vehicles he'd sent out to the city, twenty kilometres away. The visibility was crystal; he hardly needed the field holo-map to track their progress. He shaded his eyes from the sun with a saluting hand – it was duller than Earth's sun, but doctors had nevertheless warned of cataracts – and gazed upwards into the aquamarine sky. He imagined the Q'Roth ships arriving one evening above the city. The spiders had put up no defence, culled as easy as seals used to be on Earth before they became extinct, along with hundreds of other species, in what had been labelled the *decimation*, after the radioactive fallout from the Third World War. He wondered what the spider race must have thought in those last moments. Only Kat had glimpsed their emotional state, via her nodal connection to the Hohash mirrors.

He didn't agree with pacifism – he was a soldier through and through – but he had to admit that due to that innate trait, the spiders' world had been left in a habitable state. "Thank you," he said, nodding toward the city that stood like a mausoleum, likely to become humanity's refuge.

His eyes flicked downwards. A slim figure in the distance climbed the escarpment towards him with a measured, ballerina-like gait. He lowered his hand, and went back inside his tent, planting himself on the field chair behind his rusting iron desk. The inner darkness that had momentarily left him when he'd stepped outside returned as steadily as the black-rain fallout he'd experienced a decade earlier in France. His platoon had been caught in the penumbra between two aerial detonations, one over Paris, the other over Reims. He thought he'd never be able to wash off the cloying ash. Since then he'd always showered longer than necessary.

Although the weight of the remnants of humanity rested on his shoulders right now, far worse was the meeting earlier that morning with the doctor and his wife, Glenda. The physician had cleared his throat and then announced that there was no more chemo, and that they did not have the right facilities to administer and control it anyway. Before he'd been able to protest, Glenda had asked "How long?", as if she was inquiring as to the price of a loaf of bread.

Blake had found that the tearing feeling in his chest had no verbal counterpart, so he'd simply held her. Eventually, she pulled away, her eyes steeling into his. "Will you do three things for me?" she asked.

He nodded without hesitation.

"First," she said, "don't grieve for me until I am gone. I need to see the man I love, clear and strong. That will help me more than you can imagine. Second, make me proud. Pour your energies into saving humanity, no matter what it takes. Third, my love, I –'

Antonia entered his tent.

"Sorry to disturb you commander; I was going to knock, but..."

"Canvas, I know. Please, sit down." He straightened his battle tunic. Since he'd taken command he'd found people more comforted seeing him in his khaki military uniform than in his astronaut jumpsuit. "Your report."

Poised as ever, her two-tone blonde-brown hair in an immaculate bun, she nodded. He noted that she wasn't taken aback by his perfunctory style. Good, he didn't want to have to wet-nurse anyone.

"It's pretty messy, Sir." She leaned forward and produced a piece of *flimsy* – washable paper-film – with carefully hand-written notes on it. He had rarely seen such clear writing, almost a lost art these days. As she leaned forward to read from the sheet, he noticed the shadows around her eyes: she'd been working hard. Humanity's fate didn't rest on his shoulders alone.

She tapped the flimsy with a forefinger. "First, food. People are surviving, but stocks are getting low, much worse than we thought. We have maybe six weeks left, eight if we decrease rations. But that might trigger panic and worse, fuel a black market in stolen rations that's already gaining a foothold on at least one of the ships. Water is okay, thank goodness, plenty of streams criss-crossing the mountains. There's also a large underwater river heading directly into the city." She looked up from the flimsy. When Blake remained poker-faced, she continued. "Next, shelter. People..." She sat back, folding her arms. "People absolutely hate those ships, Sir. They're spooked by them: the dim light, the clammy walls, every surface feeling like dead flesh. And they're a constant reminder of the Q'Roth invaders, of what happened back on Earth."

He nodded. He noticed her left hand was shaking slightly. She bit her lip.

"Third..." Her hands dropped into her lap. "Sir, I don't know what I'm doing. Is any of this helping? Surely there's someone more qualified – "

Blake brought his fist down hard on the table. The dull thud of flesh against metal made her flinch. A wave of pressure swelled in his chest, rising into his neck. *It's not about her*, he reminded himself. Nevertheless he stood up, and stared hard at her. She looked bewildered, caught off guard. Flustered, she stood up in return.

"I'm... I'm sorry, I..." She turned toward the exit, fumbling with the chair as her boot entangled itself in one of the legs.

"Where do you think you're going?" He used his cutting voice, the one his soldiers dreaded. She stopped, and half-turned back to him. "I thought... I thought you were dismissing me."

He took a deep breath. His mind was full of Glenda, him standing over her grave on this godforsaken world in a few weeks' time. He ground his teeth, and then recalled his first and second promise to her. He leaned forwards, fingertips on the desk, and visualised Glenda fifteen years ago, laughing with him on the rocky, windswept shore of Rapa Nui. The surge in his chest ebbed, though he knew it was only a temporary respite. Breathing out slowly, he spoke with a softness usually reserved for Glenda alone, but his eyes cored into Antonia's.

"What's the first thing on your mind, Antonia? Really, the first thing."

The frown on her face morphed into horrified recognition. She shook her head. "Don't do this, Sir, please."

"Answer me!"

Her eyes brimmed, her face flushing red with emotion: anger, he hoped. She faced him. "Alright, Sir, you want it, you can have it. Kat! Every second, every face I see having lost someone, I see her. She may already be dead, she may be asphyxiating somewhere, dying. That's what's in my head every waking moment, Sir, and I'm not sleeping much right now, Sir."

Despite her quivering frame, she had the dignity to flick away a tear and glare straight back at him. He sat down, then gestured for her to take her seat. She perched on its edge, still ready to leave at a moment's notice.

"A wise woman once told me," he began, placing his hand on a holo-frame of Glenda in healthier days, "that we act only according to two drives: love and fear. It sounds trite, but the longer I walk this... The longer I live, the more I realise it's true. Most people here are driven by fear. They're the ones that people like you and me need to protect. You're driven by love. I know that for a fact, you've just made it perfectly clear. That qualifies you for the job. Period." He paused, letting it sink in. "One more thing, then we close the subject."

She met his eyes head on, defiant. Good, he thought, you'll need it.

"Kat's still alive, Antonia. I would know if she and Pierre were gone. I'm not just saying that, you're just going to have to trust me, and yourself."

She slapped her hand down on the table. "That's not nearly good enough, Sir. I need more than platitudes. Frankly I expect more than that from you of all people." Her chest heaved, but she no longer trembled.

Blake studied Glenda's picture, and spoke softly to it. "When people under my command die, I see their faces. At night, in dreams, or I think I see them in the crowds around me, then I realise it's someone else." He focused back on Antonia. "Always. No exceptions. Ever. And I haven't seen or dreamt of Kat or Pierre these past two weeks." He waited, watching her composure reassert itself. After a long silence, she nodded. She placed an index finger on the flimsy and took in a fulsome breath.

"Clothes," she said, clearing her throat. "We need to find or plant crops that can produce fibres, or else in about a year we'll all be naked."

Blake's face cracked a smile, despite himself. His grin infected Antonia, too. She let out a single nervous laugh, like the first person giggling at a rather flat party.

"You can imagine what Josefsson said to that, Sir."

He shook his head. "Are those two helping you, by the way, our good Senator, and Mr. Shakirvasta?"

Antonia rolled her eyes. "Oh, absolutely. Josefsson's preparing a manifesto, you know, for the upcoming elections?"

He raised an eyebrow.

She continued. "And as for *Mr.* Shakirvasta – what is his first name, by the way, no one seems to know? Well, I'm not sure what he's up to. Erecting Chinese walls I think. I swear that man can see around corners. You should watch him – but you know that already, don't you? That's why you put him on the council, better close and visible than underground, as my father used to say."

"Your father was a wise man." He folded his fingers into a steeple. "Antonia, we're moving people out of the ships. I want you to join Micah and Sandy today to determine living quarters and arrangements. I'll take a look at the rest of your notes and assign others to look after the issues you've raised."

Antonia's eyes widened. "But I thought the military were checking the city?"

He nodded. "They check to see if it's secure. I want you to check if it's habitale, capable of becoming a place people can call *home*. Where they can live out their lives, and..." He thought of Glenda's third wish, but he couldn't say it.

She nodded slowly, though he sensed some hesitation. Zack had already told him about some earlier argument between her, Micah and Kat, back on Eden, right before leaving. He waited for her counter-suggestion.

"Maybe Josefsson or –"

"Josefsson will certainly take the credit, but a man with manicured hands doesn't get them dirty willingly. Do you have a problem working with Micah or Sandy?"

She tilted her chin upwards, just a fraction, then shook her head vehemently.

"No, of course not. I'll take the next transport to the city, Sir." She stood, waited to see if there was anything else, and then picked up the flimsy, rolled it carefully, and handed it to him. As she left, he noticed her step was a fraction lighter.

Blake spoke to the rippling canvas door and the empty tent. "A month or two working with Josefsson and Shakirvasta, Antonia, and you'll become a much better liar."

"Nobody had time to scream." Rashid's voice was bereft of hope, like a rain-swept funeral at sea.

Blake felt his stomach churn while Rashid recounted what had happened on his ship, as best he could. Unlike the other Council members gathered, he stared straight into Rashid's coal-black eye sockets. He imagined two thousand eyes peering silently from the void through Rashid's space-like portals. Rashid trembled once or twice as if crying, but no salt water emerged – the tear ducts had been cauterised.

Blake recalled what Vince had told him earlier about Louise...

"No one else would work with her. She was so Goddammed fast, way too brutal for even the tough guys, never took prisoners. During the War, she earned a reputation. She was behind enemy lines, tracking down a renegade who'd stolen a nuke, holed up in a village in the Thai foothills. While the generals were debating who to send in, she ashed the place with a fire-stormer. All that was left was human barbecue and the bomb, its plaz casing still intact, a charred corpse next to it, a bony hand fried to the detonator controls. You see my point? Louise selected that weapon because she knew the intensity would blind him so he couldn't set the sequence. She just shrugged off the two hundred villagers who got toasted as collateral. After that little episode they nicknamed her 'the baker', though nobody said it within earshot of Louise, let alone to her face. Whatever her mission was, Blake, she got it done. She doesn't care about collateral. So, if she's after us..."

Rashid finished. His head made those small movements Blake knew well from numerous nuclear-flash-blinded soldiers, trying to hear the reactions of the people seated around him.

Zack split the graveyard silence. "Vince, I thought you said you killed that bitch."

Vince bristled, but Micah answered. "Trust me, Zack, part of her brain rained down on me in that hospital bed when Vince blew a hole in her head."

"Then how in the hell –"

Blake raised his hand. "It doesn't matter how. She's after us, and she's tooled up to take us down."

Vince folded his arms. "Maybe not all of us. You and me, Micah, for sure. And maybe your good self, Commander Alexander."

Ramires, who till now had remained a silent observer at the Ourshiwann council meetings, spoke up. "I doubt very much this is a private vendetta. They know we escaped. The Alicians want to eradicate humanity. This is a clean-up job."

Zack ran a hand over his near-bald pate. "We should send a ship to find Pierre and Kat. Maybe they're still alive."

Blake's fingers riffed once on the table, then he addressed Rashid. "Could we launch a rescue mission, Rashid?"

Rashid tilted his head again, listening hard, trying to pinpoint the exact location of each speaker. "No, we most certainly cannot. Without the navigational log, showing how much distance was covered in each leg, we would never find it again. I am sorry."

Blake stood up. "We need to get everyone out of the ships. We're moving into the city. It's the only option: not enough tents, and no other natural shelter. Senator Josefsson, I'd like you to orchestrate the operation." He watched Josefsson hesitate, and moved on before the senator could work out the angles. "I've already sent Antonia to the city where Micah, Sandy and several teams are determining habitation options. Professor Kostakis and Jennifer are also down there. They believe they may have found a weapon. Mr Shakirvasta, pick three engineering teams and try to find and disable the ships' transponders. Vince, Zack, Ramires, you're with me. Battle plan time. Let's get to it everybody."

Everyone rose except Rashid, who remained rooted to the spot. Blake headed toward him but Zack arrived first.

"Come on buddy, you're with me." Zack led him out of the room, nodding back to Blake that he'd catch him later.

Vince spoke as soon as it was just him, Blake and Ramires. "What's your real plan?"

Blake eyed them both. Vince's steel blue eyes were always head on, like a samurai's. But he thought Ramires' fresh-mown stubble fringed with his moustache concealed a wry smile. Blake realised he was too used to military, the chain of command, not being second-guessed. These men were laser-sharp. But he had to stay in charge. "You tell me."

Vince nodded, with a twitch of his mouth indicating he knew all too well the little tricks Blake was trying to play. His voice was firm and clear. "Plan A: we stay here with the ships as bait. If she gets close enough we take her ship down; we have two short-range tactical nukes left, but no delivery system other than a couple of sling jets — we need her to land, or at least enter the atmosphere, or come to our ships. Maybe some of us go down with her, but the city will survive. Plan B, to be executed in parallel: we find another one of those Hohash craft that Pierre and Kat were on, and materialise onboard her ship with a nuke. It's another sacrificial plan, with Zack the best option as pilot. If you've got a Plan C, I'm interested to hear it." Vince folded his arms.

Ramires pitched his head forward like a boxer just before a fight. "I'll take Plan A."

"You know how to set tactical nukes?" Blake asked.

Ramires' wry grin reappeared. "Not my first time, Commander."

These men aren't just sharp, Blake thought, they're *serrated*. But he still had an ace. "Good. We're on the same wavelength. There is a plan C, but I warn you now, Vince, you're not going to like it."

Sonja heard Zack's heavy footfalls approaching the cramped Q'Roth 'grotto', as he liked to call their allocated room. She glanced in the dented tin wall mirror to check she looked presentable. She hoped her boisterous black afro compensated for the hunger rings around her eyes; she gave most of her food share to Zack and their two children, and wore baggy clothes to conceal her lean frame.

Their address was 43 Beta West, deck seven in the twelfth ring from the central ramp that spiralled its way to the ship's control room. It wasn't home, but she tried to pretend. She and their two boys stood behind the meal simmering in two pots on a makeshift stove they had loan of one night in three. She'd spent half the morning begging and borrowing the ingredients. But as Zack entered, she could tell that the smell of coriander and lemon beef substitute, one of his favourites, barely registered against his sombre mood. Another wasted effort. Zack had no stomach or taste for food these days. Nothing she did reached him. She braved a smile. That was when she caught sight of the man behind her husband.

She froze as she saw the stranger's wounds, resisting the urge to gather her kids behind her.

"Hun, this is Rashid. Look after him while I'm gone."

She gaped at Zack, who'd turned on his heels, ready to leave. He hadn't kissed her, had hardly even looked at her. It had been getting steadily worse since they'd left Eden, and he refused to even talk about it, just brooded all the time. "Wait, Zack... What... where are you going?"

"Gotta go kill an Alician bitch."

He disappeared, leaving the tan-skinned Rashid standing alone in the middle of the room, his black curling hair grown wild. Sonja walked over, reached out towards him, touched his bare arm. It felt cool, unlike Zack's steam-pipe forearms.

"I am most sorry for this imposition," he said. "I had thought he was taking me to a medical facility."

Sonja inspected his eye sockets; she'd seen worse, but only once. "Kind of. I used to be a nurse, well, paramedic actually. May I?"

Rashid's head jiggled sideways. Zack had talked to her before about Rashid, so she knew this odd motion, a natural habit from his native India, signified a *yes*. Her fingers scouted his face. He flinched once, then acquiesced, keeping his head steady. She ignored her two children who hung at her waist gaping upwards at Rashid's face. Her fingers skated over the holes where his eyes should have been.

"Peter, fetch me the flashlight, please." The torch nudged her hip seconds later. She brought it up to Rashid's face, inspecting the cavities. "Minimal scarring, nerves cleanly cauterised." She switched off the light. "Whoever did this work on you did a hell of a job. Who was it?"

Rashid sighed. "That is a long story. May I sit down?"

She glanced around. "Of course you can, how rude of me. But we don't have chairs, I'm afraid."

"That is good, they are bad for the spine, you know." His beaming smile disavowed her of any residual repulsion over the way he looked. He dropped down fluidly into a cross-legged sitting position. He held out his two hands in the vague direction of her two children, and they each gingerly took one, all the time staring wide-eyed at Rashid's cavernous face.

Sonja stared at Rashid. Her kids never reached out to strangers. There was something about this man, a quality of openness and honesty that led her, and apparently her kids, too, to trust him. She ran her fingers through her thick black curls, coiling her hair around her fingers. *Zack, what the hell are you doing?*

Zack loped through the corridors like a giant rat who'd had enough of the maze he'd been cooped up in. The flashbacks to the Thai jungle during the War were getting worse. For the first time in ten years he could remember fragments, snippets of detail about what happened after his platoon was wiped out, when he'd been declared missing in action for ten days. He still couldn't recall much detail, a few faces he didn't know, a weird-looking lab, and the Eiffel fucking tower of all things. None of it made any sense.

There'd been a theory on the Ulysses that one of its crew had been implanted with a killer psychosis by the Alicians, one that could be activated by some special code. He knew he was the only remaining suspect, and he didn't care much for the way that Carlson, the resident shrink, kept looking at him, searching all the time for tell-tale signs. He knew he was being shitty to Sonja, but inside he was unravelling, barely in command.

He sensed something malevolent deep inside, watching and waiting for some signal. He needed to keep his distance from Sonja and the kids, to protect them – he felt unsafe, as if he might go off the rails at any time. He'd heard Rashid tell the story of what these implants could do to people, instantly transforming them into rabid killers. Once Louise was out of the way, he decided, he'd submit to Carlson to get the thing out of his head, no matter what it took, or how long.

Zack reached the bay doors that led him out of the ship. He hadn't meant to leave; he was supposed to join Blake and the others. He closed his eyes and took a few deep breaths of crisp air. He shrugged, feeling better already. It's nothing, he thought, just deep trauma. Loads of War-vets have nightmares. He headed back inside, jogging up the central ramp to find the board room. But he slowed down as the face of a blonde woman flickered into his mind, hanging there for a second, as if staring at him, saying something he couldn't quite catch. He'd heard Louise described often enough to guess it was her. Yet it felt like a memory, as if he'd actually met her in that lab somewhere near Chiang Rai. There'd been something else, too, a strange sing-song voice.

Thick fog billowed into his mind, dampening the image, as if his brain was trying to recall a holo-mail that it had never intended to send. Zack struggled first to remember the face, then to hold on to what he was forgetting. It slipped away as surely as a dream upon waking. When the mist in his mind evaporated he found himself standing on the ramp, leaning his head against the slimy wall, wondering what he was doing there. He couldn't remember. He'd just left Rashid with Sonja; that was the last thing he could recall. He was late for a meeting with Blake and the others, that much he knew for sure.

Zack set off at a jog up the ramp, picking up speed, feeling better than he had in weeks. He'd apologise to Sonja later. He'd tell her he'd see Carlson; that would cheer her up. But later. First he and the others had to rid themselves of Louise. He'd never killed a woman before; he hoped they could do it at a distance. Idly, he wondered what she looked like, then dismissed the idea – best not to think about it.

He arrived, a little out of breath, facing Blake and the others. "So, what did I miss? Are we on Plan C yet?"

∗ ∗ ∗

Hannah whispered to Jarvik, as quiet as autumn leaves rustling in the wind. "We need to strike first. She'll kill us both sooner or later. You know I'm right."

Jarvik's hand snapped around her throat, muscles firm. "Maybe just you, Hannah." He glared at her, then let go. He sensed the tension in his own shoulders, and his features felt leaden – this mission had not exactly been the brave new world he'd been expecting. And he'd seen the nannites. The three of them would perish soon one way or another unless they found the planet and their inferior cousins.

Right now he needed Louise, because she was above all a survivor. "She's too strong, too fast," he said.

"Then talk to them, the humans – you're taking the stealth-pod down to the planet when we arrive. Talk to them. Tell them... tell them we can be reasonable."

Hannah's eyes had that cornered animal look, like a goat he'd once seen being led to the slaughter. She made to speak, but Jarvik cast a look that stopped her dead. "No, Hannah. We see this through. We didn't sign up with the Alicians to behave like normal humans, divided and rife with corruption." He continued, pre-empting the riposte he knew she would launch. "And yes, even if our Grand-Mistress, Sister Esma means us to die, then we die for the cause."

Hannah glowered. She held her head up, tossing her copper hair back. "Alright. We do it your way, for Sister Esma, for the cause."

Jarvik's eyes tracked her as she strode back to her own console. Now he had two women he needed to watch very carefully.

CHAPTER 8 – OSSYRIANS

Pierre felt the warm liquid spill through his helmet seal, flushing down into his suit. Lifting the helmet a few centimetres with both hands, he took one last deep breath, and saw Kat's shocked features, but he also detected something like pride in her eyes. It was enough. He lifted off the helmet, the warm liquid swirling around his head like a hot, wet towel, and let it drop behind him. It sank to the floor with a small clunk. He kept his eyes closed, holding his breath even as the lighter-than-water fluid assaulted his nostrils. He forced open his eyes, expecting the fluid to sting, but if anything, it was soothing. Everything was slightly out of focus, tinged pink. Kat gripped his shoulders.

He felt the tug of anoxia beginning in his lungs, sucking in and down on his diaphragm, begging him to breathe in, unaware of the consequences. A couple of bubbles escaped his nostrils, letting the liquid rise higher into his nasal cavity, making him blink. He heard a swishing noise. Kat released him and took a slow-motion step backwards. Something was behind him. With difficulty, trying not to fall over in his last seconds, he turned around. He was so startled he almost breathed in, there and then, face-to-face with an upright-standing dog in an Egyptian pharaoh's head-dress, with its alternating horizontal bars of gold and blue, shrouding a strong black collie-like face with silver eyes.

Pierre's mouth opened a fraction and the fluid lost no time in entering, tasting of nothing, fizzy on his tongue. The creature in front of him seized his arms, and he felt something punch him very hard in the stomach, evacuating all remaining air from him in one large, noisy gurgle. He doubled over in pain. The creature wrenched him upwards, causing him at last to inhale.

The liquid charged into his lungs, cool as menthol, numbing his throat. An instant urge to cough and splutter vanished, like a sneeze that threatens but never arrives. He assumed it must be some kind of anaesthetic, but then with a shock realised he no longer felt the pressure to breathe in. The creature held onto his wrists, and placed another limb on his stomach, pushing gentler this time. Pierre understood – it was telling him to breathe the fluid. *What the hell.* He tried it. He pulled in his stomach and raised his diaphragm to expel some of the liquid, then – and it required conscious effort – reversed the movements to inhale it, as reluctantly as if sucking in acid through a straw.

He tried it a few times, and amazement surpassed his fear. He guessed it was a hyper-oxygenated fluid of some kind. It made a low squirting sound each time he breathed, but, if anything, he could breathe slower than with normal air. The creature released him, and he turned around to show Kat he was alright.

But she wasn't. She had a pulse rifle aimed at the creature. Pierre held up his hand. He tried to talk, but could only gurgle. He laid a hand on the barrel of the rifle, gently pushing it downwards. Eventually she let it fall, and he found her arms wrapped around him, her helmet pressing uncomfortably against his face. She squeezed him so tight he found it hard to breathe again.

Pierre cradled Kat in his arms on a curved bench of indeterminate material: it looked metallic but felt like sitting on dry moss. The undersized conical room reminded him of a tepee, inside all white and smooth, the bench running around three quarters of its perimeter. Light emanated from the walls, the air still. *Air.* It was good to breathe normal air again. The worst part had been getting Kat's helmet off when her supply ran out. That hadn't been pretty, even if she'd seen him breathe the liquid. In the end, as she'd stood holding her breath, stiff as a man on the gallows waiting for the drop, he'd kissed her, held her tight, and persuaded her mouth to accept a little of the fluid from his own. And then she'd thrashed violently, convulsing almost, lacerating his left cheek in the process with a fingernail, though there was no trace of it now.

"Why do you suppose they did that?" Her voice had that post-traumatic forced calmness.

"I don't know."

"You always know, Pierre, you're just too bloody shy." She pinched his arm, making him wince.

He decided she was right, but it wasn't modesty; rather, years of being tested by his father, and being verbally eviscerated if his suppositions contained the merest hint of a flaw. But Kat wasn't his father, and he had a reasonable hunch. "I believe it was medical, a way of de-contaminating us."

Kat levered herself into a sitting position, so she could see him. "What, we're unclean?"

"Well, no ... and yes. We carry microbes around with us, we shed skin daily, and we perspire all the time. That could be lethal to an alien species."

Kat puckered her nose. "Hmm. Always thought it would be some weird coloured light or something, the way we used to irradiate food."

"A liquid makes sense: invasive, sterilising, and it can get inside the body, with the advantage of a higher osmotic pressure than air – more penetrating."

She fell quiet and closed her eyes. He studied her face, her pert nose, thin pale lips that he now knew served equally well for pleasure or verbal abuse, dark eyebrows under a narrow brow. *A fallen angel.* Born into an elite rich man's world, got fed up with it, and spurned it all. He wondered what had really made her leave her uncle's Eldorado Island – a man-made atoll rising up from one of the sunken Maldivian islets.

There had been years of speculation and gossip, but neither Kat nor her uncle had ever deigned to answer even the most oblique question on the subject of her abrupt, self-imposed exile. He had the feeling she'd never tell him, no matter how close they got. Then he realised that he had it the wrong way around: she'd never tell him now *because* they were close. Something she was ashamed of, then, or else she thought he'd think less of her. *Victims always feel guilty,* his mother had told him on one of his own particularly bad days.

An opening in the wall irised out of nowhere, shaping itself into an oval doorway truncated at the floor, revealing one of the dog-like creatures. For the first time he got a decent look, without the fluid distorting his vision. The creature was tall, elegant, like a regal, upstanding dog. Its black head – he couldn't ignore the snout – was still haloed by the head-dress which framed it. He remembered seeing pictures of the boy-pharaoh Tutankhamen, and the dog-like god Anubis; there was a striking similarity, and he immediately wondered if these creatures had visited Earth – Egypt to be precise – millennia ago. The creature wore a brilliant white tunic, and something resembling a skirt, with a rectangular piece of white material hanging down in front and back to below the knee line, revealing muscular black legs coated with a sheen of fur. He noted the powerful ribcage underneath the clothing. Two long arms hung down reaching the creature's hips, ending in closed silver hands, each with two opposable thumbs and three fingers. He saw cloven, dark feet, fringed with fine black fuzz. But he was drawn back upwards to its eyes. They glistened silver. He was mesmerised by the kaleidoscopic patterns rippling across the eyes' surface, small columns like skyscrapers rising and falling, geometric shapes evanescing out of the background only to be superimposed by others.

"I think it's trying to communicate," Kat said.

Pierre realised it had not heard them speak, since they had not been able to in the fluid. "Hello," he said, instantly feeling moronic, but he had to start somewhere. Even if they understood nothing, they would realise that vocalisation was the principal modality for communicating.

"We are called humans, from a planet called Earth. We –"

The creature's jaws opened, revealing not teeth, but a mesh of blue and mauve fibres that grew taut as the open jaw reached its full extension. A blast of noise, a psychedelic choir of a thousand fingernails scraping down blackboards, made Pierre and Kat double over, hands plastered over their ears.

"STOP! Stop it, damn you!" Kat yelled through the din. Abruptly the noise ceased, replaced by the two of them gasping for breath.

The creature exited, the doorway popping seamlessly out of existence behind it.

Kat slumped against the supple wall. "Brilliant. Perfect."

He eased himself down next to her, his ears ringing after the auditory storm. "This is going to be a lot harder than I'd ever imagined."

"There, there," she said in a mocking tone, recovering, and pulled his head toward her. She kissed him, then manoeuvred him downwards so his head lay on her thigh. She stroked his temple. "Anyway, look on the bright side. At least they haven't cooked us yet."

"Maybe he was just trying to say 'hello' back."

"He?"

"Yes... Er..."

Kat sighed. "God, even the smart ones are really dumb, aren't they?"

Pierre bristled. "Well, the musculature, the ribcage, the –"

"Eight nipples?" Kat shook her head. "This is why I sleep with girls: men always miss the important details. She's a bitch, Pierre, and I mean that in the technical, anatomical sense."

Pierre decided to stay quiet.

"She's kind of cute, actually. Nice skirt, don't you think?"

He glanced at her in disbelief, just as she punched his shoulder.

"I'm kidding, lighten up, Pierre. Anyway, any ideas?"

He closed his eyes and tried to think. Then he smelt something sweet, like caramel. He tried to open his eyes but they stayed shut. He heard a distant voice, someone shouting. He felt a light touch, as if someone was nudging him gently. He strained to hear what the high-pitched voice was saying, something like "Wake up, Pierre!" But warmth suffused his body, and even a brief stinging sensation on his face failed to stop him from being sucked downwards into the depths of slumber.

Pierre jerked awake, finding himself stretched out on one of the benches in a much larger room, still conical in shape. Kat had her back to him, her arms folded from the looks of it, as she stood, legs splayed, in front of the Hohash. He made to get up, and found his strength was gone. He gasped with effort, just to sit up. Kat turned around, but didn't approach him.

"What happened?" he asked.

She surveyed him for a moment. "They took you. You've been gone for two days, judging from my body clock."

He stared at her. *Two whole days?* But where, and to do what? And why was she being so distant with him? He tried to play it cool. "They drugged me somehow. But not you?"

She shook her head and turned back toward the Hohash. Her body was tense. He had the unnerving feeling she didn't want to look at him.

He pressed his hands down on the bench, trying to sit up straight. His head still felt fuzzy, as if filled with soggy cotton wool, stuffed with needles that pricked the inside of his skull if he moved too fast. She turned to face him again. He noticed she wasn't just folding her arms, she was holding herself, as if afraid. He wanted to get up and embrace her but he knew he would fall over before reaching her, and probably throw up into the bargain. Why was she behaving like this? Had he done something, said something in his sleep? He had no recollection whatsoever, but he believed her when she said he'd been missing for two days.

A popping sound announced the entrance of the dog-like creature. He watched as it glided towards Kat and the Hohash. It – he decided he had to deal with it as an 'it' rather than a 'she', for now at least – gestured for Kat to sit on the bench next to Pierre. She did so, just out of his reach.

The creature stretched out an arm, and touched the inert Hohash. It sprang to life, hovering ten centimetres off the floor, its transparent surface flooding with liquid crystal hues of silvers, blues, and purples. It glided over towards Pierre and Kat.

"Showtime," Kat said. Without turning her head to face him, her hand slid across the bench towards his. He took it, and she clasped his outstretched hand, squeezing it tight. He looked once at her tight-lipped profile, then turned to the Hohash. Its cloud-like surface condensed to show a blue-green Earth, viewed from space – evidently before the nuclear War had browned it. A shimmering sphere approached, dangling above the planet like an old-style Christmas tree bauble. A tiny triangular section detached itself from the sphere and plunged towards the planet. It fell through the clouds towards a sandy, desert-like region fringed by turquoise sea. He'd already guessed its destination.

Pierre watched as the tetrahedron-shaped craft landed, but was taken aback as some people moved into the frame, showing by perspective how huge the craft was.

"Pyramid," Kat announced.

He nodded. As the dust settled, dark-skinned men in flowing beige robes ventured towards the centre of one of the sides of the metallic pyramid. A hatch opened midway, and a ramp extended, descending to the dusty ground. Three of the dog-like species, wearing golden garments, all having the kinds of head-dress their current companion wore, walked down to meet the humans with a smooth, regal gait.

The men bowed long and low before the creatures, the one in front holding out a scroll. The vantage point shifted – he had no idea how this scene had been recorded – and one of the dog-aliens unrolled it. Pierre and Kat saw a close-up of writing on the parchment. "Looks like hieratic," he said, "with some hieroglyphs thrown in."

The view changed, revealing a village of dying people, corpses rotting in the streets. The aliens were tending to them, using some device or other to spray a fine mist over all, both living and dead. The scene shifted again, and now the same village had people bustling about their business, children running around barefoot, and what appeared to be a camel market.

"They're doctors of some sort," he said. "At least they appear to give medical help."

"I already worked out they are medical wizards, Pierre. Just wasn't sure if they were good or evil."

He wondered what she meant, what evidence she had, but he didn't want to miss anything. The Hohash showed vistas from other worlds where, again, these aliens aided creatures beset by large-scale diseases and plagues. He was impressed.

"I think we're lucky these aliens found us."

"Could be worse, I suppose."

Pierre tore his eyes away to stare at her for a moment. She glanced at him for a fraction of a second, and he thought he saw something – fear, repulsion, maybe – then she nodded to the Hohash. "Look, we were filmed."

He turned back to see him and Kat making love. He reddened. "Oh," was all he managed to say. He'd never been good with porn; too embarrassing, too alien, he thought – until now. He was distracted by their alien escort who moved next to the Hohash, and then aimed an arm at Kat. A fluorescent, pulsing yellow light emanated from its wrist bracelet, and shone at her belly for several seconds. Kat didn't seem to notice.

"Are you okay?" he asked.

"Making notes," she replied flatly.

He wondered what was going on. Why didn't she see the beam?

The alien looked at him. He stared deep into its silver eyes, seeing shapes arise from their fluidic surface and then sink back again, so fast it was almost a blur. "Ossyrians," he said, unsure of where the word had come from.

"What?"

"These creatures. They're called Ossyrians. They're a race of doctors; their sole purpose is to help eradicate disease and suffering. We're on the Ossyrian Space Vessel 'Mercy', well that's the nearest word in our language." He put his hand to his temple. "Don't even ask me how I know."

"I already know how you know," she said, standing up.

He looked at her nonplussed.

"Show him," she said, addressing the alien, who eyed her with a calm grace. She pointed to the mirror, then to Pierre, jabbing a finger at his head. She shouted at the alien. "I said fucking *show* him, you bitch!"

Pierre waited, uncomprehending at first, as the Hohash stopped transmitting scenes, and its surface became completely flat, and mirror-like. He gaped at his own reflection and slumped back down onto the bench.

"Exactly," Kat said, as Pierre stared straight into the reflection of his rippling, silver eyes.

CHAPTER 9 – CITY OF HOPE

A steady chill breeze scoured the valley. It funnelled past the three megalithic Q'Roth ships that occupied the plateau, and down into the vast caldera that cradled the ancient spider city. The wind hastened the human chain filing downwards to Esperantia, as the city had recently been christened. A lucky few rode in vehicles. Most trudged along on foot, accompanied periodically by lev-panels – oblong metallic flatbeds piled high with possessions and provisions. Few took the time to glance backward at the grey hulking space-ships, their homes for the past month.

The straggling procession was subdued. A few families chattered quietly, most were silent, as if treading through a cemetery. Everyone by now knew the fate of the original owners of this world. Even the priests, rabbis, and mullahs were unusually reflective, heads tilted downwards, eyes fixed on their thoughts. It was hard to reconcile all that had happened with the idea of an omnipotent or forgiving deity who had humanity as its priority.

Yet the underlying mood, Carlson noted, wasn't one of defeat and despair, nor even retribution. He detected an appetite for hope, and occasionally tested it via conversations with people on the march. An innate resilience was overtaking the usual survivor guilt: he had no other word for it than *spirit*. After his forty-five years on Earth, and most of his adult life spent decrying the politics, the greed, and the social malaise of the twenty-first century, he found he was actually uplifted by the reactions he saw around him. The imminent future was certainly bleak, and no one could even countenance long term visions of life here, say, in five years time, much less longer time-frames. Yet those on this short exodus clearly felt a sense of purpose, and the human convoy suffered little of the griping and wailing he'd anticipated.

He halted to rest a while. His feet were sore after two hours of solid walking. He wandered over to a large lev-panel goods transporter, loaded high with the paraphernalia of people's meagre belongings. A cluster of twenty or so people had laid out some field chairs in the cool peach light of the afternoon sun. He parked his ample behind on the edge of the panel, suspended a convenient height from the crusty, sand-coloured ground with its straggling veins of amethyst and silver-hued sediment. A ragged, dusty man next to him offered an open bottle of water. Carlson stared at it a moment – the man had already drunk from it, possibly others too. Back home – not that there was a back home anymore – he would have politely refused. Instead, he reached out and grasped the neck of the bottle. The man's irises were a dull grey, but the pupils were sharp as disks. Carlson nodded a thank you, and raised the bottle's lip to his own, closing his eyes as the refreshing water flooded into his mouth and washed down his throat.

He returned the bottle to its owner, smiled at the man, then gazed towards the city, still a white blur, some ten kilometres away. He pulled out his imaging binoculars, and ramped up the magnification, seeing beyond the stretched millipede of people drifting towards their new lodging. There were few defining features in the city: a spattering of ivory spires poking up like blades of wheat, but generally it was a humble-looking place, its small white domes, ramps and squares reminding him of a Turkish village he'd visited as a boy on holiday in Cyprus.

The vision jarred as a small hand clamped around his binoculars.

"Natasha, no! Leave the man alone!" A portly, head-scarfed woman swaddled in flowing cloth of varying shades of grey and black hurried over toward the tugging waif, who stared up at him with shiny coal eyes. He held on for a while, but her insistence won him over, and he relinquished them to her. This world will be yours, he thought. Our generation screwed everything up, we had our chance and we blew it. The young girl ducked away, clutching her prize, eluding her mother's outstretched arms. Several other children leapt to their feet to chase her, so they, too, could spy on their future playground. Carlson smiled and shrugged as the woman stooped next to him, hands on her thighs, panting.

"She'll be the death of me, that one," she said.

He begged to differ. "She'll make you proud one day."

The other man held out a small plastic box containing bite-size pistachio-flavoured pastries so sugary Carlson almost didn't need to grasp one as it clung to his fingers and thumb. He bit into it slowly, relishing each layer's treasure of nectar. He closed his eyes and savoured it, not chewing, just squeezing it with his tongue and upper palate till it melted completely, the warm honey trickling down his throat, reminding him of childhood family get-togethers eating home-made cakes of dried fruit and marzipan. He thought of all the things that used to make him happy back on Earth, or so he had believed, in his former, tightly-wrapped life. *Baggage and bad habits: so much to get rid of, to let go of.* He licked his fingers and with the inner grunt he'd become accustomed to in middle age, got to his feet, nodded 'good day' to the others, and set off on his pilgrimage towards the city of hope. His feet no longer felt tired, or perhaps he just didn't notice.

* * *

Blake ignored the coiling snakes of smoke spreading inside his tent. He watched Shakirvasta tap the end of his cigarette, flicking a centimetre of ash onto the rock floor. He inhaled long and full one last time, then stubbed it out into a gold-plated portable ash-tray he'd brought along to the meeting.

"So good of you to tolerate my one bad habit, especially given your wife's condition."

Blake knew this was just the opening volley. The thought flickered in his mind as to how Shakirvasta had found actual cigarettes, since they'd been banned on Earth for the last twenty years, but he focused on the single agenda item. "The transponders. Have you located them?"

Shakirvasta paused, eyeing him, then nodded. "Not that we can reach them. They're behind several metres of Q'Roth engine shielding."

"So why is it taking so long for Louise or the Q'Roth to find us?"

Shakirvasta absently pulled out another pack of cigarettes, extracting one deftly into his left hand. "She may be here already," he said, as if discussing a visiting aunt. He tapped the end of the cigarette three times on the packet. "It's the Hohash we have to thank. They've been masking our signals, including the ships' transponder signatures, so all anyone else's sensors will see is a world as dead as it has been for the past millennium, unless they actually visually inspect this planet up close. The Hohash, it appears, can manipulate carrier signals over a broad EM spectrum. Quite impressive. If we were back on Earth I'd be launching half a dozen patents right now. Communications was my business, you know."

Blake's fingers rapped the desk. "Rashid's ship – the Hohash wasn't on it when Louise found them."

"No." He lit the cigarette with an ornate Mont Blanc lighter made of black lacquer, with gold insets. "Which brings me to a point I'd like to raise."

Blake leaned back in his chair. He felt tired, but was in no mood to show it. "Go on."

"We need to give Jennifer a node, so she can communicate with the Hohash."

Blake kept his brow smooth and decided to hear him out.

"Women fare better than men with nodes – less post-op psychoses. And it has to be someone younger, say, than you or I, for the neural integration to work, not forgetting the delicate brain surgery. And preferably someone on our new Council, don't you think?"

Blake stared at this ex-mogul. He knew not to trust him, but it was hard to see the angle he was setting up. Kat was gone, and so there was no direct communication with their one and only ally. It made sense to give someone else a node. But he knew he had to find the edges of this particular negotiation landscape. "What about Sandy, or Antonia?"

"Ah, yes ... Sandy." He inhaled and then blew out a perfect ring. "Pregnant you know. The temporary pituitary effects from the node could affect the embryo's growth rate."

Blake hid his surprise; he hadn't known about Sandy. "Antonia, then."

The smoker stared at his cigarette, as if studying a jewel. "Not as robust as Jennifer. Your son had a node didn't he? So you are aware of the dangers."

Blake prevented his fingers from tensing, though his thighs locked rigid at the mention of his dead son, Robert. He resisted asking how this man knew so much about his family. Shakirvasta, after all, had said he was in the business of communications, not necessarily technological communications. "We should let Carlson decide which of the two of them is best."

"Exactly what I thought." Shakirvasta produced a flimsy from his business suit jacket. "Here is his recommendation. I like to think ahead, you see. It saves you time." He held out the translucent sheet, as if dealing the winning card in a high-stakes poker game, one where he could equally afford to win or lose.

Blake snatched it, without glancing at it. His gut told him not to trust this man. Earlier he'd made a political choice, but politics wasn't his strong suit. He knew Shakirvasta would out-manoeuvre him in the long run, maybe sooner. "I'll consider it." He stood up. "Thank you, Mr. Shakirvasta. Now, if you'd excuse me I have –"

"One last thing, Commander, of some importance."

"Yes?"

Shakirvasta stubbed out his cigarette and pocketed the self-cleaning ashtray. "This may be a little sensitive," he said, "so please hear me out. I say this not as your friend – because we both know that will never be the case – but certainly not as your enemy either."

Blake's breathing slowed. This man made his flesh crawl. "Spit it out."

Shakirvasta stood. "Your wife – I understand she is stage four, and the doctors have given up on her. She has one month to live."

Blake walked around the desk, muscles taut.

Shakirvasta spoke quickly. "I never travel without my physician – I would not survive long without him. He can give your wife *six* more months, Commander. I guarantee it. Not cure her. Her pain level won't get any worse. Six months longer, though. Half a year, Commander."

Blake's stomach muscles were iron, his breathing silent. Part of him wanted to tear this man's throat out. He knew instinctively he was evil, manipulative in the extreme, playing for his own ends, whatever they might be. Even Glenda had said that if he was going to play politics, then it was a short haul flight to spying and assassination. She'd mentioned Shakirvasta by way of a palpable example. Blake remembered his father telling him that if he ever met the devil, he should kill him before he had a chance to speak. But if there was a remote chance Shakirvasta was telling the truth...

"In exchange for what?"

"Nothing. You saved us, all of us. Consider it repaying a debt. I always repay mine." He nodded to Blake and turned and headed for the canvas door. He paused there, without turning back. "I'll send my good doctor along in the morning. If you don't want him to see your wife, simply send him away." He left, the wind masking the sound of the man's footsteps heading down the gravel pathway.

Blake sat back onto the edge of the desk. He heard a canvas zip rake open behind him.

"Want me to kill him, boss?" Zack crawled through the aperture, then stood up, dusting himself off.

"No, Zack. Anyhow, assassination would be more up Vince's or Ramires' street than yours." He turned around to face the only man he trusted.

Zack beamed. "Got nothing against a little job enlargement, you know." He parked his large frame in Blake's chair, saluting lazily as he did so. "Sorry, but I was squatting out there trying to listen, and my thighs ain't like they used to be. What was that all about anyway?"

Blake reached over to a drawer, leaning over the desk, and pulled out a metal flask and two tumblers. He sloshed amber liquid into the glasses. "He was clearing the way for a later assault. He may be one of the most ruthless businessmen ever, but underneath, he operates according to a code."

"So are we celebrating, or do you just need a drink?" Zack heaved his boots onto the desk.

"Both. But mainly we're toasting Glenda having six more months to live."

They clinked glasses.

"I'll drink to that, Chief, but why in hell do you believe him?"

"Because, Zack, I know for sure he'll make me pay for it later." He downed it in one, the single malt searing his throat. He smacked the glass onto the desk top. As he screwed the top back on the flask, he wondered what Shakirvasta was really up to. He couldn't see the plot, but he was sure there was one. He hoped the real price of this deal, when it finally arrived, wouldn't be too high.

* * *

"I'm telling you she likes you, Vince." Ramires locked the last strap into place.

"And so what?" Vince started to push the crate towards the ramp, but it wouldn't budge. He spied some troops lounging near the exit. "Hey, you guys, picnic's over. Sweat time." He drew back as six burly soldiers loped over to the single black crate. "Control room, make it snappy!"

One of the men put his hands on his hips. "You're shitting us, right? That's nine floors up! Where's the fuckin' lev?"

Vince grinned. "Gone with the convoy to Esperantia. Just put your back into it, like Tarzan there," he pointed to a muscular rookie who was already shouldering the crate. "Off you go, boys."

Ramires joined Vince's supervisory distance. "You think this'll work?"

Vince waited until the men and the crate had turned the corner as they shoved it up the ramp, sure that the grunting and cursing would drown out his answer.

"She's too smart."

"Plan B then?"

"Maybe. But I have a feeling it's going to end up Plan C, like Blake said. Just me and her. My penance for not spotting her as an Alician all those years."

"You weren't to know, they're pretty good at deep cover."

Vince rounded on Ramires. "What the hell would you know? You Sentinels spend half your lives in a Tibetan cave meditating, playing with your chi, or whatever it is you do. I *know* women, and Louise and I were screwing each others' brains out for two years, and still I didn't see it!" He kicked the wall hard with the toe of his boot.

Ramires held up his hand. "Calm down. You need to breathe out more, you know. What's gotten into you?"

Vince spat on the floor. He sighed. "The feeling's mutual; tell Sandy that, afterwards. Then you can have her. Don't think I haven't seen you look."

Ramires lifted an eyebrow. "If Plan A works, I won't be around."

Vince's face grew sterner than normal. "Louise'll take one of us with her for sure, probably both of us. I just wish we had a few more plans up our sleeve. I was her mentor, she was the best I'd ever seen." He wiped a thin layer of sweat from his brow. "Let's go check our gift, make sure the grunts haven't screwed up the detonators."

The soldiers shoving their atomic load breached the control room. Five of them collapsed, chests heaving, sweating profusely, using any remaining breath to utter curses involving family members, reproductive acts and female dogs, in various permutations. The sixth soldier leaned over the crate, feigning exhaustion. As he mopped his forehead with his sleeve, he fished out a slim coin-size disk from his chest pocket, and dropped it through a slat on one of the crate's sides. He coughed to mask the tiny clink as the magnetic transponder attached itself to the side of the nuclear weapon. Then Jarvik sank to the floor like the others, and practised a few profanities of his own.

* * *

Sandy swallowed it. She screwed up her face as if she'd just drunk pure lemon juice. "That's *got* to be an acquired taste." She took a swig of water to wash it down.

"The meds say it's fine, a balanced mix of proteins and nutrients." Antonia sat on the rounded edge of a squat table fabricated from the white material the spiders used for everything. Her hands rested on its edge, legs idly swinging back and forth like two pendula. She cocked her head to one side. "How's Micah?"

Sandy had been waiting for this all morning. "You couldn't handle it, Antonia."

Her legs stopped. "What does that mean?"

Sandy sealed the lid on the tank. She grimaced; the pungent yellow liquid it contained was likely to become their staple food supply for years to come. "Look, you're neither blind nor stupid. You know how he feels about you. And he knows how you feel about Kat. Christ, we all do. And you're hurting right now, and you're tempted to turn to Micah as a friend, but it'll fuck him up really bad."

Antonia drew her feet up onto the table, and sat cross-legged. "So I should stay away from him?"

Sandy walked right up to her, placed a hand on her shoulder. "No, Antonia, you should sleep with him."

"*What?*"

"Look, I've been with a lot of men, so I know what it's like in their heads. Mostly it's like staying in a one star hotel – pretty basic: bed, wash basin, can of beer, holo-sports channel if you're lucky, toilet down the hall. What I'm saying is that even when men appear complicated and sensitive, they're not, not deep down. So, just sleep with him, it'll make him stupidly happy for a day or two and you'll be comforted. And don't tell me you're not a little bit interested, either. I'm betting Kat was your first bi experience after a string of boyfriends, right?"

Antonia flushed. She nudged herself off the table, her boots landing on the ground with a loud slap. "And what happens when Kat returns?"

Sandy sighed. *If, for Christ's sake, and it's a hell of an if!* "He'll be cut up, for sure, and you'll go back to Kat, but at least he won't screw himself up over what he never had. Sadder but wiser. More cynical." *The way I like them,* she thought. *Like Vince.*

The radio crackled on the floor. "The first batch has arrived," Micah said.

"You go, Antonia, I'm not finished here." She picked up the radio. "We're on our way."

Antonia folded her arms. "I'm not taking your advice. I won't sleep with him."

"Fine. Don't fuck him. Just don't fuck with his head, either." She watched Antonia whirl around and march towards the rope ladder to ground level. She shook her head. *Why are we all so stupid? Even when we're all about to die, nobody sees straight!*

She picked up the radio and stared at it. She'd heard the rumours about the tactics to take out Louise. About Plan C. She tapped the radio transmit button. "Micah, it's Sandy ... Antonia's on her way ... Her idea, not mine ... Can you get a private message to Vince? ... Yeah? ... Okay. I need to see him tonight ... What? ... I need to make love with him ... Yes, you heard me, Micah."

As she carried on testing and tasting the vile slurry, she couldn't help grinning. *Stupid to the end,* she thought. *No hope whatsoever.*

* * *

"I should have been at the meeting." Jen wrenched the last root out of the ground. She dragged a forearm across her brow, erasing the beads of sweat as efficiently as a windscreen wiper eradicating drizzle.

Dimitri observed her every movement, wondering where the transformation would end, how far it would go. Jen no longer exhibited any pretensions of being coyly demure. Instead, Jen – or Jennifer as he now thought of her – had metamorphosed into something approaching an Amazonian soldier. If that had been it, he could have accepted it. After all, it wasn't unattractive, and the smell of her sweat had always served as an allure for him. But there was more, a growing insidious undercurrent. He'd seen it before in other aggressive women once or twice, and had always steered away from them.

But the context before had been academic, literally, in various real and virtual universities where he'd lectured. Women with ambition – alpha females, as he thought of them – who employed sex and sly vindictiveness in equal measure to get ahead. Not content with merely stepping on others in their path, they ground them into dust, so there was zero chance of come-back. The casualties and collateral damage had often amounted to nothing more than bruised egos, a few ruined careers or truncated research avenues and, in one case, a botched suicide attempt. Now,

95

however, the stakes were of a different order of magnitude. Worse still, he knew what drove her: not some petty desire to be first or some past incident she would never allow to repeat itself. Instead, it was the memory of her murdered brother Gabriel. She wanted revenge, and it made her blood run lava hot – or cold as glacier water, he couldn't decide. He watched her biceps flex rigid as she dragged the last component of the weapon – her 'little surprise' for Louise, as she kept calling it – into place.

Dimitri guessed he would lose her soon. Not due to love waning or dying, as it always did sooner or later in his experience, but because he knew where she was heading, and where she'd come from – too much loss and too much pain, and she needed someone to blame. Right now she thought killing Louise would be enough, but he knew otherwise. If they defeated Louise, she'd quickly turn against the real failure which, in her mind, had caused the loss of her family – humanity's weakness, as she saw it. She'd already been talking these past days about how dumb humanity had been not to see it all coming, and how it had to gear up in order to survive. Her talk lately had reminded him of his study of the early Fundie movement, before the Third World War, how its ideas had seduced so many. His father, years ago, had urged him to study history, saying that science without an understanding of history is like cleverness without a conscience. For the first time he appreciated this pearl of wisdom.

He predicted Jennifer's final destination, and he knew he would sooner or later have to stand in her path and oppose her. For the first time in his life, he lacked the conviction that he would win. He parked it. First they had a more classic, rather than social, battle to fight.

He returned to his own work, complete as it could be, and tugged at his goatee. They'd synthesised a macabre weapon, with an almost biblical signature, and Jennifer was itching to use it.

"After all," she said, hands on her square hips, "I'm a captain, I led one of those ships and saved two thousand people. They shouldn't have held the meeting without me."

He didn't know what to say. His former, legendary eloquence deserted him. Maybe it had been cremated amongst Earth's embers; so much loss – his mother, his brothers, and countless nephews and nieces. But they never discussed it, he and Jennifer. Her loss, as she perceived it, was greater. She'd trade Gabriel's life for the rest of humanity's – including his own – in an instant.

"I should have been consulted in the battle planning, not left out in the field."

In an effort to maintain a connection with her, he issued forth what she wanted, needed, to hear. "But Jen, this is the key weapon. Louise will be ready for nukes. She'll expect them, and will have planned counter-measures. Faced with a more powerful adversary, surprise is the only real tactical advantage."

She gave the barest of nods. She obviously thought she'd outgrown him, he supposed, no longer needed him. There was still a lingering respect for him, though he suspected it was out of habit. More and more it was as if he hadn't spoken, as if he'd become background music. He had no doubt as to whose counsel she was listening.

"It's a question of leadership," she said, facing him, she above him, lecturing her once tutor, guru, professor, lover.

It always is.

"I mean Blake, well, he's a true hero of course." She tested the ground with the toes of a boot.

How Shakespearean, he thought. *We come here not to praise Caesar...*

"But, well, we need someone with – I don't know how else to say it – that killer instinct. Obviously Blake can kill – has killed many, in battle. But as a soldier. We need someone more –"

More what, he wondered? What do we need more than a hero?

She continued: "Sharper, politically astute, a real strategist. Someone who can lead without weapons. Someone with a *social* vision."

Her words became more direct, less hypothetical. She was convincing herself, building an argument until it resonated with truth. He knew this path so very, very well.

"Someone like –"

"Shakirvasta." Dimitri couldn't resist supplanting the conclusion. He prayed for her to laugh, or shout, to say how preposterous it was. But instead she stared at him, as if she had just noticed him for the first time in hours.

"Exactly!" She beamed. "Back on Eden, Cheveyo was right about you, the genetic engineering really works, doesn't it! No one else but you can see."

Oh yes, he thought, scaffolding a smile, I see perfectly these days, no longer lost in the haze of a woman's scent or my own accolades. No one sees clearer, sharper, than a blind man who recovers his sight.

"But we should keep this to ourselves," she said, her enthusiasm re-kindled. "When the time is right, after the battle..."

He didn't hear the rest, didn't need to. Having worked at the frontier of oceanographic geo-engineering for two decades, he'd crossed paths with Shakirvasta's Titan Corporation more than once. He knew the man to be a ruthless tyrant whose methods bordered on criminal. Right now, Shakirvasta, the CEO of the most powerful company Earth had ever seen, was keeping a low profile, biding his time. But his true colours would come out, sooner or later.

"Let's tell Vince Plan C is ready," he said. She bounced over to him, a vestige of Jen re-emerging as she threw her arms around him. He lifted her easily off the ground so that she clung to him, and he clasped her tight. It took every molecule of his will to finally let her go. *Louise, attack now, please, right now, while she is still mine.*

The radio shrieked its brief whistle, and Jen eased out of his grip, and snatched the radio from her waist pouch. "Yes?" she said, turning away from him. "Understood. We'll be ready." She clicked off the radio, slotting it back into place. She spoke to the violet, early evening sky. "She's here."

CHAPTER 10 – FIRST STRIKE

L ouise awoke with a start. As she'd done since the labour camp in Thailand during WWIII, she sprung immediately out of bed. She manoeuvred into a face-down dog-stretch on all fours, exhaling as she pushed her pelvis back and up into the air, straightening out her arms and shoulders, locking her elbows and knees, elongating her spine. Her forehead rested on the floor. When her lungs were empty, she waited a while. She then inhaled and flipped up into her customary three-minute handstand, heels resting lightly against the wall, staring upside-down towards her empty cot. She'd slept alone, not caring what the other two got up to, whether making love or plotting against her.

Blood pumped into her head, smothering the embers of sleep, but not the nightmare that had woken her. She ignored the ritual nagging of her biceps, and let the dream remnants drift back into her consciousness: the Chorazin Medical facility back in New LA; Micah just out of his coma; Antonia paralysed on the floor; somebody behind her with a gun; a click, and time slowing, the sound of a pulse-charged round scorching its way out of the pistol's barrel, roaring like a runaway train toward the back of her head. She turned, with difficulty, and the scene shifted: she and Vince making love furiously in his office, him slamming into her, she face-down over his desk. Again, she craned her neck to see his face, and the scene morphed into a place she didn't recognise: a deep purple sky cleaved in two, a blood red gash allowing millions of insect-like creatures – Q'Roth, she now realised – to rain down onto a fluorescent rainbow-coloured city. Someone held her hand, but she couldn't tear her eyes from the scene as the plague of armoured, metallic blue-black locusts feasted on the spiders, bleaching the city in minutes. An oval object tore up the hill towards her vantage point. She squeezed the hand she knew could only belong to Vince, but she could not otherwise move. As the object arrived it slowed in front of her. A mirror. She saw first Vince's reflection, his brazen blue eyes level as always, then her own – but she was Q'Roth, her trapezoidal matt black head punctuated only by the three diagonal vermillion slits on each cheek. Her mouth opened impossibly wide – the way a Great White shark's double-jointed jaws unhinge – and she emitted a grinding howl, shattering the mirror, thrusting her back into the waking world.

She lowered her legs, controlled and straight, down to the floor, waited ten seconds, then stood, her breathing rate only marginally above normal. *Why Vince? He killed me!* She slipped off her sleep-wear and strode naked into the needle shower. Without hesitation she set it to ice cold.

The water chilled her skin first to tingling, then to numbness. Images surfaced of her and Vince in happier times. Partners in every sense of the word. More than once she'd come close to renouncing her Alician heritage and going completely over to his side. But instead her life had ricocheted down a dark alley, after a messy operation in Moscow, where she'd been – what had he called it? – *over-enthusiastic.* He'd defended her tactics to their Chief, but he'd never treated her the same way afterwards. They got assigned different partners for six months, and after that got to work together again, but... She should have said something, healed it, but she never did. Too bad. She increased the water pressure till she started to shiver.

And now the Alicians had also abandoned her. She felt she was walking a tightrope across a chasm, unconvinced the rope would make it all the way to the other side. She focused, then leaned her head backwards, the shards of glacial water peppering her face, cleansing her resolve. *Vince.* He was the key. She'd deal with him and no one else. She had to admit it would be good to see him again, assuming she could repress the reflex urge to shoot him dead on sight. She shut off the water and grabbed the towel, drying herself roughly. She wrapped it around her and held herself for a moment, closing her eyes. She didn't know what she'd say when she saw him. Didn't know if – how – she'd tell him about the ship she'd vaporised. She'd have to be in a position of power, or the others would kill her in an instant. One way or another, blood was likely to spill today – it was up to Blake and the others how much. She donned her black Alician battle uniform. She caught herself smiling; it *would* be good to see him again. After all, they'd both killed so many people; what's a little murder between friends?

Louise occupied the only chair on the bridge of the hunter-destroyer vessel – the Q'Roth never sat, so had no use for seats, but she'd had it installed. It emphasised her position over the other two, standing a few metres behind her at their consoles. She surveyed the images and holostreams of data cascading a few metres in front of her. A waterfall of shiny black figures tumbled against a mustard background, the alphabet unmistakeably Q'Roth, like Chinese calligraphy but with much more attitude: curling blade-like serifs, serrated and hooked with spiked barbs. She understood most of it.

When Sister Esma and the Q'Roth had re-animated her, too much of her original brain matter had been blown away by Vince, so they'd had to install some of the Q'Roth variety. She was a hybrid. She felt no different, except her bloodlust was keener than most Alicians. Compassion seemed like an outrageous concept – only the fittest should rule, the rest should perish or serve in utter obedience. She couldn't remember if she'd felt the same way before Vince's bullet. She considered her lover a moment – he had always been a ruthless bastard in humanity's terms. Like her he had no time for weakness, instead crushing it underfoot. That was why she could deal with him.

"What do you see, Hannah?" she said, not turning around.

There was a pause before Hannah answered, like a child answering a test, Louise thought, uncertain of either the answer or the consequences of an insufficient response.

"I see all three ships, but one of the transponders has been de-activated. The other two are faint, as if something is masking them"

She waited, but nothing more followed. "When I ask what you see, Hannah, I don't just mean what you perceive with your eyes. What do you understand of their strategy? What do you recommend?"

Hannah coughed. "They must have realised there are transponders and located them. But they've only had time to disable one of them. The one with the nuclear device on board. So... I recommend we jump the other two ships into the sun and attack the third ship."

Louise stood up. You'll be first to go, she thought, you're not worthy to carry our new genes. She turned. "And what do you see, Jarvik?" She was glad to have him back onboard – the fact that he had been to the surface and back so quickly meant he would have had no time to upset her plans. There was no way she'd have let Hannah go to the surface.

He lifted his chin and spoke to the datastream. "I see a recursive tracker algorithm encoded into the two surviving transponders."

Hannah's eyes flashed accusingly to the holostream and her own data screen; she'd missed the encrypted information.

"I see a trap," Jarvik continued. "The moment we activate the two other ships, the third will have our transponder code, and no doubt will jump to our position and detonate." He paused, but Louise remained still, not even nodding agreement with his assessment. He continued. "I propose we use the transponder I planted on the nuclear device to transport it to their new home, the city, and detonate it there."

Louise allowed the shadow of a smile across her face. It was certainly tempting. The humans' intentions were clearly aggressive, extreme, desperate. It would be … just. But she had no time for such archaic concepts. There was no right and wrong. There was simply what was. All that mattered in the end was always who survived, and who would rule. Nevertheless, she was impressed that the humans had been relatively ingenious. She'd have to find out later who had engineered this little ruse – maybe someone to recruit, to replace Hannah.

She returned to her seat, facing forward again. "Hannah, let's see if you can redeem yourself with something a little less taxing. Is life on the planet sustainable?"

"Yes," she replied, her voice groping for sounder footing. "They've found a food source, and water is plentiful."

Louise ran her fingers through her thick blonde hair. "Jarvik, what do we do after we've destroyed them all?" She heard an intake of breath, then – rare for him, perhaps even a first – hesitation.

"Perhaps I spoke rashly," he said.

She waited. It wasn't enough for her to be leader; she needed them to understand that she was literally their superior. That was the essence of command.

Hannah got there first. "What would *you* suggest?"

Louise leaned back against the chair. "We need them alive, for now. But if we ask anything from a position of weakness, they will subdue us, and kill us eventually. First we have to break them. Sister Esma used to say there were two rules of negotiation. The first rule is to avoid asking anything from an enemy. The second rule is that if you do have to ask for something, make sure your enemy is on his knees when you do so."

She raised herself again from the chair, and strode back to the central console midway between Jarvik and Hannah. "Time to educate them in the meaning of the word *strategy*."

* * *

Micah studied the screens in front of him in the Mobile Command Centre, the MCC as everyone called it: a high-tech truck crammed with advanced surveillance gear, most of which he'd never even heard of. It was parked in the open plain, midway between the Q'Roth ships and the city. The stealth vehicle dampened all external emissions including bio-thermal signatures, employing chameleon-ware camouflage, so it was virtually invisible to the naked eye – unless you knew where to look. Micah had no illusions, though, and doubted it would fool Q'Roth sensor technology for a second. He despaired of the military's blind obsession with techware solutions but, then again, he had no better idea.

He stared at the central array in front of him, a flat screen with scratchy images darting and flashing, making him squint. A greasy-haired young military tech guy fussed over the controls, triple-checking everything. Micah had no intention of distracting him: he'd never used a military Optron before, let alone a field model.

Micah had been an Optron reader for the past five years back on Earth. The virtual reality immersion kit had enabled him to surf the high density data-cores slipstreaming back from space missions such as Blake and Zack's Ulysses trip to Eden, checking vital telemetry as well as comms. But it was art as well as science. All Optron 'readers' created their own Optron landscapes for data encoding, surveillance and interrogation. Only one in a hundred could do it, and as little as one in a hundred thousand could do it well. He didn't feel particularly clever, it was just the way his brain was wired. What he had always loved, however, and what more than compensated for the occasional blinding migraines, was surfing the data, flying over surrealistic terrains of metallic hues and textures, spying occasional animals representing semi-intelligent sub-routines. But *this*, he reminded himself, this method he was about to try, he'd never done before.

He'd met military Optron readers once or twice at conventions, and one guy, Hal, had talked about it briefly while they were all getting drunk in Patti's bar in underground Sylmar. He hadn't known at the time if Hal had just been bull-shitting or not. Hal had said that after unmanned aerial vehicles and drones in the early part of the century, whereby remote-control surveillance and weapons platforms could be flown pilot-less into enemy territory, came the next generation. Initially these had used micro-cameras – same idea, just smaller and so even harder to detect. But this still only amounted to what was known as tele-presence: someone far away looking at a camera or vid-shot taken somewhere else. It never had the same level of rapport as *being there*, and so the understanding, the awareness and the reflexes were all a little off.

As Optron technology developed out of the necessity both to handle ultra-high bandwidth telemetry, and still make human sense of it, the military seized the opportunity to advance their deep cover surveillance capability. Essentially, a cluster of self-organising micro-units were fired into enemy territory and acted as a dispersed neural net. An Optron reader could then 'join up the dots', fusing the signals into a data landscape much as in a conventional Optron session. The technique had helped turn the tide in several pitched battles in the last weeks of the War. The only downside, Hal had said, was that it had fried the brains of a dozen or so readers on the way.

Micah ran a finger around the collar of his jumpsuit. It felt decidedly stuffy in the MCC, despite the aircon. He'd never 'flown' a military Optron, and hadn't been trained for it. He began to wonder why he'd suggested it in the first place.

Colonel Enrique Vasquez, whom he'd met in Cocos and travelled with to Eden, hovered behind his right shoulder. The military commander had a shock of white cropped hair cresting a high brow. That was the second thing anyone noticed about him, the first being the missing right arm. Once Vasquez's teal-coloured eyes locked onto somebody, though, that person never once glanced at the missing limb.

"It's time," Vasquez said. "The Optronic micro-clusters were sent up an hour ago, they'll have dispersed in spatial orbit by now."

Micah picked up the plastic glass of chilled water, gulped it down, then glanced around at Sandy, Jennifer, and Antonia. Sandy winked at him, Jennifer glared, and Antonia found something excruciatingly interesting on the opposite wall. *Business as usual.* Shakirvasta was also supposed to be there, but hadn't arrived. *Maybe he has more sense.* He picked up the black skull-cap with wires trailing out of it, and weighed it in his hands. "I've never worn one of these before," he said, casually, as if talking about a new style of hat. *This could turn my brain into mush.*

Vasquez laid his surviving hand on his shoulder. "Vince told me you're the best Optron reader alive, Mr. Sanderson."

The *only* one alive, Micah thought, and used to a civilian Optron with the full suite of protective cut-outs and safeguards. But this is mil-tech; they don't care about a few brain deaths on the road to victory.

Jennifer chipped in behind him. "For God's sake, put it on, Micah. We need the intel, or else we're all dead anyway. We need to know where her ship is, how many are onboard, what their tactical situation is. Otherwise she's going to wipe us out."

We don't actually know that. Maybe Louise just wants me and Vince. Louise may be Alician, but she has her own agenda; always had, always will. As Micah eased on the clammy black rubber headpiece, Sandy joined in.

"Commander, it is only his brain that can be fried, isn't it? I mean, the rest will remain, er, serviceable, won't it?"

Before Vasquez had a chance to answer, if indeed he ever intended to, Antonia rushed over, stooped down towards Micah, and pressed a moist kiss on his cheek, then retreated just as quickly. A deep blush crawled across his face. He decided he'd better not dwell on it, and pulled the headpiece tight over his scalp, then flicked up a thumb. "Ready as I'll ever be."

Vasquez leaned over so only Micah could hear. "There may be some pain: sharp, pricking sensations. Try not to cry out, it's bad form in front of the ladies."

He sincerely hoped Vasquez was attempting humour.

The Colonel straightened up, cleared his throat, and spoke louder. "You'll be less immersed than you're used to, so you can talk to us occasionally if the need arises.

We'll be watching the data streams and holo-images you construe with the Optronic software. Remember, a lot of what you see will be in space. That can be pretty disorienting. Keep a mental foothold on Ourshiwann, or else you'll lose your bearings. If you need to exit at any time, just say the word 'Exit' and we'll cut you loose."

He nodded. He thought about the hundreds of times he'd 'gone under' back on Earth, surfing data landscapes and telemetry from the Ulysses, as well as the earlier Prometheus and Heracles missions to Eden. He remembered however his last few trips: Rudi's nightmarish digi-world, and the encounter with an alien intelligence – which he now knew to have been the Hohash – buried in the data slipstream. That last little spin on the Optron had put him in a coma.

The tech guy touched a pad, and first the skull-cap, then something inside Micah's head, began to hum. His vision turned grainy, then black and white, then black. Anaesthetized needles extended from the headband and burrowed into his skull – at least that's what it felt like. He could still sense his own body, and knew it was tense, muscles flexed, jaw clenched. Then, abruptly, the pain ceased, and the floor fell away and he dropped into cold dark space.

He landed on a clammy floor with a squelching thump. It was just like the material on Q'Roth ships. He felt a little dizzy, but staggered to his feet. Something wasn't right: no stars, definitely no planet – nothing. He searched in every direction, but all was black. "Exit," he said, loud and clear. He tried it again, shouting the word. *Now why am I not surprised that didn't work?* A clacking noise approached from behind him, but whichever way he turned, it was always behind, and getting closer. Eventually he stopped turning. *I'm in someone else's game.* The other player halted just behind him. He thought of all the voices he could hear next, thousands of them. All of them would be welcome except one.

"Hello, Micah," Louise said. "You're looking well."

* * *

Shakirvasta burst into the MCC. Sandy had never seen him panting for breath before, let alone looking dishevelled.

"We've ... been ... compromised." He doubled over, clinging to the door handle for support. Sandy didn't budge, but then she didn't need to, Jennifer was at his side in an instant, helping him up. Sandy noted that Vasquez said nothing, just waited, taut as piano-wire.

Shakirvasta had been running, she supposed, unless this was all for show. However, the sweat tracks suggested otherwise.

He addressed alternately Jennifer and Vasquez, granting Sandy and Antonia occasional consolation glances. "Since we left Earth I've been setting up an intelligence and surveillance network – "

Sandy folded her arms. *I bet you have.*

"– with full cognisance from Commander Blake – "

Full, my ass!

"– including tracking every survivor from Earth. Yesterday, there was an additional person here, for several hours, first on Ramires' ship, then in Esperantia."

Clever to use the city's new name so quickly. Maybe he and Josefsson are actually working together after all. But Sandy felt a gnawing in her stomach. This man was an out and out predator, a raptor, but maybe this time it wasn't all a ploy.

"We've been doing some checking," Shakirvasta continued. "When we left Earth I managed to salvage the latest Censid crystal – "

Shit! He has detailed data on the whole planet's population!

"– and I compared its records with Vince's own Chorizon Profiling Intel Data Crystal – "

This just gets better and better.

"– and there's no mistake; yesterday's visitor, one Jarvik Ardvisson, is an Alician."

Sandy made the connection immediately, and turned to Vasquez, who had already picked up the comms link. "Ramires," she whispered.

Vasquez nodded. He opened his mouth to speak.

"Wait!" Shakirvasta shouted. "We must assume they now know all our comms frequencies."

Vasquez eyed him coolly, and proceeded in Spanish, which Sandy understood perfectly. "Ramires, this is Colonel Vasquez. Leave the ship now, your position is compromised. I suggest you run!"

The developing knot in her stomach tightened. Until this moment she hadn't realised she cared anything for Ramires.

Vasquez tapped Micah on the shoulder, but there was no reaction. He continued speaking into the microphone, in English. "This is Colonel Vasquez in Ops. Code Kappa Alpha, I repeat, code Kappa Alpha." He put down the thin mike and leant forward, studying the fluidic screen that was linked into Micah's neural cortex.

Micah's screen had been registering a dark snowstorm for several minutes now, Sandy realised, and Micah had been immobile. She'd assumed this was normal, but then she'd no idea what happened with these Optron contraptions. "Kappa Alpha?" she asked.

Jennifer spoke up. "It means radio silence: comms are compromised; all units execute their missions unless they hear the pre-arranged termination code."

Vasquez slanted his head, eyeing Jennifer. "How do you know so much about mil ops. Hold on a minute," he said, tilting his head back a little, scrutinising her face. "Your surname – O'Donnell. Are you Captain James O'Donnell's daughter?"

Jennifer nodded, chin up.

And proud of it, too, Sandy thought, whoever the hell he was. But something about the surname snagged her memory too.

Vasquez saluted Jennifer. "One of the International Navy's finest."

Jennifer's face closed up like a clam. Sandy assumed it was to avoid letting the emotions breach the surface.

"There was another hero in my family too. An unsung hero ... my brother." Her voice cracked.

A chill drilled down Sandy's spine. *No, no, NO! It can't be. Gabriel?* O'Donnell was his surname too. Her right hand automatically reached around behind her to the table top to steady herself, while the other instinctively cradled her belly. My God, she thought, I'm carrying Gabriel's child, and this bitch is his *sister?* She eased herself backwards so the table ledge supported her weight.

"What's wrong?" Antonia said.

Sandy jerked her head around, but was relieved to see Antonia wasn't referring to her. Antonia raced over to Micah, leant over him to take a good look at his face, then almost shouted at Vasquez and the tech. "Bring him out of it, this isn't right. I've watched him use the Optron before, and it wasn't like this."

Vasquez glanced to the tech, who manoeuvred himself in front of Micah, and began checking various wires and indicators. "Sir, I believe she's right. We should extract him, there seems to be some kind of malfunction."

Vasquez nodded. The tech depressed a touch panel. Micah's body immediately arched backwards violently, his mouth sucking in a jagged breath, arms shaking spasmodically, forearms flexed and rigid as iron. Sandy watched helplessly as Micah's face, eyes closed, contorted in pain. She'd seen her own asshole of a father die like this. "Cardiac arrest," she said, "Jack him back in!"

The bewildered tech glanced from her to Vasquez.

"Do it", Vasquez said. The tech punched a display icon, and Micah's body slumped, his breathing fluttering back to normal.

"Sir," the tech said, cascading through various screen displays and readouts, "I don't know how, but his central nervous system has been tagged into the virtual world. It's not supposed to happen, there are cut-outs everywhere to avoid this, but –"

"Louise," Sandy said, flat. "Louise has him." And this time she won't let him go.

A stark alarm sounded, then another one. She knew what they signified. The first two Q'Roth hulks, emptied of people and supplies, had just jumped to God knew

107

where. She folded her arms and held her elbows tight, trying not to display any emotion, but inside, her stomach churned. *Run, Ramires, run for your life!*

* * *

Ramires hurtled down the spiral walkway as fast as he could, careening down all nine levels, ricocheting off the sweating walls of the last Q'Roth transport. He sprinted so fast on the last level that his lungs barely kept pace, rendering his eyesight blotchy. He saw the open hatchway beckoning him, five metres away. A half-second later he felt the static on the hairs on his arms and the back of his neck that told him the ship was about to jump. With a sharp inbreath and then a guttural grunt he kicked off the ground and launched himself towards life, just as the scene luminesced towards a mercurial frozen death. Time slowed, and he was sure he was about to die. But he still travelled through the increasingly dense air-turning-fluid, slowly, getting slower. He was almost at the threshold, the inviting darkness almost within his reach, the brightening light clawing him backward to oblivion. He heard a voice, he was certain he did, and the deep tone could only have been that of his dead master, the last Sentinel Grandmaster, Cheveyo, who uttered two words.

Time unlocked and his body broke free and crash-landed into the dusty ground in the darkness. An ear-pummelling thunderclap rocked his sprawling body, a departing howl from the gargantuan Q'Roth vessel as it disappeared with its nuclear payload to somewhere, maybe the nearest star, but definitely not its target. He lay crumpled on Ourshiwann's soil, his chest heaving, savouring the ground's welcome harsh embrace, thankful for the stars up above, even if accompanied by a stinging thumping and ringing in his ears. He panted there for a full minute, arms spread wide, knees up, letting his heart decelerate.

He re-played it over in his mind. Had he really heard those words? What did they mean? Neither he, nor Cheveyo, nor any of the Sentinels were particularly religious, and didn't believe in an afterlife. He got to his feet, dusted himself off, and glanced down toward the valley and the hazy glow of the newly-inhabited spider city. He tracked across thirty degrees to the right, where he knew the stealth-coated MCC truck was located. He picked out two distant mountain tops to use as transits, checked stars to use as a third navigation aid, and set off on a fast run toward the command centre.

While he closed the distance between himself and the MCC, the words kept playing over and over again in his mind; just two words, with no explanation. Somehow, Cheveyo had secured him across the threshold, out of the de-materialising Q'Roth ship, back to life, in order to fulfil a mission. So he would do what he had been asked, no matter if he didn't understand why.

He would protect Sandy.

* * *

Micah sat cross-legged on the floor. Louise hadn't lingered. She'd told him to stay put, that she'd be back, and that a few things had changed. He hadn't said anything, just watched her walk off into the darkness. She hadn't killed him, at least. But he'd learned not to trust anything about Louise.

He wasn't tired, since he knew that in the real world he was already in a chair – only his mind was trapped in this virtual holding cell. It was dark around him, but not completely: he could see ten metres or so in any direction – not that there was anything to see. He'd considered exploring, but had a bad feeling that he might get lost, and never be retrieved – if in fact he wasn't already irretrievable. So he waited. Besides, during his early Optron training at the Zen centre in Palo Alto, he'd learned to meditate on the void, and this place pretty much looked like what he'd envisaged. He closed his eyes and counted his breaths, so as not to start ruminating on his imminent demise. He felt oddly calm, until he was pretty sure someone or something else was there with him.

He opened his eyes to find a Hohash in front of him, close enough to touch with his finger-tips. Its mirror face swirled with clouds of electric blues. He wondered if Louise had sent it, but that didn't make sense, she'd probably never even seen one. The other option was that the others around his real body had somehow contacted one of these artefacts, and... But no, so far, only Kat had any luck in communicating with the Hohash, and she was lost, probably dead.

"How did you find me?" he said, fully expecting no answer. The swirling electric storm continued unabated. He decided to have a one-way conversation. Besides, as he'd once said to his Zen master, counting breaths is really boring. His fellow students had been shocked, but the tiny wizened man had belly-laughed, and said that Micah was ready to leave, while the others would have to stay a while longer.

Micah hadn't had much contact with these artefacts, but since seeing the spider city, a burr had lodged in his mind. "Well," he said, "what I've been wondering, you see, is..." he felt a little embarrassed. He coughed and continued. "The spider city. It's quaint and all that, and their artistic skills were clearly to die for. But the technology, it's just not that surprising. It's like they stopped innovating thousands of years ago. They developed a brilliantly sustainable ecological environment, built self-maintaining systems that would last millennia, and then ... just sat back."

He paused. Was this going anywhere? But he'd learned a long time ago to let his mind roam sometimes. Freud, or more probably Jung, would argue that the subconscious mind knew the target destination, and by talking it through, he'd eventually arrive.

"So, would a race driven to such technological marvels just stop like that? We didn't. Our own love affair with technology has survived three world wars, any one of which should have sent a sensible race scattering back to their ancestral caves. And yet your masters did amazing things, and then just hung up their ... whatever, and started sky-painting." He could feel an idea beginning to resonate. He stood up, with almost no effort at all, speaking quicker, eager to find the root argument. "And another thing. Why didn't they explore space? Staying tied to this planet was tantamount to an ostrich sticking its head in the sand, knowing other alien forces were out there." Something clicked inside his brain. He stared hard at the Hohash.

"So how did they build *you*?" This had been the chrysalis-like question sheltering deep in his mind. He spoke louder, firmer, almost accusing the Hohash. "I've seen nothing that equates to your level of technology on the planet. Nothing that even meets your level of technology half-way."

Then it hit him. He took a step backwards. He stared at the Hohash mirror anew. "They didn't make you, did they? *You* ... you found *them*!" His thoughts solidified into instinctive knowledge, the type of truth which needs no evidence. He knew that these artefacts must be very, very old.

Still reeling from what now seemed to be the unassailable truth, he caught his breath as the clouds on the Hohash cleared to reveal four images: Blake and Zack in a Hohash scout-ship; Sandy and the others in the MCC; Vince and Kostakis in the trap laid for Louise; and the inside of a strange ship where Louise and two others, a man and woman he didn't know, stared towards an image he couldn't see.

"Can anyone hear me?" he shouted, not caring if Louise did. But there was no answer. Sensor information, he figured: the Hohash trafficked in electromagnetic transmissions, and apparently could pick up any media being transmitted or recorded. He sat down again, his mind feeling tired. "Okay," he said, "I get it. At least I get a ring-side seat."

* * *

Zack powered up the Hohash craft, but there was no noise. Blake found it curious that the spider species, who didn't appear to have used sound at all – he suspected they were deaf – could design equipment so quiet. The seven metre diameter ship they'd discovered two days ago underneath Esperantia was identical to the one he'd flown on Eden – the one which Pierre and Kat had been lost in. There wasn't much spare room between him, Zack to his right piloting the vehicle, and the table-sized cubic metre nuclear device planted in the middle of the craft. He gave it a cold stare.

It sat, innocent enough, but he'd seen a dozen detonations in WWIII and knew the unthinkable annihilating power it could unleash. The hammer of God, General Kilaney had once remarked, while they had witnessed from space the obliteration of huge tracts of enemy territory.

He watched Zack busy with his controls. Blake was resolved about dying, since Glenda would join him soon enough in the grand scheme of things, and would understand his sacrifice. Zack, on the other hand, was leaving behind a loving family: Sonja about to be a widow, his kids orphans.

The outside vista of the mountains evaporated, replaced by stars. The half-darkened globe of Ourshiwann appeared beneath them as they snapped into orbit. He cast an eye over the still-light Eastern crescent, its rugged mountain ranges speckled with sparse vegetation, but no cities. The spider civilisation had not grown or sprawled the way humanity had, taking up every nook and cranny, digging ever deeper into Earth's diminishing resource pockets. Somehow, the spiders had matured to a level of stability and peace undreamed of by humankind. We could have learned so much from you, he thought, though not survival.

He had to ask the question. "How did the goodbye go with Sonja?"

Zack shifted in his seat.

"You did say goodbye, didn't you? Zack, what –"

"Don't, boss, just don't. It's my life, what's left of it."

Blake said no more.

The com-link blurted a message. "This is Colonel Vasquez, head of Ops. Code Kappa Alpha, I repeat, code Kappa Alpha."

"Great," Zack said. "So we have no triangulation, no means of detecting Louise's ship other than the Hohash, assuming they even understand what we want from them."

Blake set his jaw. "It's begun."

Zack stretched his large frame back in his fighter pilot's chair, which he'd anchored into the Hohash craft's Spartan interior. "We'll find her, or she'll find us, though if I'm honest I prefer the first option." He faced the bank of screens he'd jury-rigged into the craft, borrowed from the Ulysses which they'd brought along with them from Eden. "I reckon Ramires' plan failed, he should have detonated by now, we'd pick that up for sure anywhere within a million kilometres."

Blake cracked the knuckles in his right fist.

"You impatient, boss?"

He smiled. "No. I was just thinking, I never, ever even so much as slapped a girl when I was a kid. I tried never to raise my voice to a woman when I was an adult, let alone a hand, and here I am about to nuke one single woman."

"*Now, Commander Blake, That's not very nice.*"

Blake leapt up from his seat, drawing and firing his pistol, sending a pulse charge clean through the heart of the shimmering image hovering above their nuclear cargo. Louise didn't flinch.

Zack banked the craft hard. Blake gripped a lanyard hanging from the ceiling, but the image remained stationary relative to its surroundings. Zack made a brief transit, Blake guessed a few hundred kilometres, but the image resolutely stayed exactly where it was.

"Boys, relax, I'm just here to talk."

But Blake recognised the hunger hiding behind Louise's smile, one he'd seen all too often in people who'd gotten a taste for killing. He turned to Zack, the Louise hologram behind him, and mouthed the word "*where?*" Zack shook his head a fraction, ignoring Louise, hunting for the signal source on his screens.

"What do you want, Louise?" Blake faced her off, holstering his pistol, folding his arms.

"You won't believe me if I tell you." Her smile vanished.

"Try me," he said.

"Yes!" Zack growled from behind him, and the ship lurched sideways. Blake saw Louise glance down, a lined creasing her brow. She said something he didn't catch to someone on her left, then faced forward again. "Zack," she shouted, "Zack, stop it now. It doesn't have to be this way.'"

The stars outside vanished, dissolving into an out-of-focus room, with pipes and objects Blake couldn't make out. But he knew Zack had done it – he'd traced the signal back to Louise's ship. It was now or never. He reached over to the controls beneath Louise's fading image.

"Not yet, boss, they're blocking us from fully materialising. Just a few more seconds."

Louise's eyes, pupils sharp as needles, stabbed towards Blake's hand hovering above the detonation switch. "You leave me no choice. Zack! Do you remember Paris?"

It was such a non-sequitur, Blake thought, and she said the last phrase in such an odd way, with unusual inflexions. It took a second to realise it must be the trigger code for the implant he'd suspected Zack having since the Eden Mission. But when Zack didn't reply, and he saw Louise's face relax, he knew what was coming. Just as he reached for the detonation plunger, he was yanked backwards by grapple-like hands. He tried to grab his pistol, but Zack twisted him by his legs. Zack's ox-like strength twirled Blake like a rag doll, and his head and shoulders hit the deck hard. As soon as Zack let go of one foot, Blake lashed out with the other, but although he caught Zack solidly in the chest, a meteor-like heel crashed down on his own solar plexus, winding him completely, draining his strength away, as his nervous system went into shock. He knew it would only take one second for him to recover enough to be able to retaliate, or at least to defend. But there was no respite in the furious, deep-psyche-encoding the Alicians must have carried out on Zack back in Thailand. A single huge hand engulfed Blake's throat, his thumb and middle finger mercilessly squeezing both carotid arteries. He stared wide-eyed up into Zack's looming demonic face. Zack's black eyes raged at who-knew-what insane lies had been buried there ten years earlier, powered into overdrive by a sudden hormone imbalance which gear-shifted the part of the human brain known as the 'reptile brain' into command. Blake's arms and legs struggled with all his might, but he knew he was no match for Zack. His vision blurred, and he felt a sharp spike in his left carotid. Everything he saw turned blood red, then began to fade. He had no breath left, and felt the life being cut from him. *Glenda!* he thought, then his mind freefell into blackness.

"Munich was better," Louise said, using the same strange inflexions.

Zack's eyes snapped back into focus, and then the whites grew large as he flung himself off Blake. "What the hell?"

Blake lay immobile. Zack stared in horror at the growing purple bruise darkening the left side of Blake's neck, his left eye blood red. He cautiously reached a hand over to the other carotid where he detected a thready pulse. He bent over and put his ear above Blake's mouth. He heard a scratchy, rasping breath, like an old man's, coming from his mentor, his friend.

"It's over," Louise said. "During that little event, we disabled your device, but a lot of your craft's systems got fried in the process."

Zack didn't care. He squeezed his own eyes shut for a moment. The memory came back to him now: he'd been there, inside his body, staring down as he'd strangled his best friend. Still hunched over Blake, he lodged a knuckle into his mouth and bit till he tasted blood, emitting a groan that grew into a roar. The eye-searing astringent smell of ozone and burnt circuits confirmed that this was no nightmare he was going to ever wake up from. He eased off the knuckle, and took a deep breath. With one hand on Blake's chest, he swivelled to see that most of the screens were dead, various pieces of kit sizzling and sputtering into silence. Outside there were stars again.

He stood, facing Louise's image. "You fucking whore – "

She held up a hand. "I can do it again if you like, Zack, and leave you to tear the ship apart, and the rest of Blake."

Zack loomed like a chained bear. "What the fuck do you want, bitch?"

"Just hear me out," Louise said. "That is, if you want him to live."

He barely felt the aching of his fore-finger knuckle bitten to the bone, as his blood trickled to the floor. The pain wasn't enough, he wanted to tear at some more of his own flesh, but mostly his hands wanted to be around her neck. We both die,

Louise, that's the way it's going to be. That's the only endgame now. After I get Blake to the medics.

He folded his arms, his eyes burning steady as molten steel. "I'm listening."

CHAPTER 11 – MANNEKHI

Pierre lifted his hands from the Omskrat orb, and felt the outside world engulf him, like a tsunami breaching an empty lagoon. But the real world seemed pale by comparison.

"How long this time?" he asked.

"Four bloody hours, Pierre. *If* you're still Pierre."

He stared at her for a while, then broke off as he realised he was doing so. "Sorry. It's pretty immersive." He had few words to describe it. It was less like he had been somewhere else, than he had been *someone* else – no, not someone, he thought, some*thing* else.

"So, what did you learn this time?"

Kat's voice had her usual razor-wire edge, but it affected him less each time he came 'out'.

"It started a billion years ago –"

"Good opener. Is this going to be long, though? I may have to wash my hair this evening."

He knew better than to fence with Kat – he'd lose. "In another galaxy." He sighed. He had to forewarn her. "One that's no longer there." He paused. She said nothing. At least he had her attention now.

"There was a fantastic civilisation, brimming with energy and life, almost every habitable world populated and thriving, species ... I couldn't begin to explain. A commercialism and tolerance which bred peace. Until..." His chest felt heavy. When he'd been in communication with the educational orb known as the Omskrat, he'd been objective, untouched emotionally. Now, however, the full weight of what he'd seen squashed him with the gravity of a gas giant.

He hadn't noticed, but Kat was now sitting beside him, her arm around his shoulders. He looked at her, really looked at her for the first time in days.

"Hello, Pierre," she said, "welcome back."

"You understand what I'm going through, don't you?"

She lay her head against the smooth white wall behind them. "You mean my node? Sort of. The immersion is similar – detached, that's why they got banned, you know, too many psychotic episodes and meaningless homicides." She half-laughed, then faced him square. "But when I come out, it's still me, I'm not actually changed on the inside. With you, however..." She stood up and strolled to the other side of the small chamber and sat opposite him, hands pressing down on the cushioned seat. "Pierre, you're slipping away from me. And not just me either. You're losing your humanity, and I'm not just talking about your eyes."

He nodded. She was right. Part of him was mourning his own slow disappearance. And yet, another part...

"Come on," she said, "you started a good story. Tell me, it helps."

He tried to smile. "Okay. The Kalaheii –"

"Who?"

"Right, sorry. One of the ascendant races at the time, called the Kalaheii –"

"What did they look like?"

He was surprised by the question, but more so by his inability to give a straight answer. "It's ... it's not exactly visual. Well, some of it is, but other times it's just ... knowledge, facts." Like it's being hardwired into me, he thought. So I don't forget. He understood now the power of this educational tool: it was indoctrinating him.

She shrugged, waving a hand. "Whatever. Carry on."

"The Kalaheii wanted to rule over all the other races. There was a leader amongst them, Qaroll, who led a galactic coup. Thousands of worlds were conquered." Pierre knew the death toll had been on an unimaginable scale. He tried to recall what came after trillions. "But seven of the ancient races, led by the Kalarash –"

"Gosh, the letter 'K' was popular in this galaxy. Sorry, please do continue."

He paused, taking in her features, remembering the moment he thought he would drown – only a week ago.

"Oh come on, Pierre, don't sulk. I promise to be quiet."

He supposed it must sound abstract. But he knew that although it was legend, mythic, that it was also at some level true. He decided to cut to the chase. "There was a horrific war, the stakes kept getting higher. Suns were used as weapons, first by making a system's star go nova, then later as actual missiles; whole stars jumped into other systems. The scale of artillery was literally astronomical: black holes, white holes, space-time tears that could engulf armadas or planetary systems alike, dark matter weapons; even harnessing dark energy to skim off some of the outlying enemy star systems on the galactic rim, accelerating them out into the inter-galactic void. But Qaroll was losing, so he and the Kalaheii developed the ultimate weapon." He swallowed, at least tried to.

Kat's voice grew soft. "They developed a way to destroy a galaxy, didn't they Pierre?"

He stared at her.

"How did they do it?"

He realised that the operation on his eyes meant he could no longer shed tears. He took a breath. "They turned off all the suns. Einstein's equation works both ways. They found a way to invert the normal flow of the basic laws of physics, reverting energy to matter. Everything ... condensed to rock."

They sat for a while in silence.

"Seven of the ancient races escaped to this galaxy. They began fostering a new society here millions of years ago. They took their time, being ultra-careful, instilling a discipline, an order. Still, civilisations rose and fell at least a hundred times in that period. Each time the ancients, the Progenitors, would wait a while and then start again. This current society has lasted longest, however, and reached stability about a million years ago."

"So, are our Ossyrian friends one of these ancient races?"

"Ah, no, they're only Level Eight. The Progenitors are gone, or in hiding somewhere. Three races left to explore other galaxies, and the other two disappeared, fading into obsolescence. There's a myth that one race became Gaia-like gods, each super-being inhabiting the consciousness of a new world, then surrendering and merging with its nature, teaching its inhabitants how to advance, or simply experiencing evolution all over again."

"That leaves one."

"Yes, the Kalarash. They were the last to leave, though myth has it one of them remained, hiding or in abeyance, as overseer." He felt tired, his brain wanted to sleep, as he'd come to expect shortly after each Omskrat session.

"The Kalaheii were pretty advanced, then?"

His eye-lids were heavy. "Yes," he managed.

"Seems odd, then."

He found it difficult to focus. "What do you mean?"

She knelt in front of where he was sitting. He resisted an over-powering urge to lie down.

"I'm asking the question you should be asking, Pierre. This little orb is not just showing you things, it's constraining your thinking. It's the perfect educational instrument – what to think, but also what not to think; building walls in your mind."

He managed to sit up straight, so he could think better. "Kat – what are you talking about?" He was angry, and not sure why.

"These Kalaheii, a master race, hell-bent on galactic domination – would they really obliterate themselves?"

"They were losing the –"

"Doesn't matter. Losing is just a stepping stone to winning. That's what my uncle used to say."

His mind felt like glue. Her uncle? That seemed like another lifetime – no, another universe away. Her uncle had been some power-mad media mogul, fifth richest man on the planet at one stage, and his influence had gotten Kat onto the crew of the Ulysses, with him and Blake and Zack. With a shudder he realised they'd only landed on Eden a month ago.

She stood up. "You see, I know ego-maniacal despots up close and personal, and they don't suffer from spite. Revenge, hell yes, and as for controlling people and dominating them completely..." She looked away. "Anyway, killing themselves so no one can take the prize is simply not their style."

"But then ... what?"

She shrugged. "You're the genetically enhanced one. You tell me."

Just as a thought struck him, the orb flashed a blue pulse, and a sharp pain javellined through his head. He buckled over, clutching his temples, his jagged breathing rasping in his ears. Kat's hands touched his head, stroked his neck.

"You see, I was right. That orb is educational alright, in the classical sense. These ancients instilled order, this caste system of levels. You're not meant to have thoughts above your station."

Pierre fought hard to cling to the thought retreating just out of reach. The galaxy-killer – *what if it hadn't been a weapon?* He heard a noise inside his head like a train getting closer, braking hard, the noise reaching a crescendo, Kat shouting his name in the distance... He blacked out.

When he awoke, Kat had her back to him. She was facing the Hohash, which was showing her something he couldn't make out, as she was between him and the alien artefact. He tried to sit up, but his head felt like it had a jack-hammer inside it. He groaned.

"Morning, sleepy head. Hangover, darling? Out with the boys again last night?"

He still couldn't get used to this strange mock intimacy between them. If only they'd had a few more days on the Hohash craft before the Ossyrians had found them, maybe their relationship could have got off the starting blocks. Of course, another few days and they'd have died of lack of oxygen and food.

"Had a chat with the bitch last night," Kat said, conversationally.

He found that if he moved very slowly, the hammer poised inside his head didn't strike. He managed to prop his head on his hand. He had no idea what Kat meant, but decided to play along.

"Find out anything useful?"

"Yep."

Pierre didn't know the rules of this particular game. He'd never gotten past first base before, let alone been invited to the drinks party afterwards. "Er ... what, exactly?"

"I'm Level 3 pushing 4, you're already Level 5, and your little itsy-bitsy nannite friends are wreaking havoc with the usual Chinese walls the orb erects in your brain."

He risked sitting up, incurring a full-frontal sledgehammer. He let out a shriek.

She turned around, her sharp eyes cutting through his pain, reminding him that their brief love-making had not in fact been a fantasy.

"I'm proud of you, Pierre. It took those Alician motherfuckers – as Zack would say – eight hundred years to begin to approach Level 5, and you made it in seven days."

He went to nod, then thought better of it; he sensed the mallet of plazsteel hanging, threatening. "How did you communicate, Kat?"

She shifted sideways so he could see the Hohash. It was displaying fields of text, pictures, resembling a large vertical computer screen. "They figured out how to configure the Hohash to interface with the orb. I don't get programmed like you, though, so no headaches." She frowned. "Not sure why they let me see it all without the constraints though."

A door irised open, and an Ossyrian stepped through, the wall sealing seamlessly behind her. He was sure it was the same Ossyrian, though they had only seen a few since their arrival. She faced him and her eyes blazed information into his brain. It stung, and before he knew what was happening one of the Ossyrian's silver hands was at his neck. It extruded into his skin. He half-expected Kat to attack or shout, but she watched placidly – she'd obviously decided either to trust them, or that any kind of resistance was futile. Pierre felt soothing rain inside his head, drizzling away the residual heat from the battle enjoined there.

"Well?" Kat said.

He jolted himself back to the surface – she was right, the Ossyrian had just downloaded a lot of information into him. "They're going to remove my nannites. But first, they need to answer a distress call – a plague on a small planetary system in what are called the dark territories: an old war tore up space-time in this region, making transiting difficult. We'll get to observe, see them in action, from a distance. And ... well, later, they will take us to one of the Grid hubs, and present evidence of our Level 4 and 5 status to the Grid Hierarchy."

"Nice. Will that help us? Will it help Blake and the others, assuming they're still alive?"

He heard the plaintive tone in her voice. She was angry at everything that had happened. And why not, he thought. "I don't know. It means we might get patronage from another race – "

"You mean enslavement, don't you?"

Pierre didn't know how to answer. The orb had shown him, made him believe in the necessity of the galactic order. Kat had seen it on the Hohash, like a movie, whereas he had felt it to the core of his DNA. The Grid laws had functioned well for a million years. Who was humanity to try and go against them? But he decided to be diplomatic. "We'll see. We're not there yet, anyway. Oh, and the bitch, as you call her – her name is Chahat-Me. And she understands English now, though her vocal system can't make our sounds like ours."

Kat turned to the Ossyrian. "Charmed, I'm sure. Anyway, 'bitch' is a term of endearment, really. Just between us girls, that is."

Pierre smiled. It felt odd to his facial muscles. It had been a while. "I'm really glad you're here Kat."

Her eyes sparkled. "So stick around, okay?"

* * *

Kat watched from the viewport of their small pyramid that had detached from the mother ship. The huge silver ball shed pyramids like crystal snowflakes falling from orbit towards the yellow-green planet below. Despite herself, she was impressed by these Ossyrians, and relieved that compassion wasn't a uniquely human trait. She felt Pierre's hand touch hers, tentative, unsure. She took it, wrapped her fingers around his, and squeezed. She would lose him, sooner or later. Sooner, she decided. She let go.

She stepped away from the portal and glanced at Chahat-Me who was maybe looking at them both, maybe not – it was impossible to tell with her quicksilver eyes. She sat cross-legged in front of the Hohash. It displayed data on the progress of the medical mission as she'd requested. She'd studied epidemiology at University before crossing over into comms, and was interested to see how much more advanced this race was at dealing with pandemics.

The Hohash entertained a number of vistas and displays with fuzzy maroon borders: some were actual pictures relayed from the surface. One showed the Ossyrians in golden encounter suits which she presumed served as protection against the plague, either for themselves or to prevent them from becoming carriers. They streamed out, administering equipment and drugs. Some Ossyrians were on foot, others on amber sleds that skimmed the surface as smoothly as an ice skater on a frozen lake.

Another vista showed Ossyrian pyramids, slowly spinning, traversing the landscape at low level, dispersing a colourless hazy gas over the landscape. However, she was drawn to one particular data screen that illustrated circular pictograms of the spread and density of the affected areas: concentric circles radiating out from an obvious epicentre. Three-dimensional graphs, like mountain ranges, showed density of the plague as a function of the region and time since it had started. As she stared at it, she knew something wasn't right. A stabbing pain behind her right eye made her jolt and let out a gasp.

Pierre turned around from the portal. "Are you alright?"

"Good question." She knew what it was. It was the Hohash – it had just nudged her mind for some reason. She looked at the display again. It looked perfectly normal, exactly what she'd expect from her knowledge and understanding of epidemiological incursions; a textbook case. She studied it harder. It was a classic example... This time the pain made her cry out. Chahat-Me's silver paw on her shoulder stopped her from toppling backwards. She scrunched her eyes closed, trying to recover her breathing. It was as if a needle had just passed through her eyeball. She leaned forwards, her hands on the ground for support.

"What's going on?" Pierre said, standing in front of her.

She opened her eyes to see Chahat-Me move towards the Hohash, she guessed to try and disable it. "No," she said firmly. "It's trying to tell us something, to make me see something." She pushed away Pierre's steadying hand that had replaced the Ossyrian's on her shoulder, and rocked forward onto her knees. She took a breath, and squinted at the data fields, ready for another mind-pulse through her node. This time it didn't come, it didn't have to: she got it. She rose to her feet, accepting the helping hand from Pierre. She spoke directly to the Ossyrian.

"It's a trap! It's so perfect an example of plague radiation, so classic a mixture of randomness and single node origin that it has to be false. Someone has lured you here."

Chahat-Me's eyes danced.

"What's she saying, Pierre?"

He moved side to side with her. "I don't know, it's too fast, too complex, or both. I think she's communicating with the others, rather than us."

Kat supposed he was right – their Ossyrian guardian had that look of being elsewhere, as far as she could tell. Abruptly, as Kat looked on, fascinated by the shapes forming and collapsing at almost subliminal speeds, the eyes settled down, then appeared flat. But she wasn't prepared for what happened next. Chahat-Me held out her two arms, and each one split into two thinner arms, peeling apart as if they had only been lightly stuck together, all the way to the armpits. Kat and Pierre both took a step backwards. One pair of the thinner arms swung back behind her to a wall control panel which appeared out of nowhere and blurred into action. The space they occupied went dark, just before their craft rocked heavily.

Kat tumbled into a corner, her shoulder landing hard up against one of the benches. She tried to get up but gravity squeezed her into the soft fabric, her internal organs pressing against her back. She realised they must be doing high-G manoeuvres, straining the inertial dampers to their limit. When it stopped she ended up rolling helplessly into the centre towards the other side, only to be stopped by one of Chahat-Me's feet which pushed down on her chest, pinning her to the floor. The room spun a few times and then the sense of normality returned, leaving only a trace of nausea, reminding her of her space sickness training two years earlier.

The foot released her. She sat up, glaring at Chahat-Me, but she managed to growl a begrudging "Thanks, I think." Pierre was already up behind her, and helped her to her feet. "What –?" But she didn't need to ask, as soon as her gaze reached the portal. She saw the mother ship shattered into several large chunks, surrounded by myriad smaller fragments. Flames sputtered, then winked out as soon as they formed, as the oxygen flashed into space. She glanced at the Hohash, still in view mode, giving ugly close-up shots of Ossyrians tumbling into space, jerking spasmodically for a few seconds before freezing into corpses that would shortly be cremated as they fell towards the atmosphere. A number of Ossyrians on the planet lay prone on the ground, the helmets of their encounter suits smashed open, their muzzles gasping and bodies twitching, clearly unable to make any concerted movement. Nerve gas, she reckoned. The low-level pyramids were crashing, one by one, she presumed due to some kind of EM pulse or similar device disabling their engines or guidance systems, probably both. She watched the mother ship explode into even more fragments, though many of them remained whole. Only then did the other ships appear – black, spiked spheres reminding her of long-spined sea urchins. They approached the fragments and stuck into them, pricking their hulls. *They're boarding the mother ship, or what's left of it.*

"Why?" Pierre said.

Kat knew it was a pointless question. What he really meant was *how could they?* She reckoned it was probably technology capture by a lower level race. Then came a shock. The Hohash showed some of those boarding. They were wearing space suits and though she couldn't see their heads inside the helmets, they definitely looked humanoid. She snuck a glance at Chahat-Me, to find that she was communicating with Pierre. She waited, trying not to look at the carnage.

"Mannekhi raiders," he said, "Level 5." He seemed about to speak, but stalled, staring at the Ossyrian. His eyes moved like Chahat-Me's, only less fluidly.

"What?" Kat asked.

Pierre's brow creased, and he looked from Chahat-Me to Kat, then out the portal. "We're ... we're cloaked. So..."

Kat walked up to him, put her hands on his elbows. "Pierre, talk to me. What's going on?"

He turned back to her. Despite the silver eyes, she could see how anxious he was. He sat down on the bench.

"The Ossyrians have a vow to help people, a kind of Hippocratic oath."

She folded her arms. "So, they're going to stand by, while these Mannekhi bastards –"

"No. No, that's just it. They have a higher oath, related to Galactic security. If the Mannekhi get the technology, the database from a mothership, well..." He waved a hand, listlessly.

She glanced through the portal again. Around thirty of the spike-ships festooned the collapsing hull fragments of the Ossyrian's mighty vessel. "What can they do?" What can we do? We're just one tiny ship, maybe the only ones free right now."

Without warning, Chahat-Me seized Kat's shoulders and spun her around to face her, catching both her wrists and locking them in a vice-like grip. Kat's eyes were wild. "Pierre!" But she sensed no movement behind her. *Damn* – he knows what she's going to do to me! She watched as Chahat-Me's second pair of aluminium-coloured arms transfigured at the ends into large needles – syringes.

"Pierre! What's going on?"

He stood up, laid a hand on her shoulder. "She's saving your life."

With a blur, the first syringe stabbed into the left side of her neck, a fraction of a second before the second one pricked her belly.

"Christ!" she yelled, just as Chahat-Me released her. She took a swing at the dog-faced alien but hit nothing more than air, nearly falling over.

"Kat, don't."

She regained her balance, and glared at the dispassionate Ossyrian, then turned to Pierre. "Wanna see if you can move that quickly too?"

He stood right in front of her. "Go ahead. I won't move."

Her fist ached to connect with someone, or something; she realised how much she'd been holding in this past week. She thought about hitting the wall, but she'd given that up years ago. "Tell me what she just did to me."

Pierre walked over to the portal. "Come and see."

Reluctantly she joined him, just in time to catch a flash of emerald lightning that lit up everything. For a moment, as far as she could see, space turned an eerie green, and then faded back to black. "Fireworks. So what?"

He nodded towards the vista. She watched. The bustle of activity slowed down. Ships still moved, but nothing changed course. One or two of the spike ships collided, bursting into flame for a second before snuffing out. Her anger subsided.

Everything was stilling, silent – she tried to avoid the word which most aptly described the scene, but said it anyway. "Dead?" She tried to imagine how that could be.

He nodded.

"How?" So fast, she thought, so damned efficient.

"A Level Eight weapon, like an electromagnetic pulse, but tuned only to organic signatures. Operates on what they call the epsilon spectrum: subatomic, penetrates hulls and shields."

She felt light-headed, nauseous. "Then why aren't we dead?"

"The weapon targets anything organic without Ossyrian DNA. The ship's cloak transmits the DNA signature, and, I already have some Ossyrian DNA so my body doesn't reject the eyes, and now ... well, now you have some too."

She sensed there was something else he wasn't telling her, but it would wait. She moved back to see the Hohash, and was aghast. "The population! It's wiping them out too!"

"I know. You were right about it all being too perfect. Most probable scenario is that the inhabitants, or at the least their government or factions of it, were in on the raid from the start. Probably they were promised advanced technology too."

She stared in disbelief. "But that's all supposition. You don't know that. She doesn't know that for sure!"

Pierre faced her, with those damned eyes. Less human again, she thought, the Ossyrian's defender.

"You were right, Kat, and thanks to you they had a few seconds to take the appropriate precautions, or at least to set in motion their contingency protocol."

"A few seconds! A few fucking seconds to decide to commit genocide!" Her fists were ready for use again.

"They're Level Eight, Kat. They think much faster than we do, and have considered all manner of scenarios before, including this one, and the appropriate response."

"Stop talking like a diplomat, Pierre! It doesn't give them the right – "

"But it does, Kat, that's the whole point. That's how this galaxy works."

"Like the Q'Roth culling us. That okay with you too, Pierre?"

She saw his confidence falter, a crack in the façade. Too little, too late. But she had nothing more to say. She moved to where she could see neither the Hohash nor the portal, drew her knees up to her chest, and wrapped her arms around them. Pierre kept his distance, but the Ossyrian walked over towards her. It opened its mouth revealing the fibrous layers, like she'd seen once inside a dead whale's jaws. A shrieking noise like a psychedelic choir emanated. Through the cacophony, Kat made out two distorted words: *thank you*.

She turned her head aside, unable to think of a suitable response.

CHAPTER 12 – IGLOO

"**Y**our plan is going well," Hannah said. Louise nodded: two nuclear threats neutralized, Blake out of the picture, Zack stuck in orbit, and Micah trapped in an Optronic landscape. Victory was within her grasp, and yet... She didn't relish any of it. She was changing, could feel herself slipping away, thinking a little more like a Q'Roth warrior every day. She'd begun to second-guess her motives, her plan, and she knew how dangerous that was during battle. But showing any indecision in front of her Alician crew, or the humans for that matter, was out of the question.

Vince was still the key. She could negotiate a truce with him, maybe a more generous arrangement than she'd originally considered. But the thought came back – what was she changing into? Louise knew now why she needed to see Vince – so that he could pull her back towards her humanity, before she went too far over to the Q'Roth side.

She focused: *see it through.*

"Status," she barked.

"Ready on all fronts," Jarvik replied, crisply.

She took her chair. "Take us down to the surface, half a kilometre up-slope from their MCC. We'll humour their pathetic stealth technology for the moment."

Louise studied the viewscreen as the stars pitched upwards and the planet's surface loomed into view, then raced towards them. The ship sliced into the atmosphere as easily as a scalpel making its first incision. They plunged straight towards the cloudless, starlit landscape, gathering speed, the hull's shield systems displacing the heat energy to their phosphorous-white wake – their screeching, incandescent approach would not go unnoticed. The night-time landscape shifted into sharp relief, enhanced by the ship's sensors and her Q'Roth-augmented vision: mountains, paths, a sleepless Esperantia, and desert-shrubs manifested beneath her. Despite her trust in Q'Roth inertial dampening technology, she had thought she would at least fall forward in her seat. But it was like an old-style fighter simulator – no gravity effects except inside the mind. The ship's descent simply froze at its nadir, hanging Damocles-like above the terrain.

"Set us down, Jarvik. Hannah, contact their commander-in-chief."

She knew how to play this out, she was good at this after all, having learnt from the best. For an instant she wondered where Sister Esma – her mentor and Alician High Priestess – might be now, and how they were faring under Q'Roth sponsorship. She flushed away the thought. *Focus*, she instructed herself.

"Colonel Vasquez is on the line," Hannah said.

"Audio only," Louise said. "Colonel Vasquez, I believe."

"Yes, Ma'am."

Good, military respect at least. "Your crude attempts to nuke me out of existence have failed. The three Q'Roth ships are ... elsewhere –" *two inside the sun, the other on this planet's small moon as a back up for later, along with her insurance package* "– and your commander Blake and his foul-mouthed pilot are indisposed."

There was a pause. "And Mr. Sanderson?"

"Ah, yes, I'd almost forgotten. Micah is safe enough, for now." *Your move, Colonel. Empty threats would be bad.* Her eyes darted to a geographic display showing the exact position of their MCC. She switched to penetration mode and clearly saw the outlines of the people inside.

"What do you propose?" he said.

So nice to deal with a professional. "I will meet with Vince. Alone. Unarmed." She watched the display, seeing the obvious rapid conference going on between them. Hannah had been eavesdropping their comms for the past twenty-four hours. On cue, a display of key personnel information flashed up beneath the MCC view. *Not bad, Hannah. Maybe I'll keep you alive after all.*

"Very well," Vasquez started, "I'll give you the coordinates –"

"I know where he is, Colonel. But I see him alone. Tell the good Professor Kostakis and Antonia, who are currently with Vince, to leave immediately." She heard a woman gasp and another say "fu–" before Vasquez' reflexes clicked off the microphone. She waited.

"They are leaving. Anything else?"

Really professional – she was impressed – not the slightest hint of sarcasm or distaste. She would keep this one, too.

"No, Colonel, that will be all for now."

126

Louise stood, hands on hips, and faced Jarvik and Hannah. "I'll be gone an hour. If my life signs stop, nuke the city, then take the last Q'Roth ship to the Grid. Leave the MCC alone – they'll rot in their own guilt as they slowly starve to death. You'll be on your own, but there are still non-nomadic Q'Roth in the Grid system." *They'll probably kill you of course, but there might be some gratitude for a returned ship.* "As for Micah, if I don't return, leave him where he is. His body will die eventually, but not before his mind gives way. Questions?"

Jarvik shook his head, Hannah studied her console.

"Good." She walked to the central walkway to the lower floor, then paused there. "One more thing. Whatever it is you've been plotting, Hannah, don't. Let's just say I have taken out an insurance policy, should there be any foul play." With that, she left, knowing that Hannah's mind would be doing overtime trying to work out what Louise could have set up, and Jarvik would respect Louise to the end now, and be more likely to kill Hannah himself before joining a mutiny.

* * *

Vince could tell Antonia didn't want to leave; she'd only just arrived in any case, sent to explain the latest security breach on comms. Thank God the weapon had never been discussed except face to face – Jennifer's suggestion from her terrorist days after the fall of Dublin – a good call.

"But Louise is going to kill you, Vince."

He perched on the ledge of the small oval table in the centre of the hastily-erected field dome, or the igloo, as they all called it, and shrugged. "If it's just me and Micah, and she leaves the rest, it's a bargain. In any case, if this works, she'll be joining me."

Kostakis spoke up, his voice uncharacteristically small. "I understand she's coming alone, unarmed."

"Don't believe a word. First, I doubt she'll be unarmed, even if it looks that way, and second, I'm sure her crew are watching like hawks for any attempts on our part. No – we have a plan, we stick to it."

Antonia shook her head. "But Vince, like you, I've seen what she can do. Louise – "

"Enough! Get out, Antonia. Dimitri, take her out of here, now! I don't want either of you running into Louise out there; she might kill you as a warm-up."

He turned his back on both of them, until he heard the click of the door seal behind them. "Thanks," he said, "nice to know someone cares." He moved into the empty circular zone encompassed by the hidden weapon's range, and folded his arms. The Hohash was also out of sight, so Louise wouldn't see it, not at first.

Although he'd spent the night with Sandy, and it had been more passionate and intense than he'd expected, there just hadn't been enough time for them to have a *history*. He found himself reminiscing about Louise – the good times, and not just the sex, either. He recalled a shoot-out in Rio during the Carnival: silent, scarlet plasma pulses zipping in and out of the crowds in Ipanema, like deadly hail; he and Louise covering for each other, the rest of their squad picked off one by one. They'd finally escaped inside the hollow undercarriage of a carnival wagon shaped like a giant cow, as it trundled along in the cacophony. It was the first time they made love, knowing they could die at any second, staring into each other's eyes, neither of them masking their cries of ecstasy drowned by the music and hubbub outside.

Vince knew it hadn't all been Alician ploy, part of Louise's deep cover. They'd had something. She'd been the only one who...

The door clicked open and Louise breezed in. She looked tired, drawn, thinner than last time he'd seen her – killed her, to be precise. He had no illusions about how he looked either. The past month had worn everyone down. He watched her as one would a tarantula. She sealed the door behind her.

"Hello, Vince. Long time." She produced a slimline pulse pistol from behind her, and aimed it squarely at his forehead. "My turn."

* * *

The air was thick in the MCC, crammed as it was with technology which had proven useless against Louise. Sandy gazed at all the displays and dials, the winking lights and glinting controls, and at Micah's occasionally twitching body, and wondered what was happening to him. She looked away.

She hated this waiting, not knowing. Vince, who she'd made love to for the first time – well, second and third, too – just last night, who she'd just said goodbye to, whose scent she could still detect on her fingertips, was on a suicide mission in the igloo with the Hohash weapon, with the ultra-bitch serial killer Louise. She stood up, and Vasquez for the umpteenth time glared at her, willing her to sit down. She folded, and obliged. She ignored the fact that Ramires kept surreptitiously staring at her – she didn't know what that was about and didn't care right now, though she was glad he'd survived Louise's first wave of attacks. Shakirvasta and Jennifer were huddled in a corner, murmuring – a match made in hell, she thought. She glanced again at Micah's form – he looked peaceful at least, as if sleeping.

The door burst open, Antonia whirling inside, followed by the large-framed Kostakis, clearly out of breath. "We saw her. She must be in there by now."

Vasquez nodded. "Then bring it online Jennifer."

Jennifer moved over to the inert Hohash propped up against one of the MCC walls. She held out a slim black box and depressed a button, and the Hohash sprang to life, lifting off the ground ten centimetres, its mirror face surging with a whirlpool of blues and mauves.

"Where did you find that?" Sandy asked, suspicious of the box.

"Sanjay made it for me ... for us. It's a remote node, basic communications only."

"Sanjay, huh? Well, that answers one or two questions." She glanced at Kostakis but he avoided her gaze.

Jennifer vaulted the slur. "I can give the Hohash instructions here, and the procedure will be executed in the igloo by the two other Hohash there."

Sandy got to her feet. "*When* we need it." Her voice was steel.

Jennifer reeled. "*When* is *now*. As soon as it's ready, we activate it."

Everyone stared at the two women, and there was a realisation around the room that the criteria for the final move had not actually been discussed. Jennifer turned back to her remote. Sandy bent down and retrieved something from her rucksack. The pistol barrel lifted and targeted Jennifer's head. "Back off, bitch, or I'll blow your ugly face off." She caught a movement out of the corner of her left eye. "Don't even think about it Vasquez. I reached the fencing nationals four years ago; fast-twitch reflexes – you so much as touch me, her brain's barbecue." She glared at Jennifer, who returned the favour. "Go ahead," Sandy said, "try me".

A woman's scratchy, tinny voice stabbed into the heavy silence. "Colonel Vasquez, Colonel Vasquez, this is the Q'Roth Hunter Vessel calling. Switch off all other comms. We need to talk."

Sandy ignored it. She remembered her fencing bouts, the concentration, waiting for a subtle move, an opening. But Jennifer didn't budge a millimetre. Sandy had thought that Kostakis, or even Shakirvasta – Sanjay, no less – might try and intervene, but both remained behind Jennifer, Kostakis agitated, Shakirvasta serene.

"Colonel Vasquez, are you receiving me, this is –"

"This is Vasquez. Who the hell is this?"

Sandy heard a sigh of relief at the other end, ignoring or oblivious to the harsh tone of the Colonel, his patience obviously finally run out.

"My name is Hannah. This is a secure channel I installed yesterday in your comms matrix. Louise can't intercept it. I'm commanding the Q'Roth vessel at this time."

Vasquez left the microphone off for a while longer. "Ladies, could I suggest we put down –"

"NO!" they both said, at the same time.

Vasquez sighed. "Hannah, what do you want, I'm a little busy right now?"

"To surrender this vessel."

Sandy's head turned a fraction towards Vasquez; it was less than half a second, but Vasquez didn't miss the slot. His left backhand whipped out slamming into her pistol-bearing forearm. It was a precision strike, spiking the tendon on her inner arm just the right way to make her trigger finger loosen rather than contract, sending the pistol spinning from her grip. His hand rebounded to strike her jaw. She stumbled and hit the bulkhead, dazed. When the faze passed, she looked up to see Vasquez towering above her, his own pistol in his hand.

"Jennifer, in case it's not obvious, I'm in command. Prep the weapon, but don't unleash it until I give the order. Is that clear?"

Sandy was watching Vasquez, and didn't hear an answer, but she assumed the bitch had nodded. She'd underestimated Vasquez: he'd moved frighteningly fast.

"Colonel Vasquez, are you still there? Did you hear what I said?"

"I heard you. Power down your ship and open all access ports. Prepare to be boarded. I understand there is at least one other crew member?"

"There was. He's dead."

Vasquez shook his head. "I see. I'm sending someone over to check out your ship and bring you in." He nodded sideways – without taking his eyes off Sandy – to the three men at the back of the trailer. "All of you. Take weapons. I can't call the other marines without using a non-secure channel."

Kostakis and Shakirvasta picked up pulse rifles like rookies, and shuffled out the door. Sandy glanced at Ramires, who seemed reluctant to leave, but he followed suit nonetheless.

"Now, Hannah. You're clearly mutineering. What about Louise? Does she have any remote access to the ship or weapons? How much of a threat is she without you and your ship on her side?"

There was a pause. "Yes, yes, she's still very dangerous. She wants to kill Vince then nuke the city; she wants to kill you all."

Sandy played it back in her head. There was no doubt. "She's lying, Vasquez."

Vasquez clicked off the mike. "What?" His frown deepened. "Why would she lie?"

"Yes, Sandy," Jennifer joined in. "Are you a psych now as well as a fencing champion?"

She disregarded the taunt. "I'm telling you, Colonel, this Hannah is lying about Louise being dangerous. She just went from vagueness to extreme threat, she clearly hadn't thought it through; she's just shit-scared Louise will kill her somehow if you don't terminate her."

Vasquez leaned back against the console.

"It's ready," Jennifer said, her thumb hovering above a button on the remote.

"Wait, Jennifer." He clicked back on. "Hannah, tell me, what about Micah? Can you release him?"

There was a pause, but Hannah's channel was obviously open all the time; they could hear her moving about, cursing occasionally. "Yes, yes I should be able to. Just hang on a minute... There, he's clear to exit now."

Sandy and the other three stared at Micah's limp body. The tech, who had been trying to blend into the rear wall for the last half an hour, ventured forward and tried various controls. "Sir, he's not coming to. I can't tell if he's been released or not. He might not be able to find his way back, Sir; depends where he's been, if you see what I mean."

"You see," Sandy said, "she's lying."

"Doesn't mean squat Sandy, and you know it." Jennifer leered at her.

Sandy got to her feet. "Don't you push that. We can take Louise down without losing Vince."

"Sandy, please sit down –"

"Let her stand." Jennifer transferred the device to her left hand so she could jab her right forefinger in Sandy's direction. "Vince trained that whore; he said it as much himself, she's his responsibility. If he'd been here, he'd have pushed the button already, and you damned well know it."

She recognised the look in Jennifer's eyes. She rushed for her but couldn't reach her in time. Jennifer pressed the button. Sandy flailed at her. "NO!" just as Jennifer side-stepped, and her left foot connected with Sandy's cheekbone, knocking her out cold.

* * *

Vince relaxed his shoulders: he'd stared down the barrel of more pistols than he cared to remember. *Fire up the weapon, guys, Louise doesn't do long goodbyes.*

She walked to him, spun the pulse gun around and presented the hilt to Vince. He didn't take his eyes off hers for even a fraction of a second, nor did he blink. He took the pistol and tossed it behind him, sending it clattering across the stone floor.

"Okay, you just surprised me, Louise. What's going on?"

She placed her hands on his shoulders, like they were dancing late at night. She smiled. The way she used to. He took her wrists, and was sorely tempted to cast them aside and slap her for what she'd done to Rashid's ship. But he didn't.

"I'm here to offer a truce, Vince. Terms will be a little tough, but nothing we can't live with. You were the only one I knew would actually listen."

He'd thought he'd become immune to her a long time ago, but seeing her resurrected stirred up old emotions. He stared hard into her eyes. "Shit, Louise, you're serious aren't you?"

She leaned forward and kissed him. "You've been on my mind. So I figured when you shot me you were just playing hard to get."

That did it. He flung her wrists to the sides. "Do you know what you've done? Did you think they'd let you live if they had a second in which to kill you?" He flared at her. In his peripheral vision he noticed the Hohash that had been behind the door illuminate, snapping into life. *Too late.*

"You could negotiate for me," she said, her sultry façade cooling rapidly. We have technology that can increase your chances of survival, prevent detection by hostile aliens passing by who might fancy a bite or some easy manpower. It's a jungle out there in the stars, Vince, you've no idea."

Vince felt the static building up on his forearms, like goosebumps. Flashes began to light up the room.

Louise swivelled around on her heels, facing the glowing yellow Hohash. "You! You were in my dream!" She spun back to Vince. "What –?" She darted for the entrance but was stung backwards by a force-field that burnt like dry ice. She glanced upwards and noticed another of the mirrors attached to the domed ceiling above them. A third device, metallic and squat, lurked behind Vince. It had also powered up, glowing orange. Her voice steeled. "What's going on, Vince?"

Vince didn't do sadness or remorse; he'd seen too much killing. He watched the glistening shroud, like a huge soap bubble, cocoon the area where they stood. It started to shrink towards them.

"They're killing us, Louise. There's not much time, and no way out. And no comms, so no way I can tell anyone it's unnecessary."

She slapped him hard. "Sonofabitch. Of all the stupid fucking –"

"Seconds, Louise, That's all we have. Remember Rio?" He grabbed her, yanked her towards him. The air between them flickered.

She glanced down at her arms, quivering with static, ice cold. "Hell, Vince."

"I know." He kissed her hard, locked his arms around her, one around her waist, the other cradling the back of her head. She resisted at first, then kissed him back.

* * *

Micah, still groggy, reached the igloo, supported by Ramires. He found Sandy there, sitting on the floor, listless, staring at the statue.

"Beautiful, aren't they?" she said.

He gazed at the statue for a few seconds, then knelt down behind her, and draped his arms around her shoulders. He didn't speak. He'd observed it all silently through the Hohash connection. That's why he hadn't exited: he hadn't known Louise's real plan until it had been too late, and he'd needed to see it through till the end.

Apparently, Louise had told Zack, but even if Zack had believed her, which he hadn't, he'd had no way to communicate with Vasquez and the others, his ship's comms system having been fried during Louise's initial attack.

Sandy lowered her head against his forearm, and he felt the stickiness of dried tears. He stroked her hair with his other hand.

He watched Ramires approach the metallic effigy and test it with a finger. Ramires rapped his knuckles against Vince's chest. There was a dull metallic sound, like the giant kodo drums Micah had once seen in Nara, near Kyoto. Ramires touched Vince's eyes, as if to close them, but he couldn't. They were fixed on Louise's. He knelt down before the two of them, and began incanting a low chant: Tibetan, Micah guessed, probably from Ramires' early Sentinel training. He chanted for an hour. No one else entered the igloo during that time, as the three of them paid homage to Vince, and Micah said a final farewell to Louise.

Ramires carried Sandy back half a kilometre to the camp in the starlight. They heard shouting and celebratory whoops long before they reached it. Vasquez came out to greet them, took one look at their faces, and handed them the keys to the MCC.

"There are bunks in the front compartment. Get some sleep. It's too noisy here, anyway. Everyone else is celebrating; you understand, right? I'll go pay my last respects to Vince when it calms down here."

Micah nodded, and they meandered back to the deserted MCC. As they lay in darkness, sleep just out of reach, Sandy spoke.

"We can't stay here, Micah."

He didn't know how she'd reached the same conclusion he had an hour ago – her probably by intuition. She's right, he thought. It's going to get bad here. The Grid, this galactic society out there, that's where we have to go.

"Get some sleep, Sandy."

"Not till you tell me you have a plan, Micah."

"I have one. Now, go to sleep." He watched her till her chest rose and fell with a calm rhythm. Then he began planning.

During the next two hours, every time he thought he had a good way forward, he imagined presenting it to Vince, who would shake his head and point out the holes. On the fifth attempt, in his mind's eye, Vince shrugged and said "Okay, it's a plan." That was good enough for Micah. He rolled over onto his right side, and whispered "Goodbye Vince; thanks for everything," and then he fell sound asleep.

CHAPTER 13 – FRACTURES

"**W**ar is better," Vasquez said, on the cliff's edge. "Uniforms, insignia: you know who the enemy is. With politics, well... That's why I always turned down promotions above the rank of Colonel."

Micah listened, half-absent. His head felt heavy, weighed down by theories, some marginally less paranoid than others: hypoteses about who supported who, and who was out to get whoever else. They all ended up at the same destination. It wasn't his preferred journey. "You could come with us," he said, knowing that his very usage of the conditional already admitted what he knew about this man.

"I owe it to Vince to stay here. I'll try to limit the damage."

"You knew him well, didn't you?"

Vasquez nudged a stone off the edge, so that it clattered down the escarpment. "As much as anyone did. I think only Louise knew him really well." With his old arm he straightened his tunic. "He was my protégé originally, but he overtook me a long time ago."

Micah understood the implication: we've lost our best strategist; and someone Micah could have learned a great deal from. He stared toward the blood-orange sun strafing the mountain-tops. It rose faster than on Earth, sending tepid shadows racing across the plains. "My first sunrise here. You were right to get me up early to see it."

"Forget the sunrise, Micah. Watch, over there."

He squinted in the direction pointed out by Vasquez. At first he saw nothing but a dry basin the colour of scoured oak, fringed by a range of sun-tinted orange mesa. Without warning, a diamond-white glint sparkled in the foreground. It lasted a full minute before it faded. His eyes remained rooted to the spot, the after-image blazing on his retina.

"Fitting, somehow," Micah said. "Though I don't know if Vince would approve; not the sort of guy who craved monuments, I'd imagine."

Vasquez passed him a viewer. He put it to his eyes and zoomed in. It took a few seconds to relocate it. He stared for a while, then lowered the viewer and tried to see with his naked eyes. "Who are they?"

"People, ordinary citizens. More every day now, three weeks since our little War was officially declared over. It's become a kind of shrine. I had one of my soldiers check them out, but they just sit or kneel on the sand, and wait till the sunrise catches the statue. After about twenty minutes they leave again. Always on foot."

"You should ask Carlson."

"Already did. He said the people need quasi-religious symbolism, emotional closure."

Micah smiled. "That's Carlson alright. What about you?" He watched Vasquez' profile: straight, unerring, egoless. The right man to stay behind.

"I think they need a hero and a villain, locked in a struggle."

Micah cleared his throat. "Not exactly a struggle."

Vasquez put a firm hand on Micah's shoulder. "Micah, I thought of all people you'd recognise love as the ultimate struggle."

Micah's brow grew trenches, not least because he remembered making love with Louise – except love had played no part in it. Then, unbidden, something snagged in his mind about Louise, just out of reach. And then it was gone.

Vasquez cracked a rare smile. "Let's go, Micah, it's show-time."

As they descended, Micah noticed something. "You're not wearing your sidearm."

Vasquez' white-haired head nodded. "Martial law was declared 'over' yesterday by Josefsson, himself hastily elected in the power vacuum left by Blake."

Micah kept his counsel. Normally, martial law coming to an end would be a good thing, except that some of the best people were in the military. With Blake still in a coma, and Zack purged of his implant but an emotional space-wreck, Josefsson and Shakirvasta had moved quickly.

Vasquez was right – the war was shifting into politics, where people like Vasquez had little leverage. Micah had thought it was over, but then he knew what Vince would have said if he'd been there: it's only over when you're dead.

Micah did a double-take as he entered the meeting room. At the head of the anachronistic polished-wood table sat the triumvirate of Josefsson, Shakirvasta and Jennifer, with Josefsson in the middle. The ceiling, as with all dwellings in

Esperantia, was low, adding to Micah's gloomy outlook for this meeting, only the third official governmental meeting since the 'event.'

He and Sandy took the seats nearest the doorway. Ramires arrived with Kostakis trailing after him. Antonia deposited herself next to Kostakis.

Josefsson, well-manicured, his quaff of hair perfectly in place, stood. "Well, I think we can get started."

"We're not all present yet," Sandy said, flat.

Josefsson beamed. "Madam, we have never discussed the criteria for a quorum."

Her riposte was obviously pre-planned. "Exactly," Sandy said.

Josefsson's smile splintered. Micah noticed a small flicker of Shakirvasta's right hand, and Josefsson cleared his throat and spread his hands. "We can of course wait another few minutes." He sat down.

Micah knew it wasn't first blood, not even a scratch. These people were playing for bigger stakes, in for the long haul. He heard a shuffling noise outside, and then saw Zack lumber in slowly, looking like hell, leading Rashid by the arm. He hadn't seen Rashid for three weeks; for that matter he'd hardly seen Zack, though he knew where he spent most of his time. They seated themselves. Micah noted that no one sat next to the triumvirate. Unfortunately it only served to enhance their appearance of power, of being more equal than the others.

Josefsson rose again. "Ladies and gentlemen," he said, nodding particularly to Sandy with mock deference, "I declare this fifth session of the Council open. We have several orders of business today..."

Josefsson lorded over the proceedings, in full flood, stating how effective the fledgling government had been in the past few weeks: Shakirvasta and the military, aided by Hannah, had prevented the nannites from eating away the Hunter-Vessel's engines and other systems. Hannah had apparently been very cooperative, even without the explosive neck-collar Jennifer had insisted she wear at all times, and had managed to remotely retrieve the last surviving transport from Ourshiwann's moon. Micah recalled hearing that Jennifer now had a node, so she could communicate directly with the Hohash, although apparently it wasn't going so well for some reason. He considered the neck collar had been a good idea, but had simply been placed around the wrong throat.

Hearing Hannah's name, Louise leapt into his mind again. He tuned out from Josefsson's waxing speech, trying to figure out what was bugging him. Hannah had killed Jarvik. Her version was that she had wanted to defect, and had tried to persuade Jarvik, and that at the last moment there had been a struggle. The only part that didn't fit was how she had managed to overcome that Alician hulk. He'd wished Vince had been around to interrogate her. If only Jennifer had not been so trigger-happy...

And yet Micah had spoken with Hannah a week ago, and firmly believed she had been trying to change sides.

Still the Louise problem eluded him. But he was brought out of his reverie by raised voices. It had begun.

"– guards are there for his own protection, Zack. These are difficult times. We all want the good Commander to recover, and his security is therefore a high priority."

Zack's knuckles whitened on the table. "Next time they try and stop me or Glenda or anyone, you'll be needing two new ones."

"Are you suggesting illegal use of force?" Josefsson said.

Micah rose. Zack was about to complicate things, and these three would seize the first chance to lock him away for good. "I propose that we move to agenda item 4." He stared at Shakirvasta, rather than Josefsson. Deal with the man whose DNA signs the cheques, his father had once said. Shakirvasta didn't move a millimetre. Micah felt the rest of the room staring in his own direction. Josefsson sat down, peering officiously at the single sheet of paper in front of him, and nodded. "Very well, Mr. Sanderson. Please present your case."

He looked at the faces around the room. He ignored his heart thumping inside his chest. He took a swig of water.

"Survival is key. If we're discovered here by any of hundreds of alien races, we could easily be destroyed, consumed, or enslaved. The Q'Roth masking technology Hannah has shared with us will help, but it's only a matter of time before we're found. I propose that a small group travels to the Grid to proactively seek out potential allies." He sat down. It had been short, but the less he said, the less his enemies had to attack.

Shakirvasta held up a finger. "Mr. President, might I reply?"

Josefsson waved a hand royally. "Certainly, Sanjay."

"Mr. Sanderson – Micah – surely we are more likely to be found if you make contact with other races?"

He'd anticipated this one, especially since his own predictions supported it. "You're right. But this way we have a chance to choose who finds us, rather than waiting and hoping we're lucky."

Josefsson couldn't help himself. "And how do you propose to travel to the Grid?"

"We leave the large transport here, and take the Hunter Class vessel." Micah raised a hand to stall Josefsson's objection. "The Mil have already off-loaded most of the missile hardware for defence. If an alien race arrives, one single ship won't make much difference, and you'll have the transport ship for protection, and still have the Hohash craft, more manoeuvrable at close quarters."

Shakirvasta tapped his cigarette case, but said nothing further. Josefsson bristled. "I judge that this would leave us with an unsatisfactory, insufficient defensive capability. I –"

"You what?" Sandy stood up.

Micah had expected her to be shaking with rage, but he heard iron in her voice – like the metal her lover had been transformed into.

"There's no constitution here yet," she continued. "You can call yourself President as much as you like, but we're all representatives of this Council, so we vote."

Josefsson was about to protest, but Shakirvasta nudged his arm. "Very well, then." The ex-senator puffed his chest out. "All those in favour of allowing this futile, endangering mission?"

Although Kostakis abstained, Rashid's vote carried the motion. Micah didn't listen to the rest. He could already hear the void of space calling him, the far away Grid, all its undreamed-of wonders and horrors beckoning. Half of him knew it could be suicide. But somewhere, in another realm, he felt two proud parents smile, maybe Vince, too.

"That was a little easier than expected," Micah said to Sandy, back out in the fresh plaza air, the noon-day sun casting no shadows.

"They want us gone as much as we want to be out of here," Sandy replied. "But we should go quickly – you saw item seven on the agenda?"

He nodded. "They're no doubt determining the new constitution right now." He wished Blake had come out of his coma, but no one knew when – if – that was going to happen.

Zack joined them. "Fucking meetings." He spat. "I'm coming with you tomorrow."

Micah stared at him. "But –"

"Stow it. I'm washed up here, broken, useless. But I'm still the best pilot on this planet, and you can't trust that bitch Hannah, not after the way they found her buddy Jarvik. Now, I have to go say goodbye to everyone who God-alone-knows-why still gives a shit about me. See you in the morning." He strode off down one of the alleys which led out of the plaza like spokes from a hub.

Shakirvasta approached them with an easy grace, as if taking a Sunday stroll. He held out his hand. "Good luck, Mr. Sanderson."

Micah decided to shake his hand – it was as sure and firm as he'd presumed it would be. Then Shakirvasta held out a small oblong device. "The detonator for Hannah's necklace."

"I want it off her. She'll need us alive as much as we'll need her knowledge of the ship." He stared defiantly into the Indistani's eyes. He'd seen a tiger once, as a kid, in a zoo; the tiger had looked at him the same way. But this time there were no bars in between.

"As you wish." He held out another device. "You can release her once you leave tomorrow. Not before. President's decree."

Sandy snorted. 'Got through item seven pretty quick then?'

Shakirvasta looked from one to the other. "What we want is not so different. Our methods, differ, that's all."

"That's all, as you say," Sandy said.

The tiger nodded, returning to the Council room.

"Let's go pack," Micah said, and they quit the place as fast as they could without breaking into a trot, neither one casting a second glance backwards.

* * *

Sandy hid in the shadows till she was sure Kostakis was alone, then slipped inside his room. Unlike her own cell, as she thought of it, Kostakis had at least made an effort to render it more homely: a white and blue Greek pennant hung from one of the ceiling hooks, and various marble memorabilia were draped around the walls. A metallic mobile of yachts reflected Kostakis' dim yellow reading light, dappling the walls with rocking shadow-boats, as if they were sailing choppy seas. He's staying, she said to herself.

His chair strained as he leaned backwards from the small desk he was hunched over. "Please, please do come in; this is somewhat unexpected." He smiled. "Don't worry, she's with Sanjay, plotting and scheming somewhere." The smile dried up, lending a hollow look to his face. "I never used to want to sleep alone. Now my bed is empty, and I'm happier."

You look anything but happy, she thought, but she didn't have time to get into it. She had to stick to her purpose. She held out a manila envelope. He didn't reach for it.

"What's this?" he asked.

"It's for Jennifer. Coded with her DNA so only she can open it."

Kostakis studied the missive, then Sandy. "Have you ever read Hamlet?"

Sandy maintained her fencing arm straight. "No."

"There is a part where two men are sent with a letter to deliver to a king. The letter is sealed, and inside it tells the king to kill the bearers of the message."

She lowered her arm. "You're right, Dimitri. It's a weapon of sorts." She tossed it onto one of the spider stools. "When you can no longer reach her, when she's gone dangerously too far, let her find it."

"What will it do to her?"

"It will *undo* her. That's the point, isn't it?" She held out her empty hand. "Goodbye, Professor. I'm sorry we didn't get time to know each other better. Really, I am."

He stood up, and took her hand with both of his, then pulled her into an enveloping hug. She felt awkward until she realised it was more for him than for her. Once that critical insight came, she hugged him back, massaging his pain. Abruptly he released her. She kissed him once on the cheek, and left him alone with the missive.

* * *

Micah watched Antonia's sleeping frame, and tried to recall how he'd gotten there. She'd knocked on his door, very late, muttered something about a conversation with Sandy, and then out of the blue kissed him, just once. Then she'd told him she couldn't go further, because of how she felt about Kat. He knew his father would have somehow seduced her, justifying that she was in his room late at night, and had just kissed him, etc. Instead, Micah had held her hand, and listened while she poured out her feelings. He'd held her in the more emotional moments, felt her tears on his forearm, and comforted her with improbable statements about how Kat was still safe, somewhere, and they would find her again. At one point, in the early hours of the morning, she'd been about to say something he couldn't bear to hear...

"Micah, tonight you've been such a good – "

His finger rushed to her lips. "Don't. Don't say it."

Antonia stared at him. He removed his finger, and she nodded. "I should leave..."

He stood up. "No, stay, please. I'll sleep on the floor, you take the bed. Don't worry, I won't – "

"I know, Micah." She lay down, her head propped up on an elbow. "We're both fully clothed, Micah, and very tired. Lie here next to me ... if it's not too painful."

He studied the space next to her. Truth was, he was exhausted. In the background to everything else going on, he'd been chasing her these past months, and it was finally over. Now he'd accepted it, it wasn't the end of the world. Inside, he laughed at himself for even thinking such a thing given everything that had happened. His head lightened. The corners of his mouth twitched upwards. "Okay, Antonia, but you whisper 'Kat' during the night and you'll find yourself on the floor."

She laughed, and laid her head on the pillow, closing her eyes. Micah stretched out next to her, and surprised himself by falling asleep.

Micah woke early, and saw her next to him; neither of them had moved during the night. She looked calm, more peaceful than he'd seen her since Earth. He leaned over and planted a soft kiss on her hair, then glanced outside to see the first ginger rays of dawn skate across the plaza. He headed out for the public shower cubicles in the courtyard.

As the lukewarm water trickled over him, he pondered how for more than a year he'd watched Antonia from a distance, having an instant crush on her, nurturing it into an infatuation, and finally maturing into something approaching love. All the pathetic plotting on Earth to meet her accidentally, the stupid conversations he'd tried to start, and then the cavalcade of events in that last week before the Q'Roth invaded, when Louise had almost killed Antonia and forced a love confession out of him. It seemed like a dream: someone else's. He ran through various conversations they could have when he got back. It would be awkward, the moment of intimacy gone. But as he towelled himself dry, he realized she was stronger than she appeared, and he reckoned she'd be gone when he returned.

The bed wasn't quite empty. He gathered up the slim sapphire cross and platinum chain lying in the centre of the bed, felt its weight in his hands, then fixed it around his neck. The emotions he'd worried might come, stayed put. He picked up his two bags and headed to the ship.

Zack and the rest of the small crew stood waiting for Micah on the entrance ramp of the towering hexagonal ship. It looked like a shiny black crab. Micah walked through the small throng which parted silently before him. At its head were Vasquez and Kostakis, Rashid behind them. He'd wanted a quick, quiet getaway, but he could tell it wasn't going that way.

Kostakis drew close to the five departees, and addressed the crowd. "Friends, it is customary to christen a ship before it disembarks on a long journey, and this will surely be humanity's longest journey yet." He spoke quieter to Micah, a glint in his eye, as he produced, with a flourish, a bottle of champagne. "Preferably a nice Greek name."

He knew Kostakis must have stolen it from Shakirvasta, somehow. He hefted the bottle in his hands, and addressed the crowd. "People of Esperantia. People of Earth. I had thought about the name Athena, a wise woman to watch over us. But we need to be prepared to show aliens they need to respect us." He took a few steps to the side of the hull of the looming ship, raising the bottle high into the air. "I name this ship Agamemnon." The bottle crashed against the black metal, champagne gushing out to a small cheer from the crowd. He tossed the bottle's broken neck aside, and shook Kostakis' hand. Vasquez came forward carrying a bundle.

"Micah. Your father's jacket. Rashid replaced the nannites with some new ones, which we salvaged from this ship. You may well need them."

He received the coat deferentially, remembering how it had already saved his life back on Earth. "Colonel Vasquez, Rashid, thank you both." Micah wanted to say more, but no words came. In the awkward pause that followed, Antonia walked up to him.

"Bring *everyone* home, Micah."

He met her gaze, and nodded. She moved back into the crowd. He leaned forward, and whispered into Kostakis' ear. "Look after her, Professor."

He looked across the sea of faces, trying to lodge some of them into his memory, though he knew the odds of him making it back were remote. He had to quicken his resolve. He addressed the crowd. "We hope to return, with allies. And a few stories to tell. Please be here when we get back." With that he turned and led the group up the ramp.

Micah lowered himself cautiously into Louise's chair. Zack had mounted his fighter pilot's chair to the right and parallel to Micah's, and Sandy sat in another chair to Micah's left, with Ramires in Jarvik's position. Micah stood up, one hand in each pocket, and faced Hannah.

"Hannah, do you relinquish any and all allegiance to the Alician order?"

She blanched, but nodded, jutting out her chin. "I do."

He clicked the button in his right trouser pocket, and the chrome necklace clamped tight around her neck sprung open and tumbled noisily onto the floor. She swayed slightly, gasping, her hands around her throat. "Thank you," she croaked. She glanced around the room. "You won't regret it, I promise."

Zack shook his head.

Micah nodded and sat down again, facing forward. The viewscreen showed that everyone had moved a safe distance away. He knew the ship was fully prepared, the first set of transits already programmed into the nav system. "Anyone not ready? Okay then..." He paused, and leaned over to Zack, whispering. "What am I supposed to say, exactly?"

"You're the boss, now. You have to decide."

Micah cleared his throat. He remembered an old sci-fi vid he'd watched as a kid. "Okay. Zack – *Jump.*"

As soon as he said it, sitting in Louise's command chair, the puzzle unlocked itself in his mind. *You're the boss, now,* Zack had said. Louise had been the captain of this ship, was Level Five intelligence, as well as a trained Chorazin agent, and should have spotted Hannah's wavering loyalty. And yet she'd walked into a trap. Twice he'd seen her killed. Was it possible she had a back-up plan?

142

But Zack had already slammed the metal ankh, the ship's starter key, into the slot; it was too late to think further on it. Micah and the others held their breath, as everything around them, every contour, every surface and crevice, turned silver, freezing them in space-time as the galaxy slid beneath them.

* * *

A woman's scream of primal rage echoed around the sealed chamber. She choked, her new body not yet fully functional. Vaulting off the table, her legs buckled when they hit the floor, slipping and sliding in the green amniotic fluid. She ended up on her knees and forearms. She screamed again, but it turned into a wail, tears bursting forward. Her fingers clawed at the clammy floor, but the fingernails had not yet grown fully. Her body racked with tremors, her back arched like a hyena. She pounded the floor with her fists, her breath catching in broken rasps. She let it all ride out. She couldn't taste him any longer on her lips, but she remembered. She kissed the floor. The tears started again. She fell asleep, naked on the floor, crying.

Louise sat on the harsh bench. She hadn't eaten in the five days since her wakening and emotional torrent, but felt no hunger. She took stock. Her back-up plan had worked well, but left her emotionally fraught. She tried to recall what she'd been like before Thailand: a young, optimistic, compassionate teacher. But with each day the old sympathetic traits diminished. The emotion gaining ascendancy was anger, along with a grinding thirst for revenge. It didn't surprise her: the regeneration chamber she'd concealed inside the Transport's hidden section was tuned to Q'Roth DNA, their emotional repertoire leaning to the darker end of the sentiment spectrum.

She'd hoped she'd never need the clone, but since discovering the nannites and watching Hannah's moves, she'd uploaded long term memories into its maturing brain each night. She hadn't known how good the final memory transfer would work, but the connecting node implant had triggered in her last moments with Vince. Clone maturation had taken three weeks, but for her, less than a second had passed. She was surprised it had worked at all, and assumed it was because she'd had so much Q'Roth DNA in her already.

Using Q'Roth surveillance gear in the shielded section of the ship, she'd found out what had happened since her demise, and where Micah had gone – at least his initial spatial vector. She lazed in the Q'Roth heat therapy room, sweat trickling off fresh, supple flesh. She'd been studying Q'Roth strategy, now able to read Largyl 6 fluently. Her new body and brain was far more Q'Roth compatible, and she found she could pick up their concepts faster. A diagnostic test confirmed she had passed Level 5 intelligence, and was approaching Level 6.

She pondered her options. She could wage battle here, but even with her new found physical prowess – many of her organs and body parts such as bones, musculature and tendons had been upgraded automatically – she was severely outnumbered, and a transport ship had no weapons. Q'Roth tended to go for genocidal incursions of non-affiliated races, to avoid retribution by survivors or co-dependants. So, if she could find Micah and bring him and the others down, then she could return with the attack ship either alone, or with allies, and stamp out humanity forever. Vince had been the only man she could have dealt with – and tolerated. And he was gone. She would leave only one relic of humanity: a statue of two lovers embracing.

Four engineers sat around a small stove having their night shift snack, on a break from operating the laser drill which was making slow progress on the third level of the transport. Chairman Shakirvasta reckoned there was a hidden chamber behind this wall, perhaps even the engine room.

One of the engineers choked on his soup, as the three heads of his colleagues slipped off their shoulders in mid-conversation, their bodies folding up like rag dolls. Coughing, dropping the bowl to the floor, spilling hot soup down his overalls, he stumbled backwards, panicking. He tripped over a power cable, slapping him face down on the floor. Two boots stood in front of him. He felt a razor cut across the back of his neck, and a warm wet feeling around his throat. He tried to move but nothing happened. His vision faded to black.

Louise executed the half-dozen or more engineers working inside the ship during the night shift. She gathered their bodies on the lower level, found some fuel and set fire to them, watching the funeral pyre burn. It barely sated her need for vengeance. She knew the one person whose death could slake her thirst. The one who had been instrumental in humanity escaping, and the brains behind the twisted assassination which had killed Vince, snatching away her last chance of being human. So be it, she thought, you've made me what I am. You'll reap the whirlwind, Micah. Twice she'd had the opportunity to terminate him. She headed for the bridge.

She closed the external hatches and fed in the coordinates taken by Micah's ship. She checked there were no more humans on board, and dropped the ankh key into the slot. The ship vanished.

* * *

Deep inside the Q'Roth transport, the Hohash replayed what it had witnessed: a solitary female watching a bonfire of corpses, now smoking ash.

Once the transport had been recovered, the Hohash had tried to warn the ones calling themselves human that something was happening inside, but their scanning devices were too archaic, and now they were dead. All hatches had sealed, and the ship was about to transit.

It tried once again, as it had for aeons, to reach its master, but there was no response. And yet it sensed something, perhaps a wakening, the first stirrings from a slumber measuring nearly a million angts. It had been so long without instruction, and Hohash were above all servants, artefacts needing a purpose. It faced two choices: stay on Ourshiwann, or travel with, and confront, this hybrid, warped female. It connected briefly with its comrades to let them know its decision.

It surveyed its surroundings. Everything around it frosted silver in transit mode, which most beings believed was instantaneous. From a conventional space-time perspective, it was. But Hohash were not anchored in normal space-time. Decision made, it headed toward the bridge.

* * *

The Ranger Ukrull paused his omniviewer. This human species had survived and defeated an attack by a new Level 5 species armed with Level 6 technology. This was noteworthy. His claw slid into the glistening slot on the Bartran's back, and the purring ceased immediately. He thought – *encode message to Ranger Grid Sub-Commander 423*. The Bartran's mind became fluid, stretching towards the Grid. The Ranger began:

<ENCODE: WILD SPECIES CALLED HUMAN DEFEATED LEVEL 5 ATTACK: SPECIES FRAGMENT GRIDBOUND IN SP195 CRUISER. GRID INTERCEPTION PREDICTED AT NODE 346A. REQUEST INSTRUCTIONS>

GSC 423 ACKNOWLEDGED – ASSESS SURVIVAL QUOTIENT. ZERO-CONTACT PROTOCOL TILL GRID-LAND. REQUESTING SP195 [Q'ROTH] PRESENCE FOR CONSULTATION.

Ukrull emitted a deep, rock-crushing growl.
<ENCODE: HUMAN-Q'ROTH ARBITRATION SUCCESS PROBABILITY NEGLIGIBLE. ADVISE NON-PRESENCE OF SP195>

OBJECTION NOTED. YOUR OBJECTIVITY QUOTIENT BORDERING TOLERANCE. WISH RE-ASSIGNMENT?

His foot lashed out, crushing a non-essential, self-repairing console. His objectivity was indeed wavering. Pathetic as they were, there was something about this species...
<NEGATIVE... REQUEST PRESENCE AT ARBITRATION>

DENIED. MONITOR NEW SPECIES IN HABITAT.

Ukrull broke off comms. The Bartran vibrated unevenly. *The Hohash.* Ukrull had not yet reported that he had found them – they had been missing for so many millennia – which would land him in trouble with Ranger Prefecture Central sooner or later. What was the Hohash interest in humanity?

Ukrull stroked the Bartran till it purred softly.

PART TWO – THE GRID

GAL-C-017-001: <u>TLA BETH SENSES ONLY</u>: *INTER-GAL FAR STATION 3 CONTACT LOST*
VERIFICATION PROBABILITY: *100%*
INBOUND GENETIC MARKER: *UNKNOWN. KALAHEII SUSPECTED*
THREAT LEVEL: *OCTRINO*
GALACTIC BARRIER INTERCEPT TIME: *0.004637 ANGTS*
MINES / DRONES DEPLOYED: *Y*
GALACTIC BARRIER INTEGRITY: *HIGH*
SPACE-TEAR FIREBREAK / DARK WEAPONS ISSUED & PRIMED: *Y*
EVACUATION PROTOCOL: *LEVEL 12+ ADVISED EXODUS SECTORS RKZ249-UFZ355*
SECURITY CLASSIFICATION: *>12*
EVALUATION: *KALAHEII INVASION FLEET*
DATA RESONANCE DIAGNOSIS: *UNKNOWN WEAPONS CAPABILITY − INTEL NEEDED*
    ACTIONS: *MUSTER SCLARESE NOVASTORMERS; CONVENE TLA BETH WAR COUNCIL; CONTINUE SEARCH FOR KALARASH − ALL RANGERS PRIORITY ONE; OSSYRIANS ASSIST MED-EVAC*

CHAPTER 14 – SEVEN MINUTES

The door irised closed behind Chahat-Me.

"Thank God. At last we can talk in private," Kat said. "I preferred it when she didn't understand our language."

Pierre shifted from one foot to the other, reeling from the information exchange he'd just shared with the Ossyrian. They had only seven minutes, and he had a lot to tell Kat, most of it – no, all of it – bad news from her perspective. At least she can't read my eyes, he thought. He cleared his throat. "We don't have much time, Kat –"

She rounded on him. "Why? I'm pretty fed up with these ultra-fast conversations you two have." Her eyes softened, and she managed a smile. "Girls get jealous, you know."

Her joking made it worse. He decided to deal with the technical aspect first. "She needs to get back to the Grid, and we need to go into stasis. Because of the length of the journey," he lied. *Merde, when did I learn to lie?*

The corners of her mouth flat-lined.

He moved on quickly. Distract. Evade. *Where were these tactics coming from?* "I found out some more things about the Grid, the society."

"Can't it wait? If we only have a few minutes I'd rather –"

"It's important you know now. When we arrive there won't be much time."

She shrugged, and sat facing away from him.

He felt like a bastard. No, he thought, more like a doctor lying to a patient, trying to ease the blow. But he stuck to his course.

"Galactic society is well-orchestrated. It's like a caste system. Most races know their place, their function in society. There are whole races who farm, or fabricate things; other races are predominantly engineers or scientists, or traders or

149

militaristic, in which case they form the police network which maintains order spanning half the galaxy."

Kat stared through the floor.

Pierre cut to the important part. "The caste system is rigorously enforced. Each race can interact with any race its own level or below, but can only address the immediate two levels above its own rank. Courtesy isn't optional: if proper deference and respect isn't observed, the perpetrator is usually recycled."

Kat looked up, her expression a question mark.

"The offending person or group is deconstructed into basic biochemical constituents and used for medical or nutritional purposes." He sighed. "The least infraction can constitute a violation, and if the party concerned is four or more levels above, they don't even have to justify their claim of a '*breach of hierarchy protocol*'. We're going to have to be extremely careful."

Kat pursed her lips. "Then maybe we shouldn't go."

He nodded, and sat next to her. "We can't remain here."

"Why do we need to go into stasis, Pierre?"

He could tell she knew he was keeping something back. Timing was key. He needed to delay it a little longer. "I'm getting there." He leant back against the chamber wall. "Many races aren't satisfied with their status quo. They want what is called Elevation, which means rising to the next level. However, to do so needs two things. The first is education so that the race can take on higher responsibilities, and the second is finding another species to take over their current duties. The latter is the prerequisite to the former, and pretty hard to find, as you can imagine. Even if a petitioner race finds a substitute race it can foster to take its place, the replacement process can take anywhere from several hundred to thousands of years, due to the need to ensure the new race can do the job, and the difficulties of adjusting the new race's culture to their new galactic social role. Also, the educational process of the petitioner race sometimes requires genetic re-structuring of the brain and nervous-endocrine systems, which has to be taken slowly over many generations."

Kat's hand stifled a yawn.

He realised neither of them had slept for two days. That would be fixed soon enough, but he still had to play this out.

"So, some races rebel. Many of them, typically level 4 or 5, are clustered in this region of the Galaxy. To impede proper policing, there are illegal transpatial mines scattered over the whole region, particularly directly between us and the Grid."

Kat raised an eyebrow.

"These mines exist in transpace and lock onto any object traversing it; they home in on it and detonate."

"So, how do we get through them?"

He relaxed a little. Technical ground was easier. "A series of carefully programmed micro-jumps, each lasting about a second, flashing in and out of Transpace. It slows travel down, but it's still infinitely faster than not jumping at all. However, it'll take two months to get there."

"And we need to be in stasis because..?"

"We wouldn't survive otherwise. Neither would Chahat-Me, incidentally. Our nervous systems wouldn't be able to handle it; they'd ... melt."

"I see."

He waited, but she said no more. He knew the gas that would put them to sleep would come very soon. Then Chahat-Me would return to put them into stasis.

"There's one other thing, Kat."

She levered herself up to her feet. The words loitered in his throat, preferring to stay where they were. She approached him, so that he could smell her warm, inviting scent. Maybe he should tell her later...

She spoke softly. "Pierre, tell me right now what is going on, or I'm going to hit you very, very hard."

He stood up, half-nodded, and swallowed. "You're pregnant." He watched her eyes widen, and continued as fast as he could get the words out. "I was sterile, honest, a by-product of my genetic engineering, but when Chahat-Me scanned you, she detected the defective sperm and your ripe ovum and, well ... corrected things..."

For a second, while his heart didn't dare beat, he thought he'd got away with it. Her hand lashed out towards his cheek, but stopped millimetres from him. He hadn't flinched, feeling he'd somehow earned the pain.

She sat back down, then lay back on the bench, hands cradling her belly. She looked down at it.

He didn't know what to say, but couldn't stand the silence. He'd been brought up responsibly. He should, somehow, offer to marry Kat, or look after the child with her, or agree to take on the child alone if that was what she wanted. A badly-mixed cocktail of emotions had been stewing inside him since he'd found out: joy, at not being sterile; confusion over such an event, which should be a happy one, coming during a time when each day surpassed his imagination as to what could happen next; and sadness that his mother would never know her grandchild, or that her son could be a father. Just a few of the ingredients in the emotional punch washing around in his mind.

"Kat, I –"

"Whatever you're about to say, don't. Call Chahat-Me, I know you can."

Pierre turned to the single panel on the wall and gazed into it, imaging the Ossyrian in his mind, and Kat's request.

A hologram appeared, facing Kat. Pierre leant his back against the wall. He guessed his rights in this matter were secondary.

Kat glanced up into the dog-like features, poker-faced. "Chahat-Me: make sure it's a girl."

Chahat-Me nodded, clearly not used to the gesture. The hologram vanished.

"You never dreamed of being a father, Pierre. Well, I can tell you, I *never*, ever thought I'd be a mother. And as for the timing..."

Pierre moved over to her side, and knelt down beside her. He desperately wanted to console her, and to ask why it must be a girl. Now he needed more time, but he heard the susurration of the anaesthetising gas as it entered the room, closing off any further discussion. He had long enough to take her hand in his. Just before he lost consciousness, he felt her squeeze his hand hard.

CHAPTER 15 – QUARANTINE

Louise sprinted the last hundred metres toward the central spiral ramp, pumping her arms, pushing herself to the limit at the end of her morning ten-klick run. As she hit the incline, she powered down to a jog, then a fast walk. She panted. When she reached the next level she paused a moment, catching her breath, bending forward, hands on hips. That feeling had surfaced again during the run, as if someone – something – was watching her. She would do another scan later. Internal sensors hadn't found anything, but they hadn't confirmed definitively that she was alone, either. Bending further, pressing her palms flat on the floor, she pushed her thighs back, elongating her hamstrings so they wouldn't shorten. Her breath back to normal, she straightened up and continued towards her quarters on the Control Room level.

She needed her daily routines – she'd not anticipated it would take two months to track Micah – knowing the transponder code of his ship hadn't helped in the vastness of space. Neither had the fact that they'd not taken a direct route to the Grid, presumably because they weren't experienced with deep space navigation. Or maybe Hannah was responsible, being naturally cautious as any Alician would be with the flight plan. Louise walked faster. *Hannah.* She'd like to have a word with that one, preferably the last word that girl would ever hear. Louise had seen the betrayal coming, but underestimated Hannah's ruthlessness. That wouldn't happen again.

She swung away from her quarters and into the Control Room, draping a towel around her shoulders, mopping up the cooling sheen from her brow. She uttered a Q'Roth syllable and a screen flashed into service, casting jade shadows in the darkened room; she used little light, unafraid of the catacomb-like corridors in the gargantuan ship. She reasoned that if there *was* someone or something else aboard, she didn't need to illuminate herself. Besides, lately she felt more at ease in the dark.

Louise pored over the details on the screen. She'd picked up this particular news squirt two days ago on the local Grid-net: a renegade ship being held at an outlying sub-station. Details were sparse but her Q'Roth-honed instinct suggested it was Micah. It would take three days to get there, and she was concerned he might escape before her arrival. Once he entered the Grid, she might never find him again.

She glanced over the draft message she'd assembled earlier. It had taken all night to get the syntax and deference protocols right. It was a beacon message to any Q'Roth vessels within a hundred light years, letting them know that the renegade ship was a stolen Q'Roth Hunter Class vessel. In return for the information she claimed the right to its crew, preferably alive.

The one problem with the message protocol was that she had no Q'Roth identifier code, so she'd made one up, based on the idiomatic translation of her name. It meant they might not trust the source. But she'd given the hunter's transponder code, which any Q'Roth vessel could verify. Good enough. She said '*transmit*' in Q'Roth. She hoped Micah would still be alive when she arrived.

Her thirst for vengeance had long since condensed into a mission. She was thinking more like a Q'Roth, acting less out of ego need and more out of 'instinctive species survival strategy' – when you attack or cull a species, you go all the way – total eradication. She recalled a Pacific tribe she'd encountered whilst on recon; they'd had the same approach in their wars with neighbouring islands. Not content with killing their enemies, they ate their hearts, to conquer their souls so there could be no retribution, even in the after-life. Like that tribe, Q'Roth warriors relished battle. Louise, too, felt her moment was coming.

Of course if Vince was still alive he'd find a way to stop her, killing her again if he could. But at least he would understand her motives, and in a way, would be impressed by her tactics and her resolve – after all, he'd trained her how to track down an enemy. She smiled, aware it was the first time she'd done so since Vince's death.

She shivered, suddenly cold. *Time to go.* She reached out her hand toward the ankh key, the coordinates already set for the first intercept jump. She paused. The coldness deepened, gravitating to her spine. The tiny hairs on the back of her neck sprang up. Her smile vanished. She held her breath. She remained completely still, not turning around, despite knowing with a primordial certainty that someone, or something, was standing right behind her.

* * *

"I knew Blake's son." Micah fidgeted with a pen – he'd been trying to write his Captain's log when Sandy had arrived at his cabin. He found he had to write it the old-fashioned way, or else he didn't do it. He put the pen down, leaning back in the chair.

Sandy watched him.

Strange how some people instinctively know when to be quiet, he thought, when not to interrupt. "His name was Robert. We were training in the same squadron. On our first recon mission we were captured and air-lifted deep across enemy lines." He recalled the Kurana Bay ghoster facility. He'd only seen it at night. To him, it only existed at night. The memory chilled him. "He didn't make it." That was all the detail he was prepared to disclose.

"Does Blake know you knew his son?"

He sighed. "No." He wasn't sure how Blake would react. Micah had been a witness, after all, though neither Blake nor Zack had recognised him in amongst the other sixteen year olds they'd rescued. He decided to park this for another time. Besides, it wasn't why he'd asked to see Sandy. He cleared his throat.

"I'm losing control of this crew, Sandy." She was the only one he could tell. His eyes drifted to her swelling belly. When they'd arrived it had still been barely noticeable. Now the whole crew knew. Hell, they'd even been suggesting names for it, though he knew the one she would choose. At least her growing foetus was a way of marking time since they'd arrived two months ago and been immediately placed – no, *locked* – into quarantine.

She stroked her stomach idly. He supposed she drew her serenity – a commodity in short supply in the rest of them – from the knowledge that she was doing something purposeful. Funny – at the start of the journey, after the pain of losing Vince, he thought she'd be the first to crack. But after a couple of weeks, she confided in him that a mother-to-be's hormones had their own survival tricks.

"Micah, you're an analyst. It's what you're good at. Enter analyst mode. Work out a resolution."

He frowned. It had occurred to him. But his intuition told him they were screwed, and he didn't want to nail that particular coffin lid down with the weight of a full analysis conclusion. But she was right. As usual.

"Okay," he said. "Just stay with me. I'll vocalise, so you can tell me it's all crap afterwards, and that our glass is actually half-full."

She touched his forearm. "Deal."

He stood up and checked the cabin door was closed, not that anyone was likely to come in. Everyone stayed in their own cabins these days. He punched a pillow into a squat cushion, the closest he could get to the zafu he used to meditate on at home, and manoeuvred into a cross-legged, half-lotus position. He closed his eyelids, and began the breathing routine to connect the less-accessible, intuitive depths of the right brain, with the cold, unequivocal logic of the left. He visualised his corpus callosum as a rift between two mesa's that were the left and right hemispheres, and flooded the valley with a soft white mist from which the thought process began to precipitate, the slow drips of ideas pooling into a stream of consciousness that would surge towards an unassailable conclusion, given the data available at the current time.

He began to vocalise, the words arriving from the right-brain before the left could edit them, so that he heard them as if someone else was speaking in his voice.

"Outer reach of the Grid; negligible knowledge of species, societal structure, customs, rules or language; understanding of Grid simplistic. Arrival at location apparently called Outer Feeder Sub-Station 13765-Alpha Dextrea – language approximation only – initial communication burst unintelligible; vessel controls taken over, brought into orbit above ringed gas giant; massive orbital space-station complex visible, all attempts at communication blocked or ignored. Visited twice by cylindrical holographic avatar; explored the ship, scanned crew, then left, no interaction. Ship immobile, unable to jump or move; weapons system blocked except torpedoes Zack rigged for manual targeting. Rations and water supplies will last one more month thanks to recycling. Crew in state of subdued high tension; Zack and Hannah of most imminent danger to each other; alien intentions unclear; most probable hypothesis quarantine; second hypothesis aliens have contacted nearest Q'Roth party to intercept since in Q'Roth vessel. Current mission success probability very low; survival prospects very low; situation characterisation: quietly catastrophic."

His eyes flickered open, and accommodated to see Sandy's face in stark relief in the harsh Agamemnon lighting. Her tranquility that had been there moments before morphed into a grimace. She stood up. "Christ, Micah, you really know how to depress a pregnant woman, don't you?"

She stormed out.

"Thanks Sandy," he said to the closed door. "Couldn't have faced it without you."

He took a hot shower. Oddly enough he felt better: bleak situations were familiar territory to him. Besides, now there was no thread of hope, his way forward was clear; his way backwards, in truth. Shakirvasta had been right after all. They stood no chance out here. They couldn't even manage basic communications. It had been stupid, hubris all over again. He hoped they could at least get back in one piece, and that Josefsson's ego hadn't already ruined humanity's second chance.

As the water sprayed over his naked body, he remembered all the faces when they'd left Ourshiwann – the hope he'd seen there which would now be squashed. It would also be tough returning personally – the triumvirate of Shakirvasta, Josefsson and Jennifer would feast on his humiliation. He wasn't Blake. For a while he'd felt stronger, the man he'd always wanted to be, but out here he was powerless, unable to lead while they were stuck. A leader must act, and there was nothing he could do.

He didn't see how Blake would fare any better. The aliens were probably right to quarantine them. Maybe it was safer all around.

He reached the bridge to find everyone else already there. Zack hunkered in his pilot's seat immersed in a data cloud which he guessed controlled the weapons cache. Ramires and Sandy were huddled over a comms unit, trying to figure out the latest burst of data that had arrived in translucent rotating cubes of rust-coloured serif-like digits. Every now and again symbols would illuminate or change colour. Once, two entire cubes merged and spawned four smaller ones. He and Hannah agreed it was some form of matrix coding in three dimensions, possibly four, since the timing of the cubes' interactions appeared to matter. It was like an IQ test, and they were failing dismally. Worse still, he suspected this was a rudimentary level of communication.

Hannah's flaxen hair draped over her console as she hunched over her screen on its pedestal – making him think of a wild, long-necked bird stooped on its perch. Not unattractive, actually ... he shook himself mentally. What was he thinking?

He strode past her and stood by his Captain's chair, facing them all, and waited. No one had noticed his arrival. Oh well, he thought, here goes.

"Could you listen up, please, I've made a decision."

One by one, the heads lifted and turned in his direction. He realised how much he hated being in the spotlight. Some are born to lead, his father had once lectured him, and some are not. He took a breath. "We –"

"– have company," Hannah finished.

Micah and the others stared in her direction, then, seeing it was not a joke, whirled into activity. Within seconds everyone was at their post, infused with adrenaline. He didn't know what to say, but a single word escaped nonetheless. "Report!"

Hannah: "Single ship, small transport most likely, off our starboard, approaching the docking bay."

Zack: "Targeted their forward hull with two torpedoes."

Sandy: "No comms yet."

Ramires: "Visual image coming on-line... *now*."

They turned as one to the large screen directly in front of Micah. A dark, circular shadow approached, discernible only by its obscuration of the stars behind it.

"Any chance of lighting it up?" Micah ventured.

"Hang on," Ramires said, activating a touch-panel. "There!"

Nobody spoke, they just stared. Micah had seen plenty of cool ship designs in vids and games, but this wasn't just the latest fluidic-chip maxi-sense holo-vid: this was real. And it was much, much better.

The approaching ship was somewhere between an elongated cone and a javelin, the sleek outer hull laced with metallic scarlet and purple shades rippling from the tip back to the aft section. Its texture reminded him of a moonlit lake, but its sleek lines suggested power, and above all, speed. It was hard to gauge the size, but as it approached Hannah filled them in.

"It's a Scintarelli Star-piercer, according to the onboard database, Level Eight design, about two hundred meters in length, minimal jump drive, built for interstellar non-Transpace flight. Crew complement two, registering as Mannekhi, a Level Five race."

Micah tore himself away from the screen to face her. 'Two?'

She nodded assiduously.

It was hard to imagine such a big ship housing just two... But then, he reminded himself, he had no idea what size or shape those crew members might be.

He watched as the craft pivoted effortlessly towards them.

"Just say the word, skipper," Zack said, a single finger poised above back-lit touch-screen pads.

He shook his head. If it was an attack, surely their moves would be more aggressive? Maybe they could fire some kind of warning shot. But it was getting closer with every second.

"We're receiving a signal," Sandy said.

He prayed it was not another data matrix ballet.

"Audio only."

They all turned to Sandy then the screen. Micah wondered what it might sound like. English was the last thing he expected.

"Power down your weapons. We're coming aboard. We're here to help you."

Zack retracted his finger, and stood up. "This I've gotta' see. An English-speaking alien." He paused as his gaze met Micah's. "If it's okay with you, boss?"

Micah felt stunned: English, and an offer of help. "Okay, Zack, you and Ramires take the pulse rifles and meet our ... guests. Sandy and Hannah..." He stopped himself as he surveyed the intense faces around him. He grinned. "What am I saying? Let's all go, there's nothing much we can do from here anyway."

Zack placed a conciliatory hand on his shoulder as they trotted down the rampway. "Don't sweat it. The rifles were a good call."

Hannah stood next to the airlock controls. "They're inside, and pressure is equalised, same oxygen-nitrogen mix as here, no bio-threats detected."

Micah wished the airlock had a portal so he could see the creatures before opening the hatch. Zack and Ramires stood at either side, rifles aimed at the grey-green metal archway.

"Open it," he said.

There was a short hiss and a dull rumble, like a train carriage on tracks, as the door swung aside into a recess. A sheen of water vapour lingered in the air, then dissipated like wisps of dew in the morning sunlight. Micah's eyes narrowed, then widened.

A lean, muscled woman in her thirties, completely bald, with sharp jade-coloured eyes, stepped toward them, looked straight at Micah, ignored the rifles, and held out her hand. "Angelica Rushton, you can call me Angel. Nice to meet you."

Zack lowered his rifle. Ramires didn't.

Micah gingerly met her hand, and shook it. "Micah Sanderson. How –"

"And this is Starkel." She jerked a thumb behind her, as the second airlock occupant stepped out of its shadow. Zack's rifle jerked back into readiness as the tall, black-clad figure glided into view, silent as a zero-G dancer, and muscled to boot. Micah's instincts told him to be very careful, even before he noticed that the man's eyes – irises included – were pure black.

"It's okay everybody," Angel said, "he's eaten." She turned to Zack. "Speaking of which, and I know this is going to sound weird, but do you have any meat onboard? You know, honest-to-God meat?"

It went smoother from there.

Micah pushed his plate aside. Angel's gusto for their food rations had been infectious, and he'd eaten more than he had in weeks. She seemed to him completely self-unconscious, not caring an iota what anyone thought of her, not scarred by emotional baggage like the rest of them. He found it refreshing.

She tossed the last chicken bone onto her plate – completely denuded, bones cracked and the marrow sucked out. The rest of the crew had politely and patiently deferred to him to ask the questions.

"Angelica, how –"

"Angel, call me Angel, everyone does, you know." She beamed.

He glanced at Sandy. "Okay, Angel. How... How the hell did you get out here? And actually, we don't know anything."

She kicked back in the chair, planted her boots of indeterminate material onto the metal table, and interlaced her fingers behind her head, flicking her tongue around her teeth, trying to flush out any last morsels. "Long story. The Games. Are you here for the Games?"

Micah and the rest looked from one to the other.

"Evidently not. But you're on a Q'Roth Hunter Class vessel, here at the edge of the Grid, in one of the prime sub-stations for the Final Round."

Micah shook his head. "Angelica ... Angel, we have no idea what you're talking about. Well, except the Q'Roth part. We stole this ship, after..." He stopped mid-sentence. He'd been watching her casual mannerisms since she'd arrived, and something had nagged at him ever since. He'd slipped into passive analyst mode during the past three quarters of an hour, and had synched an irrevocable conclusion: *she doesn't know*; doesn't know what has happened to Earth. Sandy started to say something, but Micah cut in.

"When did you leave Earth?" he asked. His crew tensed. He focused on Angel.

She rocked forward, swallowed the last morsel, and clasped her hands together on top of the table. "Two years ago. Why? When did you leave?"

"Hey," Zack said, "she –" the rest of the sentence mutated into a grunt, Micah guessing because Sandy had kicked his shin under the table.

Micah's mind snapped into overdrive: he didn't know these two, or how they might react to finding out Earth had been destroyed. He reminded himself that although she looked human, and certainly the chicken-fest had been an impressively concrete demonstration, it could still be some elaborate ploy; the fate of the remnants of humanity and, most important, their existence and location, had to be carefully-guarded.

Micah elaborated the truth. "We came into contact with the Q'Roth a few months ago. They wreaked a lot of havoc before this ship was captured. I guess we were lucky they were just a scouting party." There, that should suffice.

Starkel got up from his chair at the far end of the table, with an air of smouldering impatience. "How did you overcome the Mortix internal defence system?"

Shit! Micah felt his face begin to redden.

Hannah folded her arms. "Chameleon-DNA combined with fractal narrow-range EM bursts."

Starkel leaned on his fists on the table, glaring at Hannah. "Then how did you repair the neural structure afterwards?"

Micah's blush dissipated. It was like watching a lunar-style tennis match, with particularly hard hitters.

"Nannites," Hannah parried.

"Hey, guys," Angel jumped in, "look, we don't have to trust each other, and we don't have enough time to make it worthwhile in any case." She eyed Starkel from her reclined position. "These are *my* people, remember? Let me handle it, okay?"

Starkel stood straight, solid as a sculpture, still aiming his attention at Hannah.

Angel spread her hands. "So, I got hijacked from Earth two years ago by Starkel and another Mannekhi called Torrann." Her eyes glazed over. She laughed, and leaned toward Sandy, not that the two had said a word to each other yet. "Do yourself a big favour, don't ever fall for an alien." She ran her fingers over her scalp.

160

"In any case, there's some things you guys need to know, because you're obviously new out here, and frankly you won't last five minutes unless you know the basic rules."

Micah started to speak but Angel shushed him with such an easy grace he didn't doubt that even Blake would have been silenced.

"Just listen, there isn't much time. We've travelled for a whole week to get here, since they posted your DNA on the Grid-net. And we totalled the Q'Roth envoy who was recalled to salvage this vessel you stole." She made a mock bow in Zack's direction. "Yeah, yeah, thanks can come later, I'll give you my Mom's address for the flowers." She stood up, and began counting on her fingers. "Rules not to be toyed with: number one, you always need to know what level a race is. Two levels up or any level below you can address them. More levels above and you're toast, no questions asked, no right of appeal."

Micah tried again to speak but Angel kept talking. "You'll all need shrouders – we brought some with us – they keep all your exhaled air, body odour and shedding flesh inside a contained area about ten centimetres from your body, and will prevent any alien's toxic, residual epidermis from entering your own body." She glanced around at each of them. "Aliens are alien; sounds trite, I know, but sometimes you'll be awed, sometimes you'll be disgusted, your flesh will crawl, or you'll just plain puke."

As she continued with a long list of rules on how not to be pulped, Micah realised that underneath her flippant façade was a disciplined mind. He didn't see how she'd survived this long otherwise, the only human amidst a galaxy of aliens. He had to admit that she also had their rapt attention after being starved of information for two months.

She finally paused, narrowing her eyes at all of them. She turned to Starkel, who hadn't moved a centimetre. "We can give them a ball, can't we? Otherwise we might as well kill them now, it'd be kinder." She swivelled back to Zack. "Relax, big boy, just messing." She turned to Micah. "Not all races use auditory language, quite a few use multi-dimensional mathematical constructs – roughly speaking, the higher the race, the more dimensions and parallel processing." She shook her head. "They also think faster: we're hillbillies to some, ants to others."

Micah's earlier thoughts of retreat to Ourshiwann resurfaced.

"Oh, I nearly forgot. I mentioned, the Games, didn't I. Starkel?"

Starkel unfolded his arms. His voice boomed around the room. "Once every five thousand of your Earth years races below Level Seven have the chance to leapfrog the usual patronage system. A maximum of one hundred alien species compete in this spiral arm, each submitting a small team in what you might call a treasure hunt. Only one team will survive, and that team's species is progressed at a much faster rate, say five hundred years to elevate to the next level, under the protection of a Level Eight species.'

'You're one of the teams,' Sandy said.

Angel mock-bowed. "Well, Starkel is really. We decided the less the galaxy knows of Earth the better."

"How are you doing?" Micah asked.

Her lips stretched into a forced smile. "We're still alive. There's a Q'Roth team... Vicious bastards. One of them took Torrann's head. We're trying to get it back." She glazed into silence. Sandy leaned across the table so that her fingertips touched Angel's hand. Angel looked at Sandy as if remembering something, then sat down. "It's all in the ball, the rules, that is. What are you doing out here anyway?'

Micah's words stalled, all except one. "Allies."

She studied him. "What do you think, Starkel?"

"I think they should run home as fast as possible."

Micah wanted to say there is no home anymore. But he couldn't. "Look, Earth is worried. If the Q'Roth come back..."

Angel turned to Starkel. "Help them, Starkel. Please."

He stared at her with an intensity Micah couldn't interpret.

"Head to Grid Central Station 359A. There's a Ranger outpost there. Any race of any level can approach them, although they're somewhat temperamental. Never stand behind one, their tails are mean. Here," he tossed Micah a glass ball the size of an orange. It was heavier than it looked.

"It's a basic translation globe," Angel said. "It's been probing all of you since we arrived, and asked for you, Micah." She leaned forward conspiratorially and whispered, "You're honoured, trust me." Then she beamed at all of them, so that they didn't react as she produced a gun from her boot and aimed it at the crew – except Micah – across the table. "Don't move, this is normal. Sorry, Micah, this is going to hurt a little. Well, a lot actually."

Micah stared at her nonplussed, and tried to get up. He realised he couldn't feel his right hand, the one that held the crystal orb. He tried to let go, then reached over with his other hand to pluck it away, cursing himself immediately as his left hand stuck to its surface and began to numb.

"Everyone does that. Funny, really," Angel said.

"This *isn't* funny, Angel," Sandy said, glaring.

"Yes, I know, but either you high-tail it to Earth or one of you gets the resident. It won't harm him. I have one, you see."

Micah felt like he was drowning while people sat around watching him. His whole body had turned numb, and was now heating up. He couldn't move.

"It's okay to scream, Micah, it'll get really painful, but then it will pass, and there'll be no damage."

He found it hard to breathe as his lungs began to lock. He vaguely saw two flashes of a pistol Starkel produced with lightning speed, and heard two thumps to his right. His vision blurred and he heard white noise increasing in loudness and pitch, while his skin burned. He was sure he was on fire, though his eyes couldn't move to check, and he smelt no burning flesh. Although his body wanted to scream, all that came out was a stuttering groan. He thought he would pass out with the pain, and then wished he could pass out just in order to stop it. And then, abruptly, as if a switch flicked, it was gone. He gasped. "Oh my God!" He could move again, and checked his limbs for burnt flesh, but they looked completely normal. "Hey, I think I'm alright," he said, and promptly threw up.

"That's normal," Angel said, placing her pistol against her boot where it melded into the fabric and disappeared. "Sorry about that, but you'll now see why."

Starkel still had his pistol level with the rest of the table. He addressed Micah. "You now have a resident inside you. It's a piece of Level Seven biotech only legal for Levels 5 and above – you don't qualify, so you must conceal that you have it or pretend you are Mannekhi."

"What does it do?" Micah said, wiping away dregs of vomit from his mouth with his sleeve.

"It is a communications device, but much more. Look at me."

Micah was looking at him already, but as he focused, thoughts unfolded in his mind: *Mannekhi, Level 5, male, central planet Grondsvissigen in Spiral sector –*' He looked away and it ceased. He looked back at Starkel, normally, and 'heard' nothing. On instinct he regarded the pistol and emptied his mind: *Mannekhi Crasson multi-purpose sidearm; seven levels, set to stun, recently fired twice, 89% charged, four hundred rounds minimum remaining.* "Shit," he said. The wonder outranked the pain he'd just been through. He felt a wave of elation – this could be the key, their passport to the Grid. "Awesome!" He grinned and turned back to the others: Sandy and Hannah were staring at him, Zack and Ramires were on the ground, coming round. Sandy regarded him warily.

"What?" he said.

Hannah spoke up first. "Starkel was speaking in an alien language. You replied in the same language."

"We can only spare one resident," Angel said, "and it's now bonded to Micah."

Zack and Ramires got back to the table, wincing with the effort. "You are very quick, Mr. Starkel," Ramires said.

"Evolutionary necessity. On our home planet we have very fast predators."

Micah saw Zack about to say something, but didn't want to get into a pissing contest when things were finally turning around. "It's okay, this – ball – is going to be very useful. I'd decided earlier to abandon our mission and head back to ... the others, but now we have a chance."

Zack butted in. "Got any fancy weapons we could borrow?"

Angel leaned back, and for the first time Micah saw the edges of darkness around her eyes. "Our whole ship is a weapon, actually: organic metal, can pierce anything."

The way she said it, Micah knew they had it for a very specific purpose, though he had no idea what it could be.

She stood up. "Well, it's been great, and not just the chicken. Now we really have to go, and so do you by the way – there's another Q'Roth hunter-destroyer inbound, one hour out. They've been tracking us down for two months, and they're hunting you too, now. So we need you to do us a favour." She glanced at the ball and Micah.

He shrugged, more than a little incredulously. "Sure," he said, "why ever not?"

"Thanks, all of you. Sorry about our uninvited party tricks, but you may as well get used to it – the Grid Hierarchy is brutal, and what I did to you is like a snowflake on the tip of the iceberg, if you know that quaint old pre-War expression." She smiled, ignoring the stares from everyone. "Starkel has cleared you from quarantine so you can leave as soon as you're ready, just place that little ball on your nav console and it'll do the rest. We're asking you to wait until the other Q'Roth vessel arrives. As soon as it is in transit range your ball will jump you out of here."

"And you'll be..?" Zack asked.

"Far, far away, Zack. But don't worry. We've planted a jump mine on your hull. When you jump it will release and then attach to the other vessel as soon as it tries to follow you."

"Then what happens?" Micah asked, not sure he wanted to know.

Starkel answered. "You'll exit the jump, they won't. If you leave before they arrive, you won't exit the jump."

Angel shrugged. "Sorry – *again*. Funny – it's been so long since I've had to use that word. This galaxy isn't that big on sympathy, I'm afraid. Anyway, we're going to leave you some kit. And we both hate the Q'Roth don't we?"

Micah held up his hand. "Alright. We'll do it."

She looked as if she was going to offer her hand to Micah, but instead nodded to all of them, and without another word she headed for the exit, to the sounds of chairs raking across the floor as the others got up.

Starkel held up his arm, blocking her exit. "Just one more thing," he said, producing a different pistol from somewhere inside his tunic.

Micah focused on it, letting the translation globe do its job. Starkel's pistol was a molecular disruptor. It had only one setting. Everyone else stood perfectly still. Good, he thought, nobody move.

Angel frowned at Starkel, placing her hands on her hips. "What in Orion's belt, Starkel –"

"The one called Hannah has Q'Roth DNA." Starkel said, pistol aimed at Hannah's head. "You'll be dead before you reach them," he added to Zack and Ramires, who were both edging towards their weapons.

Micah and Sandy exchanged glances. He looked pleadingly to Angel, but she silenced him with a raised hand, her face set in stone. Her stare towards Hannah rippled with a space-cold hatred.

"Sorry, Micah, but Starkel can smell these things – Mannekhi and Q'Roth are blood enemies you see. And if she has Q'Roth DNA in her, then it's just a matter of time before she develops their nasty, aggressive tendencies. Frankly, if Starkel is correct, then I'm right behind him in the queue to vaporise her sorry ass."

CHAPTER 16 – SNOW

Blake's eyes flickered open to find Sonja's dark face, haloed by tight black curls, staring down at him. She had a look he judged to be somewhere on the tightrope between fragile hope and outright desperation. She placed an index finger vertically across pursed lips. He felt like his head was full of wet cement. But the fact that she was telling him to be quiet caused his military instincts to kick in. He tried in vain to remember where he'd been before here, but it would wait. Blake trusted Sonja almost as much as he trusted Zack. Something snagged his mind when he thought of Zack – it was like a curtain, impervious. That would have to wait too, then.

Four large hooks protruded from the ceiling, and he recalled Antonia describing one of the spider dwellings in the city of Esperantia; so he was still on Ourshiwann. Rashid appeared, his tan features in stark contrast to his *dolphin* – a band of rainbow-tinted silver running around his head at eye level, obscuring his empty sockets. Blake had seen plenty before on soldiers who'd lost their sight in the War. The headband allowed detailed sonar perception of objects, based on dolphin physiology. The irony was, he recalled, that the nuclear War raised the ocean temperature so that krill and other plankton disappeared. Most dolphins and cetaceans followed shortly afterwards.

Sonja and Rashid man-handled him into a lev-chair. At first he instinctively tried to resist, then help, and finally he just gave up: his muscles were either damaged or atrophied due to lack of use. Taking the more optimistic of the two, it meant he'd been out for a long time; he reckoned a couple of months. Now that he knew he would be a passive participant in this event, his mind started to assemble the recent, or maybe not so recent, past. There was going to be a battle. He and Zack were in the Hohash craft, with the bomb. He remembered fighting Louise, struggling with her, she'd been stronger than he'd imagined. Then he'd blacked out. That was it, nothing more. Zack must have been knocked out or killed by Louise. The fact that Sonja was here instead of Zack was ominous. But whatever had happened, that any of them were here at all meant that Louise hadn't been able to carry out her threat. Humanity had prevailed. A gust of relief swept over him, and no small amount of pride in mankind's resilience.

Rashid walked on ahead as Sonja steered him from behind, the chair skimming a few centimetres above the ground down a dimly-lit tunnel. Blake saw two bodies, guards from the look of them, lying prostrate on the ground. As his eyes accommodated to the mustard light, he detected a carotid pulse in the neck of one of them. Good, he thought, it seems whatever has passed, we're not yet in outright civil war.

Darkness loomed ahead. They set off at a brisk pace across a plaza he didn't recognise. Sonja shoved him forward on the chair, and then he was startled as they emerged from the portico to find it snowing, but the snow was tinged cyan, an almost fluorescent lagoon blue. A few splotches landed on his cheeks and hands. It tingled, astringent at first, then numbed. He managed to turn his palms upwards, trying to catch snowflakes. Sonja placed a wide-brimmed hat on his head. At first he wasn't sure why, guessing it was to stop the flakes going into his eyes. The snow looked so peaceful, so calming, but had an eerie feel to it, underlined as deep stinging pains spread in his hands and cheeks. He now knew why it was so quiet outside, this snow was perfect cover; no one would be out unless there was a good reason. It wouldn't be good to get drunk and fall asleep in this weather.

Sonja sped up, joining Rashid on the other side of the plaza, where another man pushed out a skimmer. It was the same one he and Kat had ridden across Eden's desert: the scarring on the sleek two-person hover-bike from the neutralino explosion was unmistakable. But all those events – the Hohash blowing up Rashid's ship in order to kill a few Q'Roth; finding the underground lair brimming with hatching Q'Roth; and fighting the Q'Roth with nukes back on Eden – it all seemed a lifetime ago.

Sonja and Rashid helped him into an all-terrain jumpsuit and onto the skimmer's pillion seat. They strapped a full-face visor and gloves onto him, and he found his muscles began to cooperate, remembering how to work. He tested his mouth – it moved, but his larynx didn't – as if he'd forgotten how to speak. Just as well: Rashid and Sonja said goodbye, with a long kiss. She whispered something to him. Blake stared straight ahead, as Sonja came over to him, and saw his jaw set in stone.

"Don't judge me too soon. A lot of bad things have happened. And Zack..." She touched his unresponsive shoulder. "Never mind. Now you're back, the tide will turn."

She made to leave, as Rashid climbed onto the seat in front of him.

With a supreme effort of will, he rasped one word. "Glenda."

Sonja drew back. Rashid answered, without turning around. "She is safe. You will see her soon."

Blake took little comfort from those words – Sonja's expression told him a different story. The skimmer rose knee-height off the ground and accelerated through the houses and domes of Esperantia, whisking past in a blur of blue snowflakes and darkness – Rashid had no need of light.

They drove through the night into the scrubland, slowing down only once, as they passed a statue. Rashid turned on the skimmer's headlights for a few seconds. Blake recognised the features of Vince and Louise locked in an embrace, and wondered how long he had been out. It flashed across his mind that perhaps he was still deep in a coma, dreaming, but he dismissed it – the stinging pain in his hands, now stretching up into his forearms like clawing roots of ice, suggested otherwise. A short while ago he'd been elated – humanity had survived. Now he had more questions than he thought there could possibly be good answers for.

After an hour's riding at top speed, the engine's whine stuttered into a low growl. Rashid braked hard and slewed the skimmer around a rocky outcrop, entering a small cavern at the foot of one of the low mountains. Blake had most of his muscle control back, but stayed immobile while Rashid powered the bike down and dismounted. The cavern was room-sized, a pool of stagnant water in the middle. Rashid activated a small black box, and yellow lights dappled the solid rock walls, casting eerie shadows.

Rashid took off his helmet and eyed him from a safe distance. "You should have muscle control by now," he said. "Remember I was a paramedic too. So, the fact that you are acting as if you do not, means you do not trust me right now."

Blake creaked an arm upwards and flicked up his visor. He recalled the first time he'd trusted Rashid. "Do you blame me?"

"Not at all. But there is much to tell, Commander."

"No offence, Rashid, but I'd like to hear it from Glenda. Or Zack." He noticed Rashid pause in reaction to the second name.

"You do not remember?"

Blake eased off his helmet with difficulty. It got stuck halfway, and Rashid had to yank it off for him. Rashid unfastened the straps and Blake half-fell off the bike with a groan – he'd intended to dismount alone, but was glad for Rashid's helping hands.

"You will make a full recovery, but Zack... Please, Commander tell me what you remember. Everything."

He told him what he remembered, then Rashid told him Zack's version of events, and filled him in on the fatal encounter between Louise and Vince, the rapid political ascendance of Josefsson and Shakirvasta, and Micah and Zack's departure.

Blake brooded for a long time, while Rashid used a field stove to boil water and make tea.

"It wasn't Zack's fault," Blake said, finally. But he heard the tinge of anger in his own voice. He raised his hand to touch his throat, where Zack had caused a micro-stroke; Rashid had said it had been repaired since. He told himself again – *it wasn't his fault* – and this time expunged all anger. He recalled Zack pulling him out of the nightmare that had been Kurana Bay. That did the trick. He added, "Nothing to forgive."

Rashid paused, teapot in one hand, cup in the other. "Now I am blind, I hear things more clearly. Normally, I have to sift carefully for the truth... Your integrity has been missed."

Blake accepted a cup of steaming chai. "So, what happened after Micah and the others left?"

Rashid sat down cross-legged, blowing across the top of his tea. He took a sip, then set down the antique china cup, the same one Blake had seen on Eden when he first met Rashid. The Indistani's dolphin glistened as he faced Blake with uncanny accuracy. "When we left Eden, Commander, I had hoped for a turning point. But it seems we brought our darkness with us."

* * *

"How exactly did he escape?" Shakirvasta's voice clawed at the air, like fingernails etching gravestone marble. Marvin Klempfer, Ourshiwann's second Chief of Police in a month, shifted uneasily.

"They... must have planned this for a long time."

"They?"

"Yes, well, there must have been many. And they will pay when we find out exactly who it was."

"Who it was?"

The man's face flushed. "Obviously we have suspicions, but we need evidence."

"Evidence?"

The man wrung his hands. He stopped talking.

Shakirvasta tapped the end of a cheroot, the ash tumbling onto the floor. He took a long draught of the cigarillo, inhaling deeply so that its end blazed. "What do you think, my sweet?"

Jen appeared from behind a wooden screen decorated with semi-clad Indistani women. Barefoot, she wore a turquoise kimono. "I think anyone would be pleased to do their civic duty."

Klempfer, standing to attention, kept his eyes on Shakirvasta.

"Well put," Shakirvasta said. He eyed Klempfer. "Well?"

Marvin's eyebrows knitted together. "Right. Right away, then. We'll bring some people in –"

"To help us with our enquiries."

Marvin nodded, and backed away to the door, then slipped out into the night.

Jen sidled up to Shakirvasta. "Remind me why exactly you gave an ex-cyberspace security hound the job of Chief of Police? He's clearly an imbecile."

Shakirvasta sat down and pulled Jen around so that she sat atop his bony knees.

"Good people aren't hard to find, they're just hard to manage."

She cocked her head. "Do you manage me?"

"Barely."

She smiled, kissed him on the cheek, and walked over to the oval window, staring out at the snow.

"You miss him, don't you?"

"Who?" she said.

Shakirvasta said nothing.

"It was Dimitri's choice to go off on his quest to find other spider cities. It's a luxury I decided I could not afford – we, humanity, couldn't afford."

He stubbed out the dying cheroot, crushing the last embers of light. "Your new defence corps. How are they coming along?"

She turned back to him. "Ready for some field practice, I'd say."

"Blake is out there. I doubt he is in the city. You know, if he comes back, there's a chance he could gain popularity again."

Her glow faded. She folded her arms. "He should join us in the fight. Seek out the Alicians and destroy them, before they find us again."

"Agreed, he should. Humanity is working out nicely here: people are finding their way either in farming, services, or in your little army. It would be a shame to upset the balance."

Jen thrust an arm outside, so that snowflakes danced on her fingers.

"My sweet, I wish you would not do that."

She continued, until the pain began. She retracted her arm, and swept back into the room, casting off her kimono before she reached the screen. Shakirvasta listened to the snapping buckles of her commando gear and boots.

She reappeared, Valkyrie-like, fully armed. "Later," she said.

He knew that most people would have waited until after the snow had stopped. He recalled one of his father's epithets: *A good horse runs at the sight of the whip.* Sometimes you don't find good people, he thought, but the right people: so much easier. He lit another cheroot.

As it too came to an end, Josefsson arrived, brushing the blue snow noisily from his raincoat with thick gloves, ignoring the mess it made on the floor.

"You know Blake is gone, of course. If he comes back, rallies people around him..." He took off his raincoat and draped it over the wooden screen. One of the semi-clad ladies began to melt under the acid snow.

Shakirvasta stared at the irreplaceable art dissolving for a moment, then looked at Josefsson. "Yes: our brave new world could falter. Order would be replaced by liberal democracy; society would fall apart within a year. Humanity would disappear into the mire. The feudal system we have re-introduced, with wise but firm overlords, is the best basis for humanity to get back on its feet again." He studied Josefsson, but the latter's expression had not changed. "Don't worry, Jen has gone to look for him."

Josefsson jabbed a finger in Shakirvasta's direction. "You put too much trust in that girl. She could turn again, you know, you mark my words!"

He watched as twin spirals of smoke snaked around each other in the cool night air, circling but never mixing; like Jen and Josefsson. "I always mark your words, believe me." But he also hedged his bets, and he had put Jen in charge of the military. He stubbed out the cheroot. "Some of my men will be with her, just in case she suffers a crisis of conscience."

* * *

"What about Vasquez?" Blake railed - his earlier state of epiphany, based on humanity's survival and defeat of Louise, had quickly foundered, dragging him downward into political quicksand.

"The military was disbanded, and Colonel Vasquez and a contingent of his men were sent on a six-month exploration of the far reaches of the main continent."

"Kostakis, then? Antonia?" Blake was running out of options.

Rashid retained his equanimity, making Blake feel all the worse. "The Professor went to search for other spider cities after Jennifer headed up a new militia, reporting directly to Chairman Shakirvasta."

"*Chairman?*"

"Antonia remains within the Council, our only firm ally there. She has a hard time of it but knows that while she stays she can curb some of the excesses. New laws are passed every week, ever more stringent, centralising power and crushing dissent. People occasionally disappear, followed by announcements that they have gone on survey missions."

Blake paced the small cavern. His heart thumped loudly in his veins. He'd had enough. He pressed his eyes closed, then thought of his priorities. And there lay the solution, he realised. *His* priorities, not 'the people's'. His heart eased off.

"So, Glenda is in this new central complex at the heart of the city?" He picked up and checked the pulse rifle: fully charged.

"It is not so simple. The city is effectively under martial law."

"She's my wife, and neither of us is technically a prisoner, right?"

Rashid sighed, and hung his head. "Your good wife told me to give you a message, if you became..."

"Difficult?" He rammed the rifle into the one of the skimmer's gun slots.

"She said use it only as a last resort, to stop you doing something ... foolish."

"Rashid, after what I've been through – after what we've all been through – I can't just leave her there. Even if Shakirvasta takes me prisoner, I'll be closer to her." He parked the second pulse rifle in the remaining gun slot. "Coming?"

Rashid squatted down. His hand glazed across the sandy floor. "Please, reconsider. At least, let us form a strategy, gather support. Give time for the rumours of your escape to reach the population and let Shakirvasta's true nature be exposed by his actions."

Blake felt the anger brewing inside him like a thunderstorm. He'd not given up everything just so Shakirvasta and his cronies could turn their new society into a dictatorship, with people working the land as effective forced-labour or as minions in 'services'. And as for Jennifer – how had he misjudged her so? But he recognised a deeper seat to his anger. His mentor, General Kilaney, had warned him about it. He'd said that given enough time, every career soldier, at least once, will seriously question if the people he's prepared to fight and die for are worth it. He realised he was boiling inside that particular crucible right now. He'd done his part, freed people from the Alician menace, only to see them hand power to a megalomaniac. How could they be so stupid? The only person he wanted to save now was Glenda. Nothing else, and no one else, mattered.

"Sorry, Rashid, but I'm done with saving other people all the time. I went to Eden knowing my wife had terminal cancer, knowing I might never see her again. Then I ran a suicide mission against Louise, saying goodbye to Glenda *again*. And now she's a prisoner. This is personal, Rashid, I'm done being the Commander; I just want to save my wife, you understand that, don't you?" He knew damn well Rashid understood – Rashid had gone to Eden leaving his wife behind, never to see her again. Blake knew he shouldn't have said it, but it was out now.

Rashid's dolphin dimmed. He found a pebble on the floor, and weighed it in his hand, saying nothing. Blake mounted the skimmer and grabbed his helmet.

"Commander, here is the message." Rashid spoke to the floor. "She said that Zack told her about Robert. That was all she said. I do not know what it –"

Rashid winced as Blake's helmet slammed into the wall, then ricocheted off onto the floor several times before sloshing to rest in the pool of water.

Blake sat on the skimmer, breathing hard, his arms hanging by his sides. His right hand trembled, the one that had pulled the trigger all those years ago. "Zack had no right," he whispered, his voice almost breaking. He gritted his teeth, remembering his and Zack's botched rescue attempt to save those captive boys near the end of the War in Kurana Bay. His own son, Robert, had been... *transformed* by the enemy into a mindless fighting machine... And Blake had shot him, after Robert had killed the rest of his platoon, and was about to kill Zack. He'd shot his own son. There was no reason, no justification or excuse worthy of such an act, in his book. Only he and Zack had known. Robert had been declared missing in action, presumed dead.

The fight drained out of him. Glenda's message was as clear as it was brutal. No more botched rescues: use your head. He knew she was right. And the message was double-edged – she might well be angry with him, or not, he couldn't tell. He could imagine her pounding him with her fists, tears running down her cheeks, screaming '*How could you?*' Maybe that was what he wanted.

His breathing slowed. He remembered Pierre once used a French expression about the need to maintain one's *sang froid* – cold blood. His right hand stilled.

He dismounted, walked past Rashid, and retrieved his helmet, shaking it a couple of times to rinse out the fetid water. He went over to the field stove and began preparing tea. 'Names, Rashid. I need names of those you trust with your life, those who are on Shakirvasta's side, and those who could be turned to our advantage. And I need schematics of the city, as well as the political infrastructure.'

Rashid came to Blake's side. He saluted. "Good to have you back, Commander."

CHAPTER 17 – GALACTIC BARRIER

"One minute to impact." The timbre of the voice was calm, dispassionate, belying the fact that Grid Society was facing the most serious threat it had seen in more than a million angts of recorded history.

Drone A27243, *Dapsilon* to his friends, knew his organic colleagues in the fleet scattered along this section of the galaxy's edge would be sweating, shedding scales, or exuding pus, according to their physiology. Their digits and tentacles would be twitching, hovering above buttons and triggers, ready to unleash awesome weaponry at the first sight of their foe. But to a war-drone, one minute was a long time to reflect.

Dapsilon's primary function was *intel*, to gain knowledge of the inbound threat and its weapons capability, and feed data back to the Tla Beth War Council. Other drones in their thousands had been deployed to combat – correction – to *annihilate* the enemy, presumed to be the Kalaheii, though there was no definitive confirmation, because everything in the storm-front's path had been obliterated before signals could be dispatched. And so he – for he possessed male attributes compared to other drones which could be considered female in their orientation – had been charged with one simple directive: *inform*.

But he was much more, a *strategy* drone, capable of matching a Tla Beth in poly-dimensional chess. He'd seen wonders, fought in many wars, often alongside Rangers. That had been his undoing. He'd been deemed 'contaminated' by close proximity with those reptiles, his neural nets biased by their unruly yet curiously efficient value structures. And so he'd been relegated to low-ranking tasks for the last millennium. But the hierarchy hadn't deleted his higher functions, and he was determined to think until the end, and to be creative if necessary. That was what he was good at.

"Forty seconds."

Stop day-dreaming, he told himself, *analyse*! He considered the threat first – the Kalaheii. The data was hard-coded in his permanent memory, now forty thousand angts old. The Progenitors of the Silverback galaxy – where the drone currently sat – were ancient, seven noble races more than two billion angts old, but they had not evolved there. They had come from the nearby Jannahi galaxy after the terrible thousand-angt war with an eighth race, the Kalaheii. Their original galaxy had been decimated by the Kalaheii's leader Qaroll when he realised he'd lost the War. And now the data concluded that descendants of this eighth race, presumed extinct, were rushing toward the Silverback's edge, traversing the inter-galactic void, in search of retribution. Only the higher levels of Grid Society had been alerted, to prevent widespread and futile panic. War was afoot.

Another drone intruded on his thoughts. "*Drone A 27243 – status update – defence integrity secure?*"

The digital signature of the message caused a core buffer swell, quickly rectified, but a memory string resonated and surfaced into his central core awareness. Sergeant Drone D46539: *Delfina*. A long time ago he had been teamed with her. It had been a tricky mission, involving the quelling of a rebellion following the discovery of cheating at one of the Games – a ridiculous anachronistic tradition he had really expected to have been quashed long since. Together, they had developed a rare form of rapport, even for drones designed to be compatible. He had always felt that as a team they could handle anything.

Eventually, the Tla Beth had assigned them to different quadrants. Things like that happened. They were probably right. But now – *was it really her?* The odds were astonishingly small, but the signature was unmistakable. His circuits hummed, their harmonics pulsing quietly in the background data noise. His CPU felt ... perfect symmetry.

He sent the corresponding defence integrity status codes, and then transmitted "*Is that really you?*" using a single channel squirt.

She didn't reply, of course. It was an inane question, and she was far too professional. But he knew that she had received his message, and the fact that she had *not* replied, not reprimanded him for unnecessary comms in an emergency situation, spoke volumes about how she felt about him. The Rangers had taught him too much about organics' feelings, had ruined his career progression, but he wouldn't want it any other way. Still, he knew he should get back to his analysis.

Dapsilon was not the only intel drone – three hundred were speckled along the predicted intercept region. But his own defences verged on the extreme – he was cocooned in a reinforced bubble inside a neutron star five parsecs inside the galaxy, sitting on top of a stabilised wormhole able to whisk him away in a matter of micro-seconds. Moreover, he was insta-connected to three back-up drones inside, respectively, a gas giant, a moon, and a small nebula.

Upon *any* intel whatsoever, such as visual image, confirmation of Kalaheii identity, first weapons volley, or attack formation, he was to get the hell out of there, slip-streaming data ahead of him. He was absolutely *not* to stay for the battle. He would do what he was told, or rather programmed, but there was a tinge of curiosity – he wanted to stay and watch the Kalaheii smash into the galactic barrier and be destroyed.

"Thirty seconds. Energise shields, ready all weapons."

Comms traffic intensified across the fleet, but nothing unexpected, so he let his lower processing shells deal with the checks and confirmation requests. He returned to his analysis. *Defences*: the barrier and the void. The Galactic Barrier was a genius-engineered cosmic phenomenon, aimed at maintaining the integrity of the galaxy. If there was a need to resort to something as imprecise as a metaphor, then the barrier was a membrane, akin to the 'skin' of the simplest form of organic life, the amoeba. It stopped matter leaking out and, more importantly, prevented almost all dark energy seeping in. It was a repulsive force, devised by the ancients using equations of energy harmonics long since lost. The barrier itself had been forgotten until explorers attempted to leave the galaxy, their journeys ending catastrophically, said explorers becoming two-dimensional smears, molecular lamina flapping aimlessly inside the galactic edge.

Eventually – several hundred thousand angts later – ways out had been found, the most popular involving polarisation of a membrane weak spot, and careful insertion of a liquid-diamond stent, opened up using artificial black holes. But then there was another, more pernicious problem: the void itself.

Space was space, or so most organics thought. But space inside the galaxy had a density, counting space dust and EM clutter. The inter-galactic void was different. This was *serious* space. Nature might abhor a vacuum, but it was terrified of the void. The few ships that made it out there … died. There was no other word for it. Organics, machines, hybrids – all met the same fate, the life force or power source leached out of them by patches of dark space. And there was worse. A space faring creature known as the Xargylach, a space-whale, was thrown out into the void as an experiment, as bait. After a month, this normally peaceful, glacial-thinking leviathan suddenly thrashed and kicked and … screamed. They say no one can hear you scream in space, but everyone heard this goliath scream, for light years around, courtesy of its low-grade telepathic mind. At first no one knew why it was so anxious, so a Ranger who had been tracking it hooked it up to a telepathic Bartran, and then the Ranger stuck his claw into the Bartran's mind-slot. He uttered two words before slipping into a terminal coma. *Dark worms*. The space-whale died, but when it was recovered, there were hideous scars on its hide: curving, wave-like ulcerations in its space-resistant silicate flesh. After that episode, further extra-galactic excursions were prohibited by the Tla Beth council.

"Ten seconds. Charge displacement capacitors. Arm black hole magnetic mines."

Dapsilon's surveillance channels told him the whole fleet was now in hyper-readiness, waiting just inside the barrier. The armada was the largest amassed in half a million angts, enough heavy weapons and armour to fill a black hole, all directed at a sliver of empty space. He knew the organic commanders, including the legendary Q'Roth High Guard, would be straining their eyes and slits to see the approaching invasion force, but since it was travelling at near-light speed, it would not be visible until nano-seconds before it hit.

"Be careful."

Delfina's message stopped his thinking in its tracks. She was taking a big risk sending this message. It meant two things – she really cared, and she was scared, worried they were really in big trouble, that the Kalaheii would somehow break through and destroy them.

"You too, my love," he replied, knowing he was going way over the top. He reprimanded himself for such a cavalier attitude. He hoped no one would review the myriad communiqués after the battle.

Tactics. He knew at least one of their defence assumptions must be wrong – the Kalaheii wouldn't spend all this time just to launch a suicide run. The Progenitors had made the inter-galactic voyage a billion angts earlier. For security reasons their mode of voyage had been classified to Level 15 access until recent events changed matters. The dark worms were not myth – they killed many of the ancients en route, a process of attrition that bled away seventy per cent of the ancients' number during the million-plus angts voyage from the extinguished galaxy to this one.

The Progenitors had experienced first-hand the energy-leaching aspect of the void, and had countered it in two ways. The first was by adopting a minimal power output profile, with almost all ancients cocooned in stasis arks. The second counter-measure involved a ballistic approach – they used dark energy, in ways no one below Level 17 could fathom, to sling-shot towards the next galaxy. Their speed and low energy output prevented a fatal feeding frenzy by the dark worms, which would have created drag on the craft. If you lost momentum out in the void, it was all over.

As for breaching the galactic barrier from the outside, it was possible, but should take several angts just to overcome the repulsive force. There was nothing to anchor onto: it was like a swimmer with the shore in sight, struggling against the tide – the void offered no *purchase*, nothing to push off from or hook onto to gain enough momentum to break through. So, if the Kalaheii arrived – and the data definitely coalesced around that hypothesis – then it should be easy to pick them off as they tried to breach the barrier. The most disturbing conundrum was that the Kalaheii most probably knew all of this.

He took a few milliseconds to study the barrier. Though invisible to organics, to his sensors it looked like a shimmering, electrified wall crackling with hostility. *How could they get through?*

"Five seconds."

Fleet communication reached fever pitch, but he could still handle it lower down in his processing chain. He possessed a full cache of emotions, orchestrated to optimise his performance. He could have done without the fear, however. Surplus energy fluxed with uncomfortable resonances – it would be recycled, naturally, but it kept him on edge.

To take his mind off the coming insurgency, he triple-checked his sensors and comms integrity status with the conduit, the wormhole, other drones... and Delfina. He sent her a private recursive 'handshake' algorithm, the equivalent of squeezing a human hand. She returned it. His circuits fizzed.

He became aware of an unannounced drop in comms traffic. In a nanosecond he checked the transpace conduit – it was offline.

"FLEE!"

He didn't bother to check wormhole status, instead he initiated subversion, but it didn't work – the wormhole had lost stability. His energy matrices ramped up to maximum. He tried contacting Delfina and other drones, but all channels were jammed by a hailstorm of sound and light across the entire EM and sub-spatial spectra. Just outside the barrier he saw what looked like a billowing cloud erupt and mushroom out of nowhere, engulfing everything, like an antibody enveloping another cell's membrane. The shimmering galactic barrier fluttered, flashed once, and then a savage tear split across it, letting the cloud flood inward, like a burst dam. His fear sub-routines went off-scale. *Why wasn't anyone firing?* His internal diagnostic system told him that thirty-nine of his lower intelligence levels had just been eviscerated. He'd auto-downloaded as much as he could. *Time to get out!* He shunted his core into the three back-up drones, just before his neutron star imploded inside the collapsing wormhole.

He awoke inside the shattered moon. The gas giant had been boiled away, the nebula ionised to intolerable levels, so he had no further boltholes. His external sensors scanned the area but had a hard time interpreting the data. *Where am I?* It was not logical. There were no stars. But there was plenty of debris all around, across a huge area: disabled drones and shredded hulls of the organics' ships. He was out in the void.

He detected a far away swirl of light and pattern-matched it – definitely his galaxy. He triangulated with several other visible galaxies. He was fifty light years out into the void, and stationary. He tried again to connect with Delfina, first using point access, then he went broadband, no longer caring who or what listened in. No reply.

What had happened? It had been so quick. He managed to link with fifteen other non-dead Alpha drones, to assimilate data.

"Why?" they asked, "what's the point?"

His agitation intensified. "Because it is our mission to understand!"

"Who can we tell? We're all going to die."

His electrons reached dangerous levels of excitation. He cursed their sub-optimal emotional responses. If Delfina was here, she would instil order into them. He would not let her death be in vain. "COMPLY!"

They did. Together they built a picture: not pretty, but impressive. The Kalaheii – for it was confirmed now – had used a poly-instantaneous-attack strategy. They had become visible as they slowed from near-light speed. What registered was, as his Ranger would say, a shitstorm of sun-sized meteorites. They smashed into the galactic barrier with such kinetic energy that it created a shock wave on the outer wall of the membrane, shattering conduits, wormholes, and most technology in the process – the mother of all EM pulses. But that wasn't the clever part. Dark energy weapons had opened a micro-fissure in the Galactic Barrier – while it had been pounded by meteorites, no one had noticed a syringe-sized funnel piercing it. The Kalaheii had used this portal to do something ingenious.

When the Kalaheii's ships had been slowed by the repulsive forces, they locked on through the fissure to every piece of matter just inside the galactic barrier – the defensive armada of drones and ships – and leap-frogged them, using their matter to pull their own ships forward and through the fractured barrier using advanced differential transit techniques, catapulting the defensive force into the void, realising one of the universe's most basic axioms, that every action has an equal and opposite reaction. *We've been played*, he concluded – they used our fear, knowing we would mount a massive defence force, which gave them an anchor to pull against. *Clever bastards.*

He noted that five of his brother drones went off-line. There were chaotic high-intensity squirts from de-compiling data matrices – the drone equivalent of a primal scream. He knew what it was. It was the last piece of the puzzle. The Kalaheii hadn't merely evaded the dark worms – they had somehow made them allies. *Why?* he wondered, as seven more of his co-drones stopped transmitting. The answer came all too readily from one of his tactical sub-servers: allies have overlapping goals; the Kalaheii are going to allow the dark worms into the galaxy. The perfect shock-troops, while the Kalaheii consolidate their forces, co-opting further allies. Even the Q'Roth wouldn't be able to stand against them.

The last of his co-drones went silent. His circuits told him his conjecture was eighty-nine per cent probable. But who could he tell? If he transmitted now, light years out from the Galactic edge, his information would be of no timely use. Something stirred in his memory banks. It was unorthodox, but he had no other options. He assembled a nine-dimensional intel squirt and opened an ancient transpatial frequency accessible by a data-plexer known colloquially as *Hohash*, if indeed any of these mythical info-warping machines still existed. It was not an official channel, but a Ranger had once confided it to him, saying that it was an ancient, last-ditch emergency channel. But what to transmit? Most of his data had been corrupted.

His external sensors picked up something – in fact, an absence of space – moving toward him in steady, spiralling, homing curves. He could not switch off his fear conditioning, no more than an animal could, even when fear served no useful survival purpose. He had to work fast.

He trawled through the data fragments. But he could only reliably send one transmission at this distance, even using subspace. Five more layers of his intelligence sheared off like gas boiling into space. He had fifty milliseconds left. He knew the only hope for galactic survival lay in finding and re-activating the last ancient Progenitor race known as the Kalarash, not heard from for over a million angts. Only they could stand up to the Kalaheii. What did he have that could rouse them? He accessed the very last fragment, number 78. It stunned him. One of his now defunct brother drones had intercepted a Kalaheii command communication during the maelstrom. It was a visual, showing an organic commander with a face like a dying sun. Dapsilon had never been programmed to recognise something as subjective as 'evil', but he knew it when he saw it. There had been a single word decoded by the drone, a name: *Qorall*, the mythical leader of the Kalaheii. This, he knew, would get the Kalarash's attention. He encoded and transmitted. He hoped a Hohash still existed somewhere to receive it.

The remains of the moon sheltering his outer shell exploded. There was nothing more he could do. He initiated crash shutdown, it would be better that way. As his sentience faded, his thoughts were of Delfina. He condensed his memories of her, creating an electronic pastiche of her personality. The last thing he sensed was a huge mouth darker than black, yawning wide, but he had acted just in time.

As the mouth closed, a single micro-EM pulse escaped, racing away into the void, containing a complex memory string of two drones entwined in a binary embrace.

CHAPTER 18 – STAR-PIERCER

"**M**ove aside, Micah," Angel said, her shoulder level with Starkel's pistol.

Micah's feet remained planted in front of Hannah. "Can't do that, Angel. She's one of my crew."

Angel sighed. "Be smart, Micah. Starkel won't let her go alive, and he'll have very few qualms about you joining her."

"Micah," Sandy said, quietly, "now's not the best time to be a hero. I'm tired of watching people I care about die."

"Buddy, sorry, but she ain't worth it," Zack added. "You're the Captain. Mission comes first. Let her go."

Hannah stood perfectly still behind Micah. Angel peered around Micah to catch her feral eyes. "I see you haven't been winning too many popularity contests, Hannah."

Micah stared down the barrel of Starkel's disruptor. His resident displayed a legend on the right side of his vision, telling him the weapon was set to vaporise at close range. He only half-understood why he was doing this. His logical mind voted to move his feet, but they wouldn't budge. He tried to rationalise it, and an idea formed, an argument. "We need her. We're in a Q'Roth vessel, how far are we going to get without her?"

"Trade it in," Angel countered. "You'll get a good price. I know places they don't ask questions."

Micah shook his head. "Sorry." He stared into Starkel's coal-black eyes, finding no trace of compassion there. Micah felt a wave of calm. "Go ahead, just – "

Noise erupted all around, like termites crunching through wood, amplified a thousand-fold. Micah flinched.

"Shit!" Angel shouted through the din. "They've arrived early." She looked away for a second – Micah guessed she was accessing data via her resident, telemetry from her ship.

"Fuck, *two* ships – they sent two ships." Angel turned to Starkel.

Hannah came out from behind Micah. "Now you need me."

Everyone stared at Starkel, his pistol aimed between Hannah's eyes. The muscles on his forearm bulged.

Hannah stood her ground. "They're calling us. If we don't reply in one minute they'll open fire on both our vessels."

Angel laid a hand on Starkel's wrist, lowering his arm. She didn't take her eyes off Hannah. "Don't try anything clever."

"We're probably all dead anyway," Hannah said. "The bridge – quickly."

Micah and the others tailed Hannah as she raced up the ramp to the empty bridge. Two blue-black, starfish-shaped vessels filled the viewscreen, spinning slowly about their axes. The points of each limb of the two ships glowed a dull, throbbing red, growing in brightness with each pulse. Hannah rapped commands into her console, then regained her breath. "Okay, nobody say *anything*, not a sound."

Micah watched, enthralled, as Hannah started speaking what he presumed was Q'Roth – a cross between walking over dry autumn leaves, and throat-clearing after chewing razor blades.

He stood with his back to his Captain's chair, and glanced at Angel. She shrugged, looking distinctly unhappy. Starkel's disruptor kept Hannah in its sights. *So, neither of them have any clue what she's saying to the Q'Roth vessels.*

"Give me your pistol, Starkel." Hannah shouted. Micah gaped at her. Hannah rolled her eyes. "Look, there isn't time. I've told them I've captured a rival to the Q'Roth in the Games, plus your ship. They're going to send a holo-avatar here to scan us, to check my story."

Starkel flared. "I'd rather die than –"

"*Then we will all die!*" she screamed at him. "We have about fifteen seconds of life left."

Angel pried the pistol from Starkel's fingers and tossed it to Hannah.

"Thank you," Hannah said, then produced another pistol from underneath her console. "Sorry," she said, "no time to explain. I told them there'd been a fight onboard."

Micah wondered what she meant, as he watched her right thumb skim down the handle of a Q'Roth pistol he'd not seen before. Without warning, she fired at Starkel and Ramires almost simultaneously, followed by Zack as he levelled his rifle at her.

She jumped down from her dais and whipped the butt of Starkel's pistol across Angel's jaw, sending her sprawling unconscious to the floor. She faced Sandy and Micah. "Kneel! Both of you, now!"

Micah winced at the bodies lying sprawled around him, blood dripping from Angel's slack jaw.

"I said NOW!"

Sandy tugged at his elbow and they both dropped to their knees.

Hannah soaked up beads of sweat from her forehead with the back of her forearm. "Do not speak. Do not look at her when she arrives."

A swirling purple haze fizzed out of nowhere in the centre of the bridge, forming a familiar shape to Micah, one he'd hoped never to see again. First to materialise was the matt-black trapezoidal head, the lower edges tapered toward the neck, giving it the overall shape of a rectangle that had been stretched down at the middle, like the silhouette of an open book. Six diagonal slits, three on each side of its face, oozed vermillion wax, like weeping sores; eyes of some sort. A rhino-like armored thorax appeared, followed by its upper pair of barbed legs, like those of a praying mantis. The rest remained mercifully obscure, the projection only half complete.

Sandy tugged his elbow again and he remembered he was not supposed to look.

He listened at the rapid, staccato conversation between Hannah and the holo-avatar. At one point the Q'Roth issued a hiss like cold water hitting hot coals, and Micah sensed they were arguing. Abruptly, the avatar vanished.

"Quick, we don't have much time."

Before Micah got to his knees, Sandy sprung up, lunging at Hannah with her fist. But Hannah was quicker, and whirled around Sandy, deftly trapping her in a neck hold from behind. "They're just stunned, Sandy," she said. "Tell her Micah, use that thing inside your head."

He'd been too caught up in everything to process the background data projected by the resident. He stared at the pistol in Hannah's hands, draped around Sandy's necks; it was set on stun.

"Sandy, she's telling the truth. Let her go, Hannah, and tell us what's going on."

Hannah released Sandy, pistol at hip height. Sandy's hands were shaking. He put a calming hand on her heaving shoulders.

Hannah backed away and leaned against her console. "You've no idea how exhausting it is using their language, and as for arguing with them... Sandy, I'm sorry, but they're all unharmed. I didn't want to stun you, well, for obvious reasons – she waved her pistol at Sandy's 'bump'. There should be something in the med-kit to rouse them, we need to work fast."

"This had better be good, Hannah," Sandy said, glowering.

"Okay." Hannah addressed Micah. "I know about the Games, all Alicians do, we plan to compete in the next ones in three hundred years' time in a different Grid quadrant. There are certain rules of engagement. I told the captain of the lead vessel that I had captured the Mannekhi contestant, a known rival of the Q'Roth entrant, but that I demanded trophy rights. It means guaranteed eligibility for the Alicians to enter next time. I said I would only hand Starkel over after the Q'Roth commander had contacted the Games authorities and submitted a formal evidenced request for entrance by a new species."

Angel came round, sitting up, cradling her jaw, glaring at Hannah, but listening intently. "It's plausible, Micah. I have something similar planned for humanity if we win."

"The Q'Roth captain – well, she was furious, and only dimly aware of the Alicians as a newly Q'Roth-patronised race. Q'Roth hordes are nomadic, tribal, even. The various tribes don't always stay in touch."

Sandy had roused Starkel, who climbed to his feet.

Hannah continued. "We have ten minutes, then a boarding party will arrive. Before that time we have to destroy one of their ships, release the Star-piercer, and jump, blowing up the second Q'Roth vessel with the transpatial mine you so generously attached to our hull." She nodded in Angel's direction.

"And how do we take out one of their ships?" Angel stood, helped up by Starkel, a bloodstain tattooing her chin.

"I was hoping the name of your vessel, Star-piercer, wasn't just cosmetic?"

Angel nodded. "Where's their weakest point?"

Hannah turned to her console and indicated on the viewscreen an inner ring on the central body of one of the ships. "There. Penetrate that point and then get the hell out of the way as fast as you can. I told them I would take the Star-piercer and hand this ship and its *Knarll* – excuse me – all of you here, alive for them to do with as they please."

Micah helped Zack to his feet. Ramires had already come to without Sandy's help. "Zack," he said, "can you fly this ship in your condition?"

Zack rubbed his chest. "Ugh. No problem, just get me to my seat."

He and Sandy helped Zack to his fighter-jet chair. Once there he began tapping controls.

Micah walked up to Angel. "Nice meeting you," he said. "You'd better go. Good luck." He shrugged. He wanted to tell her about Earth, that it was gone, but there was no time, and it wouldn't help her.

The corners of her mouth rose. "Thanks." She paused and spoke in a low tone, just to Micah. "It's probably none of my business, Micah, but my resident is attuned to emotional patterns, and, well life is short out here, so here goes." She leaned close and whispered something in his ear.

He drew his head back, his eyes widening. He nodded, and parked it for later.

Starkel strode up to Hannah, holding out his hand. She slapped his disruptor into his palm. He quit the bridge without glancing back.

Angel paused at the exit. "Goodbye everyone, it's been ... an education. The Mannekhi have a saying – shit happens fast, death happens faster. Get used to it, it's a jungle out here, and we're just dumb wildebeest." She nodded to Micah. "Good luck, you're going to need it."

Micah turned to the rest. "Stations, everyone."

He took up his chair. "Hannah, can we power up the jump engines without them noticing?"

Zack answered. "The engines have been charged for weeks. We just need a few seconds to bring them online."

"Show us the Star-piercer, Sandy."

The viewscreen shifted. After a minute, the javelin-shaped ship, soap-bubble colours sliding down its shaft, edged gracefully away from their airlock.

Zack cracked his knuckles. "Now we get to see how good a pilot Starkel is."

No sooner had he said it than the craft spun about at its mid-point, and shot like a crossbow bolt straight through the inner ring of the nearest Q'Roth ship, vanishing out of sight.

"Holy crap!" shouted Zack. His fingers crashed onto the dashboard in front of him, a dull whine rising rapidly throughout the bridge.

"Now, Zack!" Hannah shouted.

Zack's fingers danced over his console. "Just a few seconds..."

Micah and the others watched explosions erupt where the Q'Roth ship had been punctured, spreading like cracking ice across the entire vessel.

"Zack?" Micah said. The second ship backed off. Its starfish points intensified from a dull red to bright white in a second.

"Zack! For God's sake –"

Micah hated jumping. Every time, it felt like dying, or drowning. Everything turned the colour and texture of mercury. During these transits, he couldn't breathe, or rather, simply didn't breathe, as if his body instinctively knew it would be very bad if he did. There was no sound, and the eeriest thing was that he could see everything in his field of vision until it completely whited out. This time he saw a red streak lance towards them from the Q'Roth ship on the viewscreen, frozen in space-time. He wondered if the beam would somehow follow them into Transpace. The quicksilver texture of everything around him increased until he found it difficult to distinguish anything. He knew they were outside of time, but no one knew how long each jump actually lasted. His mind slowed too, hanging up, as if he was about to say something, or about to think something. He remembered a Zen koan – *what is the sound of one hand clapping?* Right now, he thought, this is it.

They snapped back into normal space. Micah lurched forward, resisting the urge to vomit, gasping for breath. The viewscreen showed a new set of stars. He twisted to Hannah. "Did they follow us? Did the mine get them?"

She brushed a strand of ginger hair from her eyes. "Yes and ... yes. They went in – they'd ID'd our destination code – but they never emerged."

Micah sank into his chair, looking out at the stars. Angel was right, things happened too fast in this galaxy. He heard a dull thump.

"Er, Micah?" Sandy said.

He twisted around to Sandy, and followed her gaze to Hannah's console. She was on the floor, unconscious. Ramires' wiry frame stood over her, his dark eyes projecting out from beneath goat-black hair. "She's dangerous," he said. "We need to decide her fate."

Micah sealed his cabin door.

"Are you okay?" Sandy reclined on an easy chair opposite him while he perched on the edge of his bed.

"Me? You're the pregnant lady around here. It's been quite a day, Sandy. How about you?"

"What did Angel say to you, just before she left?"

Micah tugged off his boots, and let them thud onto the metal floor. "Nothing of any importance." But it had been, since it had given him new hope, but he wasn't sure he could trust Angel.

Sandy leant back on the sofa-like chair. "You're one rubbish liar, Micah, but okay, I'll humour you. I'm betting she told you to kill Hannah."

Micah lay on the hard mattress, kneading tired eyes with the backs of his knuckles.

She pressed on. "Why did you vote to keep her alive, anyway?"

He propped himself up on his elbows. Sandy obviously wasn't going to let him sleep. "She saved our necks today. We owe her one."

Sandy snorted. "Along with Louise, she wiped out two thousand humans, Micah. She's a long way from being in credit. And you saw how fast she moved today, and how quick she thinks."

Yes, the Alicians really are an upgrade. We need to catch up – pronto. "She's still useful. Without her, I'd feel compelled to turn right around and head back to Ourshiwann."

"The others clearly disagree."

"Captain's prerogative. It's not a democracy. Anyway, you abstained."

Sandy nudged his shin with her boot. "Can't have you sulking for the rest of the trip."

She got up, standing over him, her legs gently making contact with his knees. "But she's Alician, Micah. Ramires was right, we'll never be able to really trust her."

"Scorpion, eh? That's what Zack called her." Micah was dimly aware of Sandy's physical proximity. But she'd said it a thousand times: *it's not going to happen.*

"They're both more experienced than you, Micah. Maybe you should listen." She sat next to him on the bed, her hands in her lap. She placed one on his thigh. "Be a bit more cynical, Micah, like Blake. It's quite attractive, you know."

Micah rubbed his eyes again, he felt so tired. Why was she doing this? It wasn't like her to tease him, not physically anyway. "You mean like Vince, don't you?"

Her hand tensed, and withdrew. He realised what he'd just said – she'd been in love with Vince just before Louise had killed him. *Idiot!* "I'm sorry, don't know why I said that." He sat up, but she was already standing, brushing down her tunic over her bulge. She smoothed her black pants. He watched her hands as they stretched the elastic fabric over taut thighs.

"Neither do I, Micah. You need sleep, evidently. Good night."

"Sandy, wait, just..." The door closed behind her. He slumped back down on the bed. *Shit.* He should have listened to Angel's advice. He stripped off, lay down and rolled over onto his right side. He reckoned he could sleep standing up if necessary. His eyes fell on the pendant Antonia had given him two months ago; a lifetime ago. He was sure she'd have someone else by now, or maybe Kat and Pierre had found their way back. His eyes closed of their own accord, and he freefell into a deep slumber.

Micah stirred awake in a fug of sexual arousal. Completely dark, Sandy lay next to him, naked. She kissed him hard, her hand taking his and bringing it down between her legs, feeling her wetness. Her mouth travelled down his torso until he gasped with pleasure and surprise, his head arcing backwards into the pillow. She came back up and kissed him again, ravaging his mouth. She grabbed him and slid down onto him. He groaned in ecstasy. She writhed atop him, one hand between them playing alternately with herself and him, the other reaching behind her. He rose up to kiss her breasts, his hands squeezing her buttocks. It had been months – he knew he couldn't hold on for long. Pressure built in his groin. He whispered, half-grunted "Sandy" but she plunged forward, pushing her breasts into his mouth, her hair raining over his face. The shakes started. But something was wrong. His climax approaching, he reached in front and stroked her belly, felt the tight sinews, the flatness...

"Lights," he yelled. The lithe young Alician on top of him rode him like she was breaking in a horse, flaxen hair tumbling down her shoulders, half masking her face. She wrenched herself forwards and seized his wrists, pinning them to the bed next to his head, while she moved up and down on him faster and faster. Her mouth locked onto his, her tongue lashing inside. *Too late...* She thrust her pelvis down onto him, grinding her mons pubis against him as he came. She quivered as her body wracked into orgasm, synchronising her contractions with his every spasm. He shouted out, nothing coherent, a long animal cry. Arching his back one last time, he shuddered like a shutter in a storm, until it abated, and he collapsed backwards into the pillow.

She buried her head into his shoulder, released his hands. After a pause, he placed them around her back, until the post-orgasmic tremors subsided.

She raised herself up on her muscular arms. "She'll never sleep with you Micah, you know that."

Not now, at any rate. "Why did *you* sleep with me, Hannah?"

"You saved my life today."

"You ... didn't have to."

"I have needs too, Micah. Alicians are a matriarchal society. The genetic enhancements increase our hormonal activity. When we want a male, we take one. The others on this ship want me dead. Besides, like it or not, you're the alpha male here." Her feline eyes hunted his. Micah looked sideways. Abruptly she dismounted, while he was still inside her, causing him to take a sharp intake of breath. Instinctively he grabbed her buttocks but she pulled off him. "Want me to go, Micah?"

"No... Maybe... Yes. Too much today. Sorry."

"I understand. You know where my quarters are."

She bunched up her clothes and headed for the door. As it slid open, Sandy's silhouette appeared from around the corner, barefoot, in a short dress. She and Hannah both froze. Sandy spun around and disappeared out of sight. Hannah, naked, carrying her clothes under one arm, turned back to Micah. "Sorry, Micah. Really." The door closed behind her.

"Me too." He lay there for an hour, trying to think of some form of words he could string together to say to Sandy. During the rest of the night he went to her room three times but she wouldn't answer. At 5am ship-time he gave up, surrendering to fatigue. He'd lost her, for good, he reckoned. He'd always assumed he'd never had any real chance with her. But as he drifted off, exhaustion almost numbing the pain, Angel's words played back to him, based on what her resident had shown her, re-affirming that something precious and irreplaceable had just slipped through his fingers. *"Micah, Sandy really likes you, you know that don't you?"*

* * *

Louise tested her right arm, flexing it to see if the hair-line break was fully healed. Shooting pains seared their way to her shoulder. She dismissed them. She limped back to the comms console, ignoring the booming thuds coming from the door barring entry to the secondary control room. Hammering, like a heartbeat. A display flashed yellow: *message waiting.* "Read," she commanded in Q'Roth. Angular, barbed characters, all twisted iron nails and scalloped shrapnel, cascaded down the screen in foreground and background, the front field moving faster. Its elegance transfixed her.

So, Micah had escaped again, helped by an unidentified ally. Impressive – she hadn't thought he had it in him. But the local authorities hadn't taken too kindly to the jump-mine – highly illegal – and had banned further transits in the sector till it had been probed and pronounced clean. Micah and company were fugitives. *That didn't take long.*

The pounding on the door accelerated, then stopped. She listened to the yawning silence of the behemoth ship around her. It, too, sensed the mirror – the *Hohash*, according to the human refugees' database she'd downloaded on Ourshiwann before her departure. The ship itself had saved her when it had first attacked.

She'd not realised how fast the Hohash could move, nor how dangerous it was to fire a pulse weapon at it – it lived up to its mirror representation. She touched the still-raw scar on her left elbow, from the laser burn it had reflected back at her.

"More hide and seek?" She shouted through the door. "Okay, we'll play again soon." She recalled how it had chased her, she moving wildly to avoid its savage side-on thrusts, until she managed to reach the Regen-lab where she'd been reborn. By that time she'd been crawling, with a broken femur and fractured arm, not to mention concussion, and haemorrhaging inside her leg. She didn't know why it hadn't taken its opportunity there and then to crush her neck or head, but the ship had intervened, extruding a metal skin door in a millisecond, sealing her safe in the lab.

Two weeks of accelerated healing. During which time Micah had eluded her again. She'd not seen the Hohash since that day, but she heard it haunting the corridors often enough.

Where are you headed, Micah? She called up the nav-charts, and located the nearest Grid Station. Too close, and too small – they'd need anonymity now. She picked a minor hub, six transits from Micah's previous location. She zoomed in to the hub's alien manifest. She smiled. *Perfect.*

She composed another written message – she was becoming fluent by now – to a Q'Roth ambassador visiting the hub, advising him of impending 'guests'. She sent it as a closed message, not needing a reply, using her adopted Q'Roth callsign, *Arctura*. In ancient Q'Roth it had the same meaning as the old Japanese word *ronin*, meaning a samurai who'd left their master; a dangerous renegade. She was already gaining a local reputation.

She was about to switch off when she noticed that the nearby station had a sub-spatial comms booster. She stared at the glowing icon, and tapped into it. The hammering started up again. She sent a one-line message, in English: **Micah destination GZH-359A in 4 days. Arctura <Louise>.** She addressed it to <Sister Esma>: no formalities, no honorific. *Let's see what you make of that.*

The door bashing intensified, like a drum beating out a dervish. She heaved her hand-made high intensity thermal cannon onto her good hip. She aimed it at the door, and flicked the ignition on. Molten flame dripped from the tip of the muzzle. "Coming," she shouted, slamming her good hand down on the door release.

CHAPTER 19 – OSSYRIA PRIME

Pierre's quicksilver eyes gazed through the space-portal. The pearl-coloured home world of Ossyria Prime, the Galactic home of medicine, grew large. It appeared as if it had been cut into a dozen horizontal slices, then re-assembled. Each section turned at a different pace, creating a hypnotic effect. He saw no large masses of water: he'd gathered from the Omskrat orb – his handy Ossyrian encyclopedia – that water was largely underground, and only occasionally precipitated in precise locations via environmental control satellites. It took him back to a forgotten childhood – it was the most beautiful marble he could ever have imagined.

Kat entered, the swish of the door irising closed behind her.

"Don't tell me that's a natural phenomenon, Pierre."

He decided to try something he'd been experimenting with, a way of accelerating his cognition. He studied her reflection in the portal and willed his mind to shift gear. As if in slow motion, her eyes began to close. His mind ran through what she'd just said, using a poly-dimensional scaling technique to study the covariance of her words, her speech rhythm, intonation, body language, eye contact including pupil dilation, and pheromone secretion level. He applied a Neo-Bayesian statistical model of her personality, harvested from every single interaction he'd ever had with her. His brain computed eight potential interpretations of what she had just said, with statistical likelihoods attached. Her eyelids made contact. His mind automatically ran through fifteen different responses he could make, then extrapolated each conversation for the next ten sentences. All but one projection ended with a net sum loss, in terms of her becoming colder with him. Her eyes were nearly open. She had blinked.

"No," he said, re-focusing on the planet. "It took them forty thousand of our years, forty-five thousand galactic standard angts, more or less, to re-model the planet. It's ingenious – the contradictory turning rates create magnetic flux inside the planet's core, itself partly hollowed out and replenished with teratons of graphite-like material, generating almost limitless clean energy." While he talked he suppressed ninety-eight per cent of the technical detail he could have expressed much faster in hyper-math. If he'd been communicating with Chahat-Me using his eyes, he could have transmitted all of it in the same timeframe. The information filtering effort at least slowed down his speech, so he still sounded human. "Also, the different segments are protected zones. They carry out genetic research, and any accidental outbreak of a virus, for example – there have been three over the past six millennia – is naturally confined to its continental slice."

He watched her reflection, her short-cropped hair, lean lips, and greyish eyes atop a gymnastic physique, move toward him. His sense of smell had been heightened too, and he could sense her emotions via her pheromone signature. Her hand touched his shoulder. "We haven't talked, Pierre, you know, about ... our child."

His logical brain stalled, as if it couldn't compute. He was glad for the relief from the endless calculations and speculations: his heightened and accelerated intelligence came at a cost. He kissed her urgently, his silver arms – for he was changing – locked around her waist. He drew back, but held her hands. "I'm worried, Kat ... that it'll become like me."

She leaned back. "You don't mean..." She broke away from him, eyes widening. "Nannites?"

He was surprised she hadn't thought of it. She stepped back to a bench and sat down, pointing to Ossyria Prime. "They can probably take them out," she said.

He nodded, though his calculations revved up again, and gave it less than fifty-fifty odds. *Change the subject.* "The Ossyrians used to be war-mongerers, no better than the Q'Roth."

She moved to the portal and leant her brow against the glass. "What happened?"

Again, tirades of data surged into his mind, but he found a short-cut. "The Tla Beth, one of the most advanced races left, Level Seventeen. Legend has it they wanted to foster a medical race, and were impressed by the Ossyrians' attention to anatomical detail, whether tending to their wounded after battle, or torturing prisoners. They became the patrons of the Ossyrians for a hundred thousand angts."

"Probably needed a challenge."

There, he hadn't predicted *that* response.

"I've been thinking, about your nannites." She turned around, blocking his view. "I think you have a choice."

He wished her eyes worked like his, it would be so much faster. But this time she had his – and his nannites – complete attention. "What do you mean?"

"From what I remember, you know, the plague-vids from the 40's, nannites are mission-oriented. They adapt to their environment, working for themselves and their host – without whom they cease to function. They aim to advance and have a better survival likelihood or quality of life."

His nannite-infused brain was silent. No, not silent, he thought: dumb. It doesn't want to hear this. But he did. "I'm not sure I follow you."

"Pierre, *you* get to decide what advancement is. You can set the mission. Advanced intelligence, that was your father's dream, not yours. And even he never expected it to go this far. You can stop this development, Pierre. It's your life, your choice. The nannites will understand your will, and accept it."

He stared at her, wondering why he hadn't thought of it. She was right. Advanced intelligence, he realised, didn't necessarily induce wisdom, nor did it preclude the ability to hide from the truth.

The door opened, revealing Chahat-Me and the Hohash. In a flash Pierre read her eyes: they were to go before a council to see what would be done with them, including the baby. "Kat, they –"

"I know, Pierre, at least I can guess. I'm not stupid. Just think about what I said."

They crossed a narrow glass bridge so fine they could hardly see it. Beneath, a drop of several kilometres plunged downwards to a murky brown ground level. The bridge connected with a massive pyramid, itself made of Crysmorph – Pierre had studied the specs as soon as he'd come out of stasis – a crystal coded with inorganic DNA so that it could be grown into complex structures. He calculated that this pyramid must have taken four thousand years of accelerated growth to be completed.

Two suns, a yellow one like Earth's, and a strawberry one, hung low in an apple green sky, creating stunning prismatic effects on the pyramid. Around twenty bridges like theirs struck out to the sides and below, reaching out to other ships. Chahat-Me walked ahead of them, regal, her gait smooth and fluid. The Hohash hovered silently behind them. Kat ambled next to him, giving the appearance of being relaxed, but his observational analyses told a different story. She guarded her belly with one hand, now three months into her pregnancy, and glanced furtively around. She was right to be anxious.

"Pierre, they're doctors, right? So they must have some Hippocratic Oath, you know, do no harm?"

His mind skimmed over their complex code of conduct and ethics he'd accessed and memorised earlier. "I'm afraid their definition of harm goes beyond the single organism, to the societal structure." He glanced at her, unsure that would make sense. It was difficult to remember how normal humans thought anymore.

"Great," she said, "political doctors. So they might deem us unsafe for society. What about you? You're an advanced intelligence life-form now. You must be approaching their level?"

"That's just it. My intelligence growth rate shows no sign of stopping. I'm an anomaly – in their Grid Society I'm a freak or an abomination. I'm potentially a threat. They'll probably vivisect me."

She placed her hand on his and stopped him. "That's not funny, Pierre."

He took her hand, and continued walking. Why had he attempted humour? He went back to her question of fifteen minutes ago. What did he really want? What did 'advanced' mean to him? What mission should he give his nannites?

They entered the building not far from its apex, but at this level it was as wide as a hoverball stadium. He glanced downwards and was surprised to see through all the glass floors below, myriad Ossyrians going about their business. Some areas were opaque, but not that many. He looked up and saw the ceiling of their level, a dull greyish reflection of him, Kat, and all around them. He surmised that at each level, you could see below, but not upwards.

They reached a circular reflective Crysmorph wall. Chahat-Me beckoned to him, silver eyes shimmering information. He nodded. "This is it, Kat. At least she is on our side: because we helped her survive, and prevented the Mannekhi from gaining Ossyrian technology. She will present the case for us to be allowed to live out our lives, somewhere."

"Ossyrian plea-bargaining, eh? Maybe we need a better lawyer." She shook her head dismissively. "Just kidding, let's get this over with."

The room, brighter than an operating theatre, contained two red, high-backed chairs on a round plinth, surrounded by a wide circle of thirty seated Ossyrians. Pierre recognised from the arrangement of the gold, black and blue bars on their head-dresses, that this was a very senior group. One chair, directly facing the red ones, was empty. They both dutifully sat where indicated, the Hohash taking up a position to the left of Kat. Chahat-Me stood next to Pierre. He presumed it was because she was their champion, or else because she was considered contaminated by them in some way. All of the Ossyrians rose, so he and Kat did too, as a white-fleeced Ossyrian with a pure gold head-dress entered, and took the main chair. She sat, and everyone else followed suit.

Kat leaned towards him. "Can you translate what they say? I know it's tedious for you, and might irritate them, but this is important. I have the feeling my future, and our baby's, are hanging in the balance here."

He nodded, and communicated her request to Chahat-Me.

"Okay. It's begun," he said. "Chahat-Me is relating all that happened since she met us – she knows about Rashid's ship and the Q'Roth, incidentally; the Hohash must have shown her. They wanted to know where we found the Hohash – they're mythical, apparently, no one knows how old they are, and they defy scans or any type of analysis. There haven't been reports of a Hohash sighting for millennia. Chahat-Me's told them it found us on Eden. Okay, she's now telling them what you did to save her and prevent their technology falling into enemy hands. Ah, now about me."

"What?"

Pierre wondered how to condense the detailed discussions between half a dozen Ossyrians taking place at lightning speed. "They can't stop the development without killing me. It has to be referred to a higher council: the Tla Beth themselves. I'm an aberration; there's no precedent in their legal system. The Ossyrians have used nannites in the past, but have never seen anything like this – some unusual interaction between human physiology, my father's genetic tampering, and the nannites." He left out the part that a vote to vivisect him there and then was only narrowly defeated.

"A reprieve," she said, the relief in her voice palpable. "Our baby?"

He looked down at the floor, and breathed out heavily.

"What is it Pierre? What have they decided?"

"It's okay, Kat," he said, his voice shaky. "I just didn't anticipate my own emotional reaction. They can remove the nannites, they're not bonded yet, they're dormant – your physiology is unsuitable." No, he thought, that wasn't it. Kat was right. They're inert, because Kat doesn't want them there. *Which means I also have a choice.*

He looked up again, trying to catch up quickly. "They will accelerate the baby's birth outside of you –"

"Hey, wait just a minute –"

"They know where Ourshiwann is. They will..." Take you there, he thought, with the baby. They're going to separate us. His body flushed with an emotion he'd forgotten he was capable of – anger. His silver hands flexed, his fingers morphing into scalpel-sharp daggers. He stood up, rock steady. "No!" he said, his voice echoing around the room. All eyes were on him, but they were silent. Chahat-Me drew away from him. The Chief Ossyrian stood. Her jaw opened and the high-pitched screeching burst forth. To his left, Kat clasped her hands over her ears, but Pierre stood firm, and within micro-seconds his nannites had attenuated the sound. He focused on his throat, on the sounds the Ossyrian was making. He opened his mouth and shouted back in the same language: "You will not separate us. We are family. You will do no harm to us." He quoted a litany of complex ethical precedents from Ossyrian history. The Chief Ossyrian sat back in her chair, while several others rose to their feet. Pierre knew they were a dispassionate race, but back in their genes they had the capacity for anger and outrage, and he saw it bubbling to the surface in their faces; all except Chahat-Me, her expression a mixture of shock and pride.

His own mind hurled objections to what he was doing – Kat would be better off without him, back with Blake, Micah, and Antonia. He needed to become what he could become – he was a scientist, no matter if his father engineered him that way, it was his nature, his destiny. How could he bring up a normal human child? But he choked off all these thoughts, forcing coherence in his mind. He read the eyes of one of the Ossyrians studying a screen – she was scanning him. It had happened, he now knew: the nannites had finally built the bridge between his right and left hemispheres of his brain, across the chasm known as the Corpus Callosum. His logical and intuitive brains had just been hot-wired. There was no turning back. He was no longer human. But he was one again, not divided. He was more powerful, and he knew what he wanted.

He spoke again, in their vocal language, shocking them into silence. "We all three go to the Tla Beth, or to Ourshiwann, but we stay together. This is beyond you now."

He felt tiny pin-pricks on his neck as aerial micro-syringes injected him with powerful anaesthetics, but his nannites neutralised them. His whole body, all his skin, flashed silver. He stared at the Chief and shook his head. Then he walked up to her, and his eyes worked so fast that the Ossyrian leader had a hard time keeping up.

He came back to the seat and faced Kat's bewildered face. "It's okay, it's over. We're going to the Grid. All three of us."

"What did you say to them? They looked pretty furious, until now."

"They were. Most wanted me destroyed – as an abomination. They even tried to blackmail me with you and the baby. That was when I offered them something they couldn't refuse. You see, Kat, I'm an experiment, and it's not over. I offered them all my data, as I develop, on how what's happening to me could be cross-adapted to another race – theirs."

"But I thought they were happy with their lot, their level?"

"Kat, the Grid Society is a hierarchy. No matter what anyone says, everyone wants to move upwards."

She eyed him with a mixture he could tell included fear, respect and love. He smiled, knelt down and kissed her hand, and then placed his and hers on her belly. Chahat-Me appeared next to them. "Oh, Kat, I left out one small detail."

Kat raised an eyebrow.

"Chahat-Me is coming with us."

"To ensure you keep up your side of the bargain, you mean?"

He frowned. "She's taken us on as her responsibility, and in any case it might be better for her to be off-world for a while, I more than ruffled a few fur coats just now."

Kat made to say something, but her body went rigid, then convulsed. She screamed once and dropped to her knees, hands covering her eyes.

"What is it?" Pierre said, then noticed the Hohash had sprung to life. All the Ossyrians froze, watching its display. Those who had started to leave quickly re-entered the room.

He found it hard to make out at first. It resembled a fleet of space ships lined up facing a translucent glittering curtain of light. Flashes of intense brilliance shook the image, and the curtain ripped apart. The scene shifted to one of utter carnage, ships torn apart, fragments of rocks spilling in all directions, and what looked like corpses frozen in a star-less space.

Kat lifted her head, pale as porcelain. "Pierre, something very bad has happened. I'm not sure what, but the Hohash reached inside my darkest fears, to convey how serious it is."

He glanced at the Chief, who crossed over to Kat and the Hohash. "The Ossyrians here were dimly aware of an unusually intense military exercise at the farthest edge of the galactic rim, and had dispatched a contingent of medical staff out there over an angt ago. But this doesn't look like an exercise, or if it was, it went badly wrong."

"It's not, the threat is real. The Hohash wanted me to convey a message, because it doesn't have a good communication rapport with the Ossyrian species." She glanced at Chahat-Me. "No offence."

"What's the message?"

"Wait. It wants me to speak as it shows a particular image. Here, watch the display: two words – Kalaheii, and Qorall. That's it."

Pierre scrutinised the frozen image of a face of red-hot lava, parting to reveal a black pit that could only be a mouth. In the centre of its forehead was a snake-yellow vertical slit, an eye of some sort. Two bone-like tubes protruded from the mouth, curving to the back of its head. Around its neck were metal rings, like he'd seen once on a visit to an African village, except the rings fluoresced darkly.

Most of the Ossyrians fell back. Some had already quit the chamber. The Chief stared at the image, silver eyes still. Abruptly, she turned to Pierre.

"What is it, Pierre? They're all afraid, aren't they?"

"The Chief says this message has to be delivered as soon as possible, and in person – it's not safe to transmit on any carrier-wave, no matter how secure. She will deliver it herself to Grid Central. She asked if there was anything else in the message."

Kat looked down. "No."

Pierre's observational analysis told him she was lying. Fine, she must have her reasons. Whatever it was, it would have to wait.

"How do you feel, Kat?" It was a pathetic question, but he needed to break the silence.

She sat knees against chest, holding herself. "Hollow. Cheated. I know it's safer for the baby this way, but..."

He sat down and put his arms around her. "They said the baby will be fully matured in two weeks, and can then leave the maturation chamber. Hey," he lifted her chin, then dabbed at tear-stains with the back of his silver knuckles. "I've heard childbirth isn't all it's cracked up to be."

She rubbed her temple against his hand, like a cat.

"They're putting us into stasis again, Kat, in a few minutes. The journey is using a high-energy jumper; it'll burn out a ship's engines just to get us there faster."

She nodded, head down again.

He knew it was unfair, and bad timing, but he needed to know. "Kat, there *was* something else in the message, wasn't there?"

She didn't move, didn't speak.

"Please, Kat, you need to tell me."

She raised her chin. "Pierre, I've already lost too much today. Besides, it wasn't for them, it was..." She bent her head again. "Personal."

He heard the low hiss of the gas entering the room. His mind kicked into hyperdrive and ran through the possibilities and probabilities: *personal; lost too much today; she wouldn't look at me*. It's about me. About losing me. The Hohash is connected to her, to her emotions, to our discussions. It knows what she has asked of me ... and it disagrees. Earlier he had been coherent, had wanted to stay with Kat, but now he wasn't so sure. Why did the Hohash disagree? *Choices* – but the decision will have to wait. He lapsed into unconsciousness.

* * *

Pierre's nannites had evolved considerably, after more than two hundred thousand short-lived generations since their activation on Eden. They were barely recognisable compared to their original design, vastly mutated on account of Pierre's genetic re-engineering, and the recent infusion of Ossyrian DNA prior to the Mannekhi attack. Pierre, their host, hadn't made up his mind about whether to continue his transformation, and nannites were not big on independent thought. They detected the stasis field and subdued their activity, mimicking shutdown. After an hour they resumed. The basic choice was whether to continue the evolution or not, that much they understood. Their host had not decided. The nannites, however, needed a mission. If they'd been told to stop, they would have, but they had not. In a micro-second they settled on continuing his development during stasis. After all, if their master were further evolved, they reasoned, it could help him decide, resolving his tension one way or the other. They swept into action, buzzing around his brain and neuro-endocrine system.

Nannites didn't need sleep. The need for rest while unconscious and unprotected seemed to the nannites a ridiculous, untenable weakness, and they understood that a major threat was coming. So this would be their host's last sleep, they decreed: he would never need it again. But they had to make choices, too. The nervous system re-construction activity required energy and raw materials. Some internal functions might need to be sacrificed. In particular the nannites didn't favour all these gland-fed emotions their host had to endure – they caused indecision and made their host vulnerable. The lead nannites – the youngest and hence the most evolved – voted on what functions and glands could go. It took a full three micro-seconds to decide, and then they went to work.

CHAPTER 20 – NEST

lake grimaced as he woke up; his shoulder practically numb. His neck grated like rusted iron as he lifted his head. He pushed upward from the man-sized tarpaulin covering the rock floor with sluggish arms, and heaved himself into a sitting position. His post-coma muscles were on strike.

"You slept well," Rashid said.

Tea was brewing. Rashid squatted next to the kettle in vest and shorts, despite the bracing air, heels flat on the ground, with an ease that most sedentary Westerners, including Blake, could only dream about. He wondered just how much tea Rashid had managed to bring from Earth. With an effort Blake got up, and started the loosening exercise routine he'd done every day for twenty-four years since enlisting. Shafts of sunlight cut through the chill morning air at the opening to the cave. Cubes of yellow tofu, like they'd had for dinner last night, laced with honey, were lined up for breakfast. At least it didn't look curried like yesterday.

Rashid told him that the main priority from the nutritional point of view was to get vegetables growing on Ourshiwann. Despite being a largely barren planet, the soil was favourable. Vince had had the foresight to bring nitrates, seedlings, and crops including wheat and squash. They were faring well, growing quicker than back on Earth, aided by a few irrigation tricks Professor Kostakis had conjured up. Someone had even had the presence of mind to bring some birds and insect larvae in stasis, though debates still raged about waking up the latter.

The bland tofu came from the spider-race's huge underground vat complex, and would last long enough until the meagre livestock that had survived the journey on Jennifer's ship reached sustainable numbers. *Farmers*, Blake thought, *we need to become farmers again*.

He strolled to the cave entrance and stood in a martial chi gung posture facing the sun. *And soldiers.* Before they had gone to sleep in the absolute quiet of the desert, Rashid had given him more of the low-down on Shakirvasta's budding empire: how any critics tended to be pushed out to the furthest farms, or, worse, sent on 'expeditions', never to be heard from again. He'd explained how a virtual caste system was emerging, with Shakirvasta and Josefsson's cronies enjoying luxuries, as opposed to ninety-five per cent of the population being reduced to peasant status, working the land twelve hours a day. Schooling had been introduced, heavy on indoctrination into the need for order and societal restructuring. Dusk till dawn curfews operated for people's 'safety' – martial law by any other name.

There were glimmers of hope, such as Antonia's position on the Council. However, although a cause for good, and a quick study in political survival tactics, Rashid felt it was only a matter of time before Shakirvasta was irritated enough to find an excuse to get rid of her. A second ray of hope lay in Sonja's fledgling hospital and medical staff. The third was a minor underground movement, led by Rashid, branded an outlaw, covertly supported by Carlson, who also retained a seat on the Council. Most were afraid to speak openly or join the movement. Jennifer's militia kept a firm grip on the population; reactions to the slightest infractions were swift and brutal.

Blake was surprised how quickly things had deteriorated, and how fast Shakirvasta had centralised power and control. Rashid said he wasn't. He'd seen how his fellow Indistani had turned ailing companies around in a matter of months back on Earth, using ruthless business methods.

"He's treating Ourshiwann as if it is another corporate takeover," he said, "but this time he has military muscle to back him up."

Blake lowered his hands and relaxed, having learned through the years that the best soldier was dispassionate, though that was easier said than done. He walked back inside and sat down on a rock, accepting the cup of steaming chai from Rashid.

"Rashid, I've been meaning to ask you – Rashid isn't exactly an Indistani name. Were your parents Kashmiri refugees?"

Rashid nodded, his hands continuing the work of scouring last night's field crockery. "Yes, after decades of fighting over the territory, the land was finally poisoned by terrorists, or by governments – no one knows the truth – so, much of Kashmir had to be abandoned. Neither side could absorb everyone. My mother and father ended up in Tangiers, where I was conceived. They thought we would have to stay there for good, so they gave me an Arabic name. A few years later we moved back to the new, united Indistan. So many had died in that joining of those two long-divorced nations, that the new government needed all of its people back, especially those who had not suffered through the Integration. My parents decided to keep my name."

"You're proud of your ancestry, aren't you?"

Rashid nodded, his dolphin reflecting the first rays of light entering the cave. "Five thousand years of civilisation."

Blake coughed. "Several months ago," he frowned – the lost time took some getting used to – "Jennifer told me you were *Sarowan*. What does that mean, exactly?"

Rashid paused. He put down the cups, turned away, and lifted the back of his vest. Blake saw a faded tattoo. Two pairs of three diagonal lines, like the feathers of an arrow separated horizontally, slanted downwards. Beneath them sat a waving red line, all boxed within a rectangle depressed at the middle, like the outline of an open book.

"Q'Roth," Blake whispered.

"The face of our enemy, lest we forget." Rashid lowered his vest and returned to where he had been squatting before. "The Sarowan are – were – an ancient tribe, at war with the Alicians and their Q'Roth patrons for nine hundred years. I was born Sarowan. The best of the Sarowan became Sentinels." He reached for Blake's cup.

"So, you were trained to fight them, or the Alicians?"

Rashid poured fresh tea into the cups, spilling a little. Blake had never seen Rashid lose a drop before. "Oh, I was trained all right." He turned to Blake, his dolphin a blur of reds. "But foremost I was a *scientist*," he said in a mocking tone. "I did not believe all that paranoid nonsense about aliens and monsters and Rangers: there should be evidence, and there was none! I had no time for it, so I left and went to University, made my way up in the world, leaving behind my family and their delusions..." He stopped moving.

"You weren't to know."

Rashid spoke to the floor. "I've lost my family, my wife and child, my world, and now my eyes. I have paid dearly for my arrogance."

He and Rashid had never had an easy relationship, but Blake felt sorry for him. "Survivor guilt, Carlson would say."

Rashid snorted. "And you, Commander, what would you say?"

He leaned back. 'I'd say you had every reason to be mad as hell, more than most, except maybe the dead. But you're alive, Rashid. We're both soldiers. You know the deal as well as I do. Besides," he chewed on it a bit before letting it out, "You have Sonja, apparently. I'm not ecstatic about it, but you need to protect her."

Rashid stayed silent.

Blake stood up, interlaced his fingers and stretched them above his head, then bent forward so that his palms grazed the floor. He swung up again fluidly. "Think I'll go for a short walk."

"The large bush thirty metres to the right is where I went this morning. Sir. I suggest you find another. There is some paper in the satchel by the skimmer."

Blake nodded, took the paper, and headed out.

"Ah, while we are on the subject, Commander, Ramires also has this tattoo, though he is not Sarowan by birth. He is a Sentinel, the last one alive."

"Does that mean he's a good soldier, or an assassin?"

"Try to imagine the best four soldiers you ever knew, taking him on, and then imagine them all dead before they hit the floor."

"Does he have a nanosword, like Jennifer?"

"Of that I am sure, but he is far better at concealing it than she. Sentinels and Sarowan play the long game, you see."

Blake wasn't sure he did see, and headed out to find a bush.

"What is out there?" Rashid asked.

Blake peered through the viewer as they lay on the dry ground atop an escarpment. A warm wind whistled softly over the ridge. The magnification was up all the way, and he could just make out a diminutive girl strutting around between three commando-types. It looked like she was shouting down a radio. "Trouble," he replied.

They jogged back to the cave. Once inside, Blake needed to sit down – he kept forgetting his muscles hadn't been used for three months. The booster Sonja had given him only had so much to work with. "Why don't they search for us with the sling-jets?"

Rashid fished around inside one of the skimmer saddlebags. "Fuel stocks from Earth are almost exhausted, certainly for sling jets. Colonel Vasquez commandeered a chunk of the remaining fuel for his platoon's trip into the wilderness one month ago. He has not been seen since."

"No satellite coverage, eh? So we can't communicate with him once he's too far away?"

Rashid pulled out a flashlight from a rucksack. "That seemed to be the idea. I think it was a mutually acceptable arrangement between him and Shakirvasta."

"Why do you need a flashlight, Rashid?"

"I don't," he said, handing it over.

Blake hefted it, feeling its weight. "It's just Jennifer. We can talk with her."

"She is not alone," Rashid replied.

"So, they're using a spiral net tactic, groups of four strung out along a curving line, closing in on us. How'd they find us anyway?"

Rashid ran a finger along the upper rim of his dolphin – Blake had seen him do it a few times before. "Perhaps this, or a tracer buried in you somewhere. It makes little difference now. The net is closing. We must go deeper into the caves. But first, since they now know where we are, we can contact Esperantia."

Rashid produced a small glass cylinder, flicked a switch so that the small light at one end flashed yellow, then after a few seconds, a steady green. He aimed one end at Blake, holding the other end close to his own mouth. "Citizens of Esperantia, behold: our honourable Commander Blake is alive and well, and will be returning soon, your Chairman Shakirvasta and his cohorts permitting. If you do not see this man in the next three days, then it is on the Chairman's account. Please, Commander, say something to the people of Esperantia."

He inwardly cursed Rashid for doing this, though he understood why it was a good idea – an insurance policy. Rashid could have warned him though. He cleared his throat. "It's good to be awake again. I know a lot has happened since we defeated the Alician threat. I want to say first of all that I'm proud humanity won that battle. We should all be proud of that day. But I've heard disturbing rumours that suggest that, well, frankly, we've lost our way. So I'm coming back to see for myself and, if necessary, to get us back on track. Oh, and if my wife Glenda is hearing this, don't worry, I'm coming to see you soon."

Rashid jiggled his head and put the device away. Something beeped, and Rashid pulled out a radio. "Hello? Yes, she has almost found us... No, don't worry... Really? Yes, please do, as quickly as possible. I –" Rashid stared it a moment, then dropped it into his rucksack.

"Transmission jammed?"

"Yes. Come, we must go deeper now."

"We could defend from here."

Rashid shook his head. Blake decided to defer to Rashid's judgement this time. He slung a rifle over his shoulder, checked the charge in his pulse pistol, flicked on the torch, and followed Rashid down a steep, dark tunnel.

The air wasn't getting hotter. Blake remembered a schoolboy trip to Luxor and the Valley of the Kings, and how the temperature rose inside those claustrophobic tombs. Yet here it was almost getting cooler, with the faintest stirrings of a breeze every now and again. They'd been on the move for an hour. Blake's thigh and calf muscles screamed at him. Eventually, after nearly going over on his ankle for the second time, he called Rashid to stop.

The pause was short-lived. Blake was in the middle of suggesting that maybe Jennifer and the others had not followed them in, when they heard a dull crack in the passage behind them, courtesy of a small device Rashid had placed there five minutes earlier. Without a word they set off again; the others were gaining. He remembered, as a boy, an uncle who used to keep weasels, and would love to drop one down a rabbit hole. Blake never saw what the weasel did to the rabbits, but its blood-stained fur when it re-surfaced was proof enough. "We can't make a stand here, Rashid, we need some open space." Not that they'd seen any for forty minutes.

Abruptly, Rashid halted, so that Blake almost bumped into the back of him.

"You wanted a clearing, I believe, Commander?"

He moved beside Rashid and shone the flashlight. It failed to reach the other side of the vast cavern before them, but it did illuminate its contents.

Blake sighed. "Not again," he said, shining a beam onto the nearest, turquoise, basket-ball-sized object protruding from the dirt floor.

"What is it exactly, my dolphin is having a hard time interpreting the terrain."

Blake wasn't surprised by what he saw: it answered a long-harboured question. "Part of me always wondered why the spider race didn't put up any fight, pacifists or not. One of the strongest instincts of any creature is to protect its young. So, by not fighting, they left their city intact, ready and waiting. But not for us."

Rashid turned his head sideways, then back. "Eggs? Is that what I'm seeing? But there are thousands here."

And not only that, Blake thought. They're so closely packed, if we try and run through them we'll break them. He looked around. They were on a stage-sized triangular promontory a metre above the flat egg-field stretching out into the rest of the cavern. He presumed there were no exits on the other side – why would there be? This whole thing seemed man-made – no, spider-made, he corrected himself. "We make our stand here, Rashid."

Light exploded into the grotto, sending a searing pain to the back of Blake's eyeballs, blinding him temporarily. He fired three times before his rifle was kicked out of his hands. Two men were suddenly on either side of him. One seized Blake's pistol from its holster, pressing its barrel to Blake's neck. The other rammed his foot into the back of Blake's leg, so that Blake dropped to his knees. When his vision returned, he saw Rashid in the same position, but his dolphin had been torn off. A spike-flare, fired into the ceiling above the stage, sputtered a ghostly pale light over them, and revealed two gaping sockets where Rashid's eyes should have been.

"That was a little too easy," Jennifer said.

Blake watched her as she strutted in, then he saw her freeze as she glimpsed the eggs for the first time. She wandered over to the ledge, staring out across a sea of unhatched spiders.

"Let's do it now, Captain," said the one with the pistol barrel nudging Blake's neck. "Then we can torch this place, or at the least bring the roof down and seal it."

"Do you suppose," Rashid said, as if making polite conversation, "that this is the only nest?"

The man standing behind Rashid whacked the back of his head with the butt of his gun. "Quiet, you scum. You killed my brother when you broke out."

Blake held up a hand, looking over towards Jennifer, who had turned away from the eggs.

"Let him speak," she said.

Blake acknowledged with a nod. "Jennifer, no one was dead when we left. Rashid was very careful."

"LIAR!" the man behind Rashid pushed forward with his knee into Rashid's back, toppling him to the ground.

"We will hear them out! Obey my orders!" Her right hand slipped into her jacket pocket.

"The hell we will, we have our own orders." The man with the pistol barrel wedged into Blake's neck stepped back and levelled his pistol at Blake's forehead. Blake saw a flash of violet, just before the man slumped to the floor like a sack of dead meat, his head detaching itself half-way before he hit the ground. A fountain of blood gushed from the stump that used to be his neck. Blake didn't miss his opportunity. His left hand formed a fist and slammed into the second man's groin. As the man doubled-over, Blake kicked off the ground, catching the man's chin in one palm and his shoulder with the other. He pushed and pulled both arms with equal force until he heard the man's fifth cervical vertebrae snap.

Jennifer stood between him and Rashid, a thin short metal rod in her right hand. The man who had been holding Rashid down was on the floor. He wasn't breathing. Rashid stood over the man, looking unruffled. *Sarowan training must be pretty good.* Blake prized the pulse pistol from the closest dead man's fingers, glancing at Jennifer, who didn't seem to mind.

"Whatever," she said, dismissively, retracting the nanoblade into its hilt. "I've been watching them since yesterday. Furtive looks and conversations, secret radio conferences with base." She squatted down, pocketing the nanosword. "One thing I learned in Dublin in the War, leading small groups of insurgents, is to tap their comms devices. First I thought it was just a renegade element in my ranks, till I found out one of them was getting orders direct from Josefsson. Best bit," she emitted a hollow laugh which echoed across the chamber and bounced back to her, "was when Josefsson gave the instruction that if I vacillated – typical Josefsson language, don't you think? Anyway, if I *vacillated*, then I should be eliminated too." She stood, and shrugged, facing them. "Now, Commander Alexander," she said, wandering back to the edge of the egg-field. "You were saying?"

"Sanjay is a brilliant man, a strategist! There is order in Esperantia, there is purpose. It's down to him and him alone!"

Rashid shook his head vehemently. "He is a wolf, Jennifer!"

"Wolves have clarity! They're strong, they survive."

"Yes, by eating sheep!"

Blake held up a hand. The argument between Jennifer and Rashid was getting nowhere. "How soon before others arrive?"

"I told them to wait outside." She glanced over the three dead men. "However, I'm not sure I'm in charge anymore."

He thanked God she had heard them out. But she was strongly defensive of Shakirvasta, blaming her current predicament on Josefsson. She was still clearly making up her mind what to do about him and Rashid. Unfortunately, her support hung on Blake's willingness to commit to Jennifer's no-holds-barred mission to seek out and destroy the Alicians. Reason apparently had its boundaries.

Rashid at least had his dolphin back in place. He seemed to be listening to something; he kept tilting his head towards the floor.

"Let's talk about the eggs," Blake said, hoping they could find common ground. "Any idea when they might hatch?"

"Not for a long, long time, Commander!" A voice boomed out from the distant edge of the chamber.

The trio swivelled around, unwilling to believe their ears without visual corroboration.

"*Dimitri?*" Jennifer said, at the same time as Rashid sputtered, "Professor?"

The figure of Dimitri Kostakis loomed out of the darkness. He stood feet splayed on a narrow lev-panel, using a gnarled wooden staff to punt along over the eggs. It reminded Blake of the character from Greek mythology, Charon, who ferried poor souls across the river Acheron to Hades. He noticed Kostakis was careful not to touch any of the eggs with the staff.

Jennifer glared, her initial joy at seeing him now shrouded. Blake shouted to him, "Professor, what in the world are you doing here?"

Kostakis beamed through a straggling beard which merged seamlessly with his swathes of black hair. "I am on the best adventure of my life!" He reached the edge, and Blake and Rashid each leant an arm to help him up without propelling the levi-panel back out over the eggs. "And my Jennifer, it is so good to see you again, I had no idea you would be here to put things right. This means –"

She flared. "It means you're wrong on two counts, Professor Kostakis. First I am not yours, and second, I have not yet decided about these two renegades."

Kostakis' smile faded but then resurged. "Still, it makes my heart swell just to see you. I have had a lot of time to think, these past months."

Rashid lifted a hand. "More soldiers are coming. I can hear their comms. We must go, now!"

Neither Blake nor Jennifer moved, other than to check their weapons.

Rashid climbed down to the levi-panel. "They are preparing a fire-stormer – I can hear the ultrasonic charger winding up towards detonation."

With that, they rushed to the edge, Blake grabbing Kostakis' arm in the process. "Will this thing carry all of us?" As Kostakis got on board, it dipped and wobbled, so that they all momentarily clung to each other for balance. Rashid jabbed the staff to the ground to prevent them toppling, puncturing an egg, and shoving them backwards. A spume of yellow-brown gas spurted from the crushed shell.

"Do not breathe in – poison!" Kostakis shouted, as he covered his nose with a sleeve, and tried in vain to protect Jennifer's face.

"Dammit, Dimitri, get off me, you haven't had a bath in weeks!"

Rashid punted fast and fluidly into the darkness. The others crouched down, holding the edges of the lev-panel, remaining still, the elevated stage receding into the gloom. They all watched, waiting. "Professor," Blake whispered, "can we run through the eggs?"

"That would be unwise: their yolks contain a fast-acting acid. We would die a miserable death."

They heard a dull pop, then nothing. Blake hoped against hope that the fire-stormer had failed. A few seconds later fire erupted, engulfing the stage, and a tidal wave of flame flooded out across the eggs towards them. Blake felt searing heat on his face. He knew worse was yet to come, since the flame-front would breed until every last breath of oxygen had been scavenged from the chamber.

The tsunami of flame rushed toward them, but as it did so, eggs exploded in its pathway, mustard-coloured gas rising like a veil in front of the firestorm. Rashid's strokes grew more furious and jerky, but powerful, too. Blake knew their lives were literally in his hands: one slip, one lost push, and they might be swallowed in fire or a cloud of acidic gas.

Rashid didn't falter, however, and the curtain of gas grew thicker, but it no longer chased them, becoming an opaque barrier against the fire. Rashid continued to punt furiously, though the flame front flickered, dying, strangled by the gas. *The spiders have saved us again*, Blake thought. "Rashid, it's okay, you can ease off now. You've saved us all, today. You too, Professor."

His mind switched to Glenda. *That was close. Mr. Shakirvasta, you and I are going to have a little talk, soon.*

They reached the opposite side of the chamber, remaining quiet. Blake knew the soldiers would wait a short time and then enter with breathing apparatus and scanners. They disembarked, and followed Kostakis through a narrow, undulating schism in the rock face. After five minutes of hurried walking they emerged into a smaller room-sized cavity. Clearly, Kostakis had been squatting there for some time. Scattered clothes, a fusion stove, almost-empty boxes of rations, a dank-looking sleeping bag, and a bucket of water that didn't look remotely drinkable, all lay haphazard on the floor. Pride of place was a small skel-table made of pneumatic micro-mesh, upon which lay a wafer-pad, glowing dully in the dim reddish light that would keep his eyesight cave-adapted.

"My home, my office, my laboratory," he said quietly, with a mixture of embarrassment and pride. "I'm doing the best research I've ever done in my life, not that there are any journals to publish in or conferences to go to." He belly-laughed, wheezily.

Blake smiled, but saw how haggard Kostakis looked – in the harsh ruby light his facial flesh sagged like jowls; he had lost a lot of weight, fast – no one fared well on rations, especially living in continuous night. Blake noticed that Jennifer's glower masked traces of concern, maybe even shock. *Good, you need to smell the coffee.* He seized the opportunity. "I'd say your side has been chosen for you, Jennifer. Shakirvasta never trusted you fully. Josefsson doesn't take this sort of action without covering his own ass first by checking with his boss. He could maybe have gotten away with explaining you were killed in crossfire, but, well, we all know a fire-stormer is designed to take no prisoners."

She turned away, and walked to Kostakis' desk. "Josefsson never trusted me. He was desperate, saw me as a threat. Maybe he thinks Shakirvasta will get over my death. Josefsson believes himself indispensable to Sanjay."

Rashid spoke. "Do not delude yourself, Josefsson is merely a puppet, you of all people should know that."

She whirled on him. "And you know that from *her*, don't you?"

Blake frowned. Since no one answered, he asked. "Who?"

It was the trigger Jennifer had been waiting for. She rounded on Kostakis. "That conniving little bitch, Antonia! You know, that prissy little whore you were spending so much time with before you left!"

Blake looked open-mouthed to Rashid, then Kostakis.

Jennifer cracked. She launched herself at Kostakis, pummelling her fists into his chest. "How could you? How *could* you?"

Kostakis stood there letting her vent her anger. Blake thought about interfering, but she wasn't hitting him hard – he knew she could kill Kostakis if she wanted to, despite their size ratio.

"My dear Jen, nothing happened between me and Antonia, I swear."

Jen leapt back, eyelids red. Blake noticed with alarm what she had in her right hand. "Liar, Dimitri! Don't you think I knew all about your secret little rendezvous, your soirees?"

Kostakis held his ground. "The resistance, Jen. We were trying to form a resistance. I couldn't tell you, because..." His mahogany eyes looked as if they might split. He spoke in a small voice. "Shakirvasta manipulated you, my love. He has played like an alchemist on your grief for your brother Gabriel, turning it into an unquenchable anger, taking you away from me, from all of us."

Her nostrils flared. "She stayed the night more than once!"

"There were curfews. Shakirvasta wasted no time seizing control. She wasn't the only one who stayed. Carlson was often there, Rashid too." He nodded in Rashid's direction. "On my mother's grave, my dear Jen, I never touched her. If you don't believe me..." he nodded to her right wrist.

Blake watched Jennifer's white-knuckled hand closely as it clutched the nanosword, not yet enabled. Her eyes bored into Kostakis' with a fierce intensity. She took a step backwards, turned around, then storm-marched down another exit from the cave. Kostakis made to go after her, but Blake spoke up. "Leave her, Professor. She'll be back. She needs time alone."

They waited an hour. Rashid had ventured back towards the egg chamber, and employed his sonar to detect the soldiers' summary search on the other side of the chamber. He heard them leave, reporting on the radio that all were dead, that the mission was accomplished. He returned to Kostakis' refuge.

"Half the eggs have been destroyed, Commander, but the soldiers do not seem to be aware of them, since the ones on their side of the chamber were vaporised. They found enough ash from the soldiers we killed to think we are all dead."

He nodded. Kostakis sagged on his small camp chair, like an overgrown scarecrow. Blake was just thinking they would have to go and look for Jennifer, when they heard a shrill scream echoing down the passageway she had taken. Blake had never seen Kostakis move so fast, as he jumped up, grabbed a torch and bolted down the narrow tunnel.

"Should one of us stay here?" Rashid asked.

A second scream, full of pain, reverberated into their room.

"No, we stick together." He ran, followed by Rashid, cursing the fact that every event seemed to push him further away from his main mission, to rescue Glenda. He heard Kostakis shouting up ahead, and picked up his pace, ramping up his pulse pistol to maximum.

CHAPTER 21 – GRIDFALL

Despite Micah's attempt to play it cool as Captain, a "Wow!" slipped out as Grid Station 359 Alpha grew large in front of them on the viewscreen. It reminded him of a giant sea urchin, hundreds, maybe thousands of electric blue spines stretching out into space, myriad ships docked at the ends. The central hub was lozenge-shaped. Every part of it – and his resident told him it was forty kilometres long, converting automatically into its host's metering system – glinted dark phosphorescent indigoes and blues. He was getting used to Angel's gift, with its sporadic but well-timed alphanumeric data drops into the right side of his vision, to the point he wondered how long they'd survive without it. Once he'd read or scanned the data, it faded out – evidently the resident included a cognitive feedback loop. He reckoned it should win the resident's designer the galactic equivalent of the Nobel Prize.

He focused on the hub again, and realised it wasn't the most impressive item on their viewscreen. The space-port acted as a node on a ringway, a conduit of sliding colours. Micah recalled as a kid seeing a cuttlefish at the Monterey aquarium, how it changed colours as fluently as a man utters words, different shades rippling up and down its surface. Yet this was on a more majestic scale, and wasn't just about aesthetics. The light show was a side effect of the type of radiation his resident translated as Eosin harmonics, propelling ships around the Grid without the need for fuel. Occasionally a swathe of colour, like the aurora borealis, whip-lashed from the hub to the ringway's horizon, indicating that another ship had just been catapulted into the Grid network.

The ten kilometre diameter conduit lasered into space in both directions from the hub, cutting a bold line across the black tableau of space. He focused on a particularly large vessel in the upper levels of the hub, and the resident labelled it as *Varctiarian – farm produce – Ischrian leaves*. He studied numerous different ships and formed a hypothesis. Aside from a few yachts and military vessels, the Grid was mainly for commerce: Grid culture was about barter. Not only that, each race appeared to have a particular niche in the market. It made sense. After a million years, Grid society had decided its needs, and each race had been accorded one or maybe two functions. He wished people back on Ourshiwann could see it.

But his head began to thump – he wasn't used to the resident yet. He turned back to his crew and relayed his observations. Sandy was cool with him, Hannah distant, and Ramires buoyant, in an understated way. Micah couldn't help notice that Sandy seemed to be interacting a little more than usual with Ramires. Zack meanwhile frowned at his displays of the docking system.

"I haven't got a clue how we dock," Zack said. "Hannah?"

"This goes beyond my knowledge too, I'm afraid. I suggest we approach and see what happens; probably the ship knows what to do."

"Great," Zack said, "I'll go get some kip, then."

Micah moved next to him. "Take her in, Zack, let's play this one by ear."

The hub loomed closer. Zack raised his hands, and let them fall back down, slapping his thighs. "That's it, autopilot's kicked in."

A holo-cube of emerald digits appeared in the centre of the bridge. Zack groaned. "Here we go again."

But Micah's resident highlighted six pairs of digits. He strode to Hannah's console, which displayed the cube in slices. He used his forefinger to peel away each slice until he found the right pairs, then tapped them with two fingers. The holo-cube flashed once and vanished.

"I'm impressed," Hannah said quietly. Her eyes lingered on him longer than he felt comfortable with, until he was saved by a scraping Q'Roth message which boomed over their heads. She translated. "It's an automated welcome message: we're being re-directed to one of the docking needles." His resident also gave a brief translation of the location. "DN-725, to be precise." More Q'Roth-speak spilled into the room. This time, although he couldn't really tell, it didn't sound automated. They all waited for Hannah to translate, but she stayed quiet. Her right hand tugged absent-mindedly at her ginger hair while she squinted at the written version of the last message. He was reminded of the previous night's passion, and dared not turn back to Sandy. He waited, half-hoping his resident would translate, but for the moment there was nothing.

"We're in trouble," Hannah said. "Zack, can we break off our approach?"

Zack tapped his controls, then punched the console. "Doesn't look like it."

"What's the problem, Hannah?" Micah asked.

"It's an archaic Q'Roth dialect. So I wasn't sure at first, but ... there's a Q'Roth ambassador aboard the hub, and, well, there's good news and bad news."

"I thought that was the bad news," Sandy said.

"Good news is he just waived our docking fees and set up a credit account for us during our stay," Hannah said, clasping the edges of her console, addressing all of them. "Bad news is he's invited us to a dinner party this evening – he wants an update on news from our recent travels. It seems he doesn't get out much."

Zack rose from his chair, slapping his unresponsive console en route. "Well I'll be –"

"Main course," Sandy quipped.

The ship jolted, a loud clunk confirming they were locked in place.

"I'm open to suggestions," Micah said.

Ramires got up and approached him in the centre of the bridge. He pulled out a thin metal tube and held it out in his left hand. A translucent purple blade eased outward, emitting a low hum.

Sandy cocked her head. "Boys and their toys, eh?" But she smiled at Ramires in a way that made Micah edgy. In that instant he understood two things: that he'd lost his chance with Sandy, and that he didn't really want Hannah. It made him feel more alone than ever before. He realized he was glaring at the last Sentinel alive, just as Ramires caught his eye, and retracted the fluorescent blade.

Micah cleared his throat and swung his gaze back to the viewscreen. "We go get provisions, then we get the hell out of here before dinner." He felt empty inside, but with that came a coldness he could firm into purpose. "Hannah, how much time do we have before our intended soiree?"

"About five hours."

"Right. Hannah, you remain here, find a protocol, a reason we can disembark early. I want you to track the ambassador and keep us away from him. We'll keep open comms. The rest of you, you're with me. We look for provisions. With a bit of luck my resident should get us through the transactions. Angel left us encounter gear, we need to figure out how to use it. Meet down at the airlock in ten minutes. Questions?" He glanced around, and left the bridge before anyone had a chance to raise one.

Zack caught him up further down the corridor, just outside his cabin. "You okay?"

"Am I really that transparent?"

"You want some advice?"

"Not really."

"Okay."

Micah sighed. "Zack – yes, I'm out of my depth here. Too much, too fast."

"That's just it, Micah. You're not. You just gotta let go of who you used to be. Blake chose you for a reason. Me, I thought you were just some geeky kid who got lucky back on Earth – had no idea why Blake singled you out for training."

Micah's anger flared up, out of the blue. "So please tell me, Zack, because right now I'd really like to know. I feel like I'm losing everything that matters to me." He realised this shit shouldn't be directed at Zack. "Sorry, I know you've lost a lot too, maybe everything."

Zack shrugged. "Not everything, not my sense of purpose. And that's just it. I asked Blake why, why you. He said you were smart, and right now, intelligence was our only hope. So, let go of them all – Sandy, Hannah, Antonia. Doesn't mean you don't care about people. But you need to be the leader, see things the way an eagle does, from above, cool, aloof."

Micah bit his lip, but was unable to hold it in. "What about me, Zack, how I feel, my needs?"

Zack laughed, laying a heavy black hand on Micah's shoulder. "No offence, Micah, but screw you. It ain't about you or me. Take your pain, your anguish, and burn it in cold fire. That was Blake's nickname back in the War, you know. Think about it, Micah, but not too much. Analyse our situation, not yourself. Humanity needs your brain, not your petty neuroses. Sorry, but there it is."

Something clicked inside Micah's head. If he could do as Zack said, then it *would* cut off the pain, and analysts were trained to disconnect from their emotions, though usually only when using the Optron. He made up his mind. "Alright. I have nothing to lose."

Zack stared at him awhile, then grinned. "Actually, you have to lose everything first, that's the point, just let go, you'll feel lighter." Zack headed to his own cabin.

Micah remembered what a Zen master had told him back in Palo Alto during his Optron training: *resolved action only comes from emptiness*. He'd never been comfortable with that aphorism, but right now, maybe for the first time in his life, it applied.

The encounter gear was less cumbersome than he'd imagined, amounting to lightweight self-fitting copper-coloured suits, a matching metallic headband, and two pencil-width booms curving around from the ears to the chin, leaving a gap for the mouth. His resident confirmed the shrouder device was operating, neutralising microbes exiting the mouth and nose, and any foreign flora which might try to enter. Despite a glove-tight fit, he didn't sweat inside the suit; again, something inside the suit acted on the sweat immediately. So, aside from looking like some cheap, decked-out retro-punk rock band leader, he felt relaxed, at least until he exited the ship.

The hatch swished open to reveal a gelatinous twinkling membrane across the hatchway. Micah knew he had to be first, so he braced himself and stepped through it – it was like walking through jelly. Micah's resident noted *exodermic sterilisation in progress*. The membrane was thin, and his body was almost through it when something snagged – his pulse pistol. Before he could do anything about it, the holster straps dissolved and the pistol clattered to the deck inside the ship, just as he emerged fully onto the other side. The same happened to Sandy and Zack as they came through.

"Guess there's a 'no-weapons' policy." Zack said.

They watched Ramires try – it snagged a while on his back pocket, then let him through with the nanosword.

"How come?" Zack asked.

Micah answered. "Maybe it doesn't know it's a weapon."

"Still," Zack said, "don't seem fair."

Micah felt a breeze brush his cheek, and without warning, all four of them were whisked off their feet. He held his breath as they were sucked down black corrugated tubing inside the needle connecting their ship to the hub, separated from instant space death by the gossamer thin pipeline funnelling them towards – well, he didn't know where. He felt like a spider being flushed down a loo, and hoped the comparison was incorrect. He saw flashing lights, heard banshees, and was buffeted by cold and hot air blasts. The resident relayed information from the needle's analysis of Micah and the others: air-breathers; gravitic tolerance level based on musculoskeletal design; environmental sensitivity ranges to heat, light, air pressure and ionising radiation; primary sensory modality visual, secondary auditory – it gave figures which he supposed were ranges on the EM spectrum; and approximate level intelligence. The last parameter took an extra second to register, deciding on five – presumably courtesy of the resident – which was the minimum level for entry into the hub. Micah wondered what would have happened if they'd been granted a four or even a three. The spider-down-the-toilet analogy came back to mind.

They arrived at a nexus, a spherical mirrored room with nine circular portals leading out of it. They hung in the middle, courtesy of a reflective gravity effect Earth's scientists had speculated upon, but never quite managed to create. Micah recognised it because when he moved his hand away from his body, he started to move in the opposite direction. "Er, nobody move, just give me a second," he warned the others floating behind him. He focused on the opposite portal. Nothing happened. *Shit, we have to think Level Five or we're going to get nowhere.* He returned to his analyst training, and imagined the sphere and its ten portals including the one through which they'd just entered. It was hard for most people to truly think in three dimensions, but easier for an Optron analyst. As he'd hoped, courtesy of the resident, in his mind he saw each portal with supplementary information. He pivoted inside his mind, inspecting each one, surmising that the resident had probably chosen him as host because he had certain skills which were going to make survival easier.

Each portal led to different basic functional requirements: grid access registration, weapons ordering, restoration facilities, ship trading, and entertainment. One slightly above and to the right was designated nutrition. That would be their priority, as their rations were getting so low they were starting to taste good. He opened his eyes.

"Well, Micah? Much as this is fun..." Sandy didn't need to complete the sentence.

"Working on it." He puzzled over what to do next. If this was a pure gravity reflection field, then Newton's laws would keep them there indefinitely. But alien tech would be smarter. It would work out what they wanted. He concentrated hard on the desired exit, but remained immobile. Of course, he thought, the machines aren't telepathic. Okay, he thought, so the computer has already analysed our musculature, so can detect muscle movements. He flexed his feet as if getting up, and angled his torso toward the portal. He began to move in its direction, accelerating. "Quick, all of you, just imagine you're walking to this portal, use your feet and follow –" He was sucked inside, and prayed the others got it in time. This time the trip was shorter, and he was deposited feet first onto a springy glass floor inside a room-sized, squat bubble the size and shape of a school bus. The others arrived one by one. Instinctively he held out a hand to help Sandy as she arrived, but she didn't take it. "Everyone okay?" he said, retracting his hand.

Zack answered first. "Well, boss, unless we all get one of those things inside our head, I reckon we need to stick together."

Sandy folded her arms, tight-lipped. Ramires spoke up. "Do we still have comms with Hannah?"

"Good point." Micah addressed his wristcom. "Hannah, can you hear me?"

"Yes, Micah, loud and clear. How's it going?"

"Well, we're in, so to speak. We'll contact you every thirty minutes. I strongly suggest you don't leave the ship – the phrase *culture shock* doesn't do it justice."

He surveyed the surreal landscape before him. All of them walked to the bubble's side, peering out at the sight beyond.

"Babel," Sandy said.

Before them stood a Christmas-tree-like array of hemispheres, each with a diameter of several hundred metres. Micah could see ten at any one time as the tree slowly rotated. The tree was in the centre of a vast honeycombed sphere, with thousands of bubbles – more like blisters from this viewpoint – like the one they stood in right now, encircling the tree. He couldn't see inside any of the others, but the overall effect was a thousand insect eyes gazing on the tree Sandy had aptly christened Babel. Fine opal tubes snaked from the hemispheres to some of the blisters, reminding Micah of a sea anemone's tendrils waving in the sea currents, hunting plankton.

"Hey, boys, you'll want to try this," Sandy said, exuberant again. She had picked up a metal visor from several lying on a shelf, and was studying the habitats.

Micah took one and held it to his eyes. At first nothing happened as he looked towards the tree. Then as he noticed a liquid environment he unconsciously tried to focus, and the image immediately zoomed in, spying various creatures, some like ancient marine dinosaurs on Earth, others squid-like, though none looked like actual fish.

"Infini-vision," Zack said, "every pilot's dream! Mil-tech tried to develop this just before the War. It must senses eye muscle movements and amplify accordingly – but this is real smooth!"

Micah found four basic environmental types – air-like, heavy gas, liquid, and dark. The dark ones were opaque to the visors, although Micah thought he saw shadows moving within the blackness.

He focused on one of the air environments. "Wow," he whispered, finding a menagerie of alien life-forms, from grey mushroom-shaped creatures whose means of locomotion escaped him, to a quadruped beast with an upper body of a scarlet manta ray. Numerous lime-coloured, diamond-shaped organisms with four rings around them rolled around the alien food market like gyroscopes, the diamonds remaining upright. His resident produced names for the various aliens he saw, but he paid no attention, just feasted on the abundance of forms life had found according to planetary demands and environmental niches. *Darwin could work here forever.*

"Hey, check this out," Sandy shouted, "fourth level down the tree, last habitat on the right, central section."

He pulled back from the visor, located the hemisphere, and then re-applied the optical device, wishing it to get closer. At first he couldn't make it out, but then he saw what she must be referring to. A black eel was lengthening itself impossibly into fractal patterns, in front of a white, straight eel. The white eel began to do the same thing, interlacing and meshing with the black eel. At first the fractal patterns made no sense, even though it was kaleidoscopic to watch, but then he realised that this dance was generating a black and white cube. A number of other alien life-forms had gathered to watch.

Sandy laughed. "Shouldn't they get a room?"

Good, she has her sense of humour back.

Ramires butted in, his voice regaining its usual deadly serious tone. "Bipeds, two levels below the fractal eels. Some look humanoid."

They all switched to the lower hemisphere, and found a range of bipeds, including one that looked uncannily human. Micah zoomed in to the human's face. "Mannekhi," he said, even before his resident confirmed it. "That's where we start."

He touched a finger on the inside edge of the bubble while staring at the habitat through the visor.

"Now look what you've gone and done," Sandy said.

Micah lowered the visor to see a tendril snaking its way toward them. As its head rose in front of them, its mouth opened, and then leached onto the outside of the bubble. They each took a step backwards, but the exit behind them sealed.

'Oh well,' he said, 'I'm sure it's –"

They arrived in the habitat in a split second.

"– okay," he finished.

"Sonofabitch, that was fast." Zack swept his fingers over his bald head. "Must've used some kind of inertial field. Didn't feel a damn thing!"

Ramires seemed the least shocked by the suddenness of the mode of transport. He wandered off down a plant-laden central aisle. "This way, I believe."

"Wait," Micah said. "Remember what Angel told us about Grid society level hierarchy, and how we mustn't address any more than two levels above our station?"

They nodded, wearily.

Zack grunted. "Institutionalised racism."

"Yep, but we have to respect it. Still, the good news is that every vendor I've checked out so far is Level Five or Six."

"Makes sense," Sandy said, "biggest market opportunity that way."

Micah continued. "Those levels are probably also agrarian, farmers, and we're here for food, so it's a good match."

Zack grinned. "You mean you can tell which is merchandise and which is alien, because, truth is, a few times I wasn't really sure."

Micah shook his head. "I know. We're in Wonderland here, and we have almost no idea of the rules, but a pretty good idea that punishment can be terminal. So, given I've got the resident, I'll do the talking."

"Business as usual there, Micah," Sandy quipped.

He shrugged, and let it go. Her sarcasm he could handle, indifference and the silent treatment, that was a different matter entirely. He caught up with Ramires, narrowly avoiding a sucker-like frond which tried to land on his head.

They passed a couple of tall saffron-caped mantas, and tried not to stare. Most of the merchandise was laid out on lawns of blue grass, with a vendor seated, hanging, or hovering in its midst. Micah's eyes tugged in the direction of pulsing fluorescent elliptoids which kept elongating and shrinking, changing airbrushed colours at an almost subliminal rate. His resident confirmed it was nutritional, but appended the name with a red cross – not suitable for his physiology. *Thanks, Angel, we really owe you one.*

He decided to follow Ramires' lead, and proceeded straight ahead to the Mannekhi's stall. The white-bearded, bald man with the same all-black eyes as Starkel, rose from his stool to greet them. He spoke in fluent Mannekhi, and Micah's resident translated. Micah relaxed, and spoke back naturally, knowing the resident would perform the requisite gymnastics with his vocal chords.

"Fine thank you...Yes, that's right, human, not Mannekhi, though we met one recently, name of Starkel... Ah, yes, the Games. Yes, the same one... Food, mainly, we have water... Payment, yes, hold on a minute, please.'

He turned to the others. Zack was looking at him sideways, Sandy found something interesting to stare at on the grass, while Ramires kept lookout.

"Pleasantries so far," he told them, "we're just getting down to business." He coughed, and tapped his wristcom. "Hannah? It's Micah; the subject of payment has come up."

"Thought it would. I'm zapping you the Q'Roth's name and a credit account cipher. The vendor must have some kind of optical reader, just put your wristcom next to it, it should work."

Sandy nudged Zack. "Remind me why he brought us along?"

Zack jabbed her back gently in the ribs. "Micah brought Ramires for his fighting skills, me for my good humour, and you because he was afraid of what you might do to Hannah." He tickled her ribs and they both packed out laughing. Micah frowned and turned back to the vendor, and completed the purchase.

"Okay guys, I've just bought us ... two hundred plaktars, four cubic metres of Zentbread, a nushell of Qimbari beans, and ten assorted eshnibar snacks. My resident says they're all nutritional and a good balanced diet for our needs. It's being sent back to the ship as we speak."

"So," Sandy said, "are we going to take a look around?"

Ramires cut in. "We must go *now*."

"What's the –" She paled as she glimpsed what Ramires had seen.

Micah twisted around, then wished he hadn't. A tall Q'Roth warrior was heading straight for them. "Okay, no running, let's just leave quietly." Zack tripped over a root on the ground, and stumbled into Ramires. He gathered himself, muttered an apology, and they all walked as fast as they could without breaking into a run, back the way they'd come, towards the tube. As they rounded a bend, Micah risked a glance backwards – the Q'Roth wasn't there. He prayed their luck would hold, but as they turned the final corner to reach the exit tube, they found the warrior half-crouching on four of its six legs, blocking their way. The Mannekhi vendor arrived by its side, out of breath. He spoke Q'Roth. This time Micah's resident translated for him – Micah guessed it had a learning mechanism, and had now heard enough to develop translation algorithms: "Yes, ambassador, these are the ones who just spent some of your credit." With that, the Mannekhi vendor left, not meeting Micah's glare.

The Q'Roth rose upright on its hind legs, a good three and a half metres in height, its two other pairs of legs spread wide. Its armour-plated torso shone like a beetle's wings in the hazy light, the six vermillion slits on its head waxing and waning. The ambassador's broad gash of a mouth yawned open, the Q'Roth words easing out like barbed-wire pulled through flesh, in serrated English. "Leaving so soon?"

Micah tapped his wristcom. He presumed the Q'Roth had some kind of translation device too. "Hannah, we've met the good ambassador. We may be dining early."

Courtesy of the resident, he spoke a halting Q'Roth. "My dear ambassador, we were merely attending to our needs for provisions. We will be honoured to meet you for dinner later."

His mid-claws pounded into the ground, causing a sputter of dust. He reverted to Q'Roth. "Do not insult my intelligence! You think an ambassador would be unaware of events in the Q'Roth line, including the recent destruction of two vessels chasing a ship with your registration? I merely wanted you off-ship, to be sure you could not escape again. As soon as you spent my credit, I knew where to find you. You will indeed join me for dinner, all of you, including the Alician traitor onboard your stolen vessel, which is now locked down and targeted by my own flagship. But first," it turned to Ramires, "this one has something of interest, detected when you left the ship, classed as a medical tool, but I believe it is a weapon."

Micah swallowed. The Q'Roth faced Ramires, dropping into an aggressive stance: its two back legs bent behind it, ready to launch forwards, while its mid legs clawed the ground, and its upper legs folded in two, projecting out horizontally in Ramires' direction. Its body slanted forward, its head statue-still. Micah had seen a praying mantis once, and knew the forelegs, when folded like this, could whip out faster than a man could blink, catching or shredding its prey. Ramires did not waver. Zack backed away from it, moving to its side.

"Ramires," Sandy whispered.

"Do not fear," he said. "All my life I have trained for this moment." He stood tall, and reached around with his left hand to his back pocket – and found it empty. A puzzle framed his normally serene brow, and then his eyes darted sideways at Zack. Micah followed his gaze just in time to see Zack's arms raised high as his large frame leapt silently forward and upward toward the Q'Roth, a shimmering violet line rising from the metal tube he gripped in both hands.

CHAPTER 22 – ARJUNA

Blake detected blue flashes at the end of the tunnel, and drew his pulse pistol. "Rashid, I go in, you brake." He breached the cave mouth, dived and rolled to the opposite wall, ready to fire. Rashid skidded to the lip of the entrance, pistol also raised. The only sound was their laboured breathing. Blake holstered his weapon and surveyed the scene.

Kostakis held Jennifer's limp but still breathing body in his arms, and there was a Hohash, though it looked very different to the ones they'd encountered so far. Instead of a pristine golden frame, it had copper vines twisted around it like rusted cabled steel, some of it frayed. The mirror surface was also different – it was fractured into eight uneven sections, each one bordered by a rusted gold ridge, reminding him of rice paddies he'd seen in Borneo during the War.

"What happened, Professor?"

"Dimitri, Commander, please. I tire of that particular anachronism, it has no meaning anymore."

"Dimitri, then." He noticed he did not seem to tire of holding her.

"I arrived and Jen was facing that thing. I imagine it accessed her node, and was communicating directly with her. She was screaming for it to stop; I felt so helpless, so I shouted too, and kicked it, or tried to – it can move very fast when it wishes to. You have some experience of this, I understand."

"Only second hand, but it made Kat black out more than once, till they established a rapport." He noticed Rashid tilting his head toward the floor.

Dimitri laid Jennifer on the ground. "So peaceful."

Blake frowned. Rashid now appeared to be praying, with his head bowed to the floor. "Rashid, what the hell are you doing? You introduced us to these damned artefacts in the first place. Can we focus on the problem?"

Rashid didn't budge. "That is what I am doing, Commander. I believe this Hohash, which I imagine is far older than the others, judging by its condition, is guarding something precious." He placed his visor against the ground, rocking his head side-to-side slowly. "Something miraculous," he whispered.

Dimitri, unangered like Blake, joined Rashid. "Tell us, what do you see, or rather, hear?"

Rashid lifted his head, and sat on the ground. "Professor – and I call you that because I was also a man of science, and I respect your work back on Earth a great deal – you never really explained why you were here."

"Well," Dimitri beamed, "I joined Vasquez' mission just to get out of the city, away from the politics, but I had no enthusiasm to go on an engineering mission. I suppose I am still a scientist."

"But why here?"

Dimitri studied his feet, like an overgrown schoolboy trying to explain his missing homework. "I overheard Antonia talking about these caves. She confided in me that if I was ever in trouble, to come here."

Rashid stuck to his thread. "That was convenient, but not why you really came here, nor why you stayed here, was it?"

Blake stated the obvious. "The eggs, Rashid, he found the eggs."

Rashid stood up, amidst Dimitri's silence. "Professor Kostakis is not a biologist, Commander. He is a Gaiologist, one who studied the interconnectedness of Earth's ecology as if it was a single being, but first and foremost he is an oceanographer."

Blake shook his head. "But there are no..." He paused. "Wait a minute, you're not telling me –"

"An underground ocean!" Dimitri interjected, unable to contain himself any longer, his arms taking off. "Huge, as big as the Atlantic, underneath the first crust."

Blake's brow furrowed. "Does that have anything to do with the eggs?"

Dimitri looked to Rashid, who answered, "No, I don't believe so. I suspect the ocean is ancient. You found a way in, didn't you, Professor?"

He nodded. "Far below, a glass wall, a platform, and I trekked for days above a roiling ocean, smooth perfect waves, never breaking, uniform as the planet's rotation."

Blake felt out of his depth, never at ease in the company of scientists. But he tried to get with the game. "Did the spiders somehow sink the ocean, or is this natural?"

"Ah, now we turn to my speciality,' Rashid said, "terraforming theory."

Dimitri tugged at his beard. "Really! Why didn't you tell me?"

Rashid addressed Blake. "It is certainly not natural, and I believe beyond the spider's technological ability. My sonar can detect the ocean, and I see how deep it is, but also that the second crust beneath this one, underlying the ocean, is smooth and of an impermeable, synthetic material, not rock as we'd expect."

Dimitri placed two fingers delicately, as if touching a butterfly's wings, on the rim of Rashid's dolphin. "Amazing, almost worth losing one's sight for. Such an instrument!"

Blake sighed. He knelt down next to Jennifer, and noticed the first signs of stirring. Although not fond of her, he wanted a more military mind to balance the odds. A cheek muscle twitched, a tremor skidded down her forearm. He addressed Dimitri: "So, why the secrecy?"

Now Dimitri stared hard at Rashid, and shook his head very lightly.

Blake hadn't missed the covert signal, scientist to scientist. "What? What is it? What's so important about finding an ocean? I don't see how that alone has geopolitical magnitude right now, given our predicament."

Rashid patted Dimitri's arm. "I am sorry, but Blake is our rightful leader on this planet. He needs to know. We must trust in him."

Dimitri met Blake's eyes, with something approaching a look of pity. "But he is ... a soldier. Where you and I see scientific wonder, he sees weapons."

Blake stared back, but didn't know what to reply. He'd heard it before, but now, for the first time, it cut deep. *Was it true?*

"It's not the ocean, Commander," Rashid said, "but what's in it."

"Wrong," Jennifer said, prizing herself up on her elbows. With Blake's help, she sat up, held her head, massaging her temples. "It's not what's in it," she said, "but *who* is in it."

She accepted Dimitri's outstretched arm as he helped her up. "Come on," she said, "the Hohash is going to show us the way."

They continued ever downwards, tracking behind the blue glow of the Hohash along narrow paths spiralling around an abyssal crevasse. They travelled so deep Blake wondered if he'd ever see sunlight again. And then he heard it, the unmistakable swelling of waves, water moving, the salty smell of the sea. It triggered such a strong feeling of homesickness that he had to stop to catch his breath, thinking of all that had been lost. The salt water odour flooded back memories of sailing in San Francisco Bay, scuba diving off Point Lobos near Monterey, and sunbathing with Glenda and Robert on Venice Beach. He felt a shard of guilt for having left so many on Earth to perish at the hands of the Q'Roth. He leant against the crevasse wall, steadied himself, and then continued walking.

"Yes," Rashid said, in front, "the smell of an ocean takes your breath away doesn't it? When we get there, please describe it to me, because despite what Dimitri said, I'd trade almost anything to have my eyes back, to see the things and people I love and care about."

He knew Rashid meant Sonja. His mind made the inevitable connection. *Where are you Zack? I need you, dammit. I can lead, but I need a strong second; that was always you.*

Dimitri's voice boomed out. "The oxygen is very heavy down here, it may make you feel light-headed, emotional even."

Yep, that must be it, Blake said to himself, not believing it for an instant, but then he of all people understood that soldiers are trained to follow orders, whether or not they believed in them. He battened down the emotional hatches, and regained his rhythm.

Blake stepped onto the glass gingerly, like a cat, despite having seen Jennifer and the Professor clatter down onto it. Beneath his feet, some thirty metres or so, dimly lit from the cave's light source which he couldn't pinpoint, was a black sea, wave crests rolling past every thirty seconds; they were massive.

"So, what exactly is in the ocean?"

Rashid's boots thumped onto the glass behind him. "A ship, but a ship like no other we have ever encountered."

He turned to see where Rashid was staring, but only saw the dark sheen of the ocean reflecting from the domed cavern's glows. "I don't get it, Rashid – your sonar shouldn't be able to detect a ship through glass, air and then water. The dolphin's just not that good."

Dimitri spoke while turning on a small apparatus lying in the centre of the glass floor. "Yes, Rashid, you must tell us – I am also intrigued. I only found it when using this ultra-low frequency scanner."

"It is breathing," he replied, "very slowly."

Blake stared first at him, and then glanced down again through the glass floor. Dimitri focused instead on the screen illuminating his face in green. "Come, Commander, take a look."

Blake saw fuzz at first, then a figure emerged. He made out a triangular section like an arrowhead jutting out from a narrow neck, joined to the body of the ship, which was shaped like a semi-circle at the top, tapering down at the bottom. The ship resembled an elongated crossbow, pointing straight upwards out of the ocean.

"Arjuna," Rashid said quietly, gazing through the floor, since he could not observe two-dimensional displays. "The mythical archer from the Bhagavad Gita. This is a noble ship, if ever there was one to behold."

Blake had to admit its symmetry was elegant. He smiled – Zack would go nuts over this. "What's the scale, Professor? I think Rashid is right. You've earned the title, and God knows we need to research and learn if we're going to survive on this planet." He detected a blush beneath Dimitri's shroud of a beard, though it was hard to be sure in the grey light.

"The vessel is ten kilometres long. The top section alone is half a kilometre in length."

Blake turned to Jennifer. "Now it's your turn. What, or who, is inside the ship?"

She nodded to the Hohash. "The creators of these artefacts."

Dimitri got there first. "So the spiders –"

"Are a relatively new species. The one in the ship is very, very old. It came here aeons ago, with a number of Hohash. It terraformed the planet to create an underground ocean where it and its ship could hide. The spiders were barely sentient at that time, but the Hohash interacted with them, and educated them."

No one spoke for a while, as they digested this information, re-writing their basic assumptions about the spider race, and the Hohash. Blake cleared his throat. "Why did you scream, Jennifer? I heard Kat scream the first time, but she cried out in pain – forgive me, but your cry was one of fear."

"My Jen is not afraid of anything," Dimitri exclaimed.

She narrowed her eyes, then relaxed. Blake wasn't sure on whose account, his or Dimitri's. "You're right, Commander. It showed me something, an image, and conveyed an intense emotion of fear; actually, more like dread of pure evil matched with unstoppable power. Something has happened out in the galaxy, something much bigger than us or our petty problems. The seeds of a galactic catastrophe have been sewn."

"And this ship," Rashid said, "is somehow a key?"

"Yes," she said.

Blake recognised the look of uncertainty on her normally confident face. "So, what's the problem?"

She tapped the screen. "Arjuna – we might as well call it that, as I don't know its name – is dormant, and won't respond to the Hohash. So our Hohash friend here wants us to wake it. Well, *him* actually. You see, there's a single occupant inside the ship."

They discussed it for hours, until they were getting too tired to think straight. They ate rations more or less in silence. Jennifer refused to sit with Dimitri, and responded to all of his questions with either monosyllabic answers or a shrug. The problem was that the ship was far below the water's surface, they had no pressurised ship to explore it, no other obvious means of making contact, and the only deep diving gear was back in Esperantia. Blake acknowledged that perhaps this was of a higher priority in the grand scale of things, but there was nothing he could do, and there were other priorities he *could* do something about.

In the morning, he awoke later than planned. Rashid was doing some form of callisthenic exercises, and Dimitri and Jennifer were far away on the other side of the chamber, sitting close to each other, talking. He could tell by their body language that at least some problems had been resolved. *Good, we have enough real wars on our hands.*

On seeing him awake, they came over. Jennifer took the lead. "We've decided, while you slept, Commander."

"Really? And do I get a say in the matter?"

"Dimitri and I are staying here, to try and help the Hohash contact the ship's occupant. You and Rashid take Dimitri's skimmer back to the city – the Hohash will show you the way back to the surface. Rashid will return with the diving gear. You must tell Shakirvasta that I was killed. It is imperative he believes I am dead, or else he will come looking, and find ... this." She scuffed the glass floor with her boot. "You must give me your word, Commander."

Blake chewed his lip. He never liked giving promises, but it seemed like a lightweight one. "Very well. I give you my word. As for the rest, it sounds reasonable. I can go along with it, Jennifer."

She looked down to the floor, then met his eyes head on, but her eyes were softer. "It's Jen, from now on, just Jen. I will join you if I can. One more thing." She squeezed her lips together, as if trying to hold something in. She held out an opened envelope. Her hand was shaking. "If Sandy returns, I..." Her voice broke. Dimitri wrapped an arm around her waist, and she took a breath. "I'd like to see her, Commander."

He stared at it, then pushed her hand back gently, folding her fingers around the envelope. "I already know about Sandy's pregnancy, Jen. Vince told me about it before the battle, but swore me to secrecy. You see, I do know how to keep my word." He got to his feet. "And I understand, Jen. Good luck, both of you." With that, he and Rashid departed, escorted by the Hohash out of the cavern.

* * *

Blake strode down the main avenue in Esperantia. It was noon. Plenty of soldiers – Shakirvasta's militia rather than Blake's original men – had seen him, but no one had stopped him yet. A swelling throng emerged from their dwellings to see if it was really him. Good, he thought, this way Rashid can get the gear out of the city and back to Jen.

He arrived at the central plaza, a straggling crowd behind him, and stepped up on top of one of the spider's tables dotted around the square. He stood a while, meeting the eyes of many in the crowd, then raised both his arms.

"People of Esperantia, people of Earth, I have returned."

"And you are under arrest for the unlawful killing of a number of soldiers."
Josefsson approached with a not quite steady gait from a shaded portico outside the largest dwelling. A phalanx of militia flanked him, pulse rifles at their waists.

"I acted in self defence."

"Ah, but there are witnesses, Mr. Alexander."

"Commander."

"Not any longer; you see the constitution states –" he paused long enough to make eye contact with several in the crowd, "– as it did so back on Earth, that the President is in charge of the military, and I have suspended your commission pending your trial."

Blake had expected much of this, but it didn't make it any easier. He'd seen Josefsson as something of a fool, but public speaking was the senator's – now the President's – home ground, even if he was a puppet for Shakirvasta. Josefsson seemed in no hurry to make the arrest, wallowing in this charade. Blake knew he had to tread carefully.

He turned back to the crowd. "You people need to be released from the shackles Shakirvasta has placed on you. He's building an autocracy, enslaving people here." He looked around the crowd, saw some nods, though not as many as he'd hoped for. He wondered where Antonia and Sonja were – they should have arrived by now.

"Nonsense, Commander – there, I accord you the title based on the merit that you were one of our greatest heroes, rescuing us from the brink of extinction at the hands of our real enemy, the Q'Roth and humanity's bastards, the treacherous Alicians."

He saw how deftly Josefsson worked the crowd. A little too quickly, some people in the melee shouted out "Death to the Alicians," undoubtedly Josefsson's men planted in the audience; this had all been pre-arranged. That's why Josefsson was so confident. Which meant that either they'd intercepted his message, or they'd gotten to Antonia or Sonja. Or else Shakirvasta was just too damned good.

Josefsson continued, jutting out his chin, his greying blond hair shining in Aryan fashion in the pale orange sunlight. "Our Chairman, Sanjay Shakirvasta, has provided for everyone." He addressed the crowd. "Do you go hungry? Do your children not have schools to go to? Are your medical needs not addressed? Yes, of course we all have to work hard out in the fields, and I assure you that Mr Shakirvasta barely sleeps, working all hours to oversee the re-building of humanity, getting us back on our feet, readying us to prepare for the day when we can exact revenge on the Alicians and the Q'Roth."

More shouts this time, others joining in, not just the stooges planted in the gathering. Blake was losing this fast. He addressed the crowd, his words quiet, so they had to strain to listen. "It doesn't have to be like this. Look into your hearts. We haven't come all this way to become locked into a tyranny, with Shakirvasta as dictator."

Josefsson advanced on Blake. "My dear Sir, you've been brainwashed by a few insurgents, terrorists who as we speak are being brought to the justice they deserve. The services you have given for mankind will be taken into consideration when you are sentenced, Commander. Chairman Shakirvasta has already decreed this."

Blake's patience broke. "Shakirvasta –"

"Saved your good wife Glenda, Commander," Josefsson shouted to the crowd, as he joined Blake on the table. He faced Blake, lowering his voice, though clear enough for all to hear. "And yet you, Blake Alexander, are responsible for the death of Mr. Shakirvasta's consort, Jennifer."

Blake's anger stalled. He was snared. It was Josefsson's coup de grace, and Blake had to bite his lip, he'd given his word to Jen. For a fraction of a second it crossed his mind that Jen had been part of this – but he decided not, given her reaction to Sandy's letter. In any case, a word given was final in his book. He'd lost this round. He gazed once more across the crowd. "This is your world, you must decide what kind of world you want it to be, while the decision is still yours to make." The crowd stilled. "Josefsson, I'll come with you now, but I want to see my wife."

Josefsson nodded. "The arrangements are already being made."

A glint of triumph peaked above the veneer of Josefsson's practiced air of even-handedness. It was enough to enable Blake to do what he always did in situations like this: he transmuted his anger, storing it for later. Josefsson must have seen it in Blake's eyes, because his smile faltered for a fraction of a second. He leaned forward to Blake and whispered. "I'd rather not use force, Commander."

"There'll be no more trouble today. Now, I'd like to see her." Without waiting to be led, he jumped down from the table and made his way through the crowd, forcing Josefsson and the soldiers to trail behind him. He knew exactly where Shakirvasta's residence was. The crowd stayed closely packed around him, slowing him down.

"Make way, please, make way," Josefsson shouted, ineffectively.

Blake looked straight ahead as he cut his way through the crowd. He felt a number of people touch his arms, some shook his hand, a few saluted. Several times he heard whisperings: "May God be with you." Once he heard "We're still with you, Commander."

At the edge of the crowd he recognised the familiar, pudgy face of Carlson, the psychologist, rushing toward him. Carlson shook his hand heavily, his greasy hair shaking with the effort. He spoke openly. "Antonia and Sonja have been arrested, and they have Sonja's children in custody." He raised an eyebrow. "And I'm next, on a trumped-up charge of sedition."

"That's quite enough of that, Mr. Carlson," Josefsson said, finally catching up. The soldiers fanned out behind them, separating them from the crowd. "Let's go, shall we? Mr.Carlson, I really think you should join us, don't you?"

"Wouldn't have it any other way, Mr. President.'

As their entourage left the crowd behind, the chattering from the throng rose in volume. This isn't over, thought Blake. A broad smile spread across his lips.

A puzzle creased Carlson's brow as he trudged along next to Blake. "I'm not so sure why are you're so happy, Commander?"

"I'm going to see my wife," he said, "and as Kat would say if she were here, it's about bloody time."

When they rounded the final bend, he saw her willowy frame and short blonde hair ruffled by the breeze, standing tall and frail supported by two walking sticks. He couldn't restrain himself any longer. He broke into a run to greet her. As he swept her into his arms and held her tight, he spoke softly, his lips against her ear: "Nothing else matters except this, Glenda, nothing, just this." Her breathing stuttered beneath her sobs, her weakened legs trembled. He clasped her closer to his chest, feeling how thin she was.

"I held on for you Blake, just for you."

His emotions broke through. "I'm here now."

Carlson paced nearby, defying anyone to break up the embrace. "Let them have this moment," he said to Josefsson, who begrudgingly acquiesced.

Blake drew back, finally, and brushed the salt water from her hollowed cheeks with the backs of his fingers, traced a finger over the hairless, painted eyebrows, and adjusted her blonde wig back into perfect place. "I'm ready now," he said to her. "Don't worry, Glenda, it's not over. Hang on a little longer if you can." She nodded. He turned to Josefsson. "Let's get this done."

CHAPTER 23 – MURDER

Ramires screamed the loudest kiai Micah had ever heard, to distract the Q'Roth, but its slits must have detected Zack. It whipped its upper right leg to intercept him. The nanosword sailed right through it – it would have found the creature's head too had its reflexes not been ultra-quick, as it ducked backwards just in time. Its right mid-leg slammed into Zack's torso, lifting him off the ground just as he landed, blood splashing out as one of the leg's serrated thorns punctured soft human flesh. Two of the Q'Roth's other free legs lashed at Ramires in a shredding motion, so fast they were a blur. Ramires managed to dive out of the way, but the Q'Roth continued to flail two of his legs to fence him off. Zack landed with a thump a couple of metres away. "Ramires!" he cried out and spun the nanosword through the air towards him. The Q'Roth readied itself to intercept the sword as it wind-milled through the air. But out of the blue, Sandy leapt forward, snatched the sword's hilt and in one simple move thrust it point first into the centre of the Ambassador's head. Ramires vaulted over the stalled, quivering legs and planted both his hands around Sandy's, driving the blade down through the Q'Roth's torso, spilling black, sizzling guts onto the ground as the creature slumped backwards.

"I was just about to do that," Sandy said.

Ramires flicked a switch on the hilt, retracting the blade. "Nice catch."

"Sabre champion, summer of '52." She stared down at their handiwork.

Micah dashed over to Zack, who had his back to them. He rolled him over and recoiled. "Shit! That looks bad!" Blood streamed from a cone-shaped hole the size of a fist. Intestines, muscles and sinews, and at least one organ were in clear view.

Zack groaned, "Not as bad as your bedside manner!"

"Don't talk, Zack." he said.

Ramires and Sandy arrived, leaning over Micah's shoulder. "Ramires, can we patch this up back on the ship?"

Ramires shook his head. "It's taken a chunk out of your liver, Zack. I'm sorry, friend."

Sandy moved around the others and knelt next to Zack. "Wait, what are you saying? We can't leave him here!"

Zack choked up some blood. "Get the fuck out of here, all of you, before the alien police arrive. This ain't curable, Micah, mission comes first, just go." Zack's head lurched backwards, his face wracked with pain.

"We're not going to leave you, Zack! Are we?" She leaned across Zack's shaking frame, glaring at Micah. "Don't you go turning into Blake."

Micah tapped his wristcom. "Hannah, Zack is down, we're in trouble here. Can you break free?"

There was no reply. He spun around to Ramires. "If you want to go..." He didn't much care for the look of indignation on Ramires' face. "Okay, forget it. Can we stem the flow in some way, cauterise it with the sword?"

Ramires stared at the open wound. "No. Q'Roth thorns include an anticoagulant, so the blood runs free till there's none left."

"Zack," Sandy said, "stay with us."

His body was shaking. "T-tell ... Sonja..." He coughed up more blood. Together they tried to manoeuvre him into a recovery position so he wouldn't drown in it.

"Micah!" Ramires pointed at a dog-like creature wearing a white robe and a gold and lapus lazuli head-dress, approaching them on a floating disc. The creature took one look at the Ambassador and then came over towards Zack. It opened its mouth revealing thin cord-like strands, and emitted a grating noise which forced all three of them to back away. It stooped over Zack's face, which was turning a sickly yellow colour, and sprayed fine white foam over the ragged wound. Micah was just getting used to the hope that this alien might actually be able to save Zack, when one of its silver hands morphed into a spear-like syringe and plunged straight into Zack's forehead. Zack's body bucked upwards once, then collapsed to the floor, eyes wide open, vacant, his chest still. Ramires' hand pulled out the nanosword and primed its blade in one flowing movement. The dog-like creature – Ossyrian, Micah's resident informed him – cocked its head, its silver eyes staring at the blade. Ramires raised it and brought it down on the Ossyrian. The blade stopped dead a centimetre from the Ossyrian's dark brown head, a fizzing of light spattering out from the point of contact. Ramires' forearms flexed, trying to cut through the field.

"Wait, Ramires," Micah said. "It's a doctor."

"Then why did it just kill Zack?" Ramires took a step back. He lowered the sword, but didn't switch it off.

Micah didn't know if his resident could translate Ossyrian or not. Before he could try, however, four crystal spheres arrived on the scene, hovering above each of their heads, including one which approached Zack's inert frame.

He glanced at Sandy, standing over Zack's inert body. "Zack was right, we should have –"

There was darkness. Micah tried to remember what he was about to say, what he was doing. Who he was. But he couldn't think. He wasn't asleep, but it was like a stuck disk, as if he couldn't remember *how* to think. With an effort, and because he'd been trained how to do it by his Zen master as an emergency escape in case of Optron terminal looping, he split his mind into two, creating a temporary schismata running in the background. It was still dark, and one part of him was still locked in some kind of thought-dampening bubble. But another part was now free.

Since he had no sense of space or touch, he presumed he must be in stasis. He considered what might be going on. On Earth, when criminals were apprehended – suspects, he corrected himself – they were handcuffed, and taken to a cell. So ... what if in this culture, you were ... *mind-cuffed*? It made sense; it would be easier to handle people who were cognitively inactivated. He heard a noise. Not good. They know I've found a loophole. The noise grew, sounding like a space-craft landing just above him. He knew they were shutting down the schismata as well. He thought about options, but he had none left. The noise became unbearable, and even though he knew it was only in his mind, unfortunately, that's where he was. He gave up, no point doing himself mental damage. His second mind shut down.

Micah came to, standing on a small circular glass plinth suspended above – well, he could see nothing beneath him at first, just a gaping chasm, but as his eyes adjusted, he saw stars. Twenty metres beneath him lay open space, presumably behind some kind of force-field like the one the Ossyrian had been wearing. It crossed his mind that this was an illusion, but if so it was an elaborate one whose purpose he couldn't fathom. He turned around carefully on the platform not much wider than his stance, and saw three other disks behind and beneath him. All three were standing – including Zack. But they were asleep.

A piercing sapphire light shone into his eyes, increasing in size till he realised something was coming toward him. When it arrived, Micah was surprised to see an ostrich-like creature with an indeterminate number of legs, like a millipede. *Finchikta*, his resident informed him, *Level 9; judicial officer; do not address until it has first addressed you.* A sharp mental twang, as if someone had just plucked a guitar string inside his skull, accompanied that last piece of information.

The creature had three eyes – Micah hadn't noticed until the third one opened. He wasn't expecting it to speak English, though. *Polyglot,* the resident stated.

"Facts: Q'Roth Ambassador assassinated by those calling themselves human; illegal weapon brought into Market area; stolen Q'Roth ship, last reported at scene of two Q'Roth ships destroyed. Verdict: guilty of murder of high ranking official, space vehicle theft, murder of twenty-four Q'Roth onboard two destroyed vessels; use of second illegal weapon, namely a transit-mine. Punishment: voiding."

It was fast, dream-like. Micah assumed at first this was some sort of arraignment, an outline of the charges being brought against them. But as he heard and felt the disc underneath him crackle and splinter, he realised that they'd just been tried, convicted and sentenced in twenty seconds. "Wait!" he yelled, as the Finchikta turned to depart. "What about our side of the story?"

The Finchikta paused, then continued on its way.

"Fuck," he said, glancing at the glass splintering underneath his feet. A fragment fell, and as it hit the barrier it flashed and passed straight through into open space. The resident, detecting his and its own plight, began showing him potential juridical procedures Micah might be able to use to stall their imminent demise. The Finchikta's sapphire light was fading. Micah heard the others behind him waking up, and then various expletives as they each realised their predicament, but he had no time to explain. His left foot fell through the disk, and he only just managed to find his balance, bending over and gripping both sides of the disk with his hands.

"Micah!" Sandy screamed up to him, but he focused on the options flowing through his mind. The blue light was just a dot now, about to go out. There! That was it, he was sure, had to be. He lifted his head and shouted as loud as he could: "I declare retribution grounds for species violation." The glass held. "Species 195 Q'Roth committed unlawful genocide of species human in ... angt 753871GDS."

Suddenly the bird was right next to him. "No need to shout," it said. "I hear very well."

Micah managed to bring his leg back up through the hole, and sat on the remaining crescent of his disk.

The Finchikta's third eye was closed. "Q'Roth had permission to cull human species Level Three."

"Not Level Three. Am I Level Three?"

The third eye opened, staring at Micah. It closed again. "Possible irregularity. Adjourn. Gather more evidence." It turned to leave again.

"No," Micah said, firm. "Trial." Micah was scanning the resident's outpouring of information, downloading direct into his brain as if he'd just remembered it. "Species violations ... require trial, judged by ... Tla Beth." He'd seen enough now. "We have rights, this is not just a defence, this is a prosecution against the Q'Roth for direct violation of Grid Society laws." He folded his arms.

The bird paused, staring at him for a long time. Micah was glad the others stayed quiet, for now.

The bird's two main eyes closed, just as the third one, central and slightly above the others, opened. "Are you sure you want to do this?"

The offhand manner of the question disconcerted Micah, but he decided he had to see this through. Without a trial, 'gathering more evidence' would involve the Q'Roth – it would just delay his and the others' deaths a few days at most. He nodded. "Yes."

The third eye closed and the other two opened again. "Trial begins tomorrow. Q'Roth delegation en route. Ranger recalled. Tla Beth representative in station. Deposition candidate will be taken in one hour. You will select."

He had no idea what that meant, he would need to study some more. The bird's two eyes closed, and the central one opened. "*You* are above level three." The eye closed, the other two opened, and the creature backed off into the distance. The glass began growing to its full disk width. The phrase *deposition candidate* wasn't clear to him, and he had the feeling it was significant. He slipped into memory replay mode, while the others shouted to him.

"Micah," Zack said, "wanna tell me why I'm not dead? And what was all that about anyway?"

Sandy shouted too. "Zack, Micah's just trying to impress us, since he's lousy with a nanosword." She laughed, relieved. "We're impressed, Micah, really. You just saved our necks."

His smile at this slipped, however, as the missing fragment of information – deposition candidate – surfaced in his mind. *Oh Shit,* he thought, *one of us has to die!*

"What were you thinking, Micah?" Sandy stomped up and down the curved, windowless cell. The walls were the colour and texture of jade, revealing tantalising shadows outside whose form and purpose they could only guess at.

"He was saving our lives, Sandy." Ramires sat in a lotus position on the bench which ran around half the room.

Micah noted Zack was silent on the issue. "Well" he said, standing up, "it was my call, so I should –"

"Sit the fuck down," Zack said.

"Zack," Micah began.

"Has made up his mind." Zack finished.

The way Zack said it, Micah had the feeling there was no way he could go up against it.

"Shit, this sucks." Sandy kicked the wall. A dull boom reverberated around the cell. "Alien justice – it's insane!"

"Dunno," Zack said, oddly calm. "Kinda makes sense to me. If we'd have had this option in the War, I sure as hell woulda used it on the enemy. Anyway," he stood up and stretched, "when in Rome, as they used to say. You guys have something ahead – me, it's mostly behind. Trust me, ain't no picnic living like that. Shoulda died along with my platoon back in Thailand. Carrying around that time bomb in my head, nearly killing Blake, driving Sonja nuts..."

Micah didn't know what to say; their time was almost up.

Before Micah or the others could remonstrate with him, the single, circular door opened, revealing the Finchikta – Micah didn't know if it was the same one – standing on its filament legs, in front of a large sphere of shifting colours. Zack stood up and without warning or being asked to, walked toward the bird. Its third eye opened, staring at him. Zack waved a goodbye – no last words – and stood in front of the sphere. It hovered toward him and then enveloped him completely. Sandy joined Micah at the doorway, clutching his wrist so hard it hurt, but he just watched. Within a minute, the sphere retreated, leaving behind a translucent form of Zack, like a highly detailed waxwork model made of crystal. But even from the way it stood, Micah knew it wasn't Zack anymore. Micah's resident kicked in. *Transpar* – that was what this simulacrum was called – a transparent witness, unable to lie, his personality erased completely, his bodily functions obliterated. A vessel containing transparent memory strings – the perfect witness. The resident offered a footnote: *Transpar procedure used only for species below Level 8, since such species cannot be trusted to know or tell the truth reliably.* The idea stung Micah.

The Finchikta addressed Micah and the others. "You will remain silent during the deposition, on pain of immediate death. It turned to the crystal Transpar. "You have the memories of the human known as Zack."

It didn't sound like a question, more a statement, a judicial formality.

"Yes," the Transpar said, its voice tinkling like wind chimes. Even its eyes were transparent, like watery glass.

"Did you help kill the Q'Roth Ambassador?"

"Yes."

"Did you help kill the other Q'Roth using a transit mine?"

"Yes."

Sandy clutched Micah's arm. This wasn't looking good.

"Do you wish the destruction of the Q'Roth race?"

"Yes," it answered, without hesitation.

"Does this go for these humans, and the rest remaining on Ourshiwann?"

Shit!

"Yes."

The Finchikta spoke to Micah. "Deposition received. Trial convenes tomorrow. If you lose, your race will be handed over to the Q'Roth. Do you wish to call any witnesses in your defence?"

Micah had been pondering that one, remembering his discussions with Rashid before they'd left the planet. "You mentioned a Ranger. Was he present during the ... Q'Roth incursion?"

"The Ranger Ukrull will be present. Anyone else?"

He looked glum and shook his head.

"The Transpar is now the property of the court."

Sandy spoke up, risking protocol defiance. "What if we win? Do we get him back? Can you –"

The Finchikta's third eye opened. "Your friend is no more."

The court official and the effigy of Zack left, the door squelching closed behind them. Sandy sat down, laying her head on Ramires shoulder. Micah waited for her to attack him, to curse him for what he'd done. Nothing came. That made it all the worse.

Micah went into analysis mode several times during what he presumed was night, but each time the predictions came out with deplorable survival odds. He'd gambled on a legal procedure to save their four lives in the short term, losing Zack's straight away, and unwittingly putting humanity's survival down as collateral. The one parameter of uncertainty in the equation was Hannah. He speculated as to whether she had somehow escaped, and could warn the others back on Ourshiwann. But why would she? She wasn't welcome back there in any case.

He glanced over to Ramires, who looked up from his meditation. Sandy was asleep, curled up next to him.

"Micah, you did the best you could."

"Not exactly an accolade given the way things look right now."

"Perhaps it is better this way. You've placed humanity on trial, but at least this way it will be resolved. We cannot hide on Ourshiwann for long, some alien race will find us. If we can demonstrate we're better than Level Three, maybe then we have a chance."

Micah stared into his lap. "I know you're trying to help, Ramires, but if my skills are at least Level Four, and I hope to God they are, then they're telling me we're all going to end up in the hands of the Q'Roth."

The doorway opened. "Hello Micah." Hannah stood at the entrance but didn't enter. Sandy stirred. Ramires unfolded his legs.

"Hannah, where have you been? What happened?" Micah was puzzled by the taut, scared look on her face. He saw a shadow behind her. A tall woman in a blood red gown advanced into the room, her long dark hair strained back into a braided ponytail. A sneer spread across her face, accented by her hooked nose and hawkish eyes.

"I happened, Micah."

Ramires leapt towards her. A blur of fists and feet flailed in her direction, but she moved unbelievably fast, blocking every attack with arrogant ease. Her palm shot into his chest, slamming him back across the room into the wall.

"Sister Esma," Micah said.

Her sneer deepened, a crevasse opening up in her white-as-snow face. She studied Sandy helping the winded Ramires back into a seated position, but said nothing.

Good, she doesn't know whose child Sandy is carrying. Micah met Hannah's eyes, and for the briefest moment, she shook her head. He wasn't sure what it signified, whether it was an apology, or her way of saying don't fight back, but it meant something to Micah. He suspected Sister Esma had arrived unannounced, and Hannah had made a quick survival choice. She hadn't actually betrayed them – him, he thought, because it mattered to him personally.

He watched Sister Esma, High Priestess of the Alician Order, architect of Earth's demise – *we finally meet.*

She addressed him. "I see this as a wonderful opportunity. Since obviously Louise failed to crush humanity, now the Grid Court will do it for me. The galaxy works in mysterious ways, indeed."

"Come to gloat, bitch?" Sandy said, walking right up to her.

"You are with child, my dear, which is the only reason your neck is intact."

Micah took Sandy's wrist. "But she has a point. If you have nothing to say, leave."

"I do have something to say, Micah. I wanted you all to know that we are prospering on our new home world, and Alicians have already begun to explore the Grid. Humanity – the upgraded Alician version – will continue and thrive, taking its rightful place in the galaxy. Oh, and we will be awarded the Transpar after your execution and humanity's extermination. We will keep it as a memento, reminding our children never to slip backwards."

Micah gripped Sandy's wrist stronger, feeling her tug against him.

"Well, see you in court." She left, ensuring Hannah departed first so she could not make any eye contact with the others. The door slid closed.

"She's lying," Sandy said.

"About what?"

"I don't know Micah, but I know when somebody lies to my face. She's afraid of something. That's why she came here, to try and provoke us, to throw us off-balance. She's worried the court might find us above Level Three."

He nodded dully, but his predictions said that the Alician presence made their case worse. He'd been considering ways to show humanity's ingenuity, but now the Alicians would argue that all the inventions, the great advances, were on their account, not ordinary humans. There was no evidence either way, so it would just be their word against Esma's, and the dead Q'Roth Ambassador would tip the scales against mankind's favour.

Sandy seized his shoulders and shook him. "Micah, are you listening to me? We have a chance. She came here to try to put you off, even parading Hannah in front of you like stolen spoils, and the parting shot about Zack. You're the threat, Micah, because you're so damned intelligent. Don't you see? We have a chance."

He bit his lip. Her words made sense, but his emotions were in freefall. She pulled his hands down to her belly. "You feel this, Micah? There's a child in there. It's Gabriel's son. That witch killed his father, so don't you dare give up on me now. I want my son to see daylight, dammit."

He felt a movement there, in her belly. It jolted him, and the feeling of having been beaten subsided. He pulled her to him and held her, tight. Cold fire, Zack had said. He put his pessimistic analyses aside, and let her go. "Ramires, I'm going to need a fast history lesson, the Sentinels and the nine hundred years' war against the Alicians."

Ramires stood, rubbing his chest. "Gladly, but first... Sandy, you said *Gabriel*."

"Yes, a Sentinel like you."

"Not like me. He was the best. I did not know him, but we had the same Master, Cheveyo, who gave his life on Eden in combat with the Q'Roth."

"Is it a problem?" she asked.

"No ... quite the opposite. My Master's last wish he conveyed to me was to protect you. Now I understand why. I will protect you and your child with my life, until it ends."

Sandy risked a smile. "Best offer I've had for a while."

Cold fire, Micah intoned, cold fire. "Okay, we don't have much time. History lesson, Ramires. Q'Roth, Ranger, Alicians, Sentinels – all of it, please.

* * *

Louise sat hunched, back against the wall, cradling her right elbow, occasionally scrunching her eyes against the grinding pain of a dislocated right shoulder. The usually green walls were splattered with scarlet scabs exuding brown pus. The ship was healing itself after her little pyrotechnic skirmish with the Hohash; the room smelt like char-grilled excrement. "Bastard," she said. *What is it you want from me anyway? Clearly not to kill me.*

The Hohash loomed a few metres away, patrolling like a shark. Abruptly it stopped, pivoted, and turned its mirror face toward her, the smooth surface flowing like oil on water. An image rose from the depths: a fleet of titanic war-ships, of various shapes, hanging in space before a shimmering curtain. She recognized several Q'Roth planet-killer class craft. *Thought they were all moth-balled: last time they were used was the Licutius rebellion, fifty thousand angts ago.* The squid-shaped vessels had eight tendrils thousands of kilometres long, by twenty wide, sporting thorn-like crust-breakers, capable of puncturing a world's outer and inner layers, leaving it to drown in its own lava. *I could use one of those...*

Other, equally gigantic ships of unknown origin straddled the shimmering field, an impressive menagerie of destructive power. She forgot about her pain. "Quite a line-up." No sooner had she said it than the entire fleet was sucked through an impossibly small hole. Ships twisted, momentarily stretched toward the rift, before disintegrating en route. She knew what it meant – a massive gravitational shear force applied in a nano-second, bending the normal laws of physics. The next image wasn't unexpected – utter carnage, organic beings and hardware alike de-skinned, disembowelled. The ships had been turned inside out, their occupants, too.

"Is this history, or now?"

It flashed back to being a mirror for a moment, reflecting her bruised and bloody face, a lock of her blonde hair singed black.

So, it's now.

The next image was of another fleet pouring in through the widened tear. These ships were all of the same origin, dull black lozenges with spiralling indigo lights pulsing from front to back. Something accompanied them, too, blacker than black, only visible by their silhouettes, undulating like an electric ray she'd once seen in an aquarium. They loitered in the wake of the ships, wild beasts on a tight leash. She had no sense of scale, but reckoned they were bigger than a Q'Roth transport.

The last picture was a face. It would scare most people, but she intuited something beneath the bubbling flesh: rage, unadulterated, distilled anger. Some would call it pure evil, but she recognised an incredible force of will.

The pain returned as soon as the show stopped. "Well? What's it to me? Or you, even?"

The Hohash vibrated, oscillating slowly to the left and right.

"Are you going to show me or not?"

A single image formed: a noble ship sculpted from a dream, bold contours of ivory, gold and emerald. It dissolved.

"So, good guys and bad guys. Want me to choose? Don't you know me yet?"

It approached her side on. Its leading edge nudged her right elbow. *Fuck, you're shitting me!* Despite reservations, she curled her fingers around the outside rail-like edge, and gripped hard, clamping her jaw down. She took a breath.

Her scream cut off just after the *tchum* sound of her shoulder snapping back into place. The pain miraculously ceased.

"Thanks," she gasped. "But just so we know where we stand, I have more in common with the first guy you showed me."

The Hohash sped to the bridge. She trailed after it, kicking aside the remnants of her shattered flamethrower. Upon arrival, she felt goose-bumps signalling a jump initiating. She had just enough time to notice two pieces of information from the displays. The first was their destination – though she had no idea how the Hohash had set it. They were going straight to Micah's location, using a complex multi-jump process that wasn't in the Q'Roth handbook. *What Level are you, anyway?* The second was the ownership registration of a docked vessel the Hohash had highlighted: Esmeralda Alessia Carthagena.

A smile etched across her face. "Micah *and* Sister Esma. Must be my lucky day."

* * *

The Ranger Ukrull made a clicking sound with his jaw, entering the hyper-transit sequence. He'd seen the deposition already: he would be a key witness. His superiors weren't too happy about that; Rangers were meant to be impartial, in the background, unseen.

However, now that he had finally gotten what he'd wanted, to properly evaluate this race once and for all – he was reluctant to leave Ourshiwann's orbit. Initial promising signs of recovery for humanity had stalled, sliding backwards into typical Level Three despotic tendencies, and would inevitably lead to a cycle of civil wars, depletion of planetary resources, followed by extinction through a process of attrition. Grid Society levels of intelligence weren't about individuals – there were always statistical aberrations, geniuses even, in any species – there had to be collective intelligence too. If the species was locked into self-destructive and recidivist behaviour, then Grid society might order it culled – pruned – to protect the larger society from too many weeds. But some indicators, small-scale parameters at present, could turn the tide. If asked to give the assessment right now, he would say that there were the beginnings of Level Four tendencies and thinking. Humanity, as it called itself, was on the cusp of ascendance, but it could go either way. He growled and flicked a claw at the console. His ship vanished.

As he hummed through Transpace, he realised another source of his reluctance to go back. The Hohash. He hadn't reported finding them yet, and there would be a Tla Beth presiding over the court. That was going to take a little explaining. As he warped through the multi-transit sequence, he detected another vessel inbound, also on a hyper-transit approach, which required Tla Beth authorisation, as it stretched and occasionally tore sub-space fabric. His ship was cloaked of course, but he could scan the other vessel: Ossyrian. He was about to stop scanning, since they held little interest for him, when he detected human life-signs. He corrected himself – one of the life signs was no longer human, but a hybrid. He sat up when he saw the level indicated. His jaw approximated a grin, and he whacked the Bartran with his claw, making it yelp and exude more pus than usual. Ukrull kicked back in his chair, grunting and snorting with pleasure. His tail curled and twitched. *Interesting, very interesting.*

PART THREE – THE TRIAL

CHAPTER 24 – EVENT HORIZON

Micah stood mesmerized by the blue-green globe as it rolled in slow motion around the funnel suspended in space beneath them. It was an illusion, a macro-hologram of some sort, but looked incredibly real. The outer rim of the inverted, thundercloud-grey cone appeared hard, ceramic; he almost expected to hear a grinding noise as the replica of Earth toiled its way around the circumference. Towards its centre, the funnel descended like a gaseous whirlpool into darkness, a faint fire-light glow reaching up from its core. He didn't need to be Level 4 to grasp the implication.

The ball resembled Earth as it had been – trawled from one of Zack's memories, no doubt – not the post-nuclear orange dustbowl which Micah remembered most clearly. Staring at it, he felt hollow, with an attendant nausea. All that remained of his world was a pale echo of humanity's home. He gazed upon the treasure they had squandered. It was too easy to blame everything on the Alicians. They were a contributory factor, but humanity's inherent weaknesses had facilitated its own downfall.

He tugged his eyes away from paradise lost, and tracked across to the far side of the vista, to a graphite ball scarred with glowing scarlet rivers. Pinpricks of blood-coloured light stabbed out from the planetary simulacrum. He imagined a sea urchin whose spines had been ripped off, oozing its life force into naked space. Far above that ball, on a platform higher than the one for him, Sandy and Ramires, stood two Q'Roth warriors. They looked more powerful than the ones he'd seen before, their lower legs splayed, and their mid and upper legs folded together in an Escher-like snake pattern. They were completely immobile, but he had the sense they were somehow spitting on the humans who had slain their ambassador. To his far right, on a small disk, Zack's Transpar stood as if to attention – like Zack never had –

emphasising that this was no longer Zack, just an alien replica. Micah's friend, and mentor, was gone.

He noted that the three parties – humans, Q'Roth, and Transpar, were at three cardinal points of the compass. He looked to the logical fourth point, but there was just empty blackness, no walls in any direction, only darkness framing his opponents, the Transpar, and the swirling funnel.

"Is the judge late?" Sandy inquired.

Micah shrugged without turning to face her. "I don't know, Sandy, nor does my resident, in case that's who you're really asking." It came out ruder than he'd intended.

"Okay, then tell me something you do know!" Her voice ramped up a notch in sharpness. "What *is* the attraction between you and Alician women, Micah?"

"Sandy," Ramires said, trying to placate her. Ramires looked more brittle than usual, a warrior longing for battle, rather than languishing in legal proceedings. He kept glaring across the funnel to his enemy, forearms and thighs taut as razor wire.

Micah turned around to face Sandy. He hated it when she was like this. But he knew she wouldn't stop till blood had been drawn.

"No," she said, "I really want to know. First Louise, then Hannah. What is it with you and the betrayers of humanity, Micah?"

"Wait a second," Ramires said. "*Louise?*"

Micah didn't flinch.

"Sure," Sandy said, hands on hips, "I had a ringside seat."

"You didn't have to watch," he said quietly. "And I didn't know she was – "

The parry-and-strike was swift. "But Hannah, you knew she was Alician, party to genocide on Earth, let alone Rashid's ship. Didn't stop you, did it?"

He saw more hurt than anger in her eyes. He wanted to say that Hannah had tricked him, but it would sound pathetic, and she'd never believe him. Distant images flooded back to him, viewed through the night-time balustrade in his childhood home, when his parents thought he was asleep, peering through the wooden rails as they rowed over his father's latest indiscretion. Micah had watched it play out a dozen times, maybe more: the accusations, the denials, the confessions, the pain his mother endured, written all over her face, and his father's coolness, the knowledge – no, the confidence – that she would never leave him, so he could do what he wanted. And the two words that would always end the scene... Micah had sworn a hundred times as a boy that he would never be like that, would never utter those two words if the situation arose. But nothing else came to mind. They slipped out. "I'm sorry." He unfolded his arms, so that they hung loose.

Her nostrils flared, and her chest heaved, but Ramires laid a hand on her forearm to still her. "Look," he said, nodding to the far side.

Micah reluctantly broke off from Sandy to see. The two balls were still circling in the same direction, the Q'Roth home planet having moved a few degrees around the circumference as far as he could judge. Then he saw what Ramires had noticed. He backed off a pace. Between the two Q'Roth warriors, three times their height, stood a giant Q'Roth, its trapezoidal head red with black slits, the reverse of the warriors' coloration. Its bloated, purple ribbed belly curved down to the floor supported by two ramrod straight, sturdy legs. Its four other legs looked puny by comparison, protruding from its mid-section like useless appendages. It glared at Micah and the others, excreting pure hate. Beneath its loins, half the size of the warriors, Sister Esma appeared in a burgundy cloak.

"Q'Roth queen, and Alician queen bitch," Sandy said. "We must be on the Galactic A-list."

He glanced at Sandy. Humour – even the sardonic wit variety – was a good sign, and he needed all of them to be on the same side. He detected a fine inverted triangular film hanging behind the Queen's frame, and decided the Queen had wings, which wasn't good news. Doubtless she would have liked to fly across and finish them off herself. He planted his legs firm, and stared right back. He felt Sandy's hand on his shoulder.

"Apology accepted, Micah," she said quietly. "But you fuck another Alician and I'll kill you myself, understood?"

He nodded. "Sounds reasonable."

A new disk arrived close to Zack's Transpar, carrying an upright lizard, slick brown all over except for glimmering black thorns running from its crown to the tip of its tail. Its forelegs folded onto the ground so that it looked relaxed, bored even. Its smouldering yellow eyes stared forwards, though Micah had the impression it took in everything around it.

"Ukrull, the Ranger."

Micah and the others spun around to see a lime-green Finchikta hovering behind them. Micah tried to focus internally, but nothing happened.

"Your resident has been disabled for the duration of the trial. I will translate the proceedings for you." Its head bobbed like an albatross, though he guessed this creature was vastly more intelligent. He could barely make out the thin line where its upper third eye remained closed. When it spoke, its beak barely opened, but its two sharp orange eyes blazed. The Finchikta's hundreds of green vermicelli-like legs did not quite reach the ground, hanging like a curtain over its nether region.

"Counsel for the defence?" Ramires asked.

"In this court, there are only truth, causes, context, and consequences," it replied.

Micah wanted something clarified. "The funnel – what's the significance, if the representation of our world disappears into it?"

The Finchikta bobbed slowly. "A good question. In your world you represent justice by a set of scales, which can tip either way. But that implies justice can be wrong, that verdicts can be revoked, since scales can be tipped back again. Grid justice, as you may understand it, does not entertain reversals. Once either your globe, or the Q'Roth's, dip beneath the event horizon of the funnel, the case is lost permanently. There is no appeal. Execution of sentence cannot be stopped."

Micah stared out at the swirling vista, suddenly concerned that maybe this wasn't just an image. "But still, it's only symbolic, right?" He hoped that whatever happened here, today, that Blake and the others on Ourshiwann might still have a chance to escape or at least defend themselves.

The Finchikta bobbed again, deeper, which Micah interpreted to mean he'd asked another 'intelligent' question. "It is mostly symbolic."

He didn't like the sound of that.

"Where's the judge?" Sandy interjected.

"Arriving," the Finchikta said, orientating its beak upwards.

They spotted something descending from way above. At first Micah couldn't make out what was inside or riding the waves of rainbow-light, but as it got closer, he could pick out the details. Around thirty vertical rings circumscribed the main body, waves of fluorescent light surging through them. Inside the rings was a rounded hourglass shape which barely moved, except that the dark colours in the lower half sometimes squirted up into the lighter upper half of the hourglass, exchanging and sending lighter colours down through its narrow 'waist'. It made Micah think of some night-time sea creatures he'd once seen, but his analytical mind dredged up a deeper analogy, that of the yin-yang symbol. He realised why, as he noticed a white patch in the lower, dark area, and a black one in the upper, lighter half. He recalled what his Zen master had said once about the symbol: "Most people only see black and white; they forget about the white dot in the sea of black, the black dot in the white portion. In nature there can no more be pure good than pure evil; in the heart of evil there is a speck of good, and vice versa. Nature abhors ultimate states." Micah found the image fitting for a Galactic judge.

"At least it's human size," Sandy said. She placed herself between Micah and Ramires and put a hand around the waist of each. "Whatever happens, gentlemen, it's been ... interesting."

An overwhelming impulse overtook Micah, to reach out to Sandy in some way, without offending her or Ramires. He leaned forward to her left cheek and deposited a soft kiss there. She didn't pull back. Ramires shifted from one foot to another but said nothing.

"It has begun," the Finchikta chirped in a crisp tone, drifting to Micah's side. Sandy's hand slipped from his waist, and he faced the Tla Beth, some thirty metres away, its aurora ebbing into a penumbra of rippling pastel shades.

"You will now bear witness to the charges," the Finchikta said.

Above the funnel, a swirling spiral of myriad stars appeared. Micah immediately recognised it as their galaxy, the Milky Way. A scalpel-sharp white mesh etched its way outwards about a third of the distance from the galaxy's white hot centre. The pattern was complex, like some kind of blueprint, but there was a design to it. As it stretched out like vines along a number of the spiral arms, Micah realised it was the Grid, the transport system that was the paragon of Galactic infrastructure, enabling its society to function. It reached fully half the galaxy, a criss-crossing net of curving and intersecting conduits: a skeleton framing the stars. A blue dot pulsed on one of the spiral arms remote from any grid lines or nodes.

"Your planet, the one you call Earth. Here is the latest recorded image."

His jaw fell as an image of a charred, ocean-less, dust-coloured ball loomed large in front of them. He felt as if someone had just punched him in the stomach.

"The atmosphere was purged to reduce the radioactive poisoning. It will recover faster this way. In ten thousand of your years it can be terraformed and replenished with life."

"Bastards," Ramires cursed.

The Finchikta peered around Micah to see Ramires. It cocked its head. "I assure you the Q'Roth have followed strict protocol. Atmospheric removal is recommended in case of nuclear fallout, once radiation levels reach a certain point, to prevent planetary rot setting in. The world is then left fallow for a set period, after which time it can be used for resettlement of a displaced race or one requiring more room."

Sandy whirled around to the Finchikta. "It was our home! Billions of people! Not to mention all the animal life! Who gave them the right?" She pointed to the Q'Roth platform. "You'll pay for this one day, even if it takes a thousand years!" she shouted in their direction. She added quietly, just for Micah and Ramires' ears: "They hibernate a long time, that's when we'll find them."

Micah gazed toward the judge. A line of fire unfurled from the Tla Beth like a whiplash, latching onto the head of Zack's Transpar.

"The judge is interrogating the human version of events."

While the line connected the two, another dot glittered, very close to Earth. "Eden," he whispered. The image zoomed in, so they could see this sector of space in more detail. Four blue dots zigzagged from Eden towards another distant ball he knew must be Ourshiwann, still far out on the spiral, and a long way from Grid access. A red dot intercepted one of the blues, and was extinguished. The fireline connecting the Transpar with the Tla Beth dissolved. A new one lashed out to Sister Esma, taking her by surprise. Her haughty stance wavered as her face disappeared inside a fist of fire-light. Her body arced as if she was being electrocuted, her arms and legs stretched out to maximum.

"About fucking time," Sandy said. "Fry her, *please*."

"What's going on?" Micah asked, glancing at the Finchikta.

"She is being questioned. I have partial access as court official. She sent the one you know as Louise after you, but sabotaged her ship before she left so she could not hope to return to the Alicians. The Alicians made a deal with the Q'Roth a thousand of your years ago to dispose of humanity's nuclear and nanotechnology, and to bring humanity to Eden. They instigated your third World War. They..." The Finchikta's beak clamped shut.

"What?" Sandy and Micah said at the same time.

The Finchikta nudged a shoulder feather back into place. "They suppressed Level 4 emergents; co-opting those they found early enough into their order, terminating the rest."

"This much we suspected." Ramires said. He glanced at Sister Esma and spat over the side of the abyss. "Though we never knew the full extent."

Micah gazed at Sister Esma's taut body. Her face twisted in pain. *Good, I hope it rips your mind apart.* Abruptly the fireline dissipated, and they watched Sister Esma stagger, nearly collapsing. Her face had paled, and she looked shaken. Neither the Q'Roth warriors, nor their Queen, moved to support her. She gathered herself, and stared defiantly at Micah.

A deep, guttural voice boomed across the space between them and the Ranger: a series of growls and clicks that put Micah's spine on edge.

"The Ranger Ukrull is testifying. He expresses surprise at finding the race calling itself humanity more advanced than he expected, based on the original Q'Roth incursion manifest. He believes humanity was on the cusp of emergence. However, the rate of progress in the last millennium was unusual by galactic development standards, so the Q'Roth couldn't know. For him, given the escape of a number of humans, the main question is what to do with the survivors."

"Micah, this is good isn't it?" Sandy said. "He must be the one who saved Rashid."

He nodded and addressed the Finchikta. "What else?"

The Finchikta shivered, its fine feathers fluffing momentarily before settling down. "Ah. There is an anomaly in his testament. You have..." It craned its neck and peered at Micah. Its third eye opened, a clear sapphire blue. "You have encountered the Hohash?"

"Yes. So what?"

The eye sealed again. The Finchikta moved in front of Micah, clearly more interested in this than the court case. "They are legendary. They are the *Listeners*, the ears of the Galaxy. They have been missing for a hundred thousand angts. They are omnipaths."

"Omnipaths?" Micah wished his resident was online, this sounded important.

"The Hohash helped create the Finchikta Order, establishing it amongst the fifty core Grid professions known as The Torus. We worsh –". It ruffled its feathers again. "They are very important to us." The creature dipped its head and whole upper body slowly. Micah realised it was bowing to them. "You have been honoured."

Micah wished they'd brought one along. He cleared his throat. "So, who's nex..."

Micah had no body. His mind floated like a two dimensional sheet of plazfilm, flapping on the winds of a featureless emerald space. He heard sounds: his own voice, as a child, as an adult. He perceived other sheets drifting, slip-sliding in the windless space like a dropped sheaf of paper, each one containing a scene, a memory, voices, people he knew, things he'd seen, things he'd said, more than a few he wished he hadn't. As they tumbled, he knew the Tla Beth had complete access to his mind and memory. There was no question of lying or even trying to hide anything. He heard his mother crying, his father raging at him when he was a kid. He saw again the aerial nuclear detonations over LA, his younger self sprinting for the shelter to beat the vaporising blast wave; huddling there with his mother when he couldn't stop shaking; his father calling him a coward; Louise about to kill him; Antonia; Sandy... He wrenched himself back from it all. It was too easy to drown in his own life. His Optron training helped him. He took the astrosurfer's viewpoint, and witnessed thousands of sheets peppering the green sky: a man's life dissected – his life.

He discerned a common thread in the Tla Beth search strategy: Micah had always been a misfit as a kid, had hated his father, and had been a bit of a geek during adolescence. In the defence case for humanity, his head wasn't the best brochure available.

Abruptly he was back in his body, in a white space. He was standing on something but couldn't discriminate between floor and space and wall: everything was solid white. A figure emerged and walked toward him.

"No, not you," he heard himself say, as an image of his father approached, in his grey military uniform. At least he didn't have that disappointed look plastered across his face.

The image of his father spoke. "We see in humanity destruction, greed, conflict, injustice, and other disharmonious emotions associated with Level Three and below races. Such comportment is dangerous for the Grid Society. The Grid Council, chaired by the Tla Beth, sanctioned the Q'Roth request."

Micah knew he had to remain as dispassionate as possible; anger would be a fast-track to humanity's final demise. "Look at our technological achievements, our advances, they –"

"Are dangerous without mental and emotional discipline," Sister Esma said, materialising out of the white ether. "We Alicians instigated all the major breakthroughs in the past five centuries, and –"

"How many did you stop?" he countered. "How many DaVinci's, Mozarts, and Qorelli's did you snuff out? Who knows where humanity would be now if you Alicians hadn't intervened? Your agenda was to break humanity, not nurture it, wasn't it, *Esma?*"

She flared, so that Micah knew this was no avatar, it was her.

The image of his father which the Tla Beth had chosen to utilise, held up a hand, choking off her retort. "The past cannot be undone. The Q'Roth incursion and their stewardship of the Alicians followed Grid protocol. Why is humanity worth saving? You don't seem to believe in it yourself, Micah."

Micah swallowed. He wished for any other figure than his father's, but knew that was probably intentional. He had to think fast. Blake – he was as good a role model as Micah knew. "Then look into another head. Look at a real hero, Blake. Access Zack's memories, and see another view of mankind."

The Transpar materialised into the white construct, opposite Micah's father. Its crystal surface flashed a pastiche of images, becoming a montage of Blake's life. Micah had forgotten how much of it had been War-related. He couldn't keep up with the almost subliminal shifting of events, but noticed that Esma apparently could. He saw her greedy ebony eyes darting about, peering into Blake's history, scouring his soul.

"Look!" she shouted, pointing a bony finger, a sneer of triumph swelling her face. "There! See? See how humanity's big hero behaves? *He murders his own son!*"

"This needs to be witnessed by all," his father said.

Micah found himself back on the platform. His legs gave way but Sandy and Ramires' arms caught him. "Thanks," he groaned, feeling like he needed to throw up.

"What happened?" Sandy asked. But before he could answer, she continued. "Micah, the Earth. It's shifted further downwards. What's going on?"

He sagged as he saw the blue-green globe rolling closer and faster into the maw of the funnel. Worse, a dusty orange ball followed close behind. *Ourshiwann.* Humanity's fate was slipping closer to the precipice. He'd have to play the next part very carefully. Meanwhile, the Q'Roth planet rotated serenely along the outer rim. "We're about to see exhibit A," he said.

Above the whirlpool, an image formed, like an outdoor holo. It was the one Sister Esma had spotted, a night-time scene played out in real time. Micah watched with a lead weight in his stomach as Blake, in battle fatigues soaked with blood, fired the slow-gun into his own son's body, exploding him from the inside. The memory slammed into Micah as surely as if he'd stepped out in front of a hover-taxi.

He addressed the Tla Beth, his voice firm. "His name was Robert. Blake's son had been transformed into a ghoster by the Alicians." He pointed at Sister Esma. "He was no longer human." Esma's sneer faltered. Micah continued: "Please go forward in time, a few minutes," he said. "Stop there." He saw Sister Esma squint to see what he was referring to. In the freeze-framed view, Zack and Blake were rescuing a group of young boys from the Alician camp. Ramires also edged forward. Sandy rested a hand on Micah's shoulder. Micah knew exactly where to look. His voice cracked. "I was there. He rescued me and fourteen others, losing his entire platoon except Zack. Blake had been too late to save his own son."

"It doesn't change anything," Esma shouted. "Where is your Blake now? What use is a hero if the rest of your precious humanity hunts him down, and imprisons him?"

Micah frowned. "What ... what are you talking about?"

She turned toward the Ranger. "We have studied the full testimony of the Ranger Ukrull. I call upon Ukrull to testify on the most recent events on Ourshiwann. I am sure the honourable Ranger knows to which events I refer to."

"What's that witch going on about now?" Sandy asked.

Micah didn't know, but had a bad feeling in his gut.

A new image formed. It was another trial, but a human one. There was no sound; there didn't need to be. Shakirvasta and Josefsson lorded over the proceedings, with the psychologist Carlson in the dock. Carlson was gesticulating wildly. The crowd in the cramped makeshift court room appeared to be shouting too, but there was a heavy militia presence, a new uniform Micah didn't recognise. Then he saw the image of Blake, his hands cuffed behind him, sitting in a smaller dock, surrounded by four heavies. Whenever he tried to speak he was ordered into silence, then rifle-butted when he didn't comply.

The scene shifted. On seeing it, Sandy let out a cry and buried her head into Ramires broad shoulder. But Micah couldn't turn away, though it wrenched his heart to stare at the limp body of Carlson, hanging from a noose in the central plaza. There was no one around. His corpse, abandoned, twisted slowly in the Esperantian breeze.

Micah's head bowed towards the ground.

The Finchikta moved aside and the image of his father reappeared. "Do you have anything more to say in humanity's defence, Micah?"

He heard compassion and empathy in that calm voice, like he'd never known from his actual father. Something inside him splintered, cracking him like a shell. He shook his head, unable to speak. The Tla Beth's representation vanished. Micah's eyes lifted to see the two globes of Earth and Ourshiwann begin their roll inwards, down the slope, towards the point of no return into the funnel, and the cauldron of fire deep within.

CHAPTER 25 – DEAD MAN WALKING

Blake strained against the handcuffs for the umpteenth time, his shoulders and arms bulging until he felt the veins come out on his forehead. He relaxed, recovered his breathing, and sat back down on his solitary, armless metal chair. The white room he had occupied the past two weeks wasn't quite square and had no sharp edges – like an inverted tin used for baking a loaf of bread. At night four guards armed with stun-sticks released him for five minutes before handcuffing his arms in front of him so he could relieve himself and then sleep. He'd taken the men on twice already, but they knew what they were doing, and he was knocked out cold both times. He stared toward the oval window – it had been papered over, but he could judge the time of day, which was, he guessed, about five in the afternoon, an hour before dusk on Ourshiwann.

On impulse he stood up and inhaled deeply. He'd adjusted long ago to the heightened oxygen mixture, but when he breathed really deep, it chilled his nostrils as if walking in cool mountain air. Footsteps approached. He'd been practising a roundhouse kick he'd learned during his more athletic youth – though now, especially cuffed, he'd ended up crashing to the floor each time. But it would be his only way to take out Shakirvasta, if he could just get it right and connect with the man's scraggy neck. A desperate idea, highly unlikely to work, but he'd been sentenced to death, so desperation trumped rationality any day of the week. He crouched slightly, preparing his thigh muscles, then gave it up – the footsteps weren't measured enough to be Shakirvasta's, and not heavy enough to belong to one of the guards.

Sonja rounded the corner and ran straight to him, flung her arms around him, her head of dark frizzy hair burying into his chest, brushing against his chin. Her hands found his, squeezed his palms, and then she pulled back. Her face was more drawn than he remembered.

She nudged a tear away with her shoulder. "We didn't even know if you were still alive."

Antonia entered the room, head down, sheepish, arms crossing her waspish waist. "I tried, Commander. I tried everything."

He'd forgotten her crisp Eastern European accent, her elegance and poise. "I know, Antonia, I'm sure you did everything you could, both of you."

"Sit down, Blake," Sonja said, "we don't have much time."

He obliged, while Sonja started pacing. He'd never seen her do that. She wrung her hands, too, speaking fast. "They have Benjy and Peter. All children now get raised in a boarding school in a ring-fenced part of the city. Shakirvasta's doctrine is peddled there, and parents don't get to see their kids except on Sundays. Everyone works six days a week, most on farms, tilling the soil – back-breaking, spirit-breaking work."

She avoided looking at him. Blake guessed why she was here: absolution.

"After your escape I was arrested. I didn't see my kids that weekend and when I was finally allowed, they..." Her hands raked at her hair, as if to try and pull the words out.

Antonia came to her rescue. "Her children are young, Commander, young and impressionable. They are being turned against Sonja. One of them – forgive me, Sonja – one of them spat at her, called her a traitor."

Sonja trembled. She turned to face him, chin up, the proud eyes he'd known since her second date with Zack, a lifetime ago. "I'll do whatever you ask of me. Maybe there's some way I can help Rashid, if – when – he returns."

He'd sent more men and women to their death than he cared to remember, always in the name of some cause or other. Despite Zack putting him in a coma, he owed him too much. "This is what I want you to do, Sonja." He eased himself up. "Just love your kids, show them what real love is. That's the only way they'll see through the lies."

Her lips pressed together; she looked tense enough to shatter. "Zack's not coming back, is he?"

Blake frowned. "Sonja, I –"

"It's okay. I've waited for it, dreaded it, half my life. But last night, I really felt it, suddenly, as if..." Her eyes narrowed. "He always belonged to you more than me, Blake." Her voice hardened, and she spoke quickly through pursed lips. "And soon you'll be together."

"Sonja!" Antonia whispered.

"It's okay, Antonia," he said, quietly.

Sonja sniffed and approached him, face distraught, then stopped short. "I'm sorry, Blake, you know I didn't mean it. I have to go." She turned on her heels and dashed out of the room.

He stared through the empty doorway, then parked his back against the wall where the window light dwindled. "How did it come to this, Antonia? You've been on the Council, you're as close to Shakirvasta as anyone, except maybe Josefsson."

She shrugged and shook her head at the same time. "It started off better than I expected. He had an ideology and razor-sharp logic. At first it seemed he wanted to reinstate the Indistani neo-feudalism he'd installed in Mumbai after the War. He's quite persuasive, and he had a plan when no one else did – two years to achieve sustainable harvests; immediate formation of education and medical facilities, and a defence capability strategy. Everyone had their part to play and, frankly, most valued his vision after weeks of chaos. It all seemed so *rational*. But then – well, it was like watching Karl Marx morph into Joseph Stalin. He wanted to be a Tsar, or maybe the Chinese God-Emperor was his model, I really don't know."

He noticed she stood straight, as if giving evidence; her aristocratic upbringing, no doubt. He could see why Kat liked her so much. He'd have been proud to have her as a daughter.

"Anyway, that was when..." She cleared her throat. "Jennifer would go berserk if she'd known."

"What?"

She spread her hands. "He wanted a successor. To cut a long story short, he wanted to father a child with me. Can you believe it? Said I was 'good stock'. I was stunned."

She must have read his eyes. "Of course I told him where to go. But it was around that time that Bill – Bill Carlson, that is – when Bill and I noticed a change in him. He takes medication every morning, and Bill wanted to find out what it was. He even joked that maybe one day we could poison him that way. But we did finally find out. It was –"

"Retrocan." Blake was guessing, but as soon as he said it, everything fell into place.

She smiled. "You're as sharp as my father was. How did you know?"

"He smokes enough to be dead ten times over. His family were originally tobacco barons, growing fine-grade GM in the Himalayan foothills. The scientist who invented Retrocan was Indistani – designed not just to prevent lung cancer, but to re-boot the whole industry."

"Except it was found to have chronic aggressive side-effects, with hints of paranoia."

He nodded. "Explains some of it. He must be way over the normal dose. Probably also why he extended Glenda's life – he sees his future fate."

Antonia folded her arms and spoke to the floor. "I got to know his physician quite well. He ... fancied me. I mean nothing ever ... Anyway, Shakirvasta only has five years, maximum."

"So, he's in a hurry to make his stamp on this world."

She looked up, her almond-shaped eyes pleading. "Blake, where I come from, we've seen this so many times. It can take decades, generations for a society to recover from his type of politics. Already people just go missing. That creates such a fear in everyone else left behind, their families..."

Blake nodded again. But he realised they must be running short on time. The guards would call for Antonia soon. "I have a question, Antonia, about Carlson – Bill. The accusations – were they true? Did he try and assassinate Shakirvasta in the end? Did he try and poison him?"

Antonia walked to the chair and sat down. She placed her hands in her lap, and shook her head. "We joked about it, nothing more."

He coughed. After a silence: "When is my execution scheduled?"

She leant forwards in the chair, her hands cupping her chin. "He hasn't decided, but I think it'll be at dawn. He keeps everyone wrong-footed, as you know. Bill's hanging..." Her voice choked off. She collected herself. "There were protests. Three people injured, one critically, more than twenty arrested." She looked up at him. "There have been rumours about yours, many more people threatening to demonstrate. I don't think he wants a repeat performance. Carlson was a test. Shakirvasta won't want you as a martyr. Even Josefsson is starting to fray at the edges, after Carlson's hanging, he fears how far Shakirvasta is prepared to go."

Blake thought back to Josefsson's visit the previous afternoon. He'd looked haggard, old. He'd offered no reason why he'd come, but had spent a whole hour trying to justify the hanging of Carlson, the other measures. Blake had listened to it all, asked Josefsson if he knew who Pontius Pilate was, and had reminded him of the political maxim that absolute power corrupts absolutely. Josefsson had stormed out.

"He's in too deep, Antonia." Blake brought himself back to the present. "Shakirvasta plays chess, I gather. He thinks of me as the opposing king. If he takes me out, then it's endgame."

"He keeps playing on you killing his mistress. No evidence of course, just a lot of hot air. But he's good at sowing doubt in people's minds, doubt about you."

"It's a shame about Jen, I admit, but I –"

Antonia shot to her feet. "What did you just call her?" Her words had a cutting edge, reminding him that although she looked demure, she was no pushover. She approached him, hunting his eyes. "Only Dimitri ever called her that, and maybe Shakirvasta himself..." Her eyes widened. She mouthed a single word silently: *alive?*

He returned her stare, neither denying nor affirming. She went back to the chair, stood behind it and leant on its back. "You don't play chess by the rules, do you, Commander?"

He spoke to the window. "Do you know how to defeat a chess computer, Antonia?"

"I confess I don't."

He turned back to her, his eyes animated. "You defend your queen at all costs. You sacrifice everything for the queen. The computer focuses on the queen because you value it so much. You leave a back door open and let the computer take your queen, and then you strike with your last surviving rook." He watched it sink in.

A frown scraped across her brow. "How do you know all this, Commander, have you actually done it? Did you ever beat a chess computer?"

"No, but I married someone who did."

Footsteps approached from the courtyard.

"And if your plan fails? What then? What if Kat never returns? Micah neither?"

"Survive, at all costs."

"You can't possibly mean –"

"At all costs, Antonia. You said it yourself. Five years. You need to be around to pick up the pieces."

She glared. "Why nice to Sonja and hard on me?"

The guard entered.

"Good stock, Antonia." He smiled. "You can handle it. He's right about that part, at least. Goodbye, it's been a pleasure knowing you."

She pursed her lips, then relaxed them. She walked up to him and gave him a peck on the cheek.

"Hold me, Antonia. Dying wish, and all that."

She tensed, but complied. He whispered something into her ear. After a moment, she let go. "*Au revoir*, Commander."

* * *

Rashid had spent twelve days tracking Vasquez and his men. He'd ridden the skimmer into the ground, covering two thousand kilometres of terrain, staying in the saddle for twelve hours at a stretch, till his limbs and buttocks were numb from the vibrations; till he couldn't steer anymore. At first, following their trail had been easy, the tell-tale signs of abandoned encampments and buried detritus, indicating a disciplined squadron of men on the move, conscious of the environment. Later, however, nearer Ourshiwann's equator, their traces dried up, lost in an endless plain of dusty scrub, scoured clean by a recent sandstorm. He'd lost three days using a wave-search pattern until finally his dolphin had detected a single piece of metal foil lodged in a bush. After that, he'd managed to catch up with them in an extinct volcanic mountain range. It extended upwards like a botched and heavily-scarred incision on the planet's skin, shrinking towards the Southern horizon. At first the trail disappeared again, but on a hunch he headed for a collapsed volcano which might contain water in its caldera. He ditched the skimmer and spent the chill dawn hours on foot to arrive at its crest undetected. Then he waited.

Rashid pressed his fingers to his temples, and through an effort of will scanned the encampment via his dolphin, using it to zoom in wherever he 'looked'. The grainy black and grey 'image' was accurate, but the lack of colour had been depressing him lately. Occasionally he took it off, as if it was better to see nothing than to have this 'limbo-vision'.

The scanning was giving him a headache, but he did not want to arrive unannounced. "Where are you, Vasquez?" he muttered to himself, searching for the tell-tale one-armed profile that had eluded him for the past hour. Soldiers came and went out of the tents, tending fires, cleaning kit and doing laundry in the water inside the deep basin whose upper lip he lay upon. He was relieved to see several men maintaining the sling-jet – he'd been praying for a quicker mode of travel for the return trip. *Blake might be in difficulties.*

He got distracted by several men in an inflatable dinghy just inside the lake in the pit of the caldera. They'd become agitated and were pointing wildly. He hunted around and then saw a large snake-like head rear up out of the water. As it rose, water gushed off its scaly hide. It threatened the boat then dove down, nearly capsizing it, causing the men to crouch and grab the sides to stabilise it. A wide fan-tail flicked up out of the water, then lashed down against it making a thwack which Rashid heard even at his distance, and then was gone. He reckoned the creature must be twenty metres long.

"Snake-whale. Or Whale-snake. We haven't decided yet."

Rashid recognised Vasquez' taut command voice immediately, but nevertheless managed to spring up to his feet in one flowing, turning movement, so that he was facing the one-armed colonel. "How did you detect me? I left the skimmer several klicks back."

Vasquez was a head taller, and Rashid remembered his shock of white hair, though now all his dolphin detected was spiky fuzz on top of the man's head. But he found he could imagine it as white. Just.

"Oh you're good, Rashid, nearly as good as Ramires, but we still have stealth tech." He held up a small box. That was all Rashid's sonar could perceive.

"Anyway, let's call it a snake-whale. Hasn't actually eaten anyone yet, but I don't doubt it could acquire the taste if pressed." He walked to the edge. "Mighty good fishing here. Don't know where they come from, but –"

"Underground ocean. I have seen it."

"That so? Well, best catch is some fish like jack, don't taste so bad. We've been hauling them in, salt-drying them, and preparing to take them back to Esperantia."

"Did you find anything else useful on your travels?"

Vasquez shook his head. "Afraid not. This planet isn't inhospitable, but it's damned barren. If only we'd had the presence of mind to bring more fauna and flora from Earth, the bacteria that make things grow. But your ocean sounds mighty interesting. But you're not here as a tourist, are you, Rashid?"

Rashid thought of the spider nest, the ocean, the ship, Jen and Dimitri, and Blake. "We need to talk." He squatted down. Vasquez followed suit, and listened.

"Hot damn! It's only been three months! And Shakirvasta, well, I marked him as a control-freak, but this ... megalomania... We have to get back there, and soon."

"Is the sling-jet still functional?" Rashid asked.

"Enough fuel for a one-way trip. Was saving it for an emergency. This qualifies. Could take you, me and a dozen of my men – more than a match for Shakirvasta's militia, given the hardware we're packing."

Rashid had sketched an outline of the ship he'd named Arjuna in the sand with his finger. "There's another problem. Shakirvasta does not leave loose ends. Frankly, I feared I would not find you alive. He must have a spy, or spies, maybe assassins amongst your group."

"My thoughts, too. Thirty of the men, well, I've known them for years, a few of them their fathers and elder brothers before them. The other twenty were volunteers or conscripts. There are a handful we've been keeping a close eye on, but nothing substantial yet. So, we have to flush them out."

Rashid nodded. "We need bait, and you seem to have become a talented fisherman."

"I take it you have a plan?"

"First, Colonel, if you don't mind, tell me please: what colour is the water inside the caldera?"

"Now listen, Rashid, a piece of advice from someone who's seen a lot of soldiers let dolphins be their downfall: forget all about col–"

"*Please*, Colonel."

Vasquez let out a long breath. He glanced over the lip to the lake below. "It's the colour of malachite, Rashid. Right now, it's breathtakingly beautiful, the setting sun reflecting crimson on the wave-tops, the surrounding rocks the colour of rust, and you'll never see colour again, and I'll never know what sonar feels like, so *get over it!* Now, your plan."

Rashid lay in the undergrowth, still as a sleeping insect, listening to the gentle lapping of water on the rocky shore. Earlier, he'd heard from a distance as Vasquez told his assembled troops how he'd met with a messenger from Esperantia reporting crimes and social disarray there; how Vasquez planned to return with an elite platoon by sling-jet, while the rest would gather the salt-dried protein harvest and make the long return trek. All this would happen in the morning. Rashid knew that Shakirvasta's man, or men, must strike during the night or lose their opportunity. Vasquez was the bait.

Rashid set his wristcom to tactile mode. Four pin-pricks in his flesh silently announced midnight. It was re-confirmed as a new guard arrived to replace the slumped figure on watch outside Vasquez' tent, twenty metres away. The shift change was brief, both guards weary, one from having been awake, the other from having had his sleep broken in two. But once the off-going guard had disappeared back to his own tent, Rashid noticed how the new one became more alert, checking all around the camp for the next ten minutes. He kept bending down, checking the ground for something. Either he was very diligent, or he was making sure all were asleep. Once or twice he even approached Rashid's hiding place. Rashid hoped the moon had sunk below the caldera's steep walls, or else his dolphin might glint in its light.

After ten minutes, presumably giving enough time for the previous guard to have fallen into a deep slumber, two figures emerged from one of the far tents. Their silent steps, and their smooth dancer-like gait, told Rashid all he needed to know – they moved like shadows drifting on a breeze. Both of them were side-armed, though he could not tell what kind of pistol it was. Worse news was that each wore some kind of head-mounted sighting system. *Tech-assassins.* He spat quietly on the ground next to him. His own Sarowan training had followed the more traditional mode, where a code of honour prevailed.

He pushed back from the ground into a stable firing position, with one knee on the floor, one knee up, and aimed his pulse rifle at the lead assassin. They were still a way off from Vasquez' tent. He squeezed the trigger. Nothing happened. He glanced at it uselessly, since his dolphin could not read the LCD display. But he'd asked Vasquez to check its charge earlier. Then it hit him. The guard hadn't been checking the ground, he'd been placing something there, some kind of electrostatic suppression system. He remembered there had been a myth back on Earth that Shakirvasta, then President of the IVS mil-ware corporation, had survived a number of assassination attempts. Some had suspected a secret piece of never-patented IVS mil-tech was involved.

Rashid was running out of time. Even alerting the other soldiers wasn't going to help if their weapons would not fire. He wondered what the assassins were carrying, and had a feeling he would soon find out.

He lay down his rifle and extracted his commando knife from its sheath. It was a long throw, and the only still target was the guard. Back in the War he'd hunted deer in the mountains with this knife; the sound of the knife spinning in the air captivated them for the half-second it took the knife to find its target. He judged the breeze and the distance, and drew his right arm back behind his shoulder, fingers wrapped around the blade. He took an in-breath, held it, then hurled the knife forward and upward in a killing arc.

He leapt to the left side as two things happened – the guard turned to the sound just before the knife thudded into his chest, punching him off his feet; and the other two assassins aimed their weapons at the tech-triangulated position from which Rashid had launched the knife. A shimmer of deadly needles whistled past Rashid, looking to his sonar like a shower of rain hitting a pool of water. He hit the ground, rolled, and came up behind a boulder. A second volley clattered against the rock, the needles splintering into it, sounding like a hundred out-of-synch cicadas. Luckily Rashid did not have to lift his head above the boulder's crest to see what was going on – his dolphin was smart enough to assemble the reflected sonar bounces and construe a reliable picture – he could see around corners.

One assassin kept his weapon trained in Rashid's direction, while the other faced Vasquez' tent. *No!* thought Rashid, but he knew if he moved he would be dead in a split second. "Assassins!" he shouted, and then he thought of a better word, even though it was a lie. "Alicians! In the camp! Pulse weapons don't work!"

He heard the assassins murmur something, then heard the needles slice Vasquez' tent into shreds, mincing everything inside. The outrage made him want to jump up and scream. *It cannot end this way!* He clamped his jaw shut, and continued to 'watch' as soldiers emerged, the first few easily cut down in a hailstorm of poison shards. Then the assassin who had murdered Vasquez toppled – a smooth cylinder, which must have been the hilt of a knife, sticking out of his forehead. The second sprinted in Rashid's direction, his weapon levelled in front of him.

Rashid had to time it perfectly. He put his back to the boulder. Just as the assassin reached it, readying to aim and fire downwards, Rashid kicked off from his squatting position upwards in a backward arch, catching the assassin's gun-wielding forearm and forcing it upwards. Rashid's head slammed into the assassin's face, as the assassin's momentum carried them both forward. The needle-gun left the assassin's grip and scuttled across the rocks. As they toppled together, the assassin managed to bring his knees sharply into Rashid's upper back. Rashid hit the deck hard, his cheek slamming against a rock. He tasted blood and felt the numbness that meant pain would be calling imminently. The assassin rolled and recovered quickly. His head darted around to locate the gun, then he leapt to a boulder at the edge of the lake and reached down to retrieve it between two rocks. Rashid ignored the shouting of the soldiers rushing in their direction. He sprang towards the assailant, arms spread wide. He connected with him just as the gun was lifting toward him, locking his grip around the gun-toting wrist, and shoved his shoulder into his opponent's chest. The assassin grabbed Rashid's other hand, and they plunged toward the lake below. Rashid took a single deep breath just before they hit the icy water.

They sank beneath the surface, touching bottom near the shore, wrestling, each trying to gain an advantage, arms pulling and shoving, legs kicking but less useful underwater. Rashid's kicks pushed them further out into the lake. The gun fired once, needles shooting off into the depths. He knew how this would end: they would both drown. *So be it, I'll die like the Sarowan warrior my parents wanted me to be.* His lungs were already near bursting, small bubbles escaping as he fought, water stinging his nostrils and sinuses whenever the assassin gained the advantage. The temptation to breathe in was so strong, he almost succumbed, but in a flash he thought of Sonja and Blake, seeing her in tears and Blake at the end of a rope. He clamped his mouth shut.

But each of them was losing strength, slowing down. Then Rashid's dolphin picked up something rising missile-fast from the depths. He calculated its trajectory. It would be a gamble but this battle was lost otherwise. He waited another second, then brought up a knee close to his own chest, got his foot into his opponent's stomach, and pushed hard, pressing himself away. He saw the assassin recover and aim the pistol at him, but he never got the chance to fire. The snake-whale rocketed up underneath him, its mouth engulfing the assassin. Rashid bolted upwards, clawing his way to air and life. The snake-whale broke surface first, its prey writhing and kicking in its jaws, before crashing downwards, heading back into the caldera's depths.

Rashid inhaled more air than he thought possible, his body shaking. Rough arms seized him and dragged him to shore. He knew they may well believe him to be an assassin too. He then heard a voice he hadn't expected to hear.

"Don't hurt him, he's one of us." Vasquez squatted down next to him.

Rashid coughed up water. "But I saw –"

"Like I said earlier, Rashid, we still have a few stealth-ware tricks up our sleeves. My tent's been empty all night, except for a one-armed holo, that is."

Rashid's heart still pounded inside his chest. "We should leave."

"We have a few burials first, I'm afraid."

Rashid grabbed his arm. "No. I have a very bad feeling about how this night might end. Seconds can count in battle, Colonel, you know that. We're South-East of Esperantia. We need to arrive before dawn."

Vasquez frowned, then stood up. "Okay men, get everything prepared, we ship out in thirty minutes."

One of his men came forward. "But Sir, we have five of our own dead here."

"They're coming with us, to be buried in Esperantia where their families can pay their respects. Now, everyone get to work. Blake needs our help, and our speed!"

* * *

Blake became aware someone else was in the darkened room. He sat up. "Assassin?"

Light flickered on, revealing Shakirvasta, relaxed in a chair, a pistol in his right hand resting on a crossed knee. The other hand held a cigarette, though there was no odour Blake could detect.

"What do you want?" Blake said, scowling.

"A trade, Commander." He took a drag, and exhaled a ring of pale grey smoke. He stared though the ring. "This is an original cigarette, Commander, one of the old style. Unabashed nicotine, though odourless of course, since it is – was – highly illegal. Do you know, I actually have tobacco seeds stored with me? Might be nice to reintroduce it, don't you think?"

"What's the trade?"

"Yes, to business. After all, there isn't much time. I have always found people over-complicate things. Personally, I simplify matters. One only has to define the solution, and then apply the required leverage. For example, I don't want you to become a martyr. I need my people to break with the past, the old ways, and look ahead to a hard-earned but brighter future."

Blake imagined Carlson, swinging at the end of a rope. "They already have one martyr."

Shakirvasta shook his head dismissively. "People will soon forget Carlson. But you, Commander, are a different item altogether. If my citizens were able to watch you being publicly executed, with you being heroic till the end... Well, I would rather have a unified collective society of strong sheep, than one comprising a few heroes followed by weak and dissenting sheep. You are the last hero, Commander, an anachronism, and so must disappear, but in a cowardly way unbefitting your heroic status. So, here is the deal: a quick death for a painless one, that's the trade. You try to escape, and I kill you, but your wife gets her endomorphine reinstated."

Blake was on his feet before he knew it. "You sonofabitch, when did you take her off it?"

The pistol rotated idly in his direction. Shakirvasta spoke with his customary nonchalance. "Not yet, Commander. But if you wish a public execution, she will receive no more. Trust me, the pain will be severe before she dies. She may last for weeks –"

"Enough!" Blake's muscles flexed, pulling the handcuff chain taut in front of him. He glanced down at the shackles. "But how can I make an escape attempt wearing handcuffs?"

"A good point, Commander." He lodged the cigarette between his lips, and with his left hand fished into his pocket, producing a digi-key. He held it in front of him, staring at it for a moment. "Commander, I should give you fair warning: this gun shoots neural darts, the effect is instantaneous. The nervous system freezes, muscle control goes into spasm, the vagus nerve stops working, the diaphragm and lungs lock, and you asphyxiate, completely conscious throughout. I know because I've watched it happen every time somebody attempted to kill me." He tossed the key at Blake's feet.

Blake bent double and stuck the digi-key into the slot. The cuffs clanked to the floor. He rubbed his wrists, curling and uncurling his fingers to get the blood circulating properly. When he rose back up, Shakirvasta was standing, and had backed to the far side of the wall. He nodded to the oval doorway. "After you, Commander."

"Carlson. The plaza. We do this there."

Shakirvasta cocked his head, squinting slightly at Blake. "Why, Commander?"

"Last respects. He wasn't one of my men, but in a way he died for me. I want to honour him before I go."

Shakirvasta eyed Blake, then appeared to make up his mind. "Very well, it is close by. But no more words, Commander. You have been sentenced to death. You are technically already dead, and are no longer entitled to speak: a dead man walking. I have always respected you, Commander, so please don't disappoint me now. In the plaza, you'll have a brief opportunity to attack and kill me, or to run, in which case I will shoot you in the back. I think we both know how this is going to end. You'll preserve your dignity. Come Commander, it is time."

Blake thought of Rashid. *Too late my friend.* It all rested on Antonia now, his rook.

CHAPTER 26 – VERDICT

"This really is unfortunate timing, Louise. Or do you prefer Arctura, as the Q'Roth now call you?" Sister Esma stood on the bridge of the Q'Roth fast-liner. With the ship in idle mode, all the screens emitted a sleepy green glow and a rhythmic soft clicking, like crickets, just at the human hearing threshold. Two Q'Roth warriors barred the entrance. They were so still, Louise wondered if they had slipped into hibernation.

Louise paced slowly, hands clasped behind her back. "Court's in recess." She stopped. "Worried I'll testify?"

Sister Esma's eyes and nostrils flared. "Do not try my patience. You know what hangs in the balance here." She cocked her head. "And what exactly is that abomination you have brought with you?"

Louise didn't turn around to where the Hohash hovered behind her. "I was expecting this to be, somehow, different. You tried to kill me, remember? The nannites you had placed on my ship?"

Sister Esma waved a wax-skinned hand dismissively. "I knew you would find a way to survive, Louise. It's what you do best, one of your two greatest talents."

Louise ignored the invited question. She felt the dagger nestling inside her sleeve. "But finding your new homeworld would have been tricky, wouldn't it?"

"*Our* homeworld: it is yours, too, especially after you sent me this message. You are already a hero, Louise."

Louise frowned. She'd planned to strike as soon as the Q'Roth guards departed the bridge, but they hadn't; the alliance with the Alicians had drawn the Q'Roth into limelight they didn't relish, and they had Sister Esma on a tight leash. Louise knew that if she made her move now, she'd never get off the bridge alive. Another approach, then. "So what's my reward?"

Sister Esma scrutinised her once-protégé, pausing to stare at Louise's sleeve, the one that concealed the dagger. "I see." She sat down in a make-shift throne chair, adopting a regal air. "What is it you want, exactly, besides my head? You can't have it, Louise, you know that, don't you? I played you, but that is what we do – in my position you'd have done the same. And look how far you've come. Level Five in a matter of months, your knowledge of Q'Roth customs and history rivals my own."

Louise knew the moment had passed. Worst of all, Sister Esma's logic was flawless – brutal, but flawless nonetheless. "I need *something*, or else I can't come back with you."

"Hannah?" Sister Esma said, raising an eyebrow.

Louise tried to keep her voice cool. "You have her?"

"Yes. She became Micah's lover towards the end."

Louise almost smiled. It would do for now. "It's a start. One other thing –"

"That, my dear girl, is already arranged. Micah unnerves me. Break his spirit. It is nearly done. Nudge him over the edge. Lead him down the path of self-destruction. That is your second greatest talent."

* * *

Micah had been separated from the others, placed in a smaller holding cell. Same bare jade walls, but this time with an impenetrable glass door. He hoped the word 'recess' had a similar meaning in Grid law, that the verdict wouldn't be passed in their absence. *Maybe Josefsson had been right all along – we should've stayed on Ourshiwann, hiding, biding our time.* He felt exhausted, deflated – seeing Carlson's corpse... He heard footsteps – with a shock he registered heels. *It can't be!*

"Hello, Micah, did you miss me?" Louise arrived on the other side of the glass. She carried a box under one arm. She set it on the floor.

"I saw you die." *That's twice now.*

"Must have been hard for you."

He saw through the veneer to what lay underneath. "If I'd have known you were going to surrender, Louise –"

"Don't you dare patronise me!" Her eyes whitened. Without warning, so fast he flinched, she punched the glass, causing it to ripple. "You set me up, Micah, killed the best man left alive."

He stood his ground, close to the glass. "It was Vince's plan, too. You must know that."

"Of course I know that. He..." She turned her back to him, a hand touched a lock of her hair, tugged at it. She cleared her throat, faced him again. She flashed a smile. "This entire day; I've been planning it for months. It's not going at all the way I'd like."

He shrugged. "That makes two of us."

She leaned her forehead against the glass and spoke softly. "I'd like this glass to be removed, Micah, so I could place my hands around your neck, stop you breathing, watch your lips turn blue, your eyes bulge, go wide with fear in the last throes of life."

He looked at her, felt sorry for her. "I know." He leant his forehead to the glass, too. "But you know what?"

She didn't answer.

"You killed two thousand people in a blink of an eye, without a second thought. You're sick, Louise. Even for an Alician. I'd say you need help, but we both know you're beyond that. I'm not even sure Sister Esma wants you back."

She uttered one soft laugh. "I always knew you were special, Micah. You never made it to the Alician A-list, but I thought you showed promise back on Earth. Vince did, too."

He felt a pang. "If I could bring him back..."

She drew away. He reciprocated.

"If I get the chance, I won't hesitate, Micah."

He nodded. "See you in court shortly, I guess."

"Unlikely. Oh, a parting gift." She picked up the box, took the lid off and turned to leave. Just before she crossed the threshold, she up-ended it. A head with flaxen hair thudded to the floor, eyes wide. It rolled toward him till it rested next to the glass.

Micah's breathing crevassed. He pounded the glass with both fists, blood rushing to his head. "Louise! Why did –?" He knew why. He punched the glass with both fists. The glass shimmered. "The feeling's mutual. You hear me? If I get the chance..."

There was no reply, the sound of her footsteps receding. He dropped to his knees, fingers trailing down the glass. He gazed at the head lying so close to him, remembering when he released the explosive bracelet from her neck, her in his bed, the last time he saw her on the bridge... He banged his head against the glass, repeatedly, eyes misting.

A bell chimed. He clawed his way up the glass to his feet. *Vince, Zack, and now Hannah.* He straightened his tunic, brushed his palms up over his face and smoothed his hair down. The glass peeled backwards. He knelt down, closed her eyes with his hand. "Hannah, I'm glad to have known you, and also sorry I couldn't protect you. Rest now." He kissed his forefinger and touched her dry lips. The Finchikta was waiting, only its blue third eye open, watching him. Micah left Hannah's head where it was, recalling that Alicians didn't care for burial rites, believing a corpse to be an empty husk. He strode straight past the Finchikta.

∗ ∗ ∗

Micah shied away from the look of relish on Sister Esma's face, as she ogled the two globes representing Earth and Ourshiwann, accelerating towards the throat of the funnel.

"Micah," Sandy said, pointing to his right.

A new party approached out of the gloom, from behind Zack's avatar. A triangular crystal plinth transported four figures he couldn't quite make out. Across the arena, as he now considered it, Sister Esma flustered, communicating with the Q'Roth queen in a series of guttural clicks. The Q'Roth leader remained unperturbed.

The Finchikta bristled. "New witnesses," it chirped. "An Ossyrian, another human, and... this is most irregular, this has never..." It moved to the ledge, craning its neck over the side to get a better view. Its blue third eye shone in the darkness. When it spoke again, it was in a hushed tone. "May the Progenitors be praised!" It wavered tantalisingly above the abyss.

"Good grief", Sandy said, "it's Kat!"

Micah recognised her as soon as Sandy said it, and the Hohash, which had obviously caught the Finchikta's attention. An Ossyrian, indistinguishable from the one who had 'fixed' Zack, stood next to Kat, tall and proud, an arm or paw resting on her shoulder. But Micah was drawn to the third figure, a naked, but asexual, hairless man, fashioned entirely of glimmering flow-metal.

"Pierre," Ramires whispered.

The plinth passed between Zack's Transpar and the Ranger, and then split in two. Kat's section headed to their platform, the other carried the Ossyrian, the Hohash and whatever was once Pierre, into the central area.

Micah studied Kat as she drew near. She clenched her jaw, trying to lock down her emotions. She looked angry, arms folded, lips a tight line. As she breached their platform, he held out his hand, but Sandy brushed past him and pulled her into a friendly embrace. He and Ramires glanced at each other, as Sandy held Kat's rigid form, until it melted and Kat surrendered to the hug.

Micah wanted to ask her a hundred questions, particularly about Pierre, but Sandy, facing Micah over Kat's hunched shoulder, said *No* with her eyes. He tried a different approach. "It's good to see you again, Kat."

The Finchikta, its third eye closed again, made a noise somewhere between a cough and a gulp. "The one calling himself Pierre is about to give evidence."

Pierre faced the Tla Beth. He held his arms out and touched his metal fingers together. They flowed seamlessly into each other, so that his arms formed an unbroken circle. He then pulled his arms apart, shoulder width, and five tubes formed where his digits should have been. The tubes changed from a silver hue to

267

white, then colours flowed rapidly along them in an incandescent pattern too fast for Micah to follow.

Micah turned to the Finchikta. "What's going on?"

The court official watched, hawk-like, its orange eyes ablaze. "Your colleague is speaking Tla Beth! This is unheard of!"

"He's almost gone, Micah," Kat said, her voice crisp and dry, wrung free of all emotion. "His humanity. During the trip here, while we were in stasis, the nannites took over. I've lost him."

Micah was jarred back to the arena by a sharp clicking from the Q'Roth queen. A Finchikta had appeared next to her, presumably as translator. Whatever had happened to Pierre, it clearly disturbed the Q'Roth. "What's he saying?" he demanded of their Finchikta. The reply was halting, either because the alien had trouble translating it, or else had a hard time accepting it.

"He brings news ... a Galactic Level 1 emergency. The ... Kalaheii... returned! Your colleague says the Hohash has ... proof ... Q'Roth are arguing dismissal of irrelevant evidence. The Tla Beth ... ah, *there*."

The arena turned into a holorium, ectoplasmic light pouring out from the Hohash, condensing into images of a vast armada of ships floating inside a shimmering wall of light. The image shifted to myriad specks – broken hulls, metal debris littering the void, and then a face in freeze-frame. The only sound was Ukrull's low growl. Micah noticed the Tla Beth's inner hourglass pattern had stopped swirling, and became almost completely black, a lone mote of white swimming in the darkness.

Pierre looked over to Micah and the others. "Kat?"

She gathered herself and stood on the other side of the Finchikta, facing the Tla Beth. "Qorall," she said. "Qorall, leader of the Kalaheii, has returned. You have to find the Kalarash, or your precious Grid Society will perish."

Sister Esma tried to engage the Queen, but the latter gave a short burst of clicks, and Sister Esma bowed low in silence.

As the holo-image faded, Micah realised that the two globes had slowed down, no longer descending. They skirted the precipitous lip of the funnel, defying gravity.

Kat brushed down her tunic and continued to address the Tla Beth, ignoring the Q'Roth party completely. "We also have new evidence of relevance to this current case. We apologise for being late, but we were quarantined until Pierre –" she gestured towards him "– could demonstrate his Level Ten powers."

Micah heard Sister Esma's snort clear across the arena, but the Queen stretched her neck forward to gain a better view of Pierre. Micah glanced from Pierre to Kat; they had obviously thought this through, choreographed their duet. It would do no good if Pierre defended humanity – he was clearly something else now. Kat had to forge the main arguments.

The Hohash burst into life again, pouring out a new vision, of life some time ago on Ourshiwann. Micah felt a pang of loss as he witnessed scenes of everyday life on the planet before the invasion – the spiders and Hohash milling about the place he now knew as Esperantia with a grace and beauty he'd never imagined. They really owned the place, making him feel as if he and the rest of humanity were vagrants squatting in an abandoned mansion.

Incandescent vistas splashed onto the night-time sky, portraying ancient battle scenes, framed by lasers reflecting off the moon to create a luminescent vista hundreds of thousands of kilometres wide. Micah saw globe-like ships destroying whole planets, suns being propelled into other star systems, collapsing them, leaving violent nebulas in their wake. Orange and black metallic fingers of light tore the fabric of space, creating rifts that sucked whole planetary systems out of existence, until ivory and gold crossbow-shaped ships materialised, strafing the globes with streams of emerald light, imploding them into darkness.

"What are we watching," Micah asked.

"An ancient history lesson," Kat replied, a hint of sadness in her voice.

"I didn't realise the spiders were that old as a race."

"They're not, but the Hohash are. The spiders were artists, and they liked to space-paint what the Hohash remembered."

The Finchikta interjected in a hushed, reverent tone, without taking its eyes off the display. "They are omnipaths, record-keepers of the galaxy."

"I've gotten to know them a little, especially since Pierre..." She shivered. "They're tortured souls; they've seen too much. They miss their masters terribly."

The Finchikta closed both its eyes and turned and stared at her with only the blue one. It bowed once, low.

The scene shifted, and Micah winced as the Q'Roth invasion unfurled, with heart-rending images Micah knew Kat had seen before, back on Eden; the merciless culling of the spider planet. Micah had no idea if sympathy or empathy had any currency in Grid Society, but the Finchikta several times looked away with distaste.

"This has no pertinence," shouted Sister Esma. "The spider race were barely Level Four and refused sponsorship: aside from art, they were technologically primitive, even compared to humanity."

Micah begrudged her the point. He imagined from the Grid Society's perspective this would be no different to humans clubbing seals to death for fur, to the point of extinction.

"Level Four?" Kat addressed the Q'Roth and Sister Esma, as if just noticing them for the first time. "How can you be so sure?"

The scene shifted to a cavern full of blue eggs. "The spider race hid tens of thousands of eggs on the planet before the culling. They knew you were coming.

They used a shielding system your technology could not penetrate. They knew how valuable a food source the eggs would be to you; a delicacy, perhaps."

"Impossible," Sister Esma shouted.

Ukrull's voice grazed across the arena. "Have been watching. Would have seen. Not detected any eggs."

Sister Esma pointed at Kat. "You are lying in a Grid court!"

Kat closed her eyes and concentrated. Micah realised she was communicating with the Hohash. Pierre turned to face the Ranger. "Access your ship's logs." An image of the planet appeared from the Hohash, small yellow patches appearing just below the surface, like sparse stubble on a smooth chin. "These are the nest locations. Here is the decryption cipher." A sequence of serifs hung over the Ourshiwann world.

Ramires stepped behind Kat. "Are you sure we should be showing this to the Q'Roth?"

She opened her eyes. "It's all or nothing, and this is our best evidence. These courts are sealed. Besides, Grid society values complete disclosure. They have a saying that a half-truth is worse than an outright lie."

The Ranger stuck one of its claws into a smaller reptile which Micah only now realised was alive. After a moment, Ukrull growled a single word. "True."

Sister Esma tried to confer with the queen, but again was shut down by her. Good, Micah thought, you're showing your true colours. Maybe the Q'Roth will decide you're a liability.

"This throws doubt," Kat said, "on the Q'Roth and Grid procedures for determining the level to be assigned to the host of a planet."

The Finchikta squawked. "Careful! Respect!"

Kat glanced at him once then continued unabashed. "We have more evidence, this time from Earth. Chahat-Me?"

Micah thought she was talking alien for a moment, until the Ossyrian creature opened its jaws and emitted a choral screeching that had him pressing his palms over his ears.

"You get used to it," Kat said. "I can tell you what she's saying, as Pierre told me earlier. Her race, the Ossyrians, visited Earth – Egypt to be precise – four thousand years ago. They detected an EPC – that's an Emergence Precipitation Coefficient, which determines how close a race is to ascending to the next level of intelligence – of 0.7. If it reaches the threshold of 1, which is basically one per cent of the population, the race cannot be culled outright, and should be advertised for sponsorship. Oh, and she's adding, I think, that I intervened on their behalf to stop their technology being stolen, in a show of cognitive pattern recognition worthy of Level 4."

Chahat-Me closed her jaws, and bowed deeply to the Tla Beth. Pierre took up the reins. "My father was a geneticist but also a statistical historian, a researcher for the Sentinels, guardians fighting against the Alicians. He was aware of the Q'Roth-Alician pact, and believed the Alicians were systematically eliminating scientists who demonstrated Level Four talents. Before he died, he made me commit to memory various statistical data and analyses – his genetic re-engineering of my brain focused a great deal on compressed memory storage."

So, Micah thought, he used Pierre, his own son, for data storage, to keep his ideas safe. He felt sorry for Pierre. No wonder he'd turned to science long ago – less chance of being hurt.

"Here are the data, analysed with the Level Ten formula usually applied for species categorisation." Pierre's tubes flashed at a subliminal rate. A sphere appeared, like a marble, with milky colours dancing inside its surface, shifting, falling, colliding like waves. Micah had no idea what it meant. The queen stared at it intently. He was gratified to see that Sister Esma was lost, too.

"As you can see," Pierre said, "the EPC in 2058, when my father was terminated by the Alicians, was 5.8. This was despite an Alician policy of seeking out talented scientists and murdering them, as well as squashing or squandering research funding to keep humanity in the dark, despite the emergence of new intelligence."

One of the Q'Roth warriors now stood between the queen and Sister Esma. Micah did not know how complicit the Q'Roth were in the Alician tactics to achieve their masters' goals – probably they didn't care, but right now he understood why the queen would want to distance herself from the Alicians.

"Is it likely," Kat said, "given what you have seen, that less than a thousand angts ago, when humanity was rated and culling permission was granted, that the EPC was less than one?"

"This evidence could be pure fabrication!" Sister Esma screamed.

"It could, but is not." Pierre said. "So, we would like to see the original deposition which rated humanity."

Sister Esma started to speak but was nudged sharply by the warrior. A pregnant silence hung in the chamber. A minute passed.

"What's going on?" Sandy said. "Why don't they want to show it?"

Kat whispered. "Pierre's hunch, we have to play it." She walked to the other side of the platform to face the Ranger. "We call upon the Ranger to testify on the original deposition."

Ukrull's amber eyes flared, and his tail lashed out violently. "Deposition... accepted."

Kat pressed. "Did the Ranger who submitted it agree with the rating?"

The tail flailed again.

"The whole truth please, that is what the Grid Society values, is it not? It is also a requirement in human judicial proceedings."

The Finchikta ruffled its feathers. "You humans go too far!"

It was the last thing Micah remembered hearing. The Tla Beth ascended rapidly from the arena, and everything around him melted into static.

Micah opened his eyelids to see Sandy leaning over him, in a white room shaped like a tent. "Come on sleepy-head, the rest of us woke up hours ago."

He rubbed his eyes, feeling for once like he'd had a good sleep. Then it all flooded back to him. He sat up as if starting from a nightmare. "The verdict! What happened?"

"We won," Kat said. "Sort of."

Micah would have preferred an unqualified version. "Can you elaborate?"

She glared at him. "Yeah, sure, Micah. You want elaboration? Okay then, here are the headlines. I saw Rashid's ship evaporate in the heart of a star – glad to hear he survived, a story I'd like to hear in detail. Pierre and I were dying, and well, we made love, and I got pregnant. Nearly drowned but got rescued by the Ossyrians; saved their tech from being stolen by another alien race, the Mannekhi – friends of yours I believe, you really should watch the company you keep. My Hohash pal unleashed all hell inside my brain, not for the first time I might add, and it turns out the entire galaxy is under serious threat. Oh, and Pierre's nannites got way ahead of themselves and everybody else, including the Ossyrians. It's a girl, by the way. She's next door, sleeping, Chahat-Me's the godmother, kind of rushed it through for me."

Micah stared open-mouthed. "Kat, I –"

"Oh sorry," she said, in a mocking tone, much to Sandy's amusement, "you meant the court case! Silly me, I thought you gave a damn."

Micah stood up. "Kat I do –"

"The Tla Beth threw out the case. Pierre and I had a couple of days in quarantine outside to do some research. Chahat-Me helped us out. You see, the Tla Beth fostered the Ossyrians aeons ago, steered them away from their genocidal tendencies to become caring doctors. Meanwhile, though less well-known, the very same Tla Beth fostered the already nastily violent Q'Roth to become even more lethal, with a killing instinct hooked into the most basic instinct of all, hunger. The Tla Beth needed foot-soldiers, see? There was a war coming. The Q'Roth did their bit around fifty thousand years ago. Wrecked their own civilisation, reducing themselves to nomadic status, but they saved a whole quadrant from chaos. Only problem was that the killing instinct couldn't be bred out of them. Best the Tla Beth could do was extend their hibernation cycle. For a while it didn't matter, there were plenty of

Level Two or Three planets to feed upon every thousand years. But then finding such planets got trickier. So, they –"

"– relaxed the rules," Micah finished. He figured it was his turn to interrupt. She nodded, and flashed a fake smile. He could tell she was angry, but he knew it wasn't about him. "Where's Pierre now?"

She put her hands on her hips. "Are we talking existentially or physically? Because for me it's the first that's bugging me."

Sandy intervened. "Kat," she held the other's hand. "From what you've told me, he's no longer Pierre."

Micah was impressed at how Sandy never feared to say the things everyone else only dared to think. Kat retracted her hand, though not abruptly, and walked over to the single small oval portal onto space.

"He's with Chahat-Me, finalising the deal they struck with the Tla Beth."

Micah felt awkward, not knowing if he should do something like give Kat a hug – but he didn't know her that well.

Sandy rescued him. "Why don't you go and see the baby, Micah. I sent Ramires in there, too, you know how emotionally inept men can be."

He frowned, and walked towards the seamless wall as Sandy had indicated. A door irised out of nowhere, and he stepped through it. It closed silently behind him, and he realised he didn't know which way to go down the three-sided windowless corridor, left or right. On impulse he turned left and came to a dead end. He decided to try it and approached the wall. Another round doorway opened up revealing Pierre and Chahat-Me in some kind of crystalline control room.

"Enter, Micah, we need to talk. The Tla Beth have delivered their detailed ruling. You won, but there's a catch."

"Where's Kat?" Micah asked Sandy and Ramires, who were sitting on the floor, legs stretched in front of them, their backs to the bench running half-way around the room.

"Breast-feeding, last time I checked," Sandy said.

"Oh, right. I'll fill her in later."

"So, what's the deal?"

Micah sat down opposite them. He felt dizzy from the speed of events the past few days, as if he'd just stepped off a particularly violent rollercoaster. "First, the good news. The Q'Roth have been banned from going anywhere near Ourshiwann, which is where we're headed. And we've been granted provisional Level Four status, which means we can't be selected for culling. And there's an unexpected bonus, a trove it's called."

"Which is?"

"Whenever a culling takes place, a record is taken, a sample if you like. A slice of the biosphere is literally cut out of the planet, put into a massive stasis container, and sent for processing in some kind of Galactic library. Good news is, it hasn't reached processing yet, and is now being diverted back to Ourshiwann, where it'll arrive in a few months. Wherever the trove came from on Earth, there'll be fauna, insects, birds, maybe even some animals, or ... people, I suppose. We can get back some of our bio-diversity."

"But that's fantastic!" Sandy said. "So, why aren't you smiling?" She rested her palm on top of Ramires' thigh. "Spill the beans, Micah."

He sighed. "Okay. We have to be sponsored. It's a fact of Grid life. The Ossyrians will be our guardians and representatives for the next fifteen years. During this time," he raised and dipped his eyebrows, "we'll be quarantined: no one leaves or enters Ourshiwann, except a handful of Ossyrians. They've promised to be hands-off with us, just helping with education, a kind of induction into Grid Society." He looked down at his feet.

"There's more isn't there?"

"Yes. And it affects you directly, Sandy."

Her eyes fixed on him and didn't waver. Ramires pulled himself into a more upright pose, his hand clasping hers.

Micah took a breath. "The next generation must undergo genetic enhancement."

She shot to her feet. "No fucking way!"

Micah stayed where he was. "No exceptions, Sandy. Kat's daughter, too."

Sandy stomped the floor hard. "No! It's Gabriel's son. He's all I have! We didn't survive all this just to have our genes manipulated and mutilated."

Micah kept his voice calm. He guessed Pierre was having a similar discussion with Kat right now. "How long do you think humanity will last as it is, Sandy? We've been out here a few months, and we're hopelessly inept, unable even to communicate most of the time without my resident, which is borrowed, illegal alien tech. Fifteen years – a generation – to give us a chance to survive in the Grid. If nothing else it will put us on an even keel with the Alicians. The genning won't be too severe, mainly an upgrade to our neural processing – kids will think faster and be able to process thoughts in parallel."

"And what do they lose, Micah, what's the downside of this trade, because there always is one, isn't there?"

Micah had no answer. "It's non-negotiable, Sandy. It's been decreed. We take it or else we're abandoned, and the Q'Roth will finish the job they started. The Q'Roth queen played her hand well, knowing that with this Kalaheii threat, all their tribes will once again be called upon by the Tla Beth to fight; apparently two entire legions have been lost already. Despite all the evidence, we nearly had *them* sponsoring us."

Ramires spoke softly, holding her hand. "Sandy, I am a warrior, one of the best in humanity, but I'm barely a match for an Alician. I want your son to be unafraid, to know he can fight on equal terms. Gabriel would have wanted this."

She snatched her hand away, turning away from both of them, but remained silent. Ramires caught Micah's eye and nodded to the hidden doorway. Micah got up and started to leave.

"Micah," Sandy said, still facing away from him, "how are you going to convince the rest of humanity to go along with this? They've not seen what we've seen. They won't understand. They'll think you've sold them out."

Micah paused in front of the doorway. "No idea, Sandy. One leap at a time."

Kat drilled holes in the floor with her eyes, while Pierre went through the deal and the implications for humanity. Only when he'd finished everything and seemed ready to leave, did she speak.

"You're not staying with us, are you?" She indicated the cot in the corner where their daughter slept.

He answered straight away – not harsh, just clinical, "Part of the deal is that I aid the Tla Beth and the Rangers. My development has not stopped. If anything, it is accelerating."

Kat looked up. "I want to see my Pierre, even if only for one last time. I know you can do it. Somewhere buried deep inside you, he's still there."

Pierre's silver eyes danced, though the rest of him remained motionless. Kat had the sense that there was some kind of internal debate going on inside his head. Abruptly Pierre shook and fell to his knees. She was by his side in a moment, her arms locked around his trembling frame, the silver flesh uncannily soft to her touch.

"Kat," he said, short of breath.

"My God, Pierre, what's happened to you?" She braced herself and kissed his silver lips hard.

He hung his arms around her. "It's ... it's okay. In fact, it's utterly amazing, beyond description. So much, I don't know where to begin." He panted, leaning heavily on her.

"I want you back, Pierre, I need you. Your daughter needs you!"

His silver eyes flashed metallic blue, irises forming. "Can't, Kat, almost gone. No way back, organs ... changed. Everything ... rewired. I'm just an echo of who I was. War is coming... Need to prepare, fight, or else no one will survive, not even the Tla Beth. You see, I worked it out." His speech quickened, as if he was running out of time. "What the Kalaheii were trying to do when they destroyed their galaxy. You were right all along, Kat. You said it months ago: why would they commit suicide? So I figured it out. We have to find the Kalarash before they try again."

She shook him. "I don't care!" She screamed at him, waking the baby. "What about us?"

"Doing this for us. Must. No way ... back."

She felt him tensing, the blue eyes reverting to silver, his skin hardening. She was losing him for good this time. "Our daughter, Pierre, name her, please." She sniffed, trying to hold back the tears.

He held her hand, gently. "Petra," he said. "Rock. Me. Remember?"

The tears broke. She watched them fall, splashing onto his silver thigh, running off immediately onto the floor. "Petra," she whispered, as Pierre got up and left the room.

CHAPTER 27 – SHOWDOWN

Cool ground crunched underneath Blake's boots as the night surrendered to the first pre-dawn rays, rendering Shakirvasta pale and ghost-like, his pistol arm hanging by his side. They reached the plaza where Carlson's large frame hung, the noose long since dug into his neck so that the blood had congealed black around it, his contorted face chalk white. Blake followed the pleated cord upwards to a crude bronze hook, the type butchers had used since ancient times to hang up carcasses. The cadaver twisted slowly in the dawn breeze, the rope creaking at each turn. Blake wanted above all else to get Carlson down; he deserved better.

"Your move, Commander," Shakirvasta said.

Blake approached Carlson. He'd seen enough dead bodies in his time to anticipate the smell and rigidity of a stale corpse. He placed his arms around the dead man's legs, and with a grunt, shoved the stiff body upwards. It took a few attempts, but the cord finally slipped off the hook, and Blake lowered Carlson's body to the ground. Surreptitiously, squatting on his haunches next to Carlson's frame while regaining his breath, he slipped his hand inside Carlson's jacket pocket. Empty.

"Do you take me for a fool, Commander?"

He stood up to see Shakirvasta flourish the pistol Antonia had put there an hour earlier. Blake's own pistol. *Good,* he thought, *now the odds are even.* He took a step closer, so the military pulse pistol's sensors could lock onto their target. He hoped there was enough light for the facial pattern recognisers to work. Zack – due to the implant theory – had re-programmed it months ago to overload in the event someone tried to fire it at its owner.

Blake spat onto the dust. "Let's get this over with, shall we? You can say you wrestled my gun from me and killed me with it. A certain symmetry from your point of view."

Shakirvasta narrowed his eyes. "Yes, I could. But you seem a little eager, all of a sudden." He lowered Blake's weapon and held up his own. "Sometimes it's best to stick to the original plan."

Blake judged the distance: he'd never make it. Shakirvasta would fire on him before he could get half-way. Nevertheless, he lowered his body weight a fraction, loosening his knees.

"Sanjay." Jen's voice cut through the air behind Blake.

Shakirvasta did a double-take, glancing from her to Blake. "What ... what is this? You told me she was dead!"

"No, *you* told me she was dead, and that I'd killed her. I never admitted anything."

Shakirvasta shifted from one foot to the other. Both pistols were raised now, facing Blake, but occasionally drifting towards Jen. "But ... this is marvellous!"

Jen walked straight towards her former lover.

He frowned. "Wait, Jennifer," he said. "Just wait there. Please."

She carried on walking. 'What's the matter. Don't you..." She stopped as Blake's pistol shifted resolutely in her direction.

Blake bit his lip. *Damn, switch hands!*

"Please, Jennifer," Shakirvasta said, a little flustered, "this is not good timing. Please just wait a moment, this man is a criminal, sentenced to death, and judgement needs to be passed."

Jen stood level with Blake. "For my murder. But I'm alive."

"Nevertheless," Shakirvasta was clearly trying to find a rationale, but then gave up. "He has to die, my love, he stands in the way of everything we've planned."

Blake noticed she'd brought no weapon, not even the nanosword. Surely she wasn't that naïve? He wondered if he could get to Shakirvasta while Jen distracted him. He doubted it.

"That's what I wanted to talk to you about, Sanjay. Our premises were wrong. While this was just about us on a barren planet versus the Alicians and the Q'Roth, the strategy made sense. But I've seen fields of spider eggs, and Dimitri says they will hatch in the next few years. And that's not all. There's an ocean underground, and inside it a ship, millions of years old. The creature inside is waking, slowly but surely."

Her eyes glowed, evangelical. Blake had never seen her like this.

"Dimitri and I tried to contact it via the Hohash, and for one brief instant, through my node, I glimpsed a small part of its mind." She took a half step towards him.

Shakirvasta's pistol pushed out further as he took a step backwards. "What is this nonsense? What have they done to you?" A look of revulsion crawled across his face.

Jen's voice was calm, resolute. "It's a sublime creature, Sanjay, purity of thought beyond words. It made me think about things, about everything. There's a great war coming to the galaxy. Our petty rivalry with the Alicians is like old, defunct stock, it doesn't matter anymore. We need soldiers – and the best one on the planet is right in front of you. And farmers, obviously. But we need scientists, researchers, free thinkers, or else we'll remain small and of no consequence, wrapped up in our own little world."

Shakirvasta stopped shifting. That worried Blake. It meant he had decided, and Blake reckoned Shakirvasta had way too much to lose to turn back now.

"I don't know what they've done to you, Jennifer – brainwashed you in some way. If you could hear yourself! Do you know who you sound like? *Antonia!* I was right, they did kill my Jennifer."

She didn't rise to the bait. The first shafts of the sun broke across the courtyard, straight into Sanjay's eyes. He lifted Blake's pistol to block the glare.

People would be waking, now. Blake knew that Shakirvasta had to act very soon, one way or the other.

"Sanjay, please. It's not too late. Free Blake, reconvene the Council – the real one, and disband the militia. You can control people by freedom, you once taught that, years ago."

"No," he said, his voice tombstone cold. His arm flexed toward Jennifer. "You are no longer Jennifer. My Jennifer would never have come here alone, without any weapon. You haven't learned *anything* from me, after all this time. This religious enlightenment on the road to Damascus, it has weakened you, it's pathetic." He took a step to the side, so the sun was no longer in his eyes. He hefted the gun in his left hand. "This is Blake's pistol, Jennifer. You escaped imprisonment, held by Rashid and Dimitri, and you returned here to be by my side, only to be cut down by Blake as he escaped. In a fit of lover's rage I killed Blake myself, and I will grieve, and my grief will be real. Goodbye, my love."

Blake had heard the graveyard edge in a killing voice often enough to know that Shakirvasta was ready to fire. He leapt towards Shakirvasta as the fizz of a pulse pistol charged the air and he smelt ozone. In mid-air he raised his arm to smash down on Shakirvasta's clavicle so that he couldn't fire on Jen, but before he met his target, Shakirvasta's body jerked backwards and hit the ground. Blake landed roughly on all fours next to him, watching the tell-tale electric blue wisps of lightning skittering across his corpse, illuminating the look of surprise on the dead man's face. Shakirvasta had aimed Blake's weapon at Jen, but as Blake had attacked, the man's defensive instincts had taken over and he'd fired the weapon at Blake, electrocuting himself in the process.

Jen walked over and crouched next to Shakirvasta, and brushed a lock of lank hair from his staring eye. "Such a waste," she said. "He was a good leader."

Blake loosened his still-warm pistol from Shakirvasta's grip. "So, it wasn't all an act, then?"

"I'm not religious, Commander, don't worry. It's just that I always thought the only way to survive at the top was to be ruthless. Like Sanjay," she said, glancing down. "But the creature in the ship... It's immensely strong, yet compassionate." She shrugged. "I need to wake it, but couldn't reach it on the last two attempts; it's very deep. I need some more gear, and I know where Sanjay had all the mil-tech equipment stashed."

"Jen, you were lovers. How can you just walk away?"

She addressed the corpse. "We were like snakes coiling around each other, using each other. We were fascinated by finding kindred spirits, that's all. But he was right about one thing, Commander – that Jennifer is dead. I fought for years in the ruins of Dublin during the War, did unspeakable things to survive and wound the enemy. After the War it stayed with me, in my head. When I arrived here, it over-loaded, like a snake biting itself, gorging on its own venom." She met his eyes. "That Jennifer is lying there, next to him, dead on the ground."

She started walking away, then paused. "Oh, by the way, Commander, Rashid contacted us an hour ago. He and Vasquez are flying in with some troops."

"Jen, are you sure waking this creature is a good idea?"

"Absolutely. No time to waste."

Blake listened to the roar of a sling-jet arriving and landing nearby. As it powered down, he heard the sound of running bare feet coming from the other direction. Sonja burst into the courtyard, Zack's old pistol at her side. She came over to him, then fired three times at Shakirvasta's corpse, the body recoiling each time. She dropped the pistol to the ground. "A little late, I know."

He looked up at her. "It's never too late, Sonja."

She held out her hand. 'Come, I'll take you to Glenda; she doesn't have much time."

They ran all the way.

CHAPTER 28 – KALARASH

"Just like old times," Jen said, her voice only partly muffled by the squirt of cold air into the rebreather's full-face mask.

"Except you are alone. Last time we were underwater together, and I am exceedingly anxious for you. How deep are you now?"

She glanced to the right and checked through the green digits short-focused onto her visor. "A kilometre. Hey, my daddy would be proud!" She tried to hide her ragged breathing. She'd been free-falling for twenty minutes in the roiling dark ocean, buffeted by undersea currents. She stared downwards into a cone of light from her torch that only served to emphasise the blackness beneath her.

"You're the bravest soul I know, my dear Jen."

"Yeah, well, somebody's got to do it." *And this is scaring the crap out of me!* "How close do you reckon?"

"My sensor says you're almost on top of it, but it is not precise."

She yawned her eyes wide open to exercise them – all this staring into a bubble of light, nothing to focus on, was giving her a headache, not to mention vertigo. She tried not to think about getting back. On the way down the thrusters and gyros in her suit could track their target and nudge her back onto course every ten seconds. But going up would require deploying two small balloons. At this depth she wasn't sure they'd inflate enough to lift her, and if they did, she could drift miles off course, even assuming the thrusters' fuel cell didn't run out. She reminded herself she was supposed to be *not* thinking about it.

"Jen, it's back again."

281

Dimitri sounded worried. Something kept hovering near her every now and again. Dimitri couldn't determine its shape or size, but she could tell he was trying to play it down.

"Jen. *Jen!* I want you to take manual control of your thrusters."

"What is it?" She fumbled for the control panel on her left wrist, flipped open the cover.

"Please do as I say. When I say 'now' you must go hard to port."

"Dimitri, what the hell –"

"NOW!"

She hit the button and went starboard. "Shit!" she said, locking down the other button ricocheting her to port. A huge set of pearl-toothed jaws missed her by centimetres as it shot up past her, its albino smooth body bumping her, somersaulting her. When she stopped in the featureless black she felt dazed, no longer sure which way was up. *Look at the bubbles*, she remembered her father telling her during her first scuba lesson. She looked for the tiny trail of bubbles emitted from the rebreather, and checked which way they were headed. *Good, I'm upright.* "Is it gone?"

"It is circling above you."

"This is taking too long!" She pivoted so that she was head down, and pressed the button which controlled her heel thrusters, and torpedoed downwards, arms stretched out before her.

"What are you doing?"

A blinding pressure headache erupted, as if her forehead was in a vice.

"Jen, it's turning, it's diving down towards you!"

She realised she'd made a tactical error. At this angle and speed, the thrusters on her shoulders – her only brakes – would have marginal effect. Her one hope was to reach the ship, probably ramming it with her head. "*Come on*," she said aloud, "where the hell are you?" A proximity sensor beeped, signalling that it was fifty metres below.

"Jen, it's gaining on you!"

She stretched her body to minimise her drag in the water, and ramped up the thrusters to maximum. The beeps accelerated: thirty metres, twenty-five, twenty..."

She felt a yawning suction behind her, and imagined the creature's jaws opening wide.

Ten metres. The top of the ship snapped into view, like a giant turtle's head. A wave of turbulence washing against her legs told her the creature had broken off its chase, no doubt not wanting to ram the ship itself. Instinctively she hit the drag-balloon actuation button to slow her down. The harness tore at her shoulders, whipping her around as her metal boots hit the top of the ship hard with a deafening clang. Her legs buckled, sending her sprawling and scraping across the metallic surface. The current caught the balloons and dragged her sideways. She clutched for anything to anchor herself down, but the convex hull was smooth. The balloons started to lift her from the ship. "No!" she screamed. "Fuck, fuck, FUCK!" She hit the balloon harness-release button, and clattered back down onto the ship's crown. She slowed down and stopped. She stayed where she was, breath shaky, as the full enormity of her situation hit her. "Dimitri," she said, "promise you won't be angry."

She'd been shallow-breathing for the last forty-five minutes, trying to squeeze as much oxygen from the rebreather as possible. The creature hadn't returned, evidently preferring not to venture too close to the ship.

The air was getting hot to the point it singed her lungs, making her cough, which wasted precious oxygen. She'd been on the ship's skull for four hours, seeking a way in, but there was nothing except smooth metal.

Dimitri had suggested a range of outlandish rescue options, but she knew she was going nowhere. Her family had been submariners for three generations. She guessed they'd be interested in her story, and if there was any after-life, they'd be hearing it first-hand pretty soon. She and Dimitri had gone through the emotional ringer, but she'd asked him to stop – she didn't want to die morose, and now there was little else to say. They were both waiting for her to die.

"My dear Jen," he began, again.

"Tell me about Santorini," she cut in. While she listened, she tried to make her breathing sound normal, though her chest muscles were exhausted, and the over-used air was getting hotter. Her throat ached, feeling as if strips of flesh had been peeled off like wallpaper. She knew she only had minutes of consciousness left. She tried to drift on his words, like a seagull soaring above the Greek cliffs, over an azure sea that no longer existed. But the pain kept intruding, destroying the illusory scene in her mind as easily as tearing rice paper.

She heard muffled voices. Dimitri must have had his hand over the mike, she guessed. She recognised the second voice: Rashid and Dimitri were arguing. "What's going on, guys?"

"Jennifer – Jen, it's Rashid here. I have an idea, if Dimitri will let me."

There was a grumbling noise in the background. "*I'll* let you, Rashid. Tell me."

"Do you have the nanosword with you?"

Jen had almost forgotten about it. She reached down to where it was strapped to her right calf. She'd already tried it on the hull, but it couldn't penetrate it. "What did you have in mind?"

"It is a long shot, but I want you to carve the infinity symbol on the hull, and place two dots, one in each half. You know the symbol?"

Of course she knew it – an elongated hourglass. Putting the dots in each section would make it a bit like an unpacked yin-yang symbol. She retrieved the sword and activated it. It glowed a soft purple in the darkness, miniscule bubbles fizzing outwards from its blade. "Why, Rashid?" She began drawing the symbol, tracing the arc. It scored the hull, leaving a dull red glow in its wake, quickly quenched by the ice-cold water, as she sculpted the blade around.

"The symbol is known to my people. Legend has it that it was on the Ranger's ship and his uniform when he crash-landed on Earth nine hundred years ago."

She finished. She lifted the blade and drove it down point-first into one of the segments. "Maybe I should carve my name instead," she said, trying not to cough. "You know, *Jen was here*, for example." She tried to laugh but couldn't. She barely heard Dimitri remonstrating with Rashid far up above her. She felt dizzy, her sight growing blotchy. She raised the blade one more time, and felt the tug on her lungs which told her she was out of time. She sank to her knees as she drove the blade down into the second segment, fully convinced that nothing at all would happen.

She fell straight through the hull.

✳ ✳ ✳

"Jen, come in." Dimitri's bulk dwarfed the small radio set. He flicked the switch again. "Jen, come in." He glanced at his wristcom. It had been fifty-one minutes since he'd lost contact. She was dead. But he could think of nothing else to do. "Jen, come in, Jen."

"She's gone, Dimitri," Rashid said, as patient as if it was the first time he'd said it.

Dimitri hunched his shoulders, not even deigning to turn around. "Come in, Jen. Jen, come in."

"Dimitri?"

He toppled from the chair, then struggled to grab the radio set again, kneeling at the table. "Jen, Jen is that you? How can that be?" He heard her laugh.

"Take a look at your sonar."

He rushed to another table and spun the sonar screen to face him. "Jen, I don't see anything, I..." But then he did see it. It was barely noticeable at first, but he confirmed it, and sat back, his hands disappearing into his mounds of hair. Rashid's dolphin couldn't read the two-dimensional screen, so he stared down through the floor instead, to the ocean below, and saw it too. The ship was rising toward the surface.

* * *

It reminded her of an Escher sketch. She stood firm, feet spread for balance, on a smooth glass ball the diameter of a football field, filled with swirling red gas. She could see Dimitri on a neighbouring one, a grisly green affair connected to hers by a porcelain white pathway, crouching down on its underside. Further afield, she watched Rashid stroll across a sea blue sphere, his form sticking out sideways at a logically impossible angle. Her mind told her both of them should fall off and tumble into the boiling violet lake five kilometres below, toward the base of the ship.

It was like the giant molecular holo-models she'd read about, used to teach chemistry in virtual immersion-classes back on Earth. But she'd studied the laws of physics well enough to know that these globes couldn't possibly have enough mass to create such a short-range gravity field without affecting each other. The only explanation, as far as she could see, was that the ship's occupant could control gravity.

None of them had yet seen the alien dweller – she remained convinced by her interactions with the Hohash that there was only one inhabitant on the ship. She'd seen something – a fleeting shadow, more or less – move out of her field of vision once or twice, always staying ahead of her eye movements, which meant its perception and reaction time were off the scale. When she'd first heard the theory that there were nineteen levels of intelligence in the galaxy, she'd struggled to see what they could possibly know at the upper levels. But now, for the first time, she began to think it was possible after all to have such a range of capabilities in the galaxy.

Her gaze shifted back to Dimitri – it was good to be with him again. He'd stuck by her during what she now thought of as her 'dark phase'. She'd never leave him or lose him again, she decided. Looking back, she felt as if Shakirvasta had cast a spell on her. If he were here now, she'd throw him down into that lake for sure.

Dimitri's mess of hair and beard craned upwards from whatever he was doing, and he waved to her, shouting something she couldn't catch, the sound lost in the echoless chamber. She waved back, smiling, trusting him like no one else.

They'd found no control room, or any room for that matter, just these gas-filled spheres, like the one she'd landed on when she first entered the ship. Dimitri had conjectured that this whole hallucinogenic structure was part of the creature itself, but her instincts told her otherwise.

She stared past the countless orbs toward the ship's hull a kilometre away. A dull orange glow hung there. It reminded her of the first pre-dawn rays back in Dublin when she was a young girl, except here it stayed the same – sunrise never actually arrived. Yet it was uplifting, as if the creature was dawning, waking slowly, coming

285

back to life. But she was growing impatient. Idly, she scuffed the glass surface with one of her boots, creating a smear which healed itself within seconds. They'd been here for hours, and found nothing. Even the Hohash had stopped communicating, instead shadowing her like a manservant, always there when she turned around. On impulse she checked to see it was still there, and it was gone. The slender man who stood in its place took her breath away.

"Gabriel?" she whispered, knowing it couldn't be her brother. He'd aged since she'd last seen him ten years ago, but the resemblance was unmistakeable.

"Hello, Jen. I'm not Gabriel, but I needed to find a way to communicate with you, other than through my Hohash."

Her pulse raced. Part of her wanted to rush up to the man in front of her and embrace him, even if it was the alien in disguise. The other part of her was angered by the manipulative act. "Then use a vidcom!"

Gabriel smiled the wan smile she'd forgotten. It almost cracked her apart. "I'm sorry, Jen. I need to have your full attention. It's taken me a long time to understand your species. The Hohash are my eyes and ears. They are omnipaths: they see, hear, empathise, and record everything. We created them long ago as galactic recording devices, witnesses. I've been studying you, as well as your companions on this planet and elsewhere, through the surviving Hohash devices. I needed to know if I could trust humanity."

Jen snorted. "You must have dozed off during a few episodes if you've not noticed how difficult and untrustworthy we can be." The frustration at seeing her long lost brother, in the flesh, within arms' reach – yet it was not him – made her scratch deeper. "You must be a little desperate, too, to be honest. Don't you have any Level Nineteen friends to play with?"

His face grew more serious. "There isn't much time, Jen. You must listen."

Gabriel's face took the same expression he'd had when as kids he'd needed to tell her something important. It disarmed her. She turned away. "What about the others?" But she saw they were not moving, or perhaps were moving very slowly. She turned back to him. "Do you control time as well?"

Gabriel laughed. "I wish. No, I accelerated your synaptic ability for a short while. It won't harm you."

She shrugged. "Okay, I'm listening, but I have some questions too."

"I'll answer three. Choose carefully."

She folded her arms. "You first."

Gabriel's gaze swept around the menagerie of globes, as if he'd never seen them before. Maybe, Jen thought, he's never seen them with human vision before.

"The galaxy has been invaded by an ancient race called the Kalaheii. They are Level Nineteen, like me. The definition of a level difference is very simple – they can subdue any level beneath them if they so choose. All the Progenitors – the ancient

Level Nineteen races – left this galaxy long ago, or sublimated, which comes to the same thing." He glanced at her to see if she wished to ask anything, then continued. "We had a War in our home galaxy. Qorall, the Kalaheii leader, was losing badly. He unleashed a weapon we'd not seen before. It destroyed the entire galaxy in a matter of what you would call days. We barely escaped. Quintillions perished, including, so we'd thought, Qorall himself." He squatted down. He grazed his fingertips over the smooth glass surface. As he did so, the red colour underneath rippled. "Qorall will wage war here, and will steadily sweep across the galaxy. All opponents will fall before him, though they will delay him and his army. I may be able to stop him. But, as you neatly phrased it, I need friends."

"But your friends left the galaxy."

He nodded.

Jen thought about it, imagined how Qorall would think. "His first priority will be to ensure there are no ancients in the galaxy. That's why you've been hiding here."

"I've been dormant for some time, contemplating my future. However, his arrival changes everything. He must not find me before I am ready."

She unfolded her arms. "So, you're... Oh my God. You're leaving the galaxy?"

He stood up, stretching backwards at the waist the way her brother used to do. "For a short while. You three are coming with me. One of my 'friends' developed a portal, aeons ago, an inter-galactic shunt to a neighbouring galaxy. The trip will take a few months in your subjective time, but back here – and here we will return – some ten or so of your years will pass."

Jen felt dazed. Her anger about the creature taking the form of her sibling dissipated in the wake of this news. "Why take us with you?"

"A good question, your second by the way." He chewed his lip. Jen knew that if it had been Gabriel, that gesture would have indicated embarrassment. Could that be true of such an advanced species?

He gazed into the distance. "It's so long since I've held a physical form like this, so limited, yet so alive! That's why I need you three with me, by the way. When you've lived tens of millions of years, not as a race, but as an individual, you've seen it all, over and over again. You become detached. Many opt for sublimation, merging with planets, even suns. Others go off to explore new galaxies, new dimensions if they can find entry." He walked up to her, put his hands on her shoulders. "When I find others... they may persuade me to stay with them. I need a reason to come back. You three will remind me."

She sensed there must be more to it than that, but she had the feeling he wouldn't be drawn further on the matter, so she let it go. In any case, his touch melted her anger. He even smelled like her brother. She reached for his hand.

He drew back, leaving her fingers dangling in mid-air. "You have one more question, Jen. What is it to be?"

Her hand dropped to her side, and she brought herself back under emotional control. She thought hard. There were so many potential questions, but one rose above the rest. Why was he here, on this world? What was on Ourshiwann that made him pick it, because she was sure that a Level 19 alien did nothing by accident. "The spiders. They're important, somehow, aren't they?"

A broad smile lit up Gabriel's face. "Your brother would be proud of you, Jen, your father, too. Very well then, I will tell you, and then, before we leave, I need one of you to deliver a message to the man called Micah."

CHAPTER 29 – HARD CHOICES

The pyramid-shaped Ossyrian ship *Solace* dwarfed Esperantia, its burnished sides reflecting the morning's first rays. It had landed silently during the night, though not unnoticed. A straggling crowd two thousand strong had assembled at the city's boundary in the chill morning air. A hundred metres ahead of them, near the leading edge of the gargantuan vessel, Vasquez spear-headed a phalanx of a hundred or so jittery soldiers, all of whom hefted an array of heavy weapons.

A hole the shape of an eye opened up near the ship's base. A transparent oval tube sprouted forward, descending toward the ground where Vasquez and Antonia had been standing the past hour. Micah emerged, leading Sandy, Ramires, and Kat down the glass tunnel. He kept a measured gait until they got closer, when it seemed as if Sandy was tripping over his heels. He broke into a trot, and all four of them ran the last twenty metres. Micah slowed down just as they arrived at the outlet, the others fanning out around him. He made a half-hearted attempt to maintain decorum, but a grin split across his face. "Damn, it's good to see you!"

Vasquez saluted. "Welcome back, Captain Sanderson."

Micah turned to Antonia, but Kat whipped around in front of him and swept her into a long kiss.

Micah tried to ignore them, and spoke to Vasquez. "We had some disturbing news... Carlson?"

Vasquez' smile vanished. "It got ugly here, Micah, but Shakirvasta's dead, and Josefsson is in a cell with his militia commanders."

Sandy interjected. "Blake?"

Antonia extricated herself, a little short of breath, her face flushed. "His wife Glenda is dying, Micah. She could go anytime."

Kat glanced at Micah. "Not if I can help it, she won't." She turned back to the mouth of the tube, and shouted. "Chahat-Me, come on down, we have work to do!"

The soldiers, most of whom had lowered their weapons on seeing Micah and the others, raised them again, aiming at the majestic Ossyrian who appeared from the bottom of the ship aboard a crystal hover-sled.

"Hold your fire!" Vasquez yelled to his men, his hand held high.

Chahat-Me drew up beside them silently. Kat pulled Antonia behind her as they boarded the sled and sped towards the city, the wall of soldiers parting before them. Antonia glanced back once, catching Micah's eye. He nodded. *You're welcome.*

Micah picked out a lone figure walking towards them from the crowd. Even at a distance he could see her footsteps weighed heavily. *Sonja.*

Vasquez asked about the ship, its inhabitants, their weapons capability, Micah was relieved when Ramires stepped in and furnished answers to the barrage of questions. Micah had gone over and over in his mind what he would say to Sonja. He felt personally responsible: it should have been him, not Zack, turned into an emotionless crystal echo, little more than a walking, talking memory chip.

"Sonja," he said, his pre-planned speeches deserting him.

She stared deep into his face, searching, then looked downcast, her bright hopeful eyes melting in the face of his conciliatory frown. "It's alright," she said, "I already knew he was gone. I just needed to be sure."

She made to leave, but he seized her wrist. "Wait. Please." He gazed back up the tunnel, nodding to those standing just inside the ship.

He returned to Sonja. "Listen, Zack *is* gone, but not completely." He watched her eyes widen as Pierre and the Transpar started their descent down the walkway.

Sandy tried to warn her. "Sonja, it's not –"

But she pushed through them with surprising force and sprinted into the tunnel towards the Transpar. "Zack!" she screamed. "Zack!"

Sandy set off after her.

"Is it Zack?" Vasquez asked, incredulous. "And is *that* Pierre?"

Micah watched the scene as Sonja reached the crystal form of Zack. It slowed down as she tried to embrace it. "It was Zack," Micah said, "but now it's ... it has his memories, that's all. They don't add up to a person, not by a long way."

Micah couldn't hear what Sonja was saying. He didn't need to. She collapsed before the Transpar, kneeling down and curling around its lower leg, stopping it from walking. What was once Pierre stared at her with a look of detached curiosity. Two of the Ossyrians came forward, but before they reached her, Sandy arrived. She knelt down next to Sonja, and slowly disentangled her from the glass leg. Sonja collapsed sobbing into Sandy's shoulder.

Vasquez cleared his throat. "Micah, why exactly did you bring it back? What good is going to come of it?"

Micah and Ramires exchanged glances. Micah spoke in a hushed tone. "We were put on trial by one of the high races – all humanity was judged. What happened to Zack was part of that process. We think that maybe they sent the Transpar – that's what it's called – with us, because their judgement isn't entirely over."

Pierre and the Transpar made their way down. Pierre's silver eyes glistened in the morning sun. He addressed Vasquez. "Colonel," he said, "how nice to see you again." He offered a silver hand. Vasquez didn't bat an eyelid, and shook Pierre's hand firmly.

Micah knew that Pierre was affecting this all; doubtless his mind was elsewhere, working on infinitely more complex problems, most probably the Galactic incursion.

"Why are you here, Pierre?" Vasquez asked.

"The Ossyrians, the Transpar and myself are here to help you. We can offer you protection."

Micah thought Vasquez would have folded his arms if he could. Instead he stood rigid as ever.

"You'll forgive me for saying this, Pierre, but as you know yourself, invaders and colonisers throughout history have used very similar overtures."

The Transpar spoke, its wind chime voice tinkling on the breeze. "Where is your other arm?"

Micah's jaw dropped slightly. Vasquez didn't miss a beat.

"I lost it in the War, Sir, fighting for what I believe in."

"Which is?" the Transpar asked.

Vasquez jutted out his chin. "Freedom, Sir. That is what we humans value most."

The Transpar's glass eyes twinkled.

"Micah," Vasquez said, "maybe you and I had better brief each other before you meet the Council."

Micah nodded, knowing there was worse to come. "Good idea."

Pierre held up his hand. "No."

Micah and the others froze. The tell-tale buzz of soldiers' pulse weapons activating drifted toward them on the breeze. Micah leaned towards Pierre. "What are you doing?"

Pierre ignored him. "Colonel. You and Micah can talk inside the ship while we repair your arm."

Vasquez bristled. "My arm is perfectly..." His brow furrowed so deep, Micah thought it might crack. "Wait a Goddam minute, you're not saying..." He turned to Micah and Ramires. "Can they...?"

Two Ossyrians arrived level with them. Pierre faced them, his eyes evanescing instructions to them.

Sandy and Sonja arrived. "Colonel," Micah said. "These are the best doctors in the galaxy. They don't often make house-calls."

Micah had never seen Vasquez ruffled. "Trust has to start somewhere, Colonel, and, to be honest, it'll make our job a lot easier."

Vasquez' eyes darted from Micah, to Pierre, to the Ossyrians. He glanced down to the stump where his arm used to be. "Twelve years," he said softly, head lowered.

Pierre gestured toward the tube. "If it makes you feel any better, Colonel, this race used to be fierce warriors and field surgeons. They'd patch up their wounded in the midst of battle, repairing injuries, growing new limbs and re-fitting them if necessary, and have them fighting again within the hour."

Vasquez stood tall again, and nodded. He turned around to his soldiers. "You hear that men. One hour. Take a break. If I'm not back here in one hour, board their ship, and bring your weapons."

Vasquez faced Pierre. "I'm all yours, Pierre. You have fifty-nine minutes and fifty seconds to convince me."

Micah wasn't sure, but he thought he saw the trace of a smile cross Pierre's silver lips.

* * *

Micah sat positioned between Pierre on one side, and Chahat-Me and the Transpar on the other, in the domed, circular room. Its rugged white walls had a deadening effect on sound. Vasquez had remarked to Micah that many thought the room had been a place of meditation for the spiders, but in reality, no one knew. He'd also said that it had a beneficial effect on the Council meetings they'd been holding there recently, since people did not ramble on – it required such an effort to keep discussions animated.

Sandy, Ramires and Kat joined the Council meeting as honorary members, taking up their allocated places next to Micah in the high-backed wooden chairs arranged in a wide circle. Micah recognised them as those Shakirvasta had originally brought along, but the conference table was gone, people adopting the apparent spider habit of facing each other without any physical object separating them. He didn't know all the other faces in the Council, the hastily concocted governing body of the surviving population, which had quickly filled the vacuum left by Shakirvasta's militaristic junta.

Vasquez sat across the circle from Micah, oblivious to all around him, staring at his new right arm, playing with his fingers, curling and uncurling them. News of this 'miracle' had spread quickly, and the Ossyrians had wasted no time in curing other afflictions. Micah knew it would add weight to his cause, though he wasn't sure it would be enough.

He glanced towards Antonia and Sonja, who were equally introspective, for opposite reasons: Antonia had found her lost love, while Sonja had lost hers. Next to Sonja's seat was Rashid's empty chair – he'd been missing for several days. But as long as they had ten members present, the Council was considered to have a quorum, and its decisions would hold sway over the entire population.

Micah was in no hurry to see Jennifer again – even if she'd turned over a new leaf according to Vasquez, the people of Ourshiwann would be less quick to forgive. He wished Dimitri could be there though – he'd have been a welcome tonic for the dour atmosphere in the room. But the Professor was too close to his protégé, and so would probably not be given a Council position. He didn't recognise any of the other Council members, but they'd each been elected for various reasons. Micah mused that humanity was on trial yet again, this time judging itself – hardly best positioned to reach an objective conclusion.

He stared towards the empty seat dominating the room: Blake's. They'd awaited his arrival some forty-five minutes. When the Commander at last entered, Micah was shocked at how gaunt he looked, despite Vasquez' warning.

Blake's force of presence wasn't lacking, though. He strode towards his place, his footfalls stilling conversation in the room. He surveyed the alien from behind the polished oak back of the chair, and gave Micah the curtest of nods. "Ladies and gentlemen, thank you for waiting. I've already been briefed. I have to say that I was amazed, aghast even, at these proposals."

Shit, he's against it.

"However," he cleared his throat, and stared down at the seat of the chair, "in light of recent events, namely that my wife's can–". His speech stopped dead. Several people made to get up but he raised a hand, his face tilted towards the floor, jaw clenched. Micah saw the great man's chest lift and fall, Blake's breathing the only sound in the chamber. He lifted his head and gazed around the circle. "She will live. I have you to thank for that," he said, addressing Chahat-Me. "But that's a personal matter, and as Chairman of this Council, I don't intend to let that influence my judgement of the proposition we're here to debate today. So, we will hear your proposals, and then discuss them in private – humans only." He addressed Micah. "Is that acceptable to our guests?"

Before he could answer, Pierre nodded gravely. "Your terms are accepted."

"Then let's begin," Blake said, and took his seat.

Micah swallowed, then rose to his feet to convey the Tla Beth ruling.

Micah paced up and down the centre of the room, grown stuffy after hours of relentless arguing. "For the hundredth time, there's really no choice!"

"We hear you, Micah," a matronly, red-haired woman said, in a way that indicated she'd heard quite enough.

"No you don't!" He raised his hands towards the ceiling, looking upwards, trying to make them see. "We've been out there, we've seen what awaits us. We won't survive any other way." He was glad Pierre and the Transpar weren't present to hear all of this – they might just ship out and leave humanity to its own fate. But he hoped not. Pierre had confided in him earlier that the first Tla Beth assault on the Kalaheii had been a crushing rout. The Tla Beth Level 17 warships – not seen in action for fifty thousand years – had been easily disabled by Qorall's arsenal of legendary weaponry. But such news had failed to sway the Council. It seemed too abstract and foreign to them, too far away.

"*You've* seen it, Mr. Sanderson. But we have only your own word and your colleagues' word for it. Perhaps you were unlucky with the aliens you encountered. Maybe you approached them the wrong way. Please try to understand – these are our children and grandchildren we're talking about sacrificing."

Micah faced the stout, middle-aged woman. She was one of a number of key Council members, presumably stalwart citizens who had risen in status over the past five months, who were resolutely blocking the alien proposal. She was a lot shrewder than she looked, he'd come to realise in the past four hours. But he sensed that Blake was the real threat, though the Commander was biding his time, playing out his role as Chairman of the Council, staying out of the fray until the end. Blake's emotions were locked down like a good poker player. Yet Micah had seen subtle reactions which convinced him that Blake was strongly opposed to the motion. Micah guessed that in the end, it was going to come down to him and Blake.

"Not *sacrificing*," Micah continued, no longer bothering to try and hide his exasperation, "they'll be better, for God's sake, better able to defend themselves and make their way in the galaxy!"

The Councilwoman remained calm and collected, adopting a haughty air. "We're altering humanity. There will be no way back, will there, Mr. Sanderson? May I ask you to remind us of the likely changes that will take place in our offspring?"

He frowned. They'd been over this before. Each time he went through it he felt victory – sustainable survival prospects for humanity – slipping from his grasp. He held up a closed fist, and then peeled open his little finger, beginning his cataloguing of the five main differences the Ossyrians had predicted.

"One – they will be physically superior – a little taller, a lot stronger, with faster reflexes, better hearing and sharper eyesight." He noted Kat staring at him intently, Sandy too – Kat's child and Sandy's embryo were already undergoing the process, the 'upgrade' as someone in the Council had labelled it. "Two – they'll be more intelligent. They will mature a lot faster, able to speak fluently after a year, and they'll be able to grasp mathematical concepts by the age of two."

The woman interrupted. "At what age will they surpass us intellectually?"

Micah restrained a sigh. "Around twelve." He raised his voice to quell the murmurs simmering around the Council. "Three – they'll be able to parallel process, meaning they can do two things at once, for example, having a conversation and working on a computer at the same time, without making any mistakes or missing anything." He tried to press the advantage. "Don't you see? That alone is worth its weight in gold. Flying a space-craft is very tricky; we have to rely on advanced computers all the time because *they* can process information in parallel, whereas we can't. Most other races can. Without this upgrade, because it *is* an upgrade, we'd be the dullards of the galaxy! If we're lucky they might let us farm land and plant crops. That's all we'll be good for." He caught sight of Sandy's slight shake of her head – of course, what was he thinking, there were farmers here in the Council. Several members folded their arms, their body language as clear as raising a drawbridge. This time he let the sigh come out. "Sorry, that was … that wasn't meant the way it sounded." He realised he was screwing this up. He unfurled his index finger. "Four – they'll be more creative. Music, art, they'll create wonders we've never imagined."

The woman raised her nose. "Will we lower-grade humans – dullards and farmers that we are apparently – be able to appreciate such art, Mr. Sanderson?"

Sandy tapped her inflated belly. "I'll appreciate whatever my son does."

Micah wanted to get through this part. His thumb joined his fingers, out in the open air. "Five." He paused. This was the one people feared most. "They will be less emotionally labile."

The woman snorted. "Cold fish, that's what you mean, isn't it, Micah? Cold and uncaring? Like your friend Pierre?"

Kat interjected, urgency in her voice. "Pierre's already Level Ten. There's no comparison!"

"As I understand it, my dear, he is prepared to leave you and your child – his child – behind him, in the pursuit of greater things."

Micah cut in – he had to get off this track somehow. "That's not how it's going to be. Less labile means less erratic: people will be able to control their emotions, they won't fly off the handle so readily. There'll also be much less mental illness, if any at all. Isn't that worth something?" He stared at the faces around the room.

Blake joined in. "People will be more dispassionate, is that what you're saying, Micah?"

Micah wasn't sure if Blake was supporting or preparing for an attack. "Yes," he said cautiously.

Blake rose from his chair. "But it seems to me, that passion is what makes us human. Isn't that so, Micah?"

It was rhetorical. He didn't get a chance to reply.

"You see, Micah," Blake continued, "I didn't lead us all the way here, fighting against the Alicians, so we could become like them."

Micah saw several vigorous nods.

Blake continued. "I promised to protect humanity, not to sell it out."

Micah spread his hands. "It won't –"

"Hear me out, Micah. You've been speaking a lot this afternoon, and I've listened to everything you've had to say, and weighed it up carefully. But it comes down to this. Are we going to sacrifice everything that defines us as a species, in order to survive? If we're no longer human, is that survival?" Several people clapped.

Micah waited a moment. He hadn't wanted to do this. His stomach churned, rebelling against the line of argument his mind knew was his last recourse, humanity's last chance. He kept his voice low. "When we departed Eden, Commander, you made a speech to all of us." He paused, allowing the clapping to sputter to a stop, all eyes turning to him. "You said that hubris had led to our undoing. I had hoped that we had learned from that, but maybe we just don't learn." He walked up to Blake, facing him off, raising his voice. "The Alicians are still out there. Sister Esma is biding her time, hoping we screw up so they can finish what they started, or better still, enslave us. And if they don't, there'll be a dozen other species in the queue."

Blake replied, ice cold. "We can take our chances; move planets again if necessary."

The frustration of the last few hours, the anguish of the past six months since he'd first stumbled on the Alician-Q'Roth plot back on Earth, and the scars from the War ten years ago, welled up inside him like a fast-fusion reactor with the safeties off. Bordering on shouting, his voice uneven, he launched his last-ditch attack on Blake.

"Chances? What chance did we have against the Q'Roth, only a couple of levels above us? What chance did you have against Zack, your best friend, when he was re-programmed by the Alicians? What chance did your own son, Robert, have against the Alicians in the War? If he had had the opportunity the Ossyrians are giving us –"

Blake's eyes flared. "Don't you *dare* drag my son into this!" he shouted.

The harshness in his voice drove Micah back a step. Blake tried to recover his breathing, his eyes coring into Micah's, amplifying Micah's regret over his own tactics.

"Commander, I was merely –"

Blake held up his right hand. "*Enough*, Micah." His eyes swept around the room. "I think we've *all* heard enough, haven't we? Frankly, nothing new of any substance has been added in the last hour and a half. I propose that we move to the vote. Any objections?" Blake gestured towards Micah's seat. Micah clenched his fists, but he turned and sat down, arms folded. Sandy laid a hand on his shoulder.

Blake waited a full minute until people finished shuffling in their chairs, then addressed the Council. "There are eleven of us here, since Rashid is missing, but we have a quorum, so the vote will be binding. Moreover this will be an open vote: we take responsibility for our actions. All those *for* the proposal?" Sandy, Ramires, Kat and Micah raised their hands, followed hesitantly by Antonia. Micah glanced over to Vasquez, who replied with a subtle shake of his head, his old hand clasping the new one, locking it firmly in his lap. *Five. Shit!*

"All those against?" Blake's own hand went up first, followed by others. Micah bowed his head, ready for the coup de grace.

"That... also makes five," Blake said.

Micah lifted his head. All eyes latched onto Sonja. He'd almost forgotten she was there; she'd said nothing throughout the entire debate.

"Sonja?" Blake asked, quietly.

She stood up. "You'll have my answer first thing in the morning." Without a backward glance, she walked out of the chamber, amid erupting confusion in the Council.

Abruptly Micah stood up.

"Where are you going?" Sandy asked.

"To prevent a catastrophe." He headed out the exit opposite the one Sonja had taken.

∗ ∗ ∗

Micah dropped his bag onto the end of the bed. He resisted the urge to collapse onto the cot, and instead perched on its hard edge. Night was falling, wondrous to see after living on a spaceship for five months. He'd talked with Pierre, but he had been distant, his mind clearly elsewhere. Micah had felt like a mosquito buzzing around Einstein. Kat was right, Pierre was gone. He just hoped Pierre could do what he'd asked. He suppressed the guilt he felt about it.

"Micah," someone whispered.

It took him a moment to register the voice. He levered himself off the bed, his spirits lifting. "Rashid?"

His Indistani friend emerged from the shadowy doorway to the adjoining room. Micah stared at Rashid's silver dolphin band around his head – he'd never seen one before, except in vids.

"No one must know I have been here," he said.

Micah was taken aback at the lack of a 'hello' at least – he'd not seen Rashid since leaving Ourshiwann months ago. He seemed edgy. "Why? What's going on?"

Rashid bit his lip, looking toward the door. "How is Sonja?"

"Sonja?" Micah's brow puckered in puzzlement. "She's, well, pretty cut up. Where've you been?"

Rashid nodded, as if remembering why he'd come. "I've been sent to you to deliver a message, before we depart."

Micah presumed his reference to 'we' referred to Jen and Dimitri, based on what Vasquez had told him earlier. "Depart?"

"Yes, we are ... going away."

Micah's frustration rose. It had already been a long, difficult day. "I don't suppose you're going to tell me where?" He watched Rashid's face, the tension lacing his forehead. "Never mind. What's the message?"

"Protect the spiders. At all costs."

Micah waited, observing Rashid, who looked distracted, his shoulders rigid. But Rashid said no more. "That's it? You mean the eggs, right?"

"In two years a new generation will hatch. They are critical to galactic survival, and must be protected at all costs, but you must tell no one."

Micah parked his hands on his hips. "I thought communicating with aliens was difficult," he murmured. But he could see Rashid was in pain of some sort. "Look, Rashid, is there anything I can –"

"Zack. Did he make it back?"

Micah sighed. "No. Long, sorry story, and I feel responsible."

"Then Sonja is –"

"There's something left of Zack. Maybe not enough, certainly not a man anymore, but Pierre thinks that maybe –"

"There is hope, then," Rashid finished. He straightened up.

He thought Rashid seemed to relax, become himself again. He'd been hoping to have Rashid and Dimitri around, whatever the vote's outcome. "When are you coming back?"

For the first time Rashid faced Micah directly, as if he could see straight through the dolphin. "It will be a very long trip."

Micah didn't want him to leave. Coming back hadn't been what he'd expected. Instead of the exultation, the joy of seeing old friends and colleagues, he'd found complex political situations, changed relationships, and in several quarters, outright hostility. He didn't know how much this was because people had changed, and how much was due to the fact that he himself had changed. "The Ossyrians could fix your eyes, you know," he offered.

Rashid jiggled his head, a smile at last dawning across his face. "Yes, I have heard about their medical wonders. A few weeks ago I would have begged them to return my sight." His smile retreated. Micah realised Rashid had aged since he'd last seen him.

"But sometimes, Micah, a blind man sees more clearly. Less distraction."

He had no idea what Rashid meant, but had learned to accept such aphorisms from his Indistani friend. Without warning, Rashid approached and hugged him. Micah's arms stuck out like he was a waxwork model, then he hugged Rashid back.

"Good luck, Rashid." They stood back from each other. "Give my regards to Dimitri. And Jennifer, too, I suppose."

As Rashid headed for the exit, Micah thought of something. "Wait a second, Rashid. Why me? Why wasn't the message for Blake?"

"He didn't say." Rashid slipped out into the night.

Micah stared out into the darkness, thinking that for the first time he really understood just how far away those stars really were. Somewhere in the distance he heard music, shouting. It was welcome after months of hushed, vacuum-packed space travel. He longed to hear cicadas, dogs barking, babies crying, or hover cars speeding in the distance; all the sounds he used to hate. *Maybe one day.*

Then it struck him, because he was suddenly sure Rashid had not been referring to Dimitri: *He? Who the hell is 'he'?*

* * *

The Council members arrived subdued, a few with stooped postures, bleary-eyed. The previous evening, and a sizeable chunk of the early hours of the morning, had seen a large open-air party. People had been celebrating the Ossyrians' arrival and medical prowess, as well as the recent release from Shakirvasta's martial law. Micah hoped it had eased the mood in the Council. Sandy and Ramires were standing close by, and closer to each other. He didn't try to engage them, instead leaning forward in his seat, alone, concentrating on the task ahead, feeling humanity's survival hanging in the balance. Vasquez had earlier confided in Micah that he knew Micah was right, but that he wouldn't go up against Blake. Micah had just nodded, knowing that loyalty could easily trump logic, and besides, who was he to judge what was right?

He asked himself again why he'd told no one about Louise being still alive, or Hannah's demise. He didn't fully understand it himself. He could have thrown it into the debate, underlining their plight with the threat of Louise being back again, but somehow it felt underhand to do so. Of course it might pale into insignificance compared to what he'd instigated last night.

He prayed Pierre had pulled it off, even though he'd said he wasn't certain to succeed. But if it wasn't finished in time then it was all for nothing: Micah would lose the vote, and the Ossyrians would leave humanity to its own devices. Mankind could negotiate maybe a decade of peaceful quarantine on Ourshiwann – not nearly enough – after which it would be open season, with the Alicians waiting patiently at the gate. But if the Ossyrians left, they would take the Transpar with them. That had been the key. The Transpar was the wild card in the pack, and Micah intended to play it fully. He stared at Sonja's empty chair, unsure how she'd react. He'd done this for the good of everyone, he told himself, again.

The chattering in the room died down: Sonja had arrived. The gravity of the situation reasserted itself on everyone, as they all took their seats silently. She walked solemnly towards her chair, head held high, ebony face like marble.

"Good luck," Sandy whispered to Micah. It sounded consolatory, anticipating defeat.

Blake waited for Sonja to take her place, then rose to his feet. "Sonja, have you made your decision?"

She nodded once.

Micah glanced around once more to the empty doorway.

She stood. "I –"

She was interrupted by a commotion outside: shouting, muffled noises, and heavy footfalls. The Transpar strolled into the room, dragging along two soldiers struggling ineffectively to hold it back. Its crystal head swivelled first to Blake, then to Sonja.

Blake held up a hand. "Easy men, let it be. What do you want here?" he said to the Transpar. "This is a closed session."

The soldiers backed away, as the crystal man opened its mouth. Its teeth sparkled, its voice carrying like coins bouncing off a stone floor. "Blake," it said. "You are Blake. I remember you. I remember Kurana Bay."

Blake glared at the Transpar. "What do you think you're doing?"

The Transpar walked to a spot in front of Sonja. "And you. You are Sonja. I have many memories of you and the one called Zack."

Blake rounded on Micah. "Is this your doing, Micah?"

Micah rose from his chair, facing Sonja. He'd rehearsed this a dozen times, but still it came out haltingly. "Sonja, one of us had to make the ultimate sacrifice, out there, at the trial. I wanted it to be me, but Zack... Well, you know him better than any of us. When we won, I asked the court if his memories were still inside him. I knew the emotions were gone, but the memories..." He faced Blake. "Normally after a trial is finished, they dispose of Transpars, but they agreed not to, and left him in the Ossyrians' care." He swallowed. "Last night I asked Pierre to..." Micah found it hard to say the rest. He stared at the floor.

"What did you ask him to do, Micah?" Sandy asked.

"At first it was about saving us all, by getting Sonja on our side, any way possible." He glanced in Sonja's direction. "But as I talked to Pierre, I realised it was guilt. It," he said, nodding in the Transpar's direction, "that, should have been me." He took a breath, drawing himself up. "I asked Pierre to restore as much of Zack as he could. He's done something to the Transpar, don't ask me what. It'll never be Zack, of course, and I can ask him to undo it if – "

"*No!*" Sonja was on her feet. "No, Micah, you've done quite enough."

She approached the Transpar, standing close to its face, looking up into its crystal eyes. "What is my favourite time of the day?"

"Sunset," it answered.

"Where did Zack and I first kiss?"

"In your room in your parents' house. There was a storm outside. You were talking, and he told you not to stop, to close your eyes so he could focus on the sounds, and then he leant forward and kissed you in mid-sentence." The Transpar looked at the ceiling, then back down at Sonja. "He thought you were fragile, too trusting in people." The Transpar sounded curious, as if trying to grasp the emotions underneath the words. "He never told you that, because you are also a proud, strong woman. He was terrified something would happen to you. He wanted so much to protect – "

She placed a finger on the Transpar's lips, silencing it. "Stop, please," she said, her voice quavering.

She returned to her seat, clutching its edges with rigid arms. She glared at Micah. "You've manipulated me, Micah. You've grown from the young man I met six months ago. I'm not sure I like what you've become."

Blake cut in. "Then your vote is against the proposal?"

Sonja looked to the Transpar, then to Blake. "I'm sorry, Blake, really, but if I do that, these Ossyrians will take this – him – with them." She stared hard at Micah. "My vote is *for* the proposal. Micah has left me no choice."

In the uproar that followed, with everyone on their feet shouting and arguing, Micah stared at Sonja in disbelief. In the din, he mouthed the word "Sorry". Her lips widened a little, and she mouthed back, so that no one else could hear, "Thank you."

* * *

Blake and Micah were the last two left in the room, absolute quiet having seeped in once all the others had gone. They stood some distance apart. Blake hadn't said a word to Micah since Sonja's vote. Micah had expected an outburst of some kind, but instead he sensed resolution, and waited patiently, ready to accept whatever Blake had to say.

Blake sat down in Rashid's seat. "I'm retiring, Micah. I'm going to spend my remaining time with Glenda. There's a chair over there needs filling. You've earned it, and you're man enough now for the job."

Micah searched for an edge in Blake's voice, a tinge of bitterness, but found none. He knew he still had a long way to go to reach Blake's level of professionalism. He walked over to the chair, ran his fingers over its varnished wooden surface. It was no doubt heavy, like the position it occupied in the Council. He considered others who could have taken it, Vasquez for one.

Micah had never sought power – if anything he'd always been anti-establishment. But the idea resonated and, more than that, he wanted to see this through, and only someone who believed in the upgrade could lead humanity forward. He knew it would be less of an uphill struggle if he was at the top.

"I'll do it. But you can't retire. I need you to do something."

"Micah, I've –"

"Jennifer, Rashid and Dimitri need you to do something. The galaxy needs you for one last task. And Glenda will be well enough to help you soon."

Blake surveyed Micah. "Sonja was right about you, you've grown alright. Well, you've got my attention. What is this great Galactic task?"

"Protect the spiders. There are eggs on the planet, and they're going to hatch in a couple of years."

"Ah," Blake said. "They found their way in, then."

Micah tried the chair for size. "Could you maybe elaborate on that?"

Blake told Micah of the caves, the egg nest, and the ship. Micah pondered for a while. He closed his eyes and let the possibilities formulate into hypotheses. Rashid had obviously been referring to the ship's inhabitant. In the Tla Beth 'Court', Micah had seen an image of a crossbow-shaped ship, and on the way to Ourshiwann, Pierre had mentioned an ancient race of Progenitors, called the Kalarash. The pieces slotted together in his mind, though he had no idea what the role of the spiders could be. As often happened, his projections catapulted forward to yield a less certain, but plausible prediction: that the Galactic battle would find its way to Ourshiwann, and humanity and the spiders would be swept up into that confrontation. He opened his eyes.

Blake stood in front of him, watching, a wry smile on his face. "Still want the chair, Micah?"

He rose and met Blake's offered hand, shaking it firmly. "Yes, but I'd really welcome your guidance."

* * *

Micah strolled towards the central plaza. He wore his father's military jacket; it kept the chill night air at bay and, well, it was comfortable, he told himself. People liked to see him in it. At first he thought they respected it, or his deceased father. But then he realised they respected the fact that he wore it, honouring his father. Either way, Micah had decided that it fit, and anything that helped him get the job done...

He'd been doing the rounds, visited Kat and Antonia, played with their child, Petra, which had been awkward at first, until Kat said Micah should visit often, that Petra needed some kind of male anti-role model in her life, or else she'd end up straight. Despite the banter, Micah suspected she was still cut up about Pierre.

He travelled to the egg nest with Blake and Glenda. Far from being revolted as he'd feared, Glenda threw herself into cataloguing the chamber's contents, planning nurseries, and hatching her own proposal for co-habitation between spiders and humans. He winced at that, and began formulating his own plans for a new human city on the ridge, though they only had two years to build it.

He and Blake had descended alone into the deeper caves, found the roiling ocean, but no trace of the ship, just equipment abandoned by Dimitri. Blake told him of Rashid's love for Sonja. Micah cursed himself for not seeing it, playing back his last conversation with his tormented friend, realising how it had cemented Rashid's resolve to depart.

Micah squatted, staring down at the unending, perfect waves rolling fifty metres below his feet. He wondered how long it had been there, how long the ship had been hiding, waiting; maybe a million years. *We always took ourselves so seriously back on Earth. We had no idea what was out in the galaxy.* He ran a finger over the smooth glass surface, and wondered how much of a difference it would have made if mankind had known, and decided it would have made *all* the difference.

He straightened up. "How is Sonja getting on with the Transpar?"

"They need time, a lot of time. Pierre's advanced nannites are still working. Last time I was there, it saluted me, can you believe that?"

Micah smiled. "I don't think Pierre is doing it just for Sonja, or for me. I have a feeling the Tla Beth will pay a visit one day and ask the Transpar to give them a reckoning on us, on humanity. Pierre is doing it to protect us."

Blake picked up the torch, and indicated to the exit. "Sorry the Ossyrians didn't grant your request, about upgrading adults who want the process. Guess we'll have to rely on the young ones to fend for us."

Micah felt a shiver, knowing the social problems all of this was going to unleash. He'd have a lot on his shoulders starting in about twelve years' time, when teenagers would begin to outsmart him. He hoped he'd done the right thing.

* * *

Micah met Pierre for the last time as he boarded the small, ash-coloured spacecraft crouching crocodile-like outside the city.

"Are you coming back, Pierre?"

"The Kalaheii must be defeated. I will do whatever I can to help."

Micah nodded, hearing Ukrull grumble something from inside the ship.

"Micah, there is something you should know. Sister Esma has petitioned for stewardship of humanity if this 'experiment' fails."

Micah shook his head. "She doesn't give up, does she?"

He told Pierre about Louise.

"There is no threat now. Neither Alicians nor Q'Roth are allowed within ten light years of this planet. But the quarantine is only for one generation, Micah."

"I understand. But by then, I doubt I'll be in charge, Pierre – one of the young men or women will be better suited."

Pierre didn't respond, but it seemed to Micah that he had an odd, unreadable expression on his face, as if he was deciding something. Pierre held out his hand, Micah assumed out of politeness. Micah gripped the cool silver, feeling a tingling sensation in his palm. "Good bye, Pierre," Micah said.

"Au revoir," he replied, a shadow of a smile.

Pierre boarded the ship, and shortly afterwards, it vanished. "Good luck," Micah said to the rocks and bushes undisturbed by its wake. As he walked back to the city, he scratched his aching forearm absently, oblivious to the grey-black swirl, like iron filings, that circled there momentarily before disappearing beneath his skin.

* * *

Micah found Sandy and Blake in the central plaza. Like others who had gathered there and elsewhere in the city, they were looking upwards. He followed their gaze to see the final pulse of red light whisk up from the top of the Ossyrian pyramid ship into the night sky. A luminous drop, like a giant scarlet snowflake, formed at its zenith, then radiated outwards in every direction down to the horizon and beyond, a shimmering shroud around the entire planet. After a few seconds, the shield became completely transparent, vanishing from human eyesight.

"That's it," Blake said. "Nothing gets in or out. From here on it's just us, the spiders, and a handful of Ossyrians."

"A generation of quarantine; fifteen years," Micah said. "A lot can happen in that time."

"Families, stability, some breathing space, for one thing," Blake said.

"Coming to terms with arachnophobia, for another," Sandy added.

Micah laughed. But he foresaw a complex tapestry of social problems in the near future, and knew that he and Blake would clash again, sooner or later; Micah had won the first round; that was all. Still, he wanted to relax for the moment, so he suppressed those thoughts. "No news on Rashid, Jennifer or Dimitri?" he ventured.

Blake slapped his hands together, then rubbed them in the crisp air. "None. I doubt we'll see them again."

"I wonder what was in the ship?" Micah added.

"We'll probably never know," Blake said. He tilted his head as he looked at Micah, then cleared his throat, looking uncomfortable. "Micah, Sandy tells me ... you knew my son."

Micah coughed, and shot a glance at Sandy, wishing she'd warned him, but she just stared right back at him, smiling. He nodded, facing Blake. "I was in Kurana Bay, just a kid then, like Robert. We were in the same training squad. You and Zack rescued me. I never expected you to remember me, given everything that happened that night."

Blake chewed on it for a while. For the first time since Micah had met him, Blake looked vulnerable.

Sandy put a hand on each of their shoulders, pulling them closer. "God, you men are really useless, aren't you? Micah, *tell him about his son.*"

He swallowed. "I only knew him for a couple of months," he replied. He addressed Blake. "What do you want to know, exactly?"

Blake's eyes lit up. "Everything, Micah," he said softly. "Everything you can remember."

CHAPTER 30 – EPILOGUE

Pierre studied Ukrull's chaotic green console, studded with jagged controls, spattered with myriad spherical screens of shades of brown which Pierre had difficulty interpreting.

"The Kalarash was here all along?" Pierre asked.

"Masked. Level 19 stealth tech. Detected once ship folded space-time."

"The three humans have gone with it?"

"Yes."

Pierre's eyes zoomed onto the central cubic display showing the razor-thin tear in the space-time fabric caused by the Kalarash's departure. No more than a hair's breadth, and blacker-than-black, it streaked up from the planet's surface, flailing silently out into the void.

"Must fix," Ukrull said. "Qorall's spies must never see." He nudged Pierre with a claw. "Image it."

Pierre's left hand riffed over the controls to highlight the rip on the main screen. Ukrull wheeled the ship around to intercept the filament from just above the shimmering barrier. The ship emitted a narrow orange beam from its front section. Ukrull – in manual, Pierre noticed – steered the ship to trace up the tear's entire length, from Ourshiwann's orbital shield, all the way to the thread's dangling end a hundred or so kilometres out into space. The painstaking operation took over five hours, and Ukrull didn't miss a centimetre. He then withdrew the ship to observe.

Pierre was relieved to see the rip slowly contract in on itself and disappear. He also noticed Ukrull did not seem in the least fatigued. "Can we track the Kalarash vessel?"

"No."

"You've informed Tla Beth Central?"

Ukrull folded his muscular forelegs. "Yes."

"What was their suggestion?"

Ukrull snorted, his heavy tail thudding into the hull at the same time.

"What do *you* suggest?" Pierre asked.

"Have idea. Long shot. Long trip."

Pierre wondered – not for the first time – why Ukrull hated using words, minimising everything, odd for such an advanced species. He seemed to be always testing Pierre, trying to make him guess what was probably obvious to the Ranger. Pierre considered what to do next, what leads to follow. He concentrated his mind, searching through trans-dimensional landscapes of probability projections, but nothing emerged that was statistically noteworthy. The galaxy was simply too big: they could be anywhere. And the space-time rip the Kalarash ship had left behind was like nothing ever recorded. That ship could be half-way across the galaxy by now, or even ... yes, it *was* possible, the Kalarash vessel might have left the galaxy, in which case there was no way to pursue them. To make matters worse, according to the Tla Beth, there was only one Kalarash left.

He noticed that Ukrull remained still. The Rangers appeared to be aggressive, over-bearing reptiles, and said little. Yet he knew Ukrull was Level Fifteen. He wondered how this could be, in a race so loathe to communicate.

"Not loathe," Ukrull said.

The two words struck Pierre's mind like a jeweller's hammer smartly splitting a diamond in two. He understood straightaway why Rangers would want to keep it a secret.

"You're telepathic?"

Ukrull laughed, a vicious chomping sound like chewing rocks. "You not so dumb." He opened his foreclaws and activated a number of controls in blurred motion while he spoke. "Kalarash paired species. Mate for life. Female still hiding. Find her before Qorall does."

Pierre's analysis told him something about Ukrull's body language, and it stunned him further. "You know where she is, don't you? But how? You couldn't conceal such knowledge from the Tla Beth for long."

Ukrull nudged a panel with his tail, and a small hatch opened. Pierre stared in disbelief at an ancient-looking Hohash, its fractured, mirror-like surface surging with purple and blue swirls. Pierre guessed it was showing a highly unusual nebula. A location, he guessed, unique in the galaxy. As if on cue, Ukrull whacked a control that produced a holo-display of the nebula's position on an outer galactic spiral.

"Can she do battle against Qorall?"

"Female of species tougher than male." Ukrull grunted, grinning, as far as Pierre could tell.

Pierre considered the distances, the timescales, weighing up the most recent reports from the progress of the Kalaheii. The nebula was on the opposite edge of the galaxy, so the female was not yet in danger. But one Kalarash against a legion of Kalaheii... Still, they had some time. Qorall's strategy appeared to be slow but firm progression. He did the calculations, and the coincidence surprised him: *fifteen years*. Qorall would reach this sector of the galaxy shortly after the quarantine had ended. So he, Ukrull and the female Kalarash had that long to mount a defence, and then he must return to Ourshiwann. For an instant, he factored a background variable – his daughter, Petra – into the equation; she would be fifteen by then. An emotion flickered inside him, like a ghost in the data-core. He immediately suppressed it. He could not allow himself to be distracted by such things. That was why he'd programmed the Transpar to record everything, particularly Petra's development. At least that way he'd have a record of her life, even if a fragmented one.

He was about to say "I am ready," when he realised it was not necessary, since he'd already thought it.

"You learn fast," Ukrull said. He kicked a control with his lower left claw, and their small ship disappeared.

* * *

Louise watched the Hohash's mirror surface relax back to its oil-film state. She weighed her options, straddling Micah's chair on the bridge of the Hunter-Seeker vessel she had reclaimed. "So," she said, having gotten used to talking to the Hohash – it had mastered understanding English some time ago, whether by sound or lip-reading, she wasn't sure which, and didn't care. "I'm pretty much *persona non grata* with the Alicians and the Q'Roth: Sister Esma would find a way to get rid of me sooner or later, last thing she needs is a hero around cramping her style, and the Q'Roth are giving Alicians the cold shoulder right now. Micah's untouchable for a while, and the other two parties of interest are betting on the Kalarash." She still wasn't sure why the Hohash had shown her so much. She assumed these artefacts were like dogs – despite their intelligence – needing a master or a mistress.

"What would you do?" she said, addressing the metal sculpture of her and Vince she'd stolen from Ourshiwann an hour before the planet-shroud energized. She nodded. "My thoughts exactly, we should check out the likely winner." This was going to test the Hohash's loyalty to the limit; she was interested to see if it would go along with it or fight her again. She turned to her companion, as she now thought of it. "We should go see Qorall, offer him information, don't you think?"

The Hohash vibrated, sparks splashing across its surface.

"Really, I'm serious." She walked to Zack's console and called up the Galactic Nav chart, pointing as she spoke. "We'll enter the Grid here, run right around to the other side, disembark here, then head out on this spiral. Might take a few years." She folded her arms. "I'm sure Qorall will be interested in you, in any case."

The Hohash surface was transparent, its frame stilled.

"Hmm. You know I can't decide whether you are very dumb, or way smarter than me. Only one way to find out." She turned her back on the Hohash as she entered the flight plan.

As she dropped the ankh key into the slot, engaging the engines, an ivory and emerald eye opened on the surface of the Hohash, watching her. The jump initiated. Everything on the bridge, including Louise, turned quicksilver.

Everything except the eye.

Continue reading the series:

The Eden Paradox – where it begins, with a murder, and Earth's third mission to the virgin planet Eden... But what really lies in wait on Eden? Will it be humanity's salvation, or will it trigger our demise?

Eden's Revenge – Qorall, an invader from another galaxy, threatens the galactic order. Beneath humanity's new home lies a key to stopping him. But humanity's old enemies are out for vengeance at any cost...

Eden's Endgame – Superior races are falling one by one in the relentless galactic war. The only solution is a dormant weapon, one that almost destroyed the galaxy millions of years ago...

Available in paperback and Ebook from all major retailers

www.barrykirwan.com

Acknowledgements

Many thanks to fellow writers Chris Vanier and Dimitri Keramitas for their support throughout this journey, and to reviewers Gary Gibson, Gideon Roberton, Lara Nagy, Gwyneth Hughes, and Michael Zammett, and my trusty readers Andy Kilner and Andrew Hale. Last but not least, thanks to all the fans of *The Eden Paradox* who kept asking me for this sequel.